RULE
OF
LAW

A JADE HARRINGTON NOVEL

J. L. BROWN

RULE
OF
LAW

A JADE HARRINGTON NOVEL

Printed in the United States of America.

For information address JAB Press, P.O. Box 9462, Seattle, WA 98109.

Cover Design by Damonza

Library of Congress Control Number: 2017901223

ISBN 978-0-9969772-3-4 (paperback)

ISBN 978-0-9969772-4-1 (ebook)

First Edition: March 2017

For Audi.

And for victims of bullying everywhere.

You are not alone.

There is a feeling among the masses generally that something is radically wrong. They are despairing of political action. They say the only thing you do in Washington is to take money from the pockets of the poor and put it into the pockets of the rich. They say that this Government is a conspiracy against the common people to enrich the already rich. I hear such remarks every day.

— Oscar Ameringer, 1932

If people throw stones at you, build something.

— Unknown

WASHINGTON, DC - ONE MONTH AGO

SHE SHOULD HAVE thrown the letter away.

Or shredded it.

She knelt before the altar of the small, quaint Presbyterian church near the White House. The nave was empty. Easter services had just ended. Her husband, Grayson, and the children waited outside. Lead Secret Service agent, Josh McPherson, stood alone by the entryway at the front of the church.

Although her hands were clasped together and relaxed, her head bowed in supplication, President Whitney Fairchild was not praying.

Instead, she was reading.

The expensive parchment paper, creased horizontally into two sections, lay on the raised carpeted step, worn from her reading it every day since her inauguration two months ago when she had first opened the envelope.

She needn't have bothered.

She had memorized every word.

Dear Senator,

I'm sure you already own this classic, but this volume is in pristine condition and, I am told, one of a kind. I've enjoyed our reading challenge, and since I'm so far ahead, I wanted to give you a chance to catch up.

Seriously, I want to thank you for the opportunity to work for you and alongside you all these years. Every day has been a joy.

I am proud of what we've accomplished and look forward to what we'll accomplish over the next eight years (yes, I said eight!). I know you will win.

I want to have one of our talks after you read this. I believe we'll have much to say to each other.

You have no idea how much I love you.

Your son,

Landon

Despite his sins, she still missed Landon Phillips.

"Mom?"

Whitney started at the sound of her son's voice.

Snatching the letter with reflexes she didn't realize she possessed, she stuffed it back into her purse.

Her son, Chandler, stood beside her, wearing a jacket, shirt, and slacks.

"What are you doing?" he asked.

"Working."

"Working and praying at the same time?"

She rose. "In this job, I do that often."

"Dad sent me in to get you. He's hungry."

She brushed the bangs off his forehead. His face was like looking at a mirror. "Dad, huh?" She looped her arm through his. "Did I tell you how handsome you look today, my favorite son?"

He grinned. "I'm your only son, Mom."

Whitney's smile faltered. "That is true."

They walked down the aisle past the stained-glass windows to the front of the church. As he chatted about the action movie they had watched last night in the theater room in the White House, her thoughts wandered.

She chastised herself for being careless. She was not ready to share the truth about Landon with anyone yet. Particularly her husband and her children.

That was close. I need to be more careful.

PART I

CHAPTER ONE

FAIRFAX, VIRGINIA

YOU HEARD THE breathing first.

Heavy breathing from one. Quick breaths through the nose from the one accustomed to fighting.

Next, you heard the whack, whack, whack as gloves met flesh.

Then, the smell: the overwhelming musk of teenage sweat.

There were no lights.

The "spectators" used the flashlights on their iPhones to illuminate the area. Some shone real ones.

The two boys in the cage wore MMA gloves, but no headgear or pads. No shirts. No shoes. But—oddly—they both wore baseball pants. One was in pro-style knickers.

Those were the rules.

Blood speckled the fighter's knickers like an impressionist painting.

Not his blood.

Watching the fight, a boy clung to the netting outside the

cage. He held it tight to hold himself up. His knuckles stuck out like small stones in the dark.

Every punch made him sick.

He didn't want to be here. If it were up to him, he would rather be anywhere else. Even home, doing homework. Or at the dentist, having a cavity filled.

But he had no choice. Attendance was required.

The fight would be over soon. The boy in the regular baseball pants was pinned against one of the poles. Each time he slipped off the pole from the sweat on his back and fell against the netting, the guy in the knickers would grab him, right him in front of the pole again, and pummel him some more. In the face. In the stomach. In the ribs.

In between punches and exhalations, the guy in the knickers shouted, "That's poppin'! That's poppin'!"

The spectators—also shirtless and in baseball pants—wore baseball caps. They chanted: *"Poppin'! Poppin'! Poppin'! Poppin'! Poppin'! Poppin'! Poppin'! Poppin'! Poppin'!"*

The gladiatorial dogfight atmosphere intensified as the fight went on. The punches landed harder. The cheering louder. The sweat shinier.

When the fighter against the pole finally faltered, the boy in the knickers threw him down and then lifted him by both ears and slammed his head to the turf.

No one made a move to help the loser.

Knickers started kicking him with the instep of his foot. "That's hot!"

The spectators chanted: *"Hot! Hot! Hot! Hot! Hot! Hot! Hot! Hot! Hot!"*

The presumptive victor mounted the prone boy, pummeling his head with vicious punches: his left ear, then right.

"Loser!" he screamed.

A regulation fight would have been declared over.

"Loser! Loser! Loser! Loser! Loser! Loser! Loser! Loser! Loser!"

"Tap out, man!" yelled one of the spectators.

"Yeah!" said another.

"Do it!" said an opposing voice.

"Fuck him up!"

"Queer bait!"

"Kill him!"

"Let him die!"

The victor's arm rose high in the air to deliver the coup de grâce, the ensuing punch anticlimactic. Blood flew from the nose and mouth of the boy on the ground, drops spraying those who were watching.

The vanquished fighter stopped moving, his long legs still. His arms extended perpendicular to his body. A crucifix without the cross. Even in the artificial light, the boy outside the cage saw the blood running freely from the prone boy's nose and mouth. Both of his eyes, blackening.

He looked dead.

The boy outside still clung to the netting. His arms shook.

He couldn't hold it in any longer.

A grumbling roiled in the pit of his stomach. The bile rose.

Leaning forward, his head between his arms, he threw up on the ground. Teammates near him jumped out of the way.

"Gross!"

"That shit better not be on my pants, man!"

"Wimp!"

"Idiot!"

"Faggot!"

The name calling hurt the boy, although he should be used to it. He battled the tears trying to escape his eyes.

He lost the fight.

He wiped his mouth with the back of his hand. Made sure his baseball cap was on tight.

And then he ran.

*

With his arms around their shoulders, to an observer, he appeared drunk. Good friends were helping him get home safely. The illusion ended when they dumped him on the front lawn of his parents' home, his head barely missing the sidewalk.

"That'll teach you," one boy said, kicking him.

"Warriors don't run," said the other.

The two ran back to the car, their sneakers loud in the quiet of the neighborhood.

Every bone and muscle in his body ached. He scarcely registered the squeal of the tires as their car sped away.

His chest rose and fell as he breathed. The only movement he was capable of.

The stars burned bright against the black sky. The Little Dipper. The Big Dipper. Perseus—or was it Gemini? He had learned about constellations during a class field trip to a planetarium three years ago. Life had been great then. When he was young.

Running away had been stupid. Where could he hide? He saw these guys every day. Two of them had grabbed him before he made it off campus. Tossing him into a car like a crumpled piece of paper, they had driven to a three-sided section of the main building. Back in the day, it had served as the student smoking lounge, if you could believe that. Now, just an area the high overhead night-lights and security cameras missed.

Two other guys had joined them—one, the fighter in the knickers—and beaten the shit out of him until he passed out.

Dew began to soak through his shirt. He wasn't sure how long he'd been lying here. The grass, mowed to the perfection of a baseball field, smelled as the boy imagined heaven would. His dad took enormous pride in his lawn.

He could lie here forever.

Turning his head, he spotted it in the moonlight. "I thought I'd lost you."

He pushed himself up, picked up his cap, placed it on his head, and gingerly made his way to the front door. Pain shot through his hand as he extracted the key from his back pocket.

Inside, quietly and painfully, he climbed the stairs. The noise of a television behind his parents' closed bedroom door masked his footsteps as he tiptoed by. Some reality show that offered a different reality than their own.

The boy entered his room at the end of the hall. Not bothering to pull off his pants or brush his teeth, he crawled into bed.

An hour later, sleep still eluded him. He reached for his nightstand and removed a bottle of pain-relief pills hidden in the drawer.

He'd taken a lot of them over the past two years.

Shaking out four pills, he swallowed them dry and lay down and waited for them to work.

As he drifted off to sleep, he remembered the name of the constellation.

Perseus. The hero.

CHAPTER TWO
FAIRFAX, VIRGINIA

WHY IS IT quiet upstairs?

Jenny Thompson's two youngest children, seven-year-old Mia and five-year-old Matt Jr., sat at the kitchen table, slurping cereal while playing games on their electronic tablets. Learning to multitask early. She often wondered whether her kids would be able to function, if forced to focus on one thing.

"Don't make so much noise," she said. "It's bad manners."

Both cut their eyes at her, briefly, and turned back to their tablets. And their slurping.

Her husband, Matt, had left for the Mercedes dealership in Fairfax City, a short distance from their home. She'd packed his lunch, attaching a Post-it note to the plastic bag safeguarding his sandwich:

I love you! See you tonight! Love, Jenny

The *i* in tonight was a heart instead of a dot.

As the general sales manager, Matt needed to be in the office early, most days arriving at 6 a.m. From the beginning of their marriage, they had decided that she would be responsible for waking, feeding, and sending the kids out the door for school in the morning. Yes, she was a stay-at-home mom—and proud of it—but that didn't mean her days weren't stressful.

Like today.

Jenny called up to her oldest son. Again. "Tyler, come on! You're going to be late!"

Her fourteen-year-old son used to be prompt and look forward to going to school. But when he hit his teen years, he became infected with the tardiness bug pandemic to most teenagers.

Removing the stainless-steel skillet from the stove, she scooped the scrambled eggs onto a plate next to the bacon. She placed it in front of Tyler's seat at the table. She poured him a glass of orange juice and texted him to hurry up.

Her younger two children chewed their food, their intense gazes never leaving their screens. Despite their ignorance of her presence, a surge of love for them swept through her. They were growing up before her eyes. She could admire them all day, but she had her priorities.

"Tyler, I'm not kidding!"

After a last glance at Mia and Matt Jr. and double checking that the stove burners were off, she said, "I'll be right back. Don't move."

Like I have to worry.

Making her way toward the front of their Colonial home, she climbed the stairs to the second floor. As she reached the top, she paused, her hand still on the wooden rail in need of refinishing. The smell of bacon permeated all the way up here.

But something was off. It was too quiet.

She shivered.

After a few moments, she realized what was wrong. She didn't hear music. Tyler always listened to music, mostly rap.

Her Caucasian offspring from the suburbs couldn't read, watch TV, or sleep without it. His favorite t-shirt sported YOLO— You Only Live Once—in gigantic yellow letters, lyrics of a song by his favorite artist, Drake. He wore the shirt so often that it had faded from its original black to a dull gray.

Jenny shook off the bad thoughts and walked—conscious of each step—down the carpeted hallway to his bedroom, stopping at the door to listen.

Nothing.

She frowned. A gnawing started in the pit of her stomach, spreading through her body and into her fingertips. She placed her palm flat on his door, before slowly balling her hand into a fist. She knocked.

No response.

She knocked again, more insistently.

Still nothing.

"Tyler, open the door."

Her hand drifted to the knob, encircling it. She squeezed and turned. But the door did not open.

It was locked, which wasn't unusual.

When he was eight years old, Tyler saw the movie *The Haunting in Connecticut* at a sleepover with friends. Ever since, he'd been locking his door before he went to bed.

Jenny backtracked to her bedroom near the top of the stairs and through to the bathroom. She grabbed the bobby pin in a drawer of the vanity, kept easily accessible for just this purpose, and returned to Tyler's door. She inserted the already straightened pin into the hole in the doorknob.

A click. Success.

Jenny inched the door open to ensure that she didn't see anything she didn't want to see. Tyler told her he had started sleeping in the nude about a year ago. When he hit puberty, he strutted around the house without a shirt, his underdeveloped chest impressive only to himself. Every real and imagined chin hair pointed out for her inspection.

Yep. He still lay in bed, shirtless, the sheet thankfully covering the lower half of his body. She pushed the door open all the way.

"Tyler, wake up, now! I mean it!"

Stomping over to the bed, she stopped short.

His face, swollen and covered with bruises, sported a black eye. The inside of his nose and the corner of his lips were crusted with blood. Her eyes scanned his torso, the bruises forming an intricate tattoo.

What the hell had happened to her son?

She grabbed his shoulder and shook him—

And pulled her hand back as if scalded. Not because he was hot. Or warm. Just the opposite. Her son was cold. His shoulder barely moved.

She cradled her son's face in both of her hands. His eyes were closed. His face cold. An angel.

A bruised and battered angel.

Sleeping.

No. This can't be.

"Tyler, baby, please! Wake up! Please, baby. Please."

She bent and placed her ear to his chest and then over his mouth.

Nothing.

She initiated CPR. Never trained, she imitated what she'd seen on a hospital reality TV show. She put her hands together and, using the pads of her palm, pressed repeatedly against his heart. She tried mouth-to-mouth resuscitation.

Still nothing.

After a few minutes, she stopped. Her efforts fruitless.

Whispering in his ear over and over, "Wake up, baby," she closed her eyes, the warm tears cascading down her cheeks and onto his.

Still cheek to cheek, her eyes moved from his headboard to the lamp on his nightstand, to his cell phone streaming with texts until she spotted the medicine bottle laying on its side next to the phone. She reached for it.

Turning the bottle around, she read the label.

It belonged to her. A long-standing OxyContin prescription she used for knee pain, a constant reminder of her high school and college playing days.

The bottle was empty.

Only then did she start to scream. And couldn't stop.

Mia and Matt Jr. burst through the open door.

"Mom! What's wrong?"

"What's happening?"

They stood next to the bed.

"Why are you crying?" Mia asked.

"Why are you in bed with Tyler?" Matt Jr. said. He pushed his older brother with both hands. "Wake up!" He recoiled and looked at her. "Why is he cold?"

"I'm calling Dad!" Her daughter grabbed Tyler's cell phone off the nightstand.

Her children's voices reached her through a thick fog. She didn't register what they were saying.

Matt and the paramedics arrived at nearly the same time ten minutes later. Her husband must have called 911. Jenny was still crying and screaming. By that time, her two youngest children had joined her.

CHAPTER THREE

ARLINGTON, VIRGINIA

JADE HARRINGTON HOLSTERED her Glock on her hip and sipped the remains of her morning coffee as she looked out at the small backyard of her townhouse. The melting snow from last week's storm, unusual for April, exposed to the world her poor yard-work skills. Brown grass surrounded the concrete patio, the only furniture a rusted wrought-iron table and chairs. She couldn't remember the last time she had sat out there.

She glanced down at her cocoa-colored cat, Card, who stared up at her, a face of unmasked devotion.

"What?"

The cat continued to stare, a slight twitch of his ears the only evidence that he'd heard her. Placing the cup in the sink, she swooped Card up to cradle him like a baby and deposited a kiss on his forehead.

"Love you. Gotta go."

The smartphone in the pocket of her gray dress pants buzzed. She shifted the cat to one arm as she fished it out. Christian. She answered. "Hey, you."

"Hey," he said, his tone somber. Unusual for him.

While FBI agents don't have partners, she worked with Special Agent Christian Merritt more than any other agent. She wouldn't want it any other way.

Depositing Card on the floor, she placed her hand on her hip, ready, bracing for the bad news sure to follow.

"What?"

"My nephew . . . my wife's sister's son . . . he, uh, died of an apparent suicide. Last night. They . . . she found him this morning." Silence. "Do you think—"

Jade had started for the front door while he spoke. Grabbing her suit jacket off the back of a chair, she scooped up her briefcase and keys from a table in the foyer.

"On my way. What's the address?"

CHAPTER FOUR

THE WHITE HOUSE, WASHINGTON, DC

SHE LOOKED ACROSS the desk at her Chief of Staff, Sasha Scott. "Ninety days."

President Whitney Fairchild sat behind the *Resolute* desk, a gift from Queen Victoria to President Rutherford B. Hayes in 1880. President John F. Kennedy was the first to use the desk in the Oval Office, as had many presidents since.

She glanced around her office: the beige carpet with the presidential seal, the plush sofas and chairs, paintings of Lincoln, Washington, Franklin D. Roosevelt, and Susan B. Anthony—she could never exclude the famous suffragette.

"It hasn't gone as I had hoped," Whitney continued.

Sasha shifted in her chair. "You haven't accomplished anything."

Whitney proffered a wry smile. "Tell me how you really feel."

With both houses of Congress controlled by the other party, resisting—she preferred "obstructing"—every issue on her legislative agenda, her first ninety days in office had not gone well. Certainly not according to plan. This Congress allowed all legislation, even measures that had been supported by Republicans in the past, to languish or die.

"Every president since FDR," Whitney said, "has been judged on his accomplishments within his first hundred days. I only have ten left."

"But that Congress gave FDR everything he asked for," Sasha pointed out.

"Resulting in the highest GDP growth in history."

"I wish time travel existed. Like in all those books you read. We could swap this Congress for that one. So, what are you going to do?"

"That is the question. Isn't it?" Whitney held out her hand. "What's on the agenda for today?"

Sasha handed her several briefing books. "You're meeting with the Gang of Twenty on comprehensive immigration reform."

"Eight. Twelve. Twenty. No matter how many members of Congress work on it, they cannot seem to come to an agreement."

"A few freshmen congressmen requested a meeting about paving the way for another pipeline through the Midwest."

Whitney didn't bother to respond.

"And the president of the National Education Association wants to hear your ideas for education in the twenty-first century."

"I'm not ready."

Sasha nodded toward one of the books. "Just repeat what's in there." She settled back in the guest chair. "Did you see Maddow?"

"About Cole's son?"

She nodded. "Should be some show today. Cole's show, I mean."

Cole Brennan, the top-rated conservative radio talk-show host in the country, was Whitney's loudest and most vocal critic. His pledge during the campaign to support her had lasted exactly one day. Inauguration Day. Since then, he had criticized her every move, every decision, every outfit, every hairstyle. He even criticized her weight. His ratings had never been higher.

This morning his eighteen-year-old son announced he was gay—and worse, a liberal—on a special edition of Rachel Maddow's show on MSNBC. That he would do so on the liberal news commentator's television show must have been a staggering blow to Cole.

"Wish I had time to listen to it. Poor kid." Whitney crossed her legs, her left index finger resting on her lips. Her thinking position.

"What's on your mind, Madam President?"

"I'm worried. When was the last time you visited a truly diverse community? People live among other people who think like them, look like them, vote like them, and pray—or not—like them."

Sasha remained silent. She had heard all this before.

"Dual economies," Whitney said. "Different classes of people living side by side."

"The difference in income between the haves and have-nots," Sasha said, "continues to grow."

"The wealthy continue to earn the majority of income, but middle- to lower-class wages stay the same."

"And it's only gotten worse since you've been in office."

Whitney frowned. "Thanks." Leaning her head back against the chair, she stared at the ceiling. "Nineteen eighty-two began the start of gated-community construction. The year of the Great Divide. Today, seventeen percent of all new homes over five hundred thousand dollars are built in gated communities."

"It's no coincidence that 'segregate' contains the word 'gate.'"

Whitney smiled. "Ooh . . . I might need to use that."

"The question is: are the gates to keep people out or to keep people in?"

Whitney thought about it. "Both." She sighed and sat up. "I'm supposed to be the president who changes this. Reverses the trend."

"It's still early, yet," Sasha said, her pen ready. "What do you need?"

Whitney gestured at the briefing books stacked on her desk. "These aren't my legacy. Inequality is at its highest level in more than a century." She brought her fist down, tapping the table. "Income *equality* is the issue I want to solve. That is my legacy. I need you to come up with a plan. A brilliant plan that will stimulate the economy, inspire the American people, and ensure that everyone shares in the benefit. Not just the one-percenters. But, most important—"

"—will get buy-in on the Hill," Sasha finished for her.

"Work with—" She almost said "Landon." It had taken her more time than it should to name his replacement for director of legislative affairs. "—Rick."

"When do you need it?"

"Yesterday."

CHAPTER FIVE

FAIRFAX, VIRGINIA

JADE PARALLEL PARKED her old Audi A4 behind the car in front of a traditional Colonial home. It wasn't one of the McMansions that had sprouted like weeds in the DC metropolitan area in the 1990s and the first two decades of this century.

Christian leaned against the trunk of a Bureau car, his arms crossed over his massive chest. His cropped blond hair stood at attention. He watched her approach.

She gave him a brief hug. It was like embracing a mountain. Pulling back to look him in the eyes, she brought her hand to his cheek. After a moment, she said, "Let's go."

A kid's bicycle lay across the walkway that bisected the well-maintained yard. They stepped around it.

He led her through the front door. A man the same size as Christian, but not as muscular, met them in the foyer. Christian gestured to Jade. "This is Special Agent Jade Harrington."

"Matt Thompson," he said, subdued, extending his hand. He showed them to the living room, one step down off the foyer to their right.

"Be right back," Matt said, turning toward the hallway that led to the back of the house.

Jade took in the immaculate room. A massive Matisse reproduction adorned one wall over the sofa, and a hodgepodge of framed photographs rested on an end table. She picked one up of Matt with a pretty, athletic woman and three kids, all smiling, their brown hair kissed by the sun. An orange promotional lifesaver ring with Carnival Dream in black lettering hung behind them. Matt's wife resembled her sister—Christian's wife, Amanda—but Amanda was blonde like her husband. Jade stared at the children's faces.

The silence in the house was deafening.

A soft voice. "Hello?"

Jade turned. Matt held his wife with both arms. She wore a pink bathrobe. Once fuzzy, it was now worn in several places. Enormous slippers in the shape of Goofy, the Disney character, adorned her feet.

Jade placed the photograph back where she found it.

"Honey, this is Agent . . . uh," Matt looked at her, apologetic.

"Jade. Jade Harrington."

"This is my wife, Jenny."

Her bloodshot eyes fluttered to Jade and widened. "Jade Harrington! The agent from the TSK case?"

Jade had solved the Talk Show Killer—TSK—case four months ago, becoming a sudden and unwilling celebrity.

Jenny knelt before Jade and hugged her legs. Crying. "I'm glad you're here. I don't understand. Why would my baby commit suicide? We were happy. We loved him so much."

Embarrassed, Jade didn't move. She looked at Christian. Matt pried his wife from Jade's legs, and guided Jenny to the sofa facing the hallway. Jade and Christian moved to chairs opposite them.

"Ma'am. I'm not here in an official capacity. Christian and I work together. I'm just here for support."

He meant more to her than that, but didn't think the situation warranted further explanation. She also didn't say she was sorry for their loss. She knew loss. No words from a stranger could comfort them.

To Jade, Jenny Thompson said: "The police just left. They took my boy."

"The coroner," Matt murmured.

"Tell me about your son," Jade said, in the soothing voice she reserved for victims' families.

"He loves rap music. Plays it morning and night. Do you like rap music?"

"This isn't really about me."

"Baseball. He loves baseball. He was proud of his cap. He wore it everywhere." Jenny smiled. "I remember when his coach gave it to him, he couldn't wait to put his initials inside it." She stopped smiling. "But he's lost interest."

Jade couldn't stop herself. "Were there any signs he was suicidal?"

Matt stiffened next to his wife. "No."

After a pause, Jenny said, "Well . . ."

Jade leaned forward, ignoring Christian's glare. "What? What is it?"

Jenny glanced at her husband. "Tyler seems different. He isn't eating as much as he normally does. And he complains a lot about stomachaches and headaches." Jenny spoke of her son in the present tense. As if he were still alive.

"Anything else different about him? How was he doing in school?"

"He used to be an A-B student. Lately, it's been Cs and Ds."

"Was he sleeping?"

Jenny shook her head, her body crumpling. She leaned against her husband, whose arms enveloped her.

Christian stood. "I'm going to check on Amanda."

"She's upstairs with the children," Matt said.

Christian shot Jade a warning look before he left.

If he didn't want me asking questions, he shouldn't have brought me. Or left me alone with them.

Jade waited for his footsteps to fade. "Did Tyler leave a note? An email? A text?"

Matt shook his head.

Jenny's head popped up from his shoulder.

"How would we know? They . . . the police . . . took everything. His laptop, his tablet, his phone." She didn't wipe away her tears. "Can you find out for us, Agent Harrington?"

CHAPTER SIX

WASHINGTON, DC

"NINETY DAYS AND nothing," he said into the microphone, shifting his bulk in the chair. "I hate to say 'I told you so,' but I told you this would happen if *those* people elected Whitney president. So, even though I hate to do it . . . I told you so!"

Cole Brennan laughed, a high-pitched giggle that seemed incongruous coming from a man of his size.

"Our new president has accomplished absolutely nothing in her first ninety days in office. Just like every Commiecrat before her. It's a disgrace."

He glanced at the TVs mounted on the yellow and orange wall, each tuned to a different network: FOX, MSNBC, CNN, ABC, and CBS. No breaking news.

"Let's try to help her out, shall we? What should she be doing? I'll take your calls now. Go!"

He gazed at the computer screen with the list of actives. "What do you think, Jonah from Oklahoma?"

"Cole Brennan! Wow, man! It's an honor to talk to you."

"I know. What's on your mind?"

"What you've been preaching for years, man. We need to stop all these illegal aliens from entering our country."

"Couldn't agree more. Our former president—God bless that ol' cowboy—reneged on his promise to build a fence. A fence is too easy to circumvent, anyway. What we need is a wall to keep them out. A great big wall. The Great Wall of the USA. Bigger than the Great Wall of China. And we need a true visionary—a man—to build it and get the Mexican government to pay for it. A win-win."

"A great wall that's free. Great idea, Cole. My town hasn't been the same since the damn aliens took all our jobs. Anything you could do to keep them out—better yet, send them back—would be appreciated."

"Don't think that'll happen during Whitney's only term, but I'll do my best. Probably going to be the opposite. Next caller. Mason from Alabama. Go!"

"Hey, Cole, love your show. How about keeping the Muslims out of our country? London elected one as their mayor, and now the mayor of New York City is one, too. They're taking over the world! What are we going to do to prevent that from happening?"

He took a sip of his ever-present sweet iced tea. "Well, she's going to let everybody in. Even radical Islamic terrorists. It's going to be like Motel 6. 'We'll leave the light on for you.' But not all Muslims are bad, Mason. There are good Muslims. We just need a stricter process to keep the bad ones out. Wouldn't you agree?"

"You can keep 'em all out, as far as I'm concerned."

"The Statue of Liberty says something like 'give me your tired, poor, et cetera, et cetera,' but it doesn't say anything about 'give me your filthy, your Islamist, your terrorist.'"

"You got that right, Cole."

He took several more calls in the same vein before wrapping up the segment. "Where is the candidate that represents our views? A real honest-to-God conservative who will make America great like it used to be. Is anybody out there? Hello? Hello?"

He sighed. "Well, everyone, we've run out of time. This is Cole Brennan protecting your life, liberty, and pursuit of happiness. Join us again tomorrow for 'The Conservative Voice.'"

CHAPTER SEVEN

WASHINGTON, DC

CHRISTIAN LEANED INTO her fourth-floor office at the Federal Bureau of Investigation headquarters, a hand on each side of the door frame. "Got a minute?"

The question that wasted her time more than any other.

Jade looked up from a case file. She glanced at the numerous files stacked neatly on her desk and back at him. "Not really."

"Tough. We have a visitor downstairs."

They navigated through the throng of agents traversing the lobby in all directions. Jenny Thompson sat on a low couch, her hands resting on her lap. She didn't rise as they approached.

Jade sat next to her. "Mrs. Thompson."

Christian remained standing next to Jade.

"I didn't tell you about the bruises. The scratches."

"On Tyler?" Jade said.

"His arms. His legs. Chest. Back. Face. Especially his face."

Jade's gut told her what had been happening to Jenny's son. Softening her voice, she said, "At your house, you mentioned some of your son's symptoms. Do you think he was being bullied?"

Jenny shook her head. "I told Matt that Tyler was going through teenage stuff. Girl problems. Teachers. Homework. Parents."

Jade waited, expecting Jenny to fill the silence. She didn't disappoint.

Jenny scrunched up her face. "If he was being bullied, I would've known."

The likelihood of Tyler telling his mother he'd been bullied was low. Not something a lot of kids—especially teenage boys—would discuss with their parents.

Jade would know.

Jenny hesitated. "They found pictures."

"Who?"

Jenny's jaw set. Voice clipped, she said, "The police found . . . pictures of him on the Internet. Naked pictures. Buck naked."

Jade glanced up at Christian.

He stared at his sister-in-law. "Tyler?"

"The police said . . ." She fell silent for a moment. "Someone took pictures of my son in the shower at school. In the locker room."

Jade started to take Jenny's hand and then thought better of it. "Is that why they think—?"

"There's a Twitter account," Jenny said, tears flowing down her cheeks. "Dedicated to my boy. A 'fan'"—she made air quotes—"account, and it has the vilest, nastiest tweets about my son. That he was gay and had a small penis and that he liked his baseball teammates a little too much. Someone tweeted: 'Nobody loves you.' It received over a hundred 'likes.'"

"Jesus," Christian said.

Jenny's voice rose, her breathing heavy. "People shouldn't

be allowed to say whatever they want on the Internet, right? And take your picture without permission? They can't get away with this. Can you do something?"

Other agents glanced at them as they passed by.

Jade said, "There's nothing we—the FBI—can do. Maybe the county police can trace who created the account."

"They said it was created from a public computer, and they're having a hard time tracing it. I want answers! I need to know who did this to my son!"

"Mrs. Thompson, you're going through a horrible time, but I must ask you to calm down."

"Calm down? Calm down? I don't want to fucking calm down. My son is dead!"

She started to rise, but Christian grasped her in a one-armed bear hug and returned her to the couch. "Jenny, if we're going to help you, you must get ahold of yourself."

She waved at Jade. "But she said there's nothing you can do. You can't fucking help me. Can you bring my son back? Can you find out who did this to him?"

Christian and Jade looked at each other, but didn't respond.

After a few moments, Jenny's breathing steadied.

Jade ventured another question. "What else did the police say?"

"They're worthless. They can't help me. No one did anything to help my son. Not even me. Tyler was smart. Cute. Almost beautiful." Jenny Thompson gave her a defiant look. "But one thing I know for sure. I know my son. And he wasn't gay."

"How can you be sure?" Jade said.

"They won't leave us alone," Jenny said, ignoring Jade's question.

Jade glanced at Christian bewildered and back to Jenny. "Who?"

"Reporters. Camped outside our house. Fire questions at us as we try to get in our car. Follow my kids to school and Matt to work. I can't watch the news."

She put her hands over her ears and bent at the waist.

Someone in the Fairfax County police department had allegedly leaked to the media that Tyler Thompson had been cyberbullied. You couldn't turn on the TV without seeing the elaborate "Bullycide" logo next to Tyler's adorable high-school yearbook picture with the faux forest behind him.

Jenny sat up. "There's more."

What now?

Christian tensed.

"The police also discovered that Tyler exchanged texts with a girl at school. I didn't know her. He never talked about her. Never showed me her picture. But from the texts I could tell he really liked her."

"Who was it?" Christian asked.

The infinitesimal smile that appeared on Jenny's face at the thought of her son's happiness disappeared quickly. "I don't know. Turns out the girl played a joke on my son. All those fucking kids ganged up on him. That bitch never cared for him. The bullying wasn't what got to him." Jenny looked at Jade. "When Tyler found out that girl was laughing at him behind his back, that's what did it.

"That's why he took his own life, Agent Harrington."

CHAPTER EIGHT

THE WHITE HOUSE, WASHINGTON, DC

WHITNEY PACKED THE stack of briefing materials into her case and made her way up to the residence. It was only seven p.m., but she needed a break.

She had the rest of the evening to herself. Grayson was in Missouri running the family firm, Fairchild Industries, and her children were off at school: Chandler was a senior at the University of Missouri, and her daughter, Emma, a sophomore at Princeton. Whitney had not seen them since Easter.

She was alone. Well, alone if you didn't count the Secret Service. Or the White House staff. Or the residence staff. Or the military staff.

Setting the briefcase on a stand by the front door, she walked to the wine refrigerator in the living area and selected a bottle of 1997 Opus One. On the sofa, she tucked her legs under her. Holding the wine glass in one hand, and the remote in the other, she flipped through the channels on the flat-screen stopping on MSNBC. Another rally in progress.

Over the last week, rallies—protests?—had broken out in several major cities across the country, the one televised now in Philadelphia. The protesters seemed to come from all walks of life. Different races. Different ages. Different genders. Different religions.

Whitney turned up the sound.

"What we're seeing now is different from the Occupy Wall Street movement of years ago," said the red-headed male MSNBC commentator in front of a fake vista of the Liberty Bell. "These protests are more urgent, more desperate, and they don't seem to be going away anytime soon."

She sipped her wine. *Because the problem isn't going away anytime soon.*

"What do they want?" the anchor in the studio asked.

"To close the gap. According to the nonpartisan Congressional Budget Office, wealth for the rich has increased two hundred and seventy-five percent while increasing only forty percent for the middle class. For the poor, twenty. The top twenty percent own sixty percent of the wealth in this country."

More like eighty-five percent. The American people underestimated the share of wealth owned by the wealthiest individuals. But people were waking up. Reports had come in that income inequality protests were not only happening in front of businesses and banks, but also gated and other exclusive communities. Protesters had barred residents from entering their own homes. Fights had broken out in airports over first-class upgrades. In airplanes over the use of the bathroom in the forward section by coach passengers unwilling to wait with the four hundred other passengers for the three restrooms in the rear.

After a commercial break, the studio anchor introduced Evan Stevens, an influential liberal blogger. Handsome, with a short, trimmed beard and dark hair combed into the latest style, Stevens was a fastidious dresser. Everything about him seemed to be studied perfection. He railed against income inequality, an issue he had been battling for a long time.

People were starting to listen.

After several minutes, she muted the television and glanced at the stand in the foyer. The briefing books awaited her. Although she had a spacious office next door in the Treaty Room, usually, when she worked from "home," rather, upstairs, she ended up here. On the sofa.

Whitney closed her eyes, trying to forget—temporarily—this issue that had concerned her for years. The issue that could undermine not just her presidency, but her country.

Income inequality.

The outside wants in.

CHAPTER NINE

FAIRFAX, VIRGINIA

STILL PUMPED UP, literally, from lifting free weights after practice, Zach Rawlins guided his BMW around the final curve before the entrance to his parents' subdivision. Since his father purchased the car and made the payments, the Beemer didn't really belong to him. A technicality his father reminded him of often.

Wending his way through the neighborhood, he needed to hurry. His father didn't like for him to be out late on a school night, especially when he had the car. Zach's mind drifted to his conversation with Kaylee after third period. She was captain of the junior varsity cheerleading squad for football, basketball, and baseball; he was captain of the JV baseball team. Handsome—everyone had told him so since he was a kid—a good student, and a jock. What's not to like?

They were perfect for each other.

Brianna, also a cheerleader, wanted to go out with him—she hinted she wanted a lot more than that—but he never settled. He wanted only the best. The best car. The best girl. He lived in the largest house in the neighborhood. If you didn't want the best, why bother?

After all, he was his father's son.

Zach slowed to turn into his driveway. For such a well-to-do neighborhood, the developers had skimped on lighting and neglected to install enough street lamps. The yard was shrouded in darkness. He looked up at the house. Most of the lights were turned off, his mother no doubt in the living room drinking a highball and watching *The Real Housewives* of some American city. He didn't understand how she could watch those shows all the time. They were stupid. All the drama.

His father probably wasn't home yet, working late at the office again. Good. No rush.

He parked twenty feet away from the garage, the inside of which was reserved for his parents' cars. Grabbing his backpack from the passenger seat, he opened the car door. Before he could slam the door closed, he heard a soft scraping sound in an otherwise still night.

What was that?

Zach turned his head to check out the yard on the side of the house where the noise came from.

Something hard hit him in the head.

"Fuck!" he screamed.

A baton? A pipe? A baseball bat? Whatever it was, it hurt like hell.

Dropping his bag, he clutched his head with both hands. He pulled his hands away, his left saturated with a dark liquid. Blood. His blood.

"I'm going to kick your ass, motherfucker."

As the anger surged through him, he cocked his arm back

to deliver a Hail Mary punch. He caught a glimpse of his assailant. And paused. Surprised.

His hesitation cost him his life.

The person hit him in the head again.

"Damn it!"

A long-ball hitter, quickness was never Zach's strength. He didn't raise his forearms in time. The assailant hit him in the exact same spot. Now that fucking hurt. He yelped and grabbed his head again, which made him unprepared for the blow to his kidney. The pain cut to his core. The air left him. He doubled over.

The next blow came to the side of his leg, followed by two more in quick succession. Something popped in his knee.

Shit, I'm going to miss the rest of the season. Need to start fighting back.

But the blows kept coming.

His mind lost track of which part of his body was experiencing which pain. He couldn't get up.

He never had the chance to fight back.

His last thought was not of his parents or his friends or his teammates. His last thought was of Kaylee. She wouldn't go out with him with his face looking like this.

Before he drifted off into eternal darkness, his head was lifted by his hair. The roots tugged at his scalp. Zach had no energy left to scream.

Before his eyes, a photograph. Before he had time to formulate a name, his face was smashed into the ground.

And then, he felt nothing at all.

CHAPTER TEN

THE WHITE HOUSE, WASHINGTON, DC

WHITNEY TURNED OFF the television. She didn't want to be, but she was right about this issue. Things were going to get worse before they got better. The quality of life must be improved for all Americans, not just the ones at the top. If people revolted, the impact would spread beyond businesses and the boycotting of their products. The republic itself could be at stake.

She hit the remote for the stereo. The Four Seasons, op. 8 by Antonio Vivaldi was already loaded in the CD player.

She closed her eyes for a moment, a deep breath drawing the music in to soothe her. Unbidden, thoughts of Grayson arose—or as the mainstream media had dubbed him, "The First First Man." Some in the alternative media called him "The First Dude."

Whitney had never asked her husband during or after the election to turn over the reins of Fairchild Industries to one of his brothers or a professional CEO. During the transition, the Right had had an apoplectic fit, clamoring for him to place the business in a blind trust. Grayson never considered it. Since she wasn't a director or shareholder, and thus neither exercised any influence nor received any direct benefit from the business, she had hoped to assuage the public's conflict of interest concerns. The conservative media still wasn't buying it.

She hadn't asked Grayson to lead a pet cause like prior presidential spouses: the war against drugs, mental health, or supporting veterans. One of his unofficial responsibilities, to be a senior counselor to her and attend select cabinet meetings, would have bored him to tears. He hadn't made any appearances on her behalf, much less visited the poor and disenfranchised in other countries or helped to shape citizens' perception of her initiatives.

He wasn't much of a First Gentleman.

But that was fine with her. She didn't need the distraction.

His current job was important. As the CEO of a multi-billion-dollar agriculture and biotechnology conglomerate, his employees and customers and stockholders depended on him. He tried to live a normal life, despite the ever-present press corps and the small Secret Service detail shadowing him. He had resisted even that, until he realized they were going to follow him around anyway.

The media, of course, was having a field day. Grayson was not only neglecting his duties as the First Gentleman, but shirking an honor and a tradition and a privilege—although not constitutionally mandated—entrusted to him by the American people.

And the American people didn't like it.

The media speculated about their long-distance marriage.

Ted Bowling, her campaign manager, had told her that a recent poll had ranked her in the bottom twentieth percentile for "family values" out of all US presidents, a ghastly result considering the competition and unwelcome news, particularly for a female politician.

She and Grayson had lived separate lives for such a long time, while she was a representative and then as a senator in Congress. Back then, they would see each other once a month. Either she would go to him or he to her. It worked for them.

Now, he always came to her.

At times like this, she missed Landon, her congressional legislative aide. Their debates about politics. Late-night strategy sessions. Reading contests. The comfort of being able to discuss almost anything with him. He would have flourished in the White House, relishing the challenge of working with an obstructionist Congress.

For the last few months, those on the Right had tried to make more of what happened. The "TSKgate" scandal had overshadowed her presidential transition. Allegations had swirled about her complicity or knowledge of Landon's crimes. And that she hadn't done anything to stop him. FOX News had accused her of being the mastermind, an accusation repeated so often that, by some, it was now considered fact. FOX would continue to fuel the conspiracy until the next scandal erupted. Created by the network, if necessary.

She glanced at her watch. Seven p.m. in Missouri. He would still be at work.

He picked up on the first ring.

"Hello, darling," Grayson said.

"Still at the office?"

"Acquiring a biotech company in California." He sounded upbeat. "How was your day?"

"Unproductive," she said.

"Why is that?"

"Most of my legislative agenda has been stonewalled. These protests across the country concern me."

"Anything I can do?"

"Run for Congress?"

"No thanks. After this acquisition, why don't I come and spend some time with you? I can make some appearances. Join you at some events."

"Excellent idea." She glanced at her briefing books again. "Darling, I must run. Work is calling. I'll call you tomorrow. Love you."

"I love you—"

Whitney hung up.

CHAPTER ELEVEN

WASHINGTON, DC

"ASK ME WHAT I did this weekend."

She studied her colleague Special Agent Dante Carlucci. He dressed for work as if he were going out. Jade never understood how he could afford such expensive suits on his salary. His features independently—dark brown curly hair, long nose, and one ear slightly higher than the other—appeared out of sync, but together, they complemented each other. Handsome, and he knew it, Dante never passed a mirror he didn't like.

Even though they'd had run-ins in the past, the status of their relationship was one of détente. They didn't entirely trust each other, maybe didn't even like each other, but over the last year they'd developed a grudging mutual respect. It didn't mean she couldn't give him shit when warranted.

"I don't care."

"It's not like that. I met someone. Her name's Laurie. I cooked dinner for her. French, my specialty."

"And?"

"We watched a movie, and I took her home."

His cologne wasn't as overpowering as usual. Perhaps this woman was a good influence on him. Maybe now Jade would be able to work near him without gagging.

"Sounds as if you have a girlfriend."

"I think I do."

"I'm happy for you. Bye."

"What about you?"

She tore her eyes away from the file she wanted to return to reading. "What about me?"

"Don't you ever go on dates . . . with anyone?"

"I don't date."

"You should. It might take the edge off."

"Take the edge off what?" Christian said, filling up the doorway to her office.

"Nothing." Jade, in resignation, set the file down. "How was it?"

Christian had spent the morning attending his nephew's funeral. He shook his head.

Jade's desk phone rang.

The receptionist: "A Lieutenant John Briggs with the US Park Police is on the line."

"Lieutenant," Jade said. "What can I do for you?"

"I saw you on the news. The Talk Show Killer. Great work."

"Thanks." She didn't take compliments well. She straightened the items on her desk while she waited him out.

"Anyway," he said, "I caught a case you may be interested in."

"I'm listening."

"There's been a murder here. In Gravelly Point Park." He paused. "It's bad."

Gravelly Point Park was located just north of Reagan National Airport.

Oops. Zoe would kill me.

Zoe, her best friend, believed it was blasphemy to call the Washington, DC airport by any other name than its original: National Airport. A true-blue liberal Democrat, Zoe might have been a little biased.

The park, a few hundred feet from one of the runways, was considered one of the best places in the United States for aircraft spotting—the hobby of watching airplanes take off and land. The site attracted all kinds of people: casual observers, aviation buffs, locals, and tourists. Jurisdiction over Gravelly Point Park fell to the US Park Police.

Why was he calling her?

Jade received calls like this often. Local police from all over the country requested her involvement in their cases. She should tell Lt. John Briggs that she was busy.

"How so?" she replied.

"The vic was a boy," he said. "Between fourteen and seventeen."

"With all due respect, Lieutenant, I still don't understand why you're calling me."

"The manner in which he died made me think of you. Well, TSK. Beat his vics with a blunt instrument, right? A baseball bat?"

Jade's heart beat faster, as she glanced over at Christian and Dante. "Are you saying this victim suffered similar injuries?"

"Did you hear about the murder of the high-school kid a few nights ago? The one killed in his parents' front yard? Next to their BMW?"

"Sure. What about it?"

"I called the cop who caught that case, and she's on her way over."

"You think they're related?"

"I think you might want to have a look, too."

Jade took one last glance at the neglected file. "We'll be right there."

CHAPTER TWELVE
SEATTLE, WASHINGTON

"DAYDREAMING AGAIN?"

Yes.

He glanced at his father standing in the hallway just outside his office. Although in his early sixties, he was still tall and fit, except for a small belly increasing in size in direct proportion to the number of craft breweries opening around Seattle. Noah was built like him.

Noah Blakeley, the chief operating officer of his family's international shipping firm and scion of one of the first families of Seattle, had been watching the local news on the TV in his office in the Pioneer Square neighborhood near downtown. Protests across the country dominated the noon broadcast.

Income inequality was a major problem. Not only in this city and in the US, but in countries around the world. A huge supporter of the president, he was skeptical of the federal government's ability to find a solution given the current dysfunctional Congress. Raising the minimum wage would be a start, but not a panacea. He had done his part. The lowest-level employees in his firm earned twice the state minimum wage. And Washington had one of the highest minimum wages in the country.

He'd met President Whitney Fairchild before, once, during her campaign, hosting the future president and most of Seattle's wealthiest Democratic contributors in his home in Madison Park, an affluent neighborhood in Seattle.

He wondered if she remembered him.

Given the net worth of his father's company, one would think Noah's office would be nicer. His television was the opposite of flat: the silver, boxy thirty-four-inch, early 2000s model sat atop a metal filing cabinet, threatening to squash it at any moment. The TV weighed over a hundred pounds.

Good luck hanging that on the wall.

His oak desk, purchased at a secondhand store, rested on a threadbare carpet, which had been traversed many miles before its installation.

Noah wasn't much better than his father. His clothes displayed his own frugality: frayed pants, partially untucked shirt, and scruffy brown shoes. People who passed him on the street would never guess he was a multi-millionaire. Like a lot of wealthy people in Seattle.

The most valuable thing in his office was the view. He gazed across Puget Sound to the hills of West Seattle. In the distance, low-hanging clouds surrounded the lofty snowcapped Olympic mountains.

Lofty. Like Noah's dreams.

He wanted to change the world. Make it a better place. Make a difference.

His father, however, dismissed his dreams, believing Noah had bought into all that talk about "white privilege" and was suffering from some kind of guilt over it. He didn't feel guilty about being Caucasian and wealthy, he just didn't think it was fair that some people were fortunate to be born white or in an environment with all the advantages.

Income inequality plagued him.

"Just thinking . . . ," Noah finally answered. He hesitated, knowing it was a waste of time. "About the foundation."

A few years ago, Noah's family had formed a philanthropic foundation, which now contributed generously to many causes. Not just in the greater Seattle area, but across the country.

"I want to run it, Dad," he said, trying to keep the desperation out of his voice. "I'd be good at it. It's a better fit for my skills and passions. I can make a difference. A real difference."

His father remained silent.

Noah rushed on. "August should run the business. He's a better businessman than I am. We should switch places. How could it hurt to try?" When he wasn't running the foundation, his older brother, August, spent most of his time sailing on Puget Sound. Noah often wondered when he stared out the window at the Sound, if his brother was staring back at him from his boat, cocktail glass raised. Laughing at him.

His father glanced out the window. "I want a detailed report of container shipments by country for the last month. Bring it to my office in fifteen minutes. And be prepared to discuss it."

He cast one last look at his son and left.

Noah unclenched his fist and grabbed the worry beads next to his desktop computer. Sitting back, he closed his eyes, and breathed deeply as he shifted each bead from his left hand to his right.

When he completed the circle, no less worried than when

he started, he faced his computer and called up the operations software to produce the report his father wanted.

As he waited for it to print, he realized that even though the worry beads hadn't fully relaxed him or relieved his stress, they had worked. Grabbing the papers off the printer, he hurried to his father's office.

They had calmed him down enough to face him again.

CHAPTER THIRTEEN

ARLINGTON, VIRGINIA

CHRISTIAN CROSSED THE Memorial Bridge and, one hand on top of the steering wheel, guided the Bureau car south on the George Washington Parkway. Jade preferred driving her own car rather than checking one out of the motor pool.

Located in Arlington, Virginia, Gravelly Point Park was separated from DC by the Potomac River. Riding shotgun, she gazed out the passenger window, ignoring the dirty water, and choosing to stare instead at the monuments of the capital city. Dante lounged in the backseat.

There was no question as to where the body had been found. Lights flashing, US Park, Arlington County, and Fairfax County police cars were parked everywhere in a haphazard, Matchbox-cars-like fashion. Christian pulled into the parking lot.

Before she could completely exit the vehicle, a man rushed up to her.

"Agent Harrington? Lieutenant Briggs."

Jade introduced him to Christian and Dante. They followed

Briggs as he sliced through a group of officers standing around the body. The officers parted. No one asked to see her badge.

Everyone knew who she was.

Briggs nodded to a forensic tech to open the body bag. The surrounding officers quieted. Other than the chirping of a nearby bird, the opening of the zipper was the only sound in the tranquil morning.

Pulling on nitrile gloves, Jade bent next to the corpse. She winced at the sight of him. So young. The injuries were similar to TSK's victims all right, except for one thing.

"This perp's right-handed," she said.

The left side of the kid's face was damaged. Beaten beyond recognition. She inspected the length of the body, but stopped at the massive quantity of blood in the genital area of the victim's jeans.

"I hope he was already dead," Dante said.

Briggs jerked his head toward the coroner's van. "It's over there."

"Jesus!" Christian said.

"We'll need to see it," Jade said, ignoring the sick expressions on Christian's and Dante's faces.

She pointed with her pinkie. "Check out the scratches and bruises." To Briggs. "Has he been ID'ed, yet?"

He shook his head.

She scanned the faces of the men and one woman standing around her. "You're from Fairfax?"

The woman stepped forward. "Detective Chutimant."

"Similar to your vic?"

The detective nodded. "The injuries are almost identical. My vic's were worse, though, if you can imagine that."

Jade could. She'd witnessed the worst man could do to his

fellow man. Woman, too. Evil was not a trait attributed to only one gender.

Standing, she glanced around the parking lot. "Who found the body?"

"A cyclist," Briggs said. "He does a twenty-mile ride every day before work. Got a flat tire and pulled off the trail to fix it. Spotted what he thought was a gym bag. When he came closer, he saw the body and the blood and called us from his cell phone." To Jade's unanswered question: "Clothes, finger-nails were clean. No blood on him. All the cars registered to him are in his driveway."

From Christian: "You think the vic was killed some-where else?"

"Believe he was dumped here, yeah," Briggs said, "but don't know for sure, yet."

"Could've rented a car," Dante said.

The ringing of a cell phone pierced the stillness of the morning. Everyone present with the same ringtone checked their phones. Each of them shook their heads, as they realized it wasn't their phone.

The ringing continued.

The officers looked at each other and then one by one down at the body.

"Ignore it," Briggs said.

"Answer it," Jade said.

A crime-scene technician knelt and removed the phone from the victim's pocket, handing it to Briggs.

"This is Lieutenant Briggs, US Park Police. Who's this? . . . Hello?"

Jade walked away from the group. Christian and Dante followed.

"The Talk Show Killer is dead," Christian said.

She waited for the plane overhead to pass. All three of them swiveled their heads to watch it land.

"Maybe someone wants us to think he's still alive," she said. "Let's go check out his—"

Dante grimaced. "Do we have to?"

Jade was already heading to the coroner's van.

CHAPTER FOURTEEN

WASHINGTON, DC

"THE WIZARDS ARE going to win it all this year."

"You're delusional."

Christian wiped his mouth with the napkin clenched in his fist, chewing hurriedly to make his point. "We have a true point guard who can also score, and a big man who can carry twenty points, ten rebounds every night. Two pieces of the puzzle we've been missing."

Perched on stools at the counter of a small sandwich shop near the Bureau, they were enjoying a late lunch, the shop empty except for them. Jade and Christian weren't regulars, but came often enough that the proprietor pounding a slab of meat behind the counter recognized their faces. After viewing the victim's severed penis, Dante begged off lunch and headed back to the office, declaring a loss of appetite.

She lowered her voice. "I've been meaning to talk to you." She scouted the restaurant to make sure she wouldn't be overheard. "I own some Anacostia swamp land. Can sell it to you real cheap. Great for condos."

He chomped, confidently, and swallowed. "You'll see."

Her phone vibrated. She didn't recognize the number.

"Harrington."

"Agent Harrington, Lieutenant Briggs again. We got a positive ID on the vic. Name's Nicholas Campbell."

"Hold on." Jade snatched the pen Christian held out to her. She grabbed the first piece of paper she saw. The one her sandwich was wrapped in ten minutes ago. "Go on."

"Age: sixteen," Briggs continued. "A sophomore at William Randolph Secondary School in Fairfax. Parents said he never came home last night."

"Did they report him missing?"

"No."

"Why not?"

"Because they knew from TV the police didn't start searching for missing persons for at least forty-eight hours."

She stopped writing. "Seriously?"

"Uh . . . yeah. I'm on my way to interview the parents now."

"Thanks for the update."

"No problem."

Jade clicked off.

Christian took a bite of his second sandwich. "What'd he say?"

She relayed Briggs's side of the conversation. Christian's chewing slowed. He swallowed hard.

"My son, Mark, goes to Randolph."

"Huh."

"So did my nephew, Tyler."

CHAPTER FIFTEEN

WASHINGTON, DC

WHITNEY WRAPPED UP her speech to over fifty local business leaders in a meeting room at the National Press Club. When she finished, the applause was polite and respectful, but unenthusiastic.

Because they realize what's coming.

During the campaign, she had promised to fix the nation's crumbling infrastructure, which would cost money. These businesspeople knew where that money would have to come from.

The response to her recent speeches was different from the frenzied, rock-star-like reception she had garnered as a candidate. She felt like a bride who, after a fairy-tale wedding and an idyllic honeymoon, learned that marriage was work and harder than anticipated. Lingering at the podium, she answered a few questions from the reporters in the audience.

"Judy," she pointed at the auburn-haired, middle-aged reporter who had accompanied her on the presidential campaign trail. A year ago, Judy had broken the news—to her and to the world—about Grayson's indiscretion. She had long since forgiven Judy, an old-school journalist doing her job. She wasn't the one who'd had an affair. Whitney had forgiven Grayson, too, although she hadn't forgotten. She stayed with him not for what he'd done wrong, but for all the things during their long marriage he had done right.

"Madam President, your one hundredth day in office is tomorrow. How would you grade your performance so far?"

"I'm glad someone is keeping track. Thanks, Judy." She waited for the laughter to subside. "We haven't accomplished as much as I would have liked. I didn't expect a Congress so . . . uncooperative. I would give myself a C. But I was a good student, and never settled for anything less than straight As. I won't settle as president either."

She answered a few questions from other reporters when her eyes alighted on Blake Haynes. She couldn't help smiling. "Mr. Haynes?"

"Madam President, does the federal government plan to respond to the protests occurring throughout the country?"

"We are monitoring the situation carefully and will plan our response accordingly."

After several more questions, she let Josh McPherson usher her toward a side door.

"Madam President."

She turned to see Blake Haynes standing there, a huge smile on his charming face. Josh's muscular body closed almost inconspicuously toward Whitney's, his eyes cutting from Blake to her.

"It's all right, Josh. Give us a moment." The Secret Service agent moved a few paces away, standing under a ceiling light that highlighted his brown pate.

Blake approached her. He offered her his left hand. She shook it.

"Ah. A lefty."

"Us lefties—literally and figuratively—must stick together," he said. "It's been a while. Since the inaugural ball. I never got a chance to thank you."

"For what?"

"For my show. The network gave it to me based on our interview."

"Glad to be of help."

"Perhaps, we can help each other."

She tilted her head.

"I was there," he continued. "In Palo Alto. Watching you speak to a bunch of Silicon Valley execs. After Beyoncé's performance, you had me at 'I should have delivered my speech first.'"

"Shouldn't that be 'you had me at hello'?"

"I like to be different. In any case, I want to return the favor. Another interview. Now that you're president. All softballs. Promise. Just like last time."

"But can I trust you?" she teased.

"Of course you can. I'm a good ol' Catholic boy. Cross my heart and hope to die." He made the sign on his chest.

She needed some favorable publicity. She glanced over at Josh. She would be late for her next appointment. Every hour of her day was scheduled. Every minute.

Holding out her hand, she said, "I need to run, but I'm sure that can be arranged."

He held her hand. "Income equality."

"Excuse me?"

"Income equality. That is your legacy." He stared into her eyes. "Let me help you."

Whitney masked her surprise as she turned away.

How did he know?

CHAPTER SIXTEEN

FAIRFAX, VIRGINIA

THEY STRODE UP to the predominately brick Fairfax County police station. Christian hustled to the glass door first and opened it for Jade.

"We're here to see Lieutenant Chutimant," she said to the officer sitting at the front desk.

As they waited, she glanced around the gleaming lobby. No prostitutes or drunks sat waiting in chairs, pleading their case to anyone who would listen. The atmosphere was quiet, purposeful, almost businesslike.

The detective strode toward them in an off-the-rack blue business suit.

"Right this way," she said.

They followed her through the metal detectors down a hallway of modern décor.

In her office, she waved to the guest chairs in front of her desk. "I'm not much for small talk."

"Neither am I," Jade said.

"I am," Christian said. Jade shot him a look.

Chutimant typed several strokes on her keyboard before turning the computer monitor to face them.

"I'd like to introduce you to Zach Rawlins."

The crime-scene photo showed a massive quantity of blood pooled beneath the boy's head. Like Nicholas Campbell, the boy found in Gravelly Point, Zach Rawlins had suffered extensive damage to the left side of his face. Jade let out a breath. TSK was dead. His involvement in this crime, impossible. Still, it was unsettling. The two boys' injuries were similar to the injuries inflicted on TSK's victims.

"Vicious," Christian said.

Jade continued to survey the photograph. "Severed penis?"

Chutimant nodded. Christian grimaced.

"Look at his face," Jade said. "Bruises and scratches just like Nicholas Campbell."

"And Tyler," Christian said, his voice soft.

"Who's Tyler?" asked Chutimant.

"My nephew. He also went to Randolph." He swallowed. "He . . . died . . . recently."

"Oh. He's your nephew." An expression, sympathetic and fleeting, passed over Chutimant's face. She wrote something down.

Christian blew out a breath. "Three deaths at one school in such a short time. It can't be a coincidence."

"It's not," the women said at the same time. Jade didn't believe in coincidences.

Chutimant continued, "Zach and Nicholas played on the baseball team."

"What!" Christian glanced at Jade.

"So did Tyler," Jade said to Chutimant.

A moment of silence hung over them.

"What else?" Jade said.

"Not much. Zach was sixteen. Worked out in the weight room that night with some of his teammates after practice. We interviewed them. The last one left at eight p.m. that night. Zach was still there. The coroner estimated TOD between seven and ten. The father arrived home from work at around ten. Found his son in the grass near a BMW. The kid's car. Driver's door open. Overhead light off. The mother was in the living room watching TV. If she'd only looked out the window, she might have seen who did this to her son."

"Or prevented his death," Jade said.

"She wasn't worried he hadn't come home from school, yet?" asked Christian.

"Apparently not. Zach sometimes stayed out until eleven. His curfew on school nights."

"Weapon?" Jade asked.

"A blunt instrument," Chutimant said. "Could've been a baseball bat."

Jade pointed at the computer. "Can you enlarge it?"

Chutimant hit a few keys. Jade leaned in to view the autopsy photo. "Any signs of struggle?"

The lieutenant shook her head. "Nothing under the finger-nails, except boy dirt—"

"Hey!" Christian said, in mock indignation.

The detective smiled before sobering. "No defensive wounds on his arms—"

"He was ambushed," Jade said.

"Pretty much," Chutimant said. "The coroner believes the bruising and scratches on Rawlins's face pre-existed the murder."

Jade sat back in her chair. "Would you mind if we talked to the parents?"

Chutimant handed Jade a slip of paper before she'd finished the sentence. "I thought you might ask. I'll email the case
file to you as well."

Jade looked down at the address.

CHAPTER SEVENTEEN

FAIRFAX, VIRGINIA

CHRISTIAN WHISTLED. "NICE . . ."

She agreed. The subdivision's long, winding roads were laid out like lazy ribbons. The meandering journey through Zach Rawlins's parents' neighborhood felt like a nostalgic Sunday drive.

Expansive yards separated McMansion-huge houses. Jade could never afford a house like this on her government salary, even if—when—she became the first female director of the FBI. But that was okay. Money wasn't her thing.

They pulled to a stop in front of the garage. Unsullied, the yard displayed no signs of police tape, investigation trash, or trampled grass. Not even a makeshift memorial honoring the victim. You wouldn't have known a murder of one of the home's occupants had occurred here a week ago.

She scanned the surrounding neighborhood. "Not many streetlights."

"Probably gets real dark here at night," he said.

She knelt in the yard, and ran her hand in an arc over the grass. *A person lost his life here. A child.*

She stood and walked with Christian to the front door. He rang the doorbell. A man of medium height and weight opened the door. A former athlete, by the way he carried himself.

"Mr. Rawlins, we're Special Agents—"

"Come in." Turning, he walked deeper into the house. Christian looked at Jade and shrugged. They followed Zach's father past a staircase leading to the second floor and down a hallway into a spacious room. Broad windows afforded a view of the backyard with a swimming pool and tennis court. She also spotted a batting cage. A weak evening sun tried to force its way into the room.

"I'm George. My wife will be down in a minute. Drink?"

"No, thank you," she said.

"Sit," he said, pointing to the sofa.

A visceral reaction exploded within her. "We're not dogs, Mr. Rawlins. We'll stand." Christian smirked, and moved to lean against the wall near the window.

Rawlins raised his hands in mea culpa. "I apologize." He motioned his hand to the sofa. "Please."

She glanced at the overstuffed sofa and chose a modern chair instead. "What do you do for a living, Mr. Rawlins?"

"I'm the vice president of logistics for the Visix Corporation, headquartered in Reston. We're one of the world's biggest shippers and distributors of petroleum products."

"I believe," she said, "you generated one billion dollars in revenue last year and earned the largest profits in corporate history."

Rawlins blinked and then nodded. "You do your homework."

A slender, light-brown-haired woman glided into the room. Her pointed chin, elevated at a thirty-degree angle, was preceded by her arm, extended as she walked toward them.

"Hello. I'm Vanessa Rawlins."

The couple sat apart on the sofa, just out of reach of each other.

"Mrs. Rawlins," she said, "I appreciate your taking the time to meet with us. We're here to ask you some questions about your son."

"Zach was a good boy. He did well enough in school. In baseball. At least, he was popular."

"He didn't work hard enough, if you ask me," George Rawlins cut in. "Could've started on varsity as a freshman last year. I started as a freshman in high school. It's not that hard. You just need to put in the work."

Christian sat in the matching chair to Jade's. "Was your son having any problems? Maybe, at school? Teachers? Girlfriends?"

Mrs. Rawlins shook her head before he could finish. "No, everyone liked Zach. He was handsome and outgoing."

"A lot like me." Mr. Rawlins's laugh came out like a bark.

"What about friends?" Jade said. "Teammates?"

"He got along with everyone," Mrs. Rawlins said. "Teachers, administrators, friends, teammates. He didn't have an enemy in the world."

He must have had one. Jade kept that thought to herself.

Mr. Rawlins looked at his wife. "Which means he wasn't trying hard enough. When you're the best, you're going to pick up enemies along the way."

"If he didn't have any enemies," Jade said, slowing her cadence, "who do you think did this to him?"

Vanessa Rawlins opened her mouth to answer and then

closed it. After a moment, George Rawlins said, "Random. Must've been a random killing. My son was in the right place at the wrong time."

"What about security? Do you have cameras?"

"Been meaning to tighten security. Infrared cameras. An invisible fence. Maybe a couple of pit bulls. I just never got around to it."

"Did your son get along with Nicholas Campbell and Tyler Thompson?"

"Nicholas was his buddy," George Rawlins said. "They all played JV baseball together. Zach and Nicholas started. Tyler sat on the bench. He was enthusiastic, but didn't have any skills." His eyes watered. "It's not fair. Zach had so much potential, while that loser Tyler—"

Christian clenched and unclenched his fist, slowly. Jade raised her hand from her lap, palm down, signaling him not to react.

"Nicholas's family belonged to the club," Mrs. Rawlins said. She lowered her voice, as if to confide in them. "The country club we belong to. But Tyler's family didn't run in the same . . . circles. A different stratum of society, if you know what I mean. Nice family, though. Wholesome."

Jade let the last word hang, the Rawlinses unaware of Christian's relationship with the Thompsons. Or if they did know, they didn't care.

Or maybe they just didn't want to live long.

"What about you, Mrs. Rawlins?" she said. "What do you do for a living?"

"I'm an executive's wife. I plan our social calendar. Entertain George's business guests. I volunteer. Serve on a few charity boards."

"It doesn't sound like much," Mr. Rawlins added, "but it's a full-time job."

Jade stared at him a beat too long. "Can you think of anything else that can help us figure out who did this to your son?"

The murdered boy's parents looked at each other before shaking their heads.

Jade cast a glance at Christian, "Anything?"

He turned to a clean page in his small spiral notebook. His words came out terse. "We're going to need the names of everyone Zach encountered that day."

After the interview, Jade strode to the car, Christian close behind her. She opened the driver's side door. "I'm driving. What did you think of the Rawlinses?"

He looked at her over the top of the car. "He's an ass."

"So is she. Don't let what she said get to you."

As she shifted into drive, his phone rang. "Yeah? . . . Are they sure? . . . Okay, I'll be there as soon as I can." He disconnected.

At the next stop sign, Jade turned, raising an eyebrow. Christian looked shell-shocked. "That was Matt. It turns out Tyler didn't commit suicide after all. The coroner said he died from blunt force trauma to the head."

The questions swirled in Jade's mind like a programmer's computer code scrolling out of control. She pressed the gas pedal as the light changed. "Tyler was murdered. Is that what these other murders are all about?"

Christian nodded absently, staring out the windshield. "He's ruled it a homicide."

PART II

CHAPTER EIGHTEEN

THE WHITE HOUSE, WASHINGTON, DC

"EMMA."

"Mom!"

Her daughter's unwavering enthusiasm for life never failed to bring a smile to Whitney's face.

"I've been trying to get in touch with you," Whitney said. "How's school?"

"I know. I'm sorry. I've been sooooo busy. Finals are coming up in a couple of weeks."

"I miss our talks every day."

"Well, Mom, you're a little busy, too. Running a country and all."

She could imagine Emma now, lying on her stomach on her dorm room bed twirling her long straight hair with her finger. Her lower legs sticking up, scissoring back and forth.

"Besides studying, what else have you been up to?"

"Not much."

"Met any interesting young men?"

"Sure, Mom. With my Secret Service escort shadowing me wherever I go? Not exactly a come-hither signal, you know? No, I haven't met anyone, and even if I had, it wouldn't be serious enough to talk to you about it."

Her daughter dated. Or did before Whitney became president. It was rare for Emma to introduce her boyfriends to her parents. Perhaps, Whitney and Grayson were too intimidating. Just a little.

"But I have been . . ."

Staring out at the Rose Garden from her chair in the Oval Office, the sound of her daughter's voice jolted her. A tone she had not heard before.

"What?"

Emma didn't answer right away. "Do you remember that income-inequality rally in Philadelphia a few weeks ago?"

"I saw it on the news."

"I was there!"

"You. Were. There."

"Yes!"

"Doing what, exactly? Watching from the sidewalk?"

"No, Mom, I was participating! I marched along with everyone else."

She tried to absorb her daughter's words. The political implications. Her safety.

The order of Whitney's thoughts was not lost on her. Why hadn't someone in the Secret Service told her? She made a mental note to follow up with the director.

"Sweetheart, are you sure that was a safe thing to do? Remember who you are now."

Whitney was referring to Emma's status as the First

Daughter, neglecting to mention that as a member of the Fairchild family, Emma belonged to the very class of people the protesters were rallying against.

"It was amazing! Sitting here in my dorm room, I realized I could no longer stand by and do nothing. During the march, I felt like I was *doing* something. People are working two jobs—sometimes three—and still unable to make ends meet. I talked to this one woman who works full-time without benefits and needs—but can't find—a second job. She has no savings. What if she gets sick or loses her job?

"I have a wonderful life. I never worry about anything. Where I'm going to sleep. What I'm going to eat."

"I know, darling, but—"

"I don't need to worry about finding a job when I graduate. Do I?"

She was right. Whitney remained silent.

"Mom, we're on the verge of a revolution. We're going to take the power away from the wealthy and the corporations and give it back to the people. I have a voice. And a platform. I want to speak for those who can't."

When did Emma start using words like "platform"?

"How did you get away from the Secret Service?"

"I can't tell you all my secrets."

"Tell me."

"I went into a friend's room. I put on one of her wigs, and just walked out with another friend."

"Don't do that again. I can't lose you."

A pause. "I'm sorry, Mom. I get it."

"Did you tell your father about the protest?"

"He's going to freak. I thought maybe you could tell him."

Some revolutionist.

After the call, Whitney speed-dialed the director of the United States Secret Service.

"You need to fire the detail assigned to my daughter the day of the Philadelphia protest and replace them with your best team."

CHAPTER NINETEEN

FAIRFAX, VIRGINIA

"ETHAN'S GOING TO kill us," Christian said the next day, as he parked the car. "Coming out here. Without official jurisdiction."

Jade placed her hand on the door latch. "You worry too much. Besides, he can't kill us if he doesn't know where we are."

"Seems like career-limiting logic to me," he said, getting out of the car.

"Bosses love employees who take risks."

"Said no boss ever who really meant it."

She waited for him on the other side. "We'll be back in the office in a couple hours. Thanks for arranging this."

"You're the one doing me a favor."

He held open one of the many blue doors to the William Randolph Secondary School. They immediately faced a massive, glass-covered trophy case filled to capacity. State championship trophies in golf, soccer (girls), football, basketball (boys and girls), cross-country, wrestling, baseball, softball, intermingled with pictures of the school's All-Americans.

A huge banner dominated the wall next to it: Home of the Warriors

This was a powerhouse sports school.

Christian led her to the administrative offices. "And, no," he said, "I don't know my way around in here because Mark is called into the principal's office a lot."

"Of course not."

"I've talked to the kids here a few times about staying in school and what can happen to them if they do stupid stuff."

A woman sat at a desk, a sign displayed on its front: All Visitors Must Sign in Here. She proffered a bright smile. "Can I help you?"

"We're here to see Mr. Trussell," Christian said.

"Is he expecting you?"

He nodded. Waving her hand at the clipboard with a sign-in sheet, she picked up the phone.

A minute later a man with a brown, buzzed haircut and a slight tan—unusual for Virginia in April—came out to meet them. He smiled and offered his hand. "Bobby Trussell. You must be Jade Harrington. Good to see you again, Merritt. Y'all come on back. We've set up a room for you."

Trussell led them down a short hallway and entered a conference room. Standard school chairs were pushed in around the exterior of four tables arranged in a square.

Jade walked to the other end of the room and sat in a chair facing the door. Trussell pulled out a chair and parked next to her. Christian leaned into a corner, crossing his arms.

"Thanks for allowing us to use this room," she said.

"So, what are y'all trying to accomplish here, exactly?"

"We want to talk to the teammates of Tyler Thompson,

Zach Rawlins, and Nicholas Campbell. And, possibly, some of the other students."

"But that's not telling me what you hope to accomplish."

"Aren't you concerned that three of your students have died in the last few weeks? Three players on the same team? Seems like a lot. Even for a school of this size."

Trussell sat back. "Of course, I'm concerned. Do you think I *like* all the media attention? The police presence? I can't wait for things to get back to normal. It's been difficult for the team. For all the students. We've brought in grief counselors on a full-time basis. What a tragic set of coincidences."

"Coincidences?" she asked, disbelieving.

"Look. We're a big school, with the largest student population in Virginia. At least one of our students dies every year."

"And now a baseball player has died every week for the last three weeks. All murdered."

He flinched. "Tyler, too?"

She nodded. "What's going on with your baseball team?"

"Heck if I know."

"Can I speak to the coach?"

"He's not here. At a coaches' conference. Down in Richmond. He'll be back tomorrow."

Christian sat on the other side of Trussell and pulled out his notebook. "What's his name?"

"Daniel. Lane Daniel."

"Tell me," Jade said, "do you think bullying is a problem here?"

Trussell flinched again at the shift in topics. Holding the lapels of his suit jacket, he glanced at Christian for help. Christian offered none.

"Not more than any other school. Kids will be kids. Some

kids think it's fun to torture other kids. Some may not realize it's bullying." He spread his hands. "I know. Doesn't make it right. Anti-bullying policies are in place. But as I said, this is a big school. A lot of places to hide here. Lots of nooks and crannies. We can't cover the entire building. Even with cameras. And that doesn't address the verbal bullying that goes on, or anything that takes place beyond these walls. Or on the Internet."

Trussell's face, flushed, looked as if it would burst if Jade poked it with a pin.

Christian gestured with his pen. "Nice ring."

Trussell stared proudly at the Harley-Davidson ring on his right hand. "Try to ride every weekend. Helps me get away from it all." He stood. "I'll go tell the assistant coach that you're ready. We sequestered the team in the locker room. Okay if I bring them in a few at a time? Otherwise, you'll be here all day."

Jade would have preferred to interview the boys individually, but he was right. They didn't have all day. Technically, she and Christian weren't here. "That's fine."

Trussell closed the door behind him.

"He's a pretty good principal," Christian said. "The kids love him."

"He can't be happy with all the negative publicity."

"This is a great public school. Not only in sports, but academically. That's why Mark goes here. Why all my children will go here."

"He's pretty protective of his school." Jade stood and stretched. "Maybe there's a reason."

*

Three athletic boys entered the room. Each reacted differently when he saw her: one's eyes widened, one's mouth opened, and one's face flushed crimson. She ignored their reactions.

From the second boy: "You're Jade Harrington! Are you really with the FBI? Like on TV?"

"Well, TV is supposed to be like us," she said. "Although they don't always get it right."

From the third boy: "Can we see your gun?"

"Maybe another time."

Second boy: "Can we take a selfie with you?"

The first boy didn't ask her any questions. He just stared at her.

"This isn't a social visit," she said. "We're here to talk to you about Tyler, Zach, and Nicholas."

Her words sucked the air out of the room. The boys glanced at each other and sat down across from them. Two of them sported scratches and bruises on their faces just like the victims, the silent boy's face unblemished. The third had a faded black eye. Either this was one unlucky group of athletes, or something else was going on here.

"Let's start with your names."

The first boy pointed to himself. "I'm William Chaney-Frost."

"Do you go by Will or Billy?" Christian asked.

"Neither. It's William." He smiled, looking at Jade. "With a hyphenated name, what do you expect?" He pointed a thumb to the second boy. "This is Joshua Stewart. And this is Andrew Huffman."

"Tell me about your relationship with Tyler, Zach, and Nicholas."

William glanced at the other two. Was it a signal to let him do the talking?

"We all played freshman baseball together last year," he said. "Won districts. We all got along. We're all on JV this year. Tyler, too. He was okay."

"As a baseball player," she finished for him.

"He wasn't very good."

"Everyone on the team got along? No arguments? No fights ever broke out?"

Joshua's face twitched. "Fights?"

William shot him a look before turning to her. "Not really."

"Who bullied Tyler?"

"The cops asked us the same thing. Tyler was such a nerd. Easy to pick on. But I wouldn't call it bullying."

"What would you call it?" she asked.

"Just messin' around."

"Tell me about Zach."

"Z was cool. Funny. A good athlete, although not as good as he thought he was. Always trying to live up to his old man."

"Any of them have girlfriends?"

William laughed. "Tyler? No." An exaggerated shake of his head. "Nicholas liked to flirt with all the girls. But Zach only had eyes for one."

"Who?"

"Kaylee Taylor."

This kid was smart and observant. And handsome in a teen-heartthrob sort of way. She questioned them for another fifteen minutes, including their whereabouts on the nights of the murders, but didn't learn anything else. The other two boys didn't say much, only speaking when addressed directly. And not much even then. They stole looks at William Chaney-Frost for confirmation or approval of their answers.

She stood, walked over to them, and handed each of them

her FBI-emblazoned business card. "Three of your teammates were murdered. That should make you nervous."

"Tyler committed suicide," William said.

Jade shook her head. "No, he didn't. Any idea who killed him?"

She got the reaction she wanted. The boys exchanged furtive glances. Only William's eye contact remained unbroken.

She waited to see if one of the other two would talk. They stared at the table. They looked scared. She needed to come back and speak to them one at a time.

"How did he die?" asked William.

As if she just thought of it, Jade asked, "Who created the 'TylerThompsonFan' Twitter account?"

Head shakes and shrugs. She wouldn't get anything more from these kids today.

"If you remember anything later," she said, "anything at all, don't hesitate to call me."

William examined her business card, and then held her gaze, as his thumb slowly caressed the raised FBI logo.

*

After interviewing the entire baseball team, the woman manning the visitors sign ushered two girls into the room. Although Jade presumed the girls would be around fifteen or sixteen years old, they could have passed for twenty-one. The first girl strode into the room in black leggings, a pullover top, and a light cardigan sweater. A touch of lip gloss her only makeup.

The girl trailing behind her wore too much makeup, in an inverse relationship to the length of her dress. The dress seemed not only inappropriate for school, but inappropriate for the cool weather outside.

The girls sat across from them.

After Jade introduced Christian, she said, "Thanks for coming to talk to us. What are your names?"

"I'm Grace," said the girl in the dress, her eyes on Christian.

"What's your last name, Grace?" Jade said.

"Angleton."

Jade looked at the other girl. "And you?"

"Kaylee Taylor."

"We want to ask you a few questions. Were you friends with Tyler, Zach, and Nicholas?"

Grace laughed.

Jade tilted her head. "Why is that funny?"

"We were cool with Nicholas and Zach, of course." Grace glanced coyly at Kaylee and back at Jade. "You could say one of us was more than friends with Zach. But I'm single." She checked out Christian and waited for him to look up from his notes. He didn't. She turned back to Jade. "We weren't *friends* with Tyler. He was a geek."

"We only knew him because we're cheerleaders," Kaylee agreed.

"And you were more than friends with Zach?"

Kaylee glared at her friend and back at Jade. "Zach and I were cool."

"You were dating?" Jade asked.

"We were *aware* of each other," Kaylee said.

"Aware."

"She was playing hard to get," Grace said.

"Shut up!" Kaylee said, lightly tapping Grace on the arm. Her smile belied her words.

"Tell me more about your relationship with Zach," Jade asked.

"We didn't have a *relationship*. He played sports. I cheered. We had a lot in common."

"Like what?"

Kaylee seemed puzzled by the question. "Like I said, he played sports and I cheered."

Jade nodded. "Got it. How are you coping since he died?"

Kaylee hesitated. "I miss him of course."

"What about Nicholas?"

"What about him?"

"Were you close?"

"Not very. He was cute. A little too short for my taste. But he had nice muscles."

"I thought he was hot," Grace said.

Jade rejoiced she wasn't still in high school. "Is there anything more you can tell me about him that isn't physical?"

Kaylee thought for a moment. "Not really. We all hung out together. The athletes and the cheer squad. I'd see him at parties and stuff."

To Grace: "You?"

"Same."

"Are you both on Facebook?"

"Facebook's lame," Kaylee said. "It's for old people."

"People your age," Grace added, helpfully.

Jade let that slide. "What about Twitter?"

They nodded.

"Would you know anything about the 'TylerThompsonFan' account?"

The two girls shared a look.

"Heard about it," Grace said.

Kaylee could not quite meet Jade's eyes. "What about it?"

"Pretty horrible stuff, wouldn't you say?" Jade said. "If someone wrote those things about you?"

"I guess," Kaylee said.

"Did either of you ever exchange texts with Tyler?"

"Never!" Grace said.

"No," Kaylee said.

"Are you sure?"

"Why would we text *him*?" Grace asked.

Jade focused on Kaylee. "And you never texted Tyler? Not once?"

Kaylee shook her head.

Jade held her gaze for a moment, then let it go. "Last question. Is there a lot of bullying in your school?"

"No," Grace said.

Kaylee shrugged. "Is that why you think Tyler committed suicide?"

It was Jade's turn to shrug.

She didn't bother to correct Kaylee about Tyler's manner of death. She would find out soon enough.

CHAPTER TWENTY

WASHINGTON, DC

BACK AT THE Bureau, they exited the elevator on the fourth floor. As they walked down the hall, Dante strode toward them, his expression a warning as he passed by. "Ethan wants to see you. Both of you."

Jade and Christian glanced at each other, but said nothing.

Dropping off her briefcase in her office, she joined him in front of her boss's door. She knocked.

From inside: "Come in."

They entered and sat in the chairs across the desk from Supervisory Special Agent Ethan Lawson. He continued to scribble something on a legal pad. A display of the FBI's motto "Fidelity - Bravery - Integrity." hung behind him. White shirt, starched and pressed, his slacks held up by black suspenders, Ethan was a dapper throwback to a bygone era.

Setting down his pen, he turned his attention to them. "What've you two been up to?"

Jade looked at Christian—who stared at the floor—and back at Ethan.

"Research," she said.

"Hmmm . . . On what?"

"A case we're working on."

Ethan gave her a familiar look. "And which case is that, pray tell?"

"Three boys died—were murdered—at Randolph Secondary School in Fairfax in the last three weeks."

Ethan rifled through a stack of files on his desk. "I can't find that file." He threw up his hands. "Oh, wait. Now I remember. It's not our case."

"Yet."

"These were tragic murders, yes . . . " He glanced at Christian. "And I understand your personal interest, but we have our own cases to solve. Let the local police handle it."

Christian looked up at Ethan. "Hell no."

Ethan blinked. "Excuse me?"

She understood why Ethan was surprised. Christian never contradicted him. Or cursed.

"Tyler is family," Christian said.

"All the more reason why you shouldn't be involved," said Ethan.

Jade, her sleeves rolled up, leaned forward and rested her forearms on her thighs, as if about to enter a basketball game. "We're not letting it go, Ethan. Besides, I have a feeling about this."

"You and your feelings." He sighed, tearing his eyes away from Christian. "Okay. What do you have?"

"Tyler Thompson died as the result of blunt force trauma to the head. He had been bullied. Zach Rawlins was murdered with a blunt instrument a couple of weeks later. The following week, Nicholas Campbell was murdered in the same manner.

Zach's and Nicholas's genitals had been mutilated. All three boys went to the same high school and played on the baseball team. All had scratches and bruising on their faces and bodies that predated their deaths. As if they fought a lot."

Ethan spun his wedding ring once. Twice. Three times.

Jade continued. "There are more deaths to come. Something's going on here. We have a serial killer on our hands. I know it."

He stopped spinning his ring. "Three murders don't equate to a serial killer. But, I'll give you two a little rope on this." He sat up, his eyes back to the work on his desk. "Don't hang yourselves."

*

In her office, she focused on some of her cases. Her assigned cases. Her attention, though, kept drifting back to the interviews that morning.

This case tugged at Jade. A psych major in college, it wasn't too difficult to figure out why. Bullied as a teenager herself, one day she decided she'd had enough. She promised herself from that day forward she would never be bullied again. And now bullying in any form, especially of women and children, compelled her to act.

Her cell phone rang. Area code 703. Virginia. She didn't recognize the number.

"Agent, uh, Harrington. This is William. From the interview today. At the school."

That didn't take long. "I remember."

"Listen . . . there's something we didn't . . . I didn't . . . say. That I should have."

"I'm listening."

"Z . . ."

"What about Zach?"

"It was Z."

She let the silence linger.

He continued. "Zach bullied T—Tyler. Well, he wasn't the only one, but he was the leader. Z was always the leader."

"Go on."

"Like I told you today. T was easy to pick on. A dweeb, kind of nerdy. Read books in public. In places where people could see him. Told people he liked math. Watched the news. Sh—stuff like that. Z liked to mess with him in the locker room. He would steal his clothes, so he had nothing to wear after he took a shower. He made fun of T's . . . uh . . . "

Jade let him hang for a moment. "Private parts?"

"Yeah."

"Do you know that someone took naked pictures of Tyler and posted them on the Internet?"

Silence. After a few beats, he said, "I knew. Everyone knew. It sucked. I'm not really proud of my classmates."

"Who killed Zach, Nicholas, and Tyler?"

"One time, T fell asleep in class, and Z taped his head to the desk. T almost started crying, asking for help. Everyone in class just sat there and laughed. The teacher finally cut him out. Z did stupid stuff like that. I guess you would call Z a bully. I didn't think of it as bullying at the time. It was funny."

Hysterical. "What about Nicholas?"

"Nic would do anything Z said. Zach would goad him into stuff."

"Why didn't you say something earlier?"

The boy hesitated. "Sometimes it's easier not to get involved. So, I say nothing."

"You didn't answer my question."

"What question was that?"

"Do you know who killed Zach or Nicholas or Tyler?"

"I have no idea."

She thanked him and hung up.

Jade was not surprised by what William had told her about Zach. She thought back to the interview with his parents. Although Zach's father lamented that his son wasn't like him, Zach had followed in his father's footsteps.

He was a bully. Just like his father.

She wondered why William had called her. To manipulate the investigation? To manipulate her?

And, if so, to what end?

CHAPTER TWENTY-ONE

THE WHITE HOUSE, WASHINGTON, DC

SASHA SAT ACROSS from Whitney in the Oval Office and handed her a briefing book. "My proposal to address income inequality."

Whitney accepted it and opened it to the first page.

"It's based on the same three Rs as the New Deal: relief, recovery, and reform," Sasha said. "Relief for the unemployed poor, recovery of the economic system, and the reform of the financial system. My proposal is the same, but with a twist. This New New Deal will be based on relief for the unemployed and underemployed poor and middle class, the recovery of the American Dream, and reform of the financial system and the national infrastructure."

Whitney nodded, pleased so far. "Go on."

"The relief program will consist of training the unemployed, expanding the earned-income and child tax credits, and raising the federal minimum wage to twelve dollars an hour."

She smiled. "I'm also proposing a thirty-five-hour work week, which will increase the demand for workers and improve work-life balance for everyone."

"That should be popular," Whitney said. "Does it apply to presidents as well?"

"Presidents are exempt."

"Pity."

To the media pundits, Sasha Scott, the black congresswoman from Texas, had been a surprising selection for chief of staff. Whitney had not known her well when they both served in Congress, but when they did work together, the woman's intelligence, strength, fortitude, devotion to her cultural roots, and passion for diversity and inclusion had impressed Whitney. Sasha was respected on both sides of the aisle, even when her direct—some would say "blunt"—communication style left some hurt feelings along the way. Strategic use of her Southern charm, however, always seemed to assuage those feelings after the fact.

Whitney's choice had been the right one. Gatekeeper, personnel manager, CEO, and fixer, the chief of staff's responsibility was to keep Whitney focused on the principal event of the day and to remove all distractions. Sasha turned out to be perfect for the job.

They didn't agree on every issue. Sasha, a devout Catholic, supported a woman's right to choose politically, but Whitney believed she struggled with the issue on a personal level.

Sasha turned the page. "The premise for the recovery program is the importance of education to social mobility. It consists of universal preschool, a cap on college tuition, and allowing students to repay student loans based on a percentage of post-graduate income."

"What about universal college education?"

"We couldn't get that through this Congress. Now, to reform. Instead of resurrecting the WPA, the Department of Commerce will oversee the building and repairing of highways, bridges, low-income housing, and parks."

"Twenty percent of our bridges are impaired and half of our highways—"

"—are not fit to drive on."

"How will we fund this?"

"Small- and mid-sized businesses will be given incentives to bid on these projects. The DOC will administer them."

"Ooh . . . I like that, too." Whitney thought a moment. "Although I'm in favor of universal pre-K, I need something that will impact the economy now. Like high-speed and inner-city rail. Or water systems."

Sasha shook her head. "According to the ASCE"— American Society of Civil Engineers—"it will cost three-point-six trillion dollars to fix this country's water and sewer systems."

"Trillion."

"Trillion," Sasha repeated. "Look at how much it cost to repair Flint."

"It was worth every penny."

"We don't have the revenue to approach it nationally in a significant way this time around."

Whitney crossed her legs. "Now, the sixty-four-thousand-dollar question: How will we pay for this proposal?"

"Increased tax rates, a limit on CEO pay, limits on tax deductions and loopholes. And eliminating pork."

She flipped through the proposal on her lap as Sasha spoke. After she fell silent, Whitney kept reading. After several minutes, she said, "This is good work. Thank you. Treasury won't be happy with all the changes to the tax code. But too bad.

Leave it with me. I'll mark it up tonight, and give it back to you tomorrow. I'll want you to float it by Hampton and Bell."

Sasha scrunched up her face. "The 'Young Guns' on the Hill?"

"Who, by the way, are not so young anymore."

"I heard that one time Hampton spoke for ten hours on the Senate floor."

"He did," Whitney said. "I was there."

Sasha shook her head. "How could you stand it? It's hard for me to listen to that whiny voice for ten minutes." Sasha closed her briefing book. "It must be nice to be Senator Eric Hampton. I wish I had the privilege of always being so . . . "

"Certain?"

Sasha nodded. "They'll kill this before it has a chance to be debated."

Whitney smiled. "Then you may want to persuade them with sugar instead of your usual hot sauce. We need their buy-in, Sasha. It won't get through otherwise."

"But do you trust them?"

Whitney had battled Hampton before on previous bills. Last year, they came to an agreement on a major piece of legislation. Just before it went to vote, he added an amendment that was anathema to Whitney's principles and one she could never support.

But she needed him this time. She had no choice. As senate majority leader, he was her best chance of selling the proposal to others in his party.

Whitney laid the briefing book on her desk. "No. No, I don't."

CHAPTER TWENTY-TWO

FAIRFAX, VIRGINIA

SHE STARED THROUGH the one-way mirror at Matt Thompson. Hands clasped on the table, he listened to instructions from his attorney sitting next to him. From his suit, the attorney didn't look like a high-priced one to Jade, but he wasn't a public defender either.

Thompson looked much better than the last time she had seen him. The reality, if not the acceptance, of his son's death had sunk in. Christian stood next to her, the anguish of seeing his brother-in-law in that room plain on his face.

Detective Chutimant had decided to bring Thompson in for questioning. She had invited Jade and Christian to observe.

She had also sent Jade the results of Tyler's autopsy report. The coroner ruled out the use of a blunt instrument. He didn't find any fingerprints on the body. This didn't surprise Jade. If Tyler was sweaty from baseball practice or struggled during the altercation, any fingerprints would have been damaged or lost. He could have unintentionally rubbed them off.

The coroner did find grass, glass, rocks, dirt, and fragments from fast-food wrappers on Tyler's skin. But no hair fibers.

Not much to go on.

The detective glanced at her now and nodded before opening the door to the interrogation room, followed by another detective from the county. The door clicked closed behind them, the sound loud in the observation room. By his slight head movement, Thompson acknowledged the detectives' entrance but didn't look at them.

Chutimant went through the interview preliminaries and then asked Thompson about his whereabouts the night Zach Rawlins was murdered.

He glanced at his attorney. The attorney nodded. Thompson cleared his throat and looked at Chutimant. "I was home. I left the dealership around eight p.m. and went straight there. My wife and I watched television until we went to bed."

"Was your wife with you the entire time?"

"Yes. Even before Tyler . . . " He looked away from Chutimant. "With two young children, we don't go out much."

"What about the night Nicholas died?"

"What night was that?"

"April twenty-seventh of this year."

Thompson cleared his throat again. "That would've been a Thursday. Same thing. Work and then home. We're basic. We lead a boring life."

The detective, her tone sharp and accusatory: "Did you kill Zach Rawlins and Nicholas Campbell?"

"No, I did not," he said.

After an hour of questioning, Christian said to her, "They don't have any evidence against him."

"Except motive." Jade stared at Thompson. "Or other suspects. Let's go talk to his wife."

*

"This is a bad idea."

"It'll take some time to release him," Jade said.

The bicycle now lay in the grass.

Christian knocked. "House is quiet. Maybe she's not here."

"Let's wait," she said.

After a couple of minutes, they turned to leave.

The door opened. Jenny, her bathrobe cinched at her chest, said, "Sorry, I was in the shower. Come on in."

They headed without invitation to the living room. Jenny stopped at the stairs, her hand on the railing. She looked down the front of her robe and over to them. "I'm going to change. Be right back."

She trudged upstairs.

Jade said to Christian, "Her hair's not wet."

He nodded, distracted. "I don't think she's washed that robe in a while."

She glanced around the living room. It appeared as it had the first time she was here. Immaculate.

"I still think this is a bad idea," he said.

"I want to see if their stories match."

Jenny returned wearing a light-blue t-shirt and jeans. "I need to pick up the kids from school soon."

Christian cut his eyes at Jade before turning to Jenny. "We came by to check on you."

"We just left the police station," Jade said. "We saw Matt."

"They're wasting their time. Matt wouldn't hurt a fly."

"They asked him where he was the night Zach Rawlins was killed."

"I could've saved them the trouble. He was here with me. Watching TV."

"How do you remember which night it was?" Jade asked.

"Because it's what we do every night. We're not the most exciting couple in the world. No one would ever create a reality show about us."

"What about the night Nicholas Campbell died?"

"Same."

"And you're sure he was with you the entire time?" Jade pressed. "Both nights?"

"Yes."

"Do you believe Matt is capable of murder?"

"No, I don't. He's a big teddy bear." She gestured to Christian. "Like him."

CHAPTER TWENTY-THREE

WASHINGTON, DC

"JADE, COME IN."

"I wanted to update you on—" She stopped in the doorway of Ethan's office. He wasn't alone. "I can come back later."

Before she turned, his guest stood.

She processed several observations about him at once.

He wore an FBI-issued badge on a lanyard around his neck. Tall, the same height as she, his biceps filled out his suit jacket. His skin was the color of light mocha. The absence of a wedding ring.

He returned her stare, his eyes, gray and mesmerizing.

"I can come back," she repeated.

"No," Ethan said, "I want you to meet Micah Alexander."

She shook his hand. "Jade Harrington."

"I know who you are," he said through straight white teeth. A slight British accent tinted his words. They held each other's gaze until a throat cleared. She looked over at Ethan.

"Micah just graduated from the academy," he said. "Today's his first day. He just joined the department."

Jade turned back to the new agent. "Welcome."

"Thank you."

"Ethan, I'll catch you later."

She turned to leave.

"Wait a minute," he said. "Take Micah with you. I've assigned him to your team."

CHAPTER TWENTY-FOUR

SEATTLE, WASHINGTON

CHIEF FINANCIAL OFFICER David Smith rushed from the CEO's office of the technology company at which he worked and down the hall to his own corner office. His employees were accustomed to seeing him hustling up and down the corridors.

He strode straight to his chair and dropped his writing pad on the desk. He spun the chair to the credenza behind him and logged onto his laptop. Checking the time in the bottom-right corner of the computer screen, he opened the browser. He navigated to the Pacific Coast Bank website, where his company kept its operating and payroll checking accounts.

He glanced at the time again. Ten minutes to make the train to Sea-Tac for his four o'clock flight. The train wasn't always on time. He may have an extra two minutes. Worst-case scenario he could call a cab, but like any good CFO, he would rather spend $2.50 than $45 of the company's money for the same service. Plus, it was faster these days to travel by train than car with Seattle's worsening traffic.

He clicked Transfer Money, selected From the Operating

Account, and typed in *1,000,000*. He clicked To the Payroll Account. It wasn't the exact amount of payroll, but enough to cover it. He could transfer the excess back later after his payroll accountant finished reconciling all the adjustments.

Spinning the chair back to his desk, he removed the security token from the center drawer. He pressed the blue button. A six-digit access code appeared in the digital display. He punched the code on the laptop's keyboard and hit Enter. The Transfer Successfully Completed page displayed on the computer screen. He emailed this page to his controller.

With care, he logged out of the bank's website and closed the browser. Tapping the Windows button and the letter L on the keyboard to lock his computer, he swept the laptop off the docking station. He stuffed it into the bag, and shoved it down the handle of his suitcase.

He grabbed his suit jacket off the hook on the back of his office door with one hand and breezed out the door with the suitcase and laptop in the other.

Thank God, transferring significant sums of money was easy and fast these days.

He would make the train.

*

As David Smith hurried to the University Street train station, the million dollars he just transferred was not deposited in the company's payroll account at Pacific Coast Bank.

Instead, the funds jetted to Switzerland, then the Cayman Islands, London, and four other locations before ending up in a different Seattle bank.

CHAPTER TWENTY-FIVE

QUANTICO, VIRGINIA

IT HAD BEEN over a year since Jade had visited Behavioral Analysis Unit 4 of the National Center for the Analysis of Violent Crime in Quantico.

Standing in the doorway of Max Stover's office, she watched him work. His hair was thinning, with only faint blond wisps remaining on top. Max was a supervisory special agent. Most people would call him a profiler. One of the agency's best. He was also Jade's mentor and godfather.

Without looking up, he said, "Are you going to stand there all day or are you going to sit down and tell me why you're here?"

Jade entered his office and removed a stack of papers and folders from the solitary guest chair, glancing around to figure out where to put it. He waved at the floor.

"How did you know it was me?"

He pointed to his ear. "I could tell by the sound of your walk. No one walks like you."

"I'll take that as a compliment."

Max stopped writing and placed the pen on his pad of paper. He pushed his glasses farther up on the bridge of his nose and looked at her. "To what do I owe this honor?"

"You look pale."

"I'm always pale."

"Paler than usual. You need to get out more."

"Now that that's cleared up, why are you here?"

"What do you know about bullying?"

Max shrugged. "Bullies are insecure. Bullying gives them power over someone or a group of people. A power they lack in other aspects of their lives. Sometimes, a bully has been bullied, and often models what has been done to him or what he sees others doing."

"Or her."

As a bullied kid, she never realized her attackers could have been victims, too. At the time, she hadn't thought much about them at all, except hoping they would all go away or die. She didn't tell Max any of this. He knew her history.

He nodded. "Women, too. If we're talking about kids, sometimes the victim's friends—or frenemies—are the meanest bullies of all."

"And with the Internet and smartphones, bullying is a twenty-four/seven endeavor."

"Your home is no longer a sanctuary. There is no safe place."

"You heard about Christian's nephew."

Max nodded.

During the conversation, she had straightened all the items closest to her on Max's gray metal desk.

"They posted photos," she said, "on the Internet of him in the locker room shower." She told him about the Twitter account, and the texts from the girl who played a joke on him.

Max watched her straighten, a smile-grimace etched on his face. "Bullying is different now than when I was growing up. Than when you were growing up. It's more psychological and socially cruel. Bullies target vulnerable groups like special-needs kids or LGBTQ kids or weak kids. And they keep coming up with creative ways to bully. It's more commonplace. Some of our politicians are the worst bullies of all."

Last year, a billionaire businesswoman threatened to oppose the incumbent president in the Republican primary. According to her, everyone in the GOP establishment was either a liar, a cheater, stupid, or out to get her. No segment of the population—except for Caucasians—escaped her wrath.

"Entertainment," Jade added.

"And games. Bullying behaviors in games are explained away as trash-talking. All these things desensitize kids—heck, all of us—to violence. By the time a child reaches eighteen years of age, she or he has watched two hundred thousand acts of violence."

"What can we do about it?"

"Adults could set a better example. Better enforcement of school policies. Tougher laws. There's no federal law against bullying. But at the micro level, victims need to tell someone and not stay silent. So they know they're not alone. And parents, teachers, and bystanders need to say something when they see it."

Jade aligned files she'd already straightened. "I wish bullies could channel that creativity and energy into something useful. More productive. Like becoming an FBI agent." She stopped and admired her handiwork.

Max glanced at his files. "Are you finished?"

She pulled her hands away. "Yes."

He removed his glasses to polish them and squinted at her. "You shouldn't take this case personally."

She examined her hands, her complexion the product of a black father and Japanese mother. The physical scars had long since healed. Her parents never knew about the bullying. Now that they were dead, they never would.

"I was a mixed-race Army brat. Always the new kid on the block. Always an outsider. It's hard to forget."

"What do they know about the perp?"

She relayed the skimpy information they had obtained so far. The killer, most likely right-handed, used a blunt instrument to murder his victims, and then severed their genitals.

"That wasn't in the paper."

"Two victims, Zach and Nicholas, both bullied Tyler Thompson, Christian's nephew."

"I like that you still use the victims' names like I taught you. It humanizes them."

"They were human beings. With lives. With hopes and dreams. What else would I call them? What do you make of the mutilations?"

Max didn't react to the shift in topics. He picked up his pen and started gently tapping it on his notepad. "We could hypothesize about that one all day. The obvious reason is the perpetrator is exacting revenge. Could these boys have raped Tyler? But it sounds as if most of the bullying wasn't physical. Maybe it has something to do with the baseball team. Any signs of resistance?"

Jade shook her head. She then described the scratches and bruises inflicted on all three victims before their deaths.

"Antemortem?" he asked, surprised.

She nodded. "I've seen them on other members of the

baseball team, too. The living members. I believe that other kids are involved. And that they may be in danger."

"Not much to go on," Max said.

"Not much is right. Christian and I interviewed the parents of Zach Rawlins. His mother is a perfectionist, and his father is a bully."

"Dangerous combination. Zach most likely never felt comfortable in his own skin. Since he wasn't perfect, his parents couldn't see him for the person he actually was. Always judging him."

Jade looked away. *Like I judge myself.*

After a moment, she cocked her chin toward the paperwork on his desk. "What are you working on?"

"Serial-killer case in Wisconsin. Someone is kidnapping, raping, and killing girls from trailer-park homes spanning a three-county area."

Jade's stomach clenched. "Get him."

"I will." He paused. "Everything else all right?"

"Great." She got up to leave.

"How's Micah doing?"

"You know him?"

He nodded. "I trained him."

"Hmph."

"He's going to be good, Jade."

"As good as I am?"

"No one's that good." He smiled. "But I wouldn't sleep on him, though."

"You don't even know what that means," she said.

"I still teach, remember?"

She stood. "I need to go."

"A piece of advice. Forget the victims were bullies. You've got a killer to catch. Get. Him."

"I will."

She nodded and moved toward the door.

"Jade," he said. She turned to look at him. "Thanks for straightening my desk."

Over her shoulder, she said, "You're welcome," and strode out the door.

Halfway down the hallway, she heard Max shout from his office: "I was kidding!"

CHAPTER TWENTY-SIX

THE WHITE HOUSE, WASHINGTON, DC

IN THE OVAL Office, Whitney reviewed her chief of staff's proposal one last time. She crossed out the sections that would hurt middle-class families, including the elimination of the mortgage-interest deduction for homes under one million dollars. She made her final changes in the margin of the document.

To be palatable to the other party, distribution of income must benefit the wealthy in some way. With her revisions, she thought the proposal would be amenable to Hampton. Bell didn't matter as much.

Sean, her secretary, buzzed her. "Madam President? Ashley Brennan is here to see you."

"Who?"

"Cole Brennan's wife."

"Oh, yes. Send her in." Whitney had not seen or heard from Cole since she had appeared on his radio show late last summer. She had never met the wife of the radio talk-show host, and had been surprised by her request for a meeting.

"Mrs. Brennan."

"Whitney . . . Madam President, thanks for taking the time to see me."

Whitney gestured toward the sofa, as she sat in a nearby chair. Ashley Brennan, blonde and beautiful and a decade younger than her husband, carried herself like the model she once had been. In an Hermès dress, she perched near the edge of the sofa, her legs crossed at the ankle, à la Jackie Kennedy.

"What can I do for you?" asked Whitney.

"My husband hasn't been kind to you on the show these last few months . . . well, ever, but I've always admired you from afar. That you stand for what you believe in. I voted for you." A small smile. "Cole doesn't know that, of course."

Whitney crossed her legs. "I'm surprised, but flattered."

"You shouldn't be. As Madeline Albright said, 'There is a special place in hell for women who do not help other women.' I still believe that." She paused. "I'm here about our son. Cole Jr. CJ. You may have heard that he came out. That he's gay."

"I did."

Ashley hesitated. "He . . . was beaten up. Badly. Yesterday. By a bunch of boys at his school."

"Oh, Ashley, I'm sorry." She placed her hand over the woman's hands. "Is he all right?"

A shrug. "He'll be all right. Nothing broken. Doctors said the bruises on his face will heal. He'll still be handsome. He's strong. Stands up for what he believes in." Ashley glanced at Whitney. "Like his dad." That smile again. "But opposite."

"What can I do for you?" When someone called or visited her, the person wanted something.

"CJ is a good kid. Never hurt anyone. Bullying has to stop. Not just for my child, but for all children."

Whitney retracted her hand. "It is a problem, the pervasiveness of bullying in our schools. In our workplaces. In our politics." She bit her lip, but said it anyway. "On the radio."

Ashley didn't respond. The silence lengthened. Whitney thought she had gone too far.

"I don't always agree with what my husband says. But he is my husband. And I support him. Always. He's devastated by what's happened. But he feels helpless. He doesn't know what he can do about it." Her eyes, vacant and sad, implored Whitney nevertheless. "Is there something that you can do? Can you strengthen federal laws to stop bullying?"

Whitney bit back her comment this time, choosing to ignore the irony that Ashley—like many Republicans— opposed the federal government's intervention in the lives of US citizens in almost everything, except for women's reproductive rights. And when they needed something.

"There is no federal law against bullying."

"Can you create one?"

"This Congress would be an obstacle. I may need your husband's help."

Ashley Brennan's back straightened with resolve. Whitney suspected that many people underestimated this woman.

"You'll have it."

"But there may be something I'll need in return."

*

"To make this work, we need to align our interest groups. Just like the New Deal Coalition. Labor, minorities, intellectuals, liberals, and small businesses. We must be the party of prosperity. Like back in the Thirties."

Whitney pumped hard on the elliptical in the gym in the White House residence as she spoke. She glanced at the electronic dashboard. Fifteen minutes to go.

Sasha shifted on the bench she had pulled up close to the machine earlier. "No luck with Hampton or Bell, so far."

This didn't surprise Whitney. In addition to the inherent intransigence of the two congressmen, Sasha's direct approach rubbed some people the wrong way. Particularly men.

Whitney smiled. "I guess you didn't take my advice and feed them a spoonful of sugar."

"I always did prefer hot sauce."

"I tried to tell you."

"I was never a great listener, either."

Whitney's legs continued to pump. "At the end of the nineteenth century, the economic inequality prevalent throughout Europe at that time almost caused a socialist revolution."

"Met with them and their LDs a few times."

"The gap in wealth has not been this wide in the United States since the Great Depression."

"I'll keep trying," Sasha said.

"Poverty is at its highest level since 1993. It's harder for the poor to climb out of poverty. It matters more than ever that you were born to the right parents." She stopped exercising. "Seven percent of the people who work are poor. *Who work.*"

"We can take on Social Security and Medicare."

"Not until my second term." She realized her response came out sharper than intended. She softened her tone. "We'll fix them on our way out."

Sasha remained silent, realizing she was supposed to shut up and listen.

Whitney resumed her pedaling. "It's going to get worse. If the American Dream dies, chaos will reign. An economist on *Meet the Press* said that if we do not address income inequality, it will create a crisis of legitimacy for the republic." Wiping her face with a towel, she threw it on the floor. She stared at her chief of staff. "Not on my watch."

"Understood, Madam President."

"'When there is no vision, the people perish,'" she said. She pursed her lips, imitating the expression Sasha often gave her. "Don't look surprised. I read the Bible, too." Whitney started pumping faster. "How many do I need?"

Sasha calculated the votes in her head. "At least ten, maybe two more from our side."

"Bell is not intellectually curious. He just parrots whatever his constituents want him to say. Offer him some tickets to my box at the Kennedy Center. Sampson, too. He'll drink everything in the fridge, so make sure it's stocked."

Democratic Senator Paul Sampson was known for two things: his love of the University of Nebraska Cornhuskers football team and his love of drink.

"What about Hampton?"

"Off camera," Whitney said, "he has an open mind. More than others in his party. I think he could be persuaded."

"If something's in it for him," Sasha said.

"Be that as it may, schedule a meeting for me to meet with the three of them. Tomorrow."

"That's a mistake."

"Duly noted. Do it anyway."

Sasha nodded, rising from the chair. "Yes, Madam President."

"Is there a problem?"

"No, ma'am. I serve at the pleasure of the president."

Whitney searched Sasha's face for sarcasm. And found none.

CHAPTER TWENTY-SEVEN

SEATTLE, WASHINGTON

NOAH BLAKELEY LIFTED a champagne flute from the tray of a passing server. He sipped the cool liquid, the bubbles just right, as he scanned the room over the lip of the glass. Standing in a ballroom in the Grand Hyatt Hotel on Pine Street downtown, the muted light from the gigantic chandelier above allowed him to observe his fellow guests without appearing as if he were doing so.

He wondered whether other cities had as many fundraisers. He could attend a different one every night, if he desired. Seattle was not known for its pretentiousness like other cities such as New York or Washington, DC, but Noah knew that was a lie. Some pretentious Seattleites just hid behind their outdoorsy Pacific Northwest façade. The same people who excluded him from their cliques. His wife, Diane, never attended these events with him. After having accompanied him to a few functions right after their wedding, she now refused.

Never one to stand still, he began to stroll around the room. He squeezed by a woman and a man in animated conversation.

The woman, wearing a tight dark-blue dress with a hint of gold at her neck, whispered to her companion in a fierce undertone. He caught the words "hacker" and "stole" and "cyber." He wanted to stop and listen, but didn't want to be conspicuous. Other snippets of conversation reached him: "money" and "million" and "IT consultants" and "beefed-up security."

What's going on?

He drained his glass. He needed something stronger than champagne and headed toward one of the bars set up in the ballroom.

A woman dressed in a black pantsuit and an expensive white shirt stood at the back of the line at the bar. Her smile always looked like a smirk to him. He looked down at his own tan slacks and mismatched brown jacket. "Kyle. Hello."

"Good evening, Noah." She waved her hand, indicating he should cut in front of her. "Feel free. You seem to need a drink more than I do."

Kyle Madison was the founder and managing director of a powerful venture-capital firm.

He squeezed between her and the woman in front of her. "Thanks."

They stood. The silence uncomfortable. Noah hated silence. "How've you been?"

"Well, thank you."

She didn't bother asking how he was, but instead scanned the room. As if searching for someone more interesting. He had always sensed that she didn't like him.

"And business?" he said.

"Never better."

"Have you heard about something going on?"

She looked at him, her dark hair cascading like waves. Like

one of those shampoo commercials. He wanted to reach out and touch it but knew she wouldn't appreciate that. Her beauty intimidated him.

"What do you mean?"

He shoved his hand in his pocket. "Just hearing things. About hackers. Stealing money."

"Sounds like a bunch of rumors to me." She spotted someone in the crowd. Or pretended to. "I see someone I need to speak to. If you'll excuse me."

Placing her glass on the tray of a passing server, she moved away from him.

Guess she didn't want another drink after all.

But he knew it was him. He had that effect on people.

Noah inspected his jacket. He pulled a loose thread at the bottom, wrapping it around his finger. And kept pulling. The thread seemed endless. *Shit!* The woman in front of him glanced down at his engorged finger, and then abruptly faced the bar. He stuffed his hand in his jacket pocket.

He did not speak to Kyle Madison for the rest of the evening.

CHAPTER TWENTY-EIGHT

THE WHITE HOUSE, WASHINGTON, DC

SARAH, HER BODY woman, poked her head into the Oval Office. "Excuse me, Madam President. Senators Hampton and Sampson and Representative Bell are here."

"Send them in. And ask Sasha to join us, please."

Whitney rose, smoothed her skirt, and came around her desk, arm extended. "Gentlemen. How good of you to come."

"Madam President," Hampton and Bell said.

Sampson said nothing.

Her eyes narrowed. "Excuse me, Paul; I didn't hear you."

"Madam President."

She indicated for them to sit on the two sofas facing each other, while she sat on a Queen Anne chair, her back to the window. Sasha entered and sat in the matching chair.

"I won't mince words." Whitney looked at Hampton and Bell. "I understand the two of you met with Sasha. What are your thoughts about the proposal?"

Hampton adjusted his black-framed glasses. "We don't need another 'Soak the Rich' proposal. If you want our support, focus on growing the economic pie rather than wealth distribution."

"Income inequality isn't the issue," said Bell. "Economic opportunity is."

"'The fact is that income inequality is real; it's been rising for more than twenty-five years.'" She waited.

The men looked at each other.

"George W. Bush," she said. "Early 2000s. The gap has widened since then. We have less economic mobility in America today than in class-conscious Europe."

"You make income inequality sound like a bad thing," Hampton said. "Howard's right. The issue is making sure that everyone has the opportunity for a better life. What they do with that opportunity is up to them."

Senator Paul Sampson rested his hands on top of his belly. "Some income inequality is beneficial. It creates an incentive for people to be productive, innovate, and create wealth."

Whitney glanced at him. *Aren't you a Democrat?* "But too much impedes economic growth and marginalizes the people at the bottom, leaving them feeling disenfranchised."

"That's not the problem," said Bell. "The quality of life for everyone is improving. Even if you're poor today, you're likely to own a smartphone, the latest Nikes, a flat-screen TV—"

Sasha sat up. "Excuse me?"

"What Howard is saying," Hampton cut in, "is that the government shouldn't be in the business of altering economic outcomes, but should instead focus on creating opportunities."

"All right," Whitney said. "Give me an example."

Hampton and Bell glanced at each other.

Bell spoke up. "Didn't you see on the news about those

two guys on food stamps who became billionaires overnight by inventing a smartphone app?"

She held up a hand, signaling Sasha to stop laughing. Turning to Bell, she didn't even try to mask the incredulity in her voice. "You're kidding, right?" He wasn't. "How often is that going to happen? Really, Howard. That's not real life."

"You make it seem as if being born poor is a life sentence," Sampson said. "My daddy was a farmer." He spread his arms. "Now, look at me."

"Yes," Whitney said. "Look at you."

He dropped his arms.

"Social mobility isn't dead," Hampton said. "The people with vision and drive, who are willing to work hard and take risks, will be rewarded."

"An economist once said that 'it's harder to climb our social ladder when the rungs are further apart.'"

He leaned forward. "For argument's sake, let's say we enact what you propose. How do you intend to pay for it? Taxing the rich is a nonstarter. There's no way we're going to sign on for any of the usual class warfare championed by you and your party."

"My party? Do you think if you say 'class warfare' enough, constituents in *your* party will forget that they are part of that middle or lower class that is falling behind, too?"

"They have so far," Sasha quipped.

Hampton's cool demeanor dissipated. "Instead of demotivating the rich with new taxes, how about easing their tax burden by eliminating the corporate tax? They'll work harder, be more productive, create more jobs, and expand the economy."

"Come on! Historical evidence proves that higher taxes don't demotivate people. Between nineteen forty-seven and nineteen seventy-seven, income taxes were high and GDP grew by almost four percent. The top one percent owned six-teen percent of the wealth versus eighty-five today. That's why Americans remember those times fondly. It was the golden age of the middle class."

"And what are *we* going to do with all those tax dollars?" Hampton said. "Our government has a propensity to be inefficient and waste resources."

"I still don't understand why so many in your party bash the federal government, when they themselves are the ones making the decisions. That has never made sense to me."

Hampton glanced at the other two men. "How about this? Instead of the American people funding social programs through the government, what if we allow them to 'self-tax' by giving directly to the charities of their choice?"

Sasha sighed, shooting a meaningful glance at Whitney.

Whitney did not try to hide her frustration. "That won't work. Not all needs can be met by established nonprofits. Poor, minority women would be forgotten. I want to return to Clinton-era tax rates, which will increase revenues by seventy-six billion dollars a year. With just that much, we're talking about improving a significant number of people's lives at a small cost to the wealthiest Americans."

Hampton had started shaking his head when she mentioned the former president from Arkansas. "No way. I can't even bring that to the caucus with a straight face. The one percent will migrate to Galt's Gulch."

"I wish we could discuss income inequality without your party resurrecting Ayn Rand."

"She has her uses," he smiled. "The one percent start companies, employ millions of people, pay their benefits, create products. Let's make it easier for them to provide that. What we really need to do is help them compete in the world marketplace so they can generate that wealth for their workers. Streamline regulations. Reduce their taxes."

"Or we can increase social benefits," Whitney countered, "such as food stamps and unemployment. History has shown that benefits stimulate the economy four to five times more than tax cuts."

Hampton shook his head again, knowing he didn't need to respond.

"A columnist once said that the rising tide is not lifting all boats, only the yachts." She decided to change course. "Minimum wage?"

Hampton smoothed his tie. "Historically, minimum-wage increases have been ineffective at improving standards of living."

She looked at him. "How would you know? Reagan and H. W. kept the minimum wage fixed for nine years, and based on real buying power, it hit a fifty-one-year low during W.'s administration."

Bell snorted. "It's easy to raise the federal minimum wage when the federal government doesn't have to pay for it. Let the states decide."

"Higher pay increases autonomy, personal freedom, and responsibility," Whitney said. She turned to Hampton. "Bottom line, it increases their buying power. Conservative principles, Eric. Ones you profess to believe in. Or used to anyway."

"You're forgetting the negative consequences. Inflation, higher prices, and layoffs in businesses that can't afford the new wage."

"With all due respect, Madam President," Bell said, "there

will always be poor people. Your party has to get over it. That's what charities are for."

Before Sasha could react, Whitney said, "Adam Smith said, 'No society can surely be flourishing and happy, of which the far greater part of the members are poor and miserable.'"

Hampton raised his hand. "Before you quote someone else, I'll concede to raising the minimum to ten-fifty. But that's it. That will lift nine hundred thousand people out of poverty."

Bell protested. "But that will cost five hundred thousand jobs."

Whitney considered it. Improving the lives of only a million people wasn't enough for her. She wasn't getting anywhere with them. She rose to signal the end of the meeting. The three men and Sasha stood, too, Sampson faster than the rest.

"We like the EITC and child-tax credit expansions," Hampton said. "We can work together on repairing bridges, roads, and schools, and modernizing our shipping ports and airports. We might even give you high-speed and inner-city rail, but we want to privatize Amtrak." Whitney shook her head. He tilted his head and offered his charming smile. "Come on. Give us something."

She said nothing.

Hampton extended his hand. "Eliminate the new tax brackets. I'll float the Clinton-era rates. No promises, though. Good day, Madam President."

CHAPTER TWENTY-NINE

WASHINGTON, DC

ETHAN LAWSON LEANED into her office. "My office. Five minutes." He left before she could respond. She mentally reviewed her active cases in preparation for whatever he might ask and grabbed her notebook.

He was hanging up his suit jacket on the mahogany coat rack in the corner as she entered. Over his shoulder, he said, "What's up?"

Jade sat in the guest chair. "Preparing to testify in the Morales case tomorrow. Merritt and I are interviewing a source in the Blanchett case later today."

"What else?"

"That's about it."

"I heard a rumor."

She gave him a blank look.

"Don't you want to know what it is?" Ethan asked.

"Not really."

He leaned back in his chair, one hand on his desk. "This is an interesting one, though. It involves you."

Jade feigned ignorance.

"Rumor has it," he continued, "that you and Merritt not only have an interest in the deaths of those three teenage boys, but you have an unofficial investigation going. An administrator for the Fairfax County school system told me that you interviewed students at one of his esteemed institutions of secondary education. I also heard you interviewed the parents of one of the victims of this case-that-isn't-ours. Observed an interview of an alleged suspect, for that same case. Any of that ring a bell?"

He didn't seem to know about their visit with Jenny Thompson.

Jade tilted her head and shrugged. "Maybe. Who did you hear that from?"

He ignored the question. "You shouldn't be involved."

"Why not?"

Ethan raised his hands in exasperation. "It's not our case!"

"More kids are going to die."

"Jade . . . "

"More. Kids. Are. Going. To. Die."

He sank into his chair. "There are rules for a reason." He twirled his wedding ring, then sighed. "Until this is officially our case . . . if you continue to pursue it, I'll place you on administrative leave."

Jade's heart beat faster. Her cheeks flushed. She shot Ethan a look and headed for the door. Holding the door open, she turned, staring at him for a moment.

"Then place me on leave."

She made sure to slam the door as hard as she could on her way out.

CHAPTER THIRTY

COLUMBUS, OHIO

"WHERE IS THE crowd?" she asked, as she accepted a bottled water from Sarah and took a quick sip.

Sasha shrugged. "Things change when you go from candidate to president."

What a difference six months make.

Sarah held the daily schedule and the ever-present stack of briefing books. Scanning the invited guests sitting in the three rows of bleachers behind the podium, she said, "Don't bother to thank Senator Harris in your remarks. He didn't show."

"Asshole," Sasha said.

As Whitney's body woman, Sarah was on call twenty-four/seven and accompanied her almost everywhere. She didn't have time for a private life, so Whitney never bothered to ask her about it. A specific document, a Sharpie for autographs, a breath mint, snacks, a messenger, her cell phone, or a sounding board, Sarah anticipated and catered to Whitney's every need. She even worked out with Whitney sometimes.

Whitney glanced up at the bleachers, a quarter of them still empty. They were both right. The senior Democratic senator from Ohio was not in attendance, which was bad form and showed a lack of respect for a sitting president. And he was an asshole.

This was the first stop on a road trip through the Midwest to get her message out about the New New Deal. In the wings of a makeshift stage at Ohio State University's St. John Arena, she waited for the governor to wrap up his introduction. She took deep, relaxing breaths until her name was announced.

"Let's do this." Handing the bottle back to Sarah, she adjusted the specially-made Kevlar vest under her suit and walked into the basketball arena.

She smiled and waved at the crowd. At the podium, she shook hands with the governor. "Thanks, Bill." She turned back toward the crowd. "How are you, Columbus?"

A lukewarm response greeted her. She didn't take it personally. She was a politician, after all.

"I'm here today to talk to you about the New New Deal Coalition legislation. Franklin D. Roosevelt once said, 'Throughout the nation men and women . . . look to us here for guidance and for more equitable opportunity to share in the distribution of national wealth . . . I pledge myself to a new deal for the American people. This is more than a political campaign. It is a call to arms.'

"No words are more true today.

"The New Deal reduced income inequality by putting eight point five million people to work, built six hundred and fifty thousand miles of highways, and one hundred and twenty-five thousand buildings. The Lincoln Tunnel, LaGuardia Airport, and the San Francisco Bay Bridge were all built during this glorious period of American achievement.

"But the legislation wasn't only about what it built. The New Deal represented what was best about our country. It was about coming together, making real change, caring about the American worker, and providing security and a sense of purpose.

"Income inequality is the defining issue of our time. Five years ago, the three hundred and eighty-eight richest people in the world were more wealthy than the poorest three-point-five billion combined. Three years ago, it was the top eighty-five people. Now, it's eight people. Eight."

She paused, allowing that number to hang in the air.

"The concentration of wealth is accelerating. No other economic system in the history of the world has ever had the concentration of untaxed wealth that we do now. This deprives the government of much-needed resources for public services and erodes trust that there is a level playing field of equal opportunity. For everyone.

"In the nineteen forties and fifties, the gap between the rich and everyone else was small. In the eighties, with technological advances, deregulation, and tax cuts for the wealthiest Americans, fortunes began to diverge; the rich got richer, but everyone else stayed about the same. I call this time the 'Great Divide.'

"Although we saw some improvement in the nineties during the economic boom and with the increasing of the highest marginal tax rate, it got dramatically worse during the first decade of this century when that administration slashed taxes, cut social services, and deregulated industries. And it has worsened ever since.

"In 1980, a CEO made about forty-two times the average worker. With the decreasing influence of unions and changing societal norms, CEO pay has climbed to over three hundred and eighty times worker pay." Whitney spread her arms wide. "Has the productivity of CEOs increased that much compared with yours?"

She waited for the shouts of "No!"

Instead, she received a low grumble of disagreement.

She'd take it.

"A CEO of a software company has a net worth of twenty-seven *billion* dollars and could spend three hundred thousand dollars an hour every *hour* until he died, and still not make a dent in his net worth.

"On the other side of the Great Divide, there are two-income families who still need government assistance to make ends meet. Who's fighting for these families?

"We even have some teenagers who must work to feed their families. Who's fighting for these teenagers?

"Twenty-five percent of the children in the United States live in poverty. That is one out of every four. In the United States! Who's fighting for our children?

"Our middle class is shrinking. Historically, the prosperity of this country flowed from the middle class. Who's fighting for our middle class?"

Whitney scanned the arena, letting the last statement sink in, gauging their response. This audience, predominately middle-class and white, must identify with this statement or her message was dead. Her historic legislation was dead.

"And everyone knows that women make only seventy-seven percent of what a man makes for the same work. Everyone *knows* this. Who's fighting for our women?

"If we do not act now, our country will continue to grow evermore divided. We can do better. The Great Divide does not need to be the status quo. My New New Deal Coalition legislation will not eliminate income inequality—a problem that has been over three decades in the making—but it will put us in a position to start closing that gap and realize our true wealth by making a significant investment in the American people.

"And I'll make that investment any day."

Whitney outlined the plan. She did not mention the changes that Hampton sent to her after their meeting. She would allow him to take credit for them with his constituents.

She wrapped up her speech, surprised at the tepid applause. Surprised because this audience would benefit the most from her plan. Pasting on a smile, she waved and met Sasha and Sarah backstage.

"You wrote an incredible speech," Sasha said.

Whitney accepted a fresh bottle of water from Sarah. "Doesn't matter if no one listens."

CHAPTER THIRTY-ONE

WASHINGTON, DC

"BOY, HAVE TIMES changed. Remember when her acolytes treated her like Jesus? And the crowds gathered forth? Like some young, talentless pop star. Now, you can't pay people to attend her speeches. And, yes, I'm talking about the president of the United States.

"This morning a paltry one thousand people showed up to hear Whitney peddling her liberal snake oil message at Ohio State University, one of several stops in the Midwest. And a waste of taxpayers' money, if you ask me.

"Let's talk about this New Old Deal, shall we?

"Are we really going back to the nineteen thirties to help solve today's problems? Can't you be more original, Ma-DAMN President?

"The New Deal built miles of highways—Cha-ching!—thousands of buildings—Cha-ching!—airports, tunnels, bridges—Cha-ching, Cha-ching, Chaaa-ching. All I hear is cash registers, folks!"

Cole was on a roll. He leaned into the studio microphone.

"Income inequality is not the defining issue of our time. What is the defining issue of our time, you ask? Well, I'll tell you. It's the disappearance of manufacturing jobs. Back in the day, people didn't need to go to college and earn fancy degrees to carve out a decent living for themselves and their families. The 'Great Divide,' my ass. It's the 'Trade Divide,' people! Eliminate those trade deals and bring those jobs back home to the good ol' US of A. Who's fighting for these workers? I am.

"And regarding CEOs, they make the big money because they make the tough decisions. Like in *Atlas Shrugged*. Anyone can dig, but we need someone to tell us where. That's what CEOs do.

"By the way, that's one book I did read. If you've never read it, I suggest you do. Along with my book, *Communism in Russia is Dead, but Alive and Well in the USA*. I wrote it almost a year ago, but it's still true today. Maybe more so. Can I get an amen?

"We have the greatest economic system in the world. Capitalism worked just fine until our federal government started tinkering with it."

Cole grabbed a hand towel to dab his forehead. "We have to take a break here to pay the bills. After the break, a special guest will be joining us. Don't go away."

CHAPTER THIRTY-TWO
SEATTLE, WASHINGTON

NOAH BLAKELEY BIT into the sesame-seed ciabatta smothered with cream cheese that he'd picked up at the Specialty's bakery on the way to the office. This was his favorite part of the day: sitting at his desk, eating breakfast, drinking his first cup of coffee, and reading the *Seattle Times*.

He opened the paper. President Whitney Fairchild had just completed a tour of Ohio, Michigan, Indiana, Illinois, and Missouri. Noah always read the editorial section of the paper first. Today's editorial was supportive of her latest speech, describing it as one of the most important presidential speeches of the twenty-first century so far. The editorialist believed it was a moral imperative for the country to address income inequality and its dire consequences before it was too late.

He agreed.

The Associated Press news article on the first page covering her speeches wasn't as positive. The correspondent reported on the unreceptive audiences, even in the president's home state of Missouri. Noah couldn't understand why. Her legislation would create jobs. Employment cured many ills.

He finished the ciabatta and sipped his coffee, wondering how he could help the president.

He turned to the business section of the paper. He slowly placed the to-go cup on his desk.

The rumors he'd heard at the Grand Hyatt fundraiser were now fact.

Several major corporations in the Seattle area had fallen victim to cybertheft. Hackers, using dummy bank sites, had siphoned off millions of dollars. One controller, acting on an email from his CEO about a secret acquisition, transferred a million dollars to a bank account via a link in the email. The email turned out to be fake. The CEO hadn't sent it. The police had not located the money.

He let the paper drop and speed-dialed his chief financial officer whose office was on the other side of the building.

"Check our bank account."

"Why?"

"Just do it."

He listened as the CFO tapped on his keyboard.

"Hurry up," Noah said.

After a moment, the CFO said, "This can't be."

Noah felt the first stirrings of fear developing in his stomach. "What is it?"

"The balance in the account is about a million dollars lower than it should be."

"Call the bank. I'll wait."

The CFO did as instructed. Through the CFO's speakerphone, Noah heard the message: "Thank you for calling Pacific

Coast Bank. All customer-service agents are busy now. Please leave a message or try your call again later."

He slowly replaced the handset.

His father was going to have a fit.

CHAPTER THIRTY-THREE

THE WHITE HOUSE, WASHINGTON, DC

BACK IN THE Oval Office the day after returning from her trip to the Midwest, Whitney reviewed the daily presidential briefing books. Although available in electronic tablet form, she still preferred to read the print version. The weight of the document in her hand reinforced the weight of the issues it represented.

Included in today's report—along with scores of terrorist threats, terrorist cell movements, a potential terrorist attack on a Planned Parenthood building in Idaho, and US and euro currency manipulations by the Chinese government—was an item about network security breaches involving substantial sums of money at several companies in Seattle. The report speculated Chinese government involvement.

The Chinese had been suspected of various attacks on US corporate and military computer networks for years, including theft of medical data, Social Security numbers, and classified information. Whitney's national security team believed that most of the attacks were government-sanctioned. What they didn't have was proof.

She called Sasha into the Oval Office. Within a minute, Sasha stood in front of her desk.

She held up the briefing book. "The Chinese?"

Sasha shrugged. "Why not? We blame them for everything else."

Whitney smiled. "Like the Japanese in the Eighties? Call ODNI"—the Office of the Director of National Intelligence—"and find out who's handling this."

Sasha made a note.

"And can you turn on the radio? Cole's on."

Sasha's neck twitched, the way it did every time she thought Whitney was doing something foolish. "Why do you want to listen to him?"

Whitney thought of Ashley Brennan. "I have my reasons."

Sasha moved to a table against the wall and turned on the radio. She settled into the chair across from Whitney.

At the end of a commercial, Cole said, "Welcome back. I'd like to introduce my special guest, Paul Sampson, the Democratic senator from Nebraska. Welcome, Senator." Whitney and Sasha shared a glance. Foreboding pressed against Whitney's chest. "What's all this I've been hearing about income inequality?"

"Income inequality isn't a bad thing," Sampson said. "It creates an incentive for people to be productive, innovate, and create wealth. Besides, the quality of life for everyone is improving. Even if you're poor today, you're likely to own a smartphone, the latest Nikes, a flat-screen TV—"

"Sounds familiar," Whitney murmured.

"Bunch of BS," Sasha said.

"But don't you think this legislation will pit Americans against each other?" Cole asked. "Don't you think it's just another attempt by you and your Commiecrat comrades to engage in class warfare?"

"The president mentioned you in a meeting recently," Sampson said. "We were discussing increasing taxes on the rich and distributing the wealth."

Whitney burned, listening. How dare he talk publicly about a private meeting.

Cole laughed. "At least she's thinking about me." He sobered. "No more taxes, Senator. Please! Americans are taxed enough."

"I agree, Cole," Sampson said. "We need to streamline regulations and reduce taxes for everyone."

Sasha's mouth opened. "What is he saying?"

Whitney held her hand up for silence.

"Switching gears," Cole said. "What are your thoughts about these protests?"

"I don't think they're helpful."

"Me neither. Instead of protesting, I think they all should be working. Don't you? Put that energy to good use. Well, I'd like to thank you for coming on the show today. Is there anything else you want to say?"

"Well, I have a lot to say, Cole, but first I want to tell you that today I burned my Democratic voter-registration card. And I registered as a Republican. I am now a proud member of the GOP, and I'm ready to take my country back."

Cole's high-pitched giggle filled the airwaves. "God Almighty, you've seen the light!"

Whitney visualized Cole with his hands raised in a televangelist pose.

"Yes, I have, Cole," Sampson said. "And my first order of business will be immigration. We're going to build that wall that Ellison was too scared to start, and we're going to place a moratorium on all non-Christian immigration to this country."

"Jesus H. Christ," Sasha said.

"I'm not sure even He can help us," Whitney said. She made a shooing motion with her hand. "Turn that off."

Sasha complied. "Without him, it will be harder to get our agenda through."

Whitney willed herself to calm down. She couldn't do anything about Sampson now. "I didn't call you in here for that. Set up a meeting with Jade Harrington."

Sasha didn't hide her surprise. "The FBI agent from the TSK case?"

"One and the same."

"What has that got to do with Sampson?"

"Nothing."

Sasha hesitated, waiting for Whitney to elaborate further on the purpose of the meeting. She didn't.

"Yes, Madam President." She turned to go, but then stopped. "This may be a little unprofessional . . . but can you introduce me to her? I'm a huge fan."

"You don't strike me as a person who gets star-struck."

"I'm not," Sasha said. "It's the magic."

"Magic?"

She winked. "Black-girl magic."

*

Later that afternoon, Sarah escorted FBI Special Agent Jade

Harrington into the Oval Office. The agent strode toward Whitney with the confidence evident in current and former athletes. Whitney had forgotten how tall Jade was. And striking. The most intriguing part was that Jade didn't seem to realize it.

Whitney rose to greet her in the middle of the room. She covered the agent's proffered hand in both of hers. "Agent Harrington. I hope you've been well."

"Yes, Madam President. It's been quite a year."

"Yes, it has. Please have a seat."

Jade sat on the sofa, as if she were invited to the Oval Office every day. Not in a disrespectful manner, but as someone comfortable in her own skin. Whitney moved to her favorite chair. She hadn't spoken to the agent since they had met in her Senate office. "I never thanked you for solving the TSK case."

The agent hesitated. "I'm sure its resolution was bittersweet for you."

Whitney gasped, but recovered quickly. She had not told anyone about Landon's letter. And the devastating secret it contained.

"Bittersweet?"

"He'd created a shrine."

"Pardon me?"

"In his apartment. We didn't disclose this to the press. He had this wall covered with pictures of you. Articles about you. From your campaigns, your marriage announcement, the births of your children."

Whitney breathed, realizing she had overreacted. "How disturbing."

"He drew this picture of you," the agent said, shaking her head. "It was amazing. The likeness, uncanny."

Whitney paused a moment, taking it all in. "I guess no matter how close you are to someone, you can never really know him. Or her."

"That's the truth," Jade said, a slight color rising to her cheeks. Whitney wondered why.

Jade pulled out a ragged notebook. If Whitney wasn't mistaken, it was the same one Jade had used to interview her last year. *Was the FBI's budget that tight?*

"Why am I here?" Jade asked.

No small talk for this one. "I have a proposition for you. What do you know about the cyberthefts occurring in Seattle?"

"Only what I read in the papers."

Whitney filled her in on the contents of that morning's PDB, which wasn't much more than what was reported in the newspapers.

"Any evidence that the Chinese are involved?" asked Jade.

"Just suspicions. Suppositions. Rumors."

"I'm still not sure why I'm here."

"I want you to be the liaison between the Secret Service and the FBI on this."

Most people were familiar with the Secret Service's responsibility of protecting the president and other high-placed government officials, but the Service also had jurisdiction over other domains, including cybercrime. As did the FBI.

Jade shifted, uncomfortable. "This isn't my area of expertise. Shouldn't you be asking someone from our cyber division?"

"I've talked to your boss," Whitney said. "Ethan Lawson, isn't it? He's approved this assignment." She smiled at the scowl crossing Jade's face. "Is something wrong?"

Jade glanced out the window. "He wants to distract me from the bullying case."

"Bullying case?"

"Never mind."

"There's something else."

Jade remained silent, probably thinking about what she would say to her boss next time she saw him. Whitney didn't envy him.

"I'm sure you're aware of the income-inequality protests taking place across the country," Whitney said.

Jade turned back to her. "Sure."

"Evan Stevens. A liberal blogger. Smart. Irreverent. Heard of him?"

"I've met him. We interviewed him about the TSK case."

"What did you discover?"

"Not much. I read a lot of his blogs. He's passionate about the causes he believes in. He turned out to be clean."

Whitney crossed her legs and smoothed her skirt. "It may be more than that. He seems to be . . . stirring up the masses. I believe he is one of the reasons these protests are having such a long shelf life. I am contemplating inviting him here. To talk to him."

"Sounds like a good idea, but I don't understand why you're telling me."

"I want you to look into his background."

Jade's eyes narrowed. "Don't you have people for that?"

"Yes, but I want you to do it. I trust you." Whitney stood, ending the meeting. She bit back a smile. "Oh . . . and Agent Lawson said it was okay."

CHAPTER THIRTY-FOUR

WASHINGTON, DC

SHE WAITED IN the queue at Peet's Coffee & Tea near FBI HQ. She thought about her conversation with the president and what she'd said about Landon. That you can never really know someone. Fairchild didn't know about her relationship with him, unless he told her, which Jade doubted. No one knew, except Zoe. And it was going to stay that way.

Her phone rang. She wanted to ignore it. She needed her coffee. Badly. She glanced at the display. A 206 number. Seattle.

Stepping outside the shop, she scanned the surrounding area. "Agent Harrington."

"Harrington, it's your favorite detective in Seattle."

"I only know one detective in Seattle."

She had worked with Detective Kurt McClaine on the TSK case.

He waited a beat. "And I'm still not your favorite? Ouch." A smile in his voice. "I need your help."

"Another murder?"

"No. Not a murder this time. It's about money. Someone

or some organization or a sovereign nation that starts with a 'C' is stealing a lot of money from the good people of Seattle."

"I heard."

"I know. From the president."

She frowned. "How do you know that?"

"I'm who you're liaising with on the local level. I need you to come to Seattle. I was informed the president cleared it with your boss."

She looked at the phone, wanting to throw it. She brought it back to her ear. "When?"

"You're booked on a flight early this afternoon your time. I emailed the details."

On the sidewalk, people walked around her on either side. Some of them slowed, their eyes widening when they recognized her. A woman with Asian features took her picture.

"I suggest you pack for a few days," he said.

Jade glanced back at Peet's. "Damn. It looks like I won't get my coffee."

"We have plenty of coffee in Seattle. I'll pick you up at the airport."

CHAPTER THIRTY-FIVE

THE WHITE HOUSE, WASHINGTON, DC

WHITNEY SWUNG HER legs onto the sofa and picked up the glass of red wine from the coffee table in front of her. A healthy pour.

Is there any other kind?

A biography about Victoria Woodhull, who, in 1872, was the first female candidate to run for president of the United States—before women had the right to vote—lay beside her. She took a sip of wine, rolling it around on her tongue. Savoring it. She reflected on her conversation with Jade Harrington.

I'm sure its resolution was bittersweet for you.

Whitney was concerned. If Landon's secret got out, her presidency would be destroyed. Or, at least, it would give the other party and the political pundits fodder to talk about for a long time. It would impact her family.

She thought about Jade. Her intelligence. Her confidence.

Her swagger. She had "It." There was something about the agent that Whitney was drawn to. A kinship.

The initial melody of Chopin's Nocturne in E-flat Major, op. 55, no. 2 trilled from her cell phone. Chandler.

"This is a nice surprise."

"Hey, Mom. What's up?"

She envisioned her son sitting, one leg bobbing up and down with nervous energy. His bangs flopping down on his forehead.

Whitney glanced at the briefing books stacked on the end table, untouched, and then back at her glass. "Taking a break from work. And you?"

"I have some good news, and some bad news. Which do you want first?"

Gripping the phone tighter, she tried to remain calm. "Bad."

"I'm not graduating until September. I can't get all my credits in without summer school."

Whitney exhaled. "That's not bad. I think it takes six years now for the average student to graduate, so you're still ahead of your peers."

"I didn't know it was a competition, Mom."

"It's always a competition. What's the good news?"

"I've decided to work for Dad after graduation."

She smiled. "That's wonderful! He's going to be happy."

"He is. I told him."

"I'm proud of you. What made you choose the family business?"

"I couldn't get a job anywhere else." Before she could respond, he said, "Just kidding. It seemed like a good way to learn how to run a big business. Besides, I don't want to end up like those protesters."

"What protesters?"

"The ones on TV. Protesting that income-inequality bullsh—stuff. I want to make my own money. Someday own my own business. Be in charge of my own destiny."

She placed her glass on the table. "Sometimes being in charge of your own destiny is not enough, son."

"Sorry, Mom, I just don't buy that. You and Dad always taught us that if we worked hard, good things would happen. To not wait for anything to be handed to us. To go after what we want."

Whitney chose her words carefully. "I still believe that, but there's more to it. Some people are born into a bad situation that is difficult to rise above. Others encounter bad luck: financially, a health crisis, the unexpected death of a provider. There are systemic issues within our economy that allow the wealthy to become wealthier, and everyone else to stay the same."

"The wealthy get a bad rap. It's not their fault they're rich. I can't wait to be one of them."

"Well—"

"Mom, I need to go. I'll call you again soon. Love you."

"I love you, too."

She looked at the phone display. Chandler was gone. She placed it on the sofa and picked up her glass. The person on the phone did not sound like her son. Their normal playful banter, absent. He sounded like a damn Republican.

She finished the rest of the wine in one gulp. The president of the United States crossed the room to the refrigerator to retrieve another bottle.

CHAPTER THIRTY-SIX

SEATTLE, WASHINGTON

DECLINING THE RECEPTIONIST'S offers for a seat or coffee or water, Jade and Detective Kurt McClaine stood off to the side of the sleek, gray front desk. McClaine, with his blond, unkempt hair, gold earring, cheap suit jacket, jeans, and a tattoo on his neck peeking out of his customary t-shirt, looked more like a handsome rock star than a detective.

"You brought the sun," he said. "That doesn't happen too often in May."

"I don't think I had anything to do with it," Jade said.

"I wouldn't be so sure," said the tall woman walking toward them. "It's rained for three weeks straight. And, please, forgive the good detective. Talking about the weather is what we Seattleites do best." She extended her hand to McClaine. "Good to see you again." Her green eyes focused on Jade. Extending her hand, she said, "Kyle Madison."

Her grip was firm. Jade held her gaze. "Special Agent Jade Harrington."

The woman turned. "Follow me," she said over her shoulder. She didn't wait to see if they complied.

Jade liked that.

Something flickered in McClaine's eye as he gestured for Jade to walk ahead of him. She followed Kyle down a long hallway, taking in the shimmering medium-length black hair, the expensive, fitted dark suit, and the high heels. She noticed everything, except the sway of Ms. Madison's hips.

Kyle's office, in the same décor as the reception area, was gray and white and black, save a red rose in the slim vase on her desk. Elegant, but impersonal. No pictures. No knickknacks. No plants. Nothing to reveal more about the woman.

Except the rose.

After they were seated, McClaine said, "Ms. Madison, can you—"

"Hold that thought," the executive said, as she pushed a button on the phone on her desk. "Kevin, can you bring in some tea, please?" She turned to McClaine. "You want me to tell Agent Harrington what happened."

He nodded.

Kyle leaned back in her chair. "I manage a venture-capital firm. We help social media entrepreneurs turn their dreams into reality by providing Series A financing so they can reach more customers, increase revenues, and grow their businesses. We're selective in the companies in which we choose to invest. You've heard of most of them. Our approach is different. We invest in the people, not the—"

Jade interrupted the sales pitch. "Where are your tombstones?"

A discreet knock on the door postponed the answer. The receptionist entered and placed the tea service on the desk.

"Thank you, Kevin," Kyle said.

He left. She lifted the silver-plated tea pot that appeared as if it cost more than Jade's monthly mortgage payment. Kyle looked at them. "Tea?"

They both shook their heads.

She poured a cup for herself. "To answer your question, I don't need to be surrounded by visual reminders of my successes. It keeps me hungry."

"How big is your typical fund?"

"Our last one was one billion."

McClaine whistled.

"Tell me what happened," Jade said.

"Obviously, a lot of money flows through here. In. And out. My CFO discovered that our account reconciliations had been slightly off consistently for months. Not by enough to cause alarm, so he didn't think it necessary to inform me. It's crazy around here. All the time. The companies, investors, entrepreneurs in residence. He chalked it up to minor errors by his staff. Rounding. A few days ago, he realized they weren't errors."

Jade leaned in. "How much was stolen?"

"One million dollars."

She glanced at McClaine and then back at Kyle. "They were testing your internal control systems to see if any red flags would be raised. When there weren't, they struck."

Kyle nodded. "That's what my CFO said."

"We'll need to talk to him."

"Certainly."

Jade turned to McClaine. "Any luck tracing the money?"

"Your local brethren are working on it. Nothing, yet."

To Kyle, Jade said: "Talk to me about your systems."

"I'll have you speak with my IT director. He will be able to help you much better than I could."

Do only men work for you?

"Agent Harrington," Kyle said, "as I told the detective," nodding at McClaine, "it's imperative that we keep this quiet. I don't want to spook our investors. We're about to embark on raising our largest fund ever. In my business, trust is everything."

"I understand."

Kyle rose, a signal for them to leave.

Jade stayed seated. "I wasn't finished."

Kyle hesitated before returning to her chair.

"We need a copy of your financial records for the last year. And I want to interview everyone in your accounting department."

"That can be arranged."

"I'll also need copies of your personal financial records during that period."

For the first time, the confident smile faltered, hardened. "I'm the victim here."

"Standard procedure," McClaine reassured her.

"To rule me out. I get it. Are we finished?"

Jade stood. "Now, I'm finished."

"*Now* . . . I'll show you out." Kyle strode toward the door, again not waiting to see if they followed.

Back out front, she spoke to the receptionist, and turned back to them. "Kevin will make arrangements for you to talk to everyone." She shook their hands again. "I would appreciate your locating my clients' money as soon as possible, and bringing the criminals to justice."

"We'll do our best," McClaine said.

Kyle turned toward her office and then back as if realizing something. "Agent Harrington, when are you going back to DC?"

"Tomorrow. Why?"

"Would the two of you like to join me tonight for a Storm game?"

"We don't have time," Jade said.

From McClaine: "What time's the game?"

"Seven."

"We should be finished with our interviews by then," he said.

"Perfect."

"But I can't make it," he said.

Jade gave him a sharp glance.

Kyle's penetrating gaze turned to Jade. "When was the last time you took in a WNBA game?"

When I was in the league. "It's been a while."

"Splendid. Then, you must come."

She didn't particularly like how McClaine set her up. Or the look that passed between him and Kyle. Jade should spend the evening drafting interview reports and preparing for her early-morning flight tomorrow.

"Sure," she said. "Why not?"

CHAPTER THIRTY-SEVEN

FAIRFAX, VIRGINIA

MARK MERRITT WAS late. Since running in the hallways was forbidden, he half-ran, half-walked down the empty school corridor, headed to his last class of the day. His homework was unfinished, but he'd worry about that when he got there. He couldn't be late. For every minute late, the teacher forced you to write a one-page essay. Mark didn't like to write. There was little he liked about school lately.

Almost there. His class was on the second floor, first classroom on the right.

He was going to make it.

As he passed by the stairwell, with his foot almost on the first step, the top of his t-shirt sliced against his throat. He couldn't swallow. The person who'd grabbed him from behind pulled him backward. He tripped over an outstretched foot, his feet leaving the floor. He heard laughter. His head banged against the linoleum, an instantaneous explosion of pain followed by tiny stars.

That hurt.

He was dragged under the stairs.

Touching the back of his head, he felt a bump forming. He

opened his eyes and saw three people. They looked like boys, but their heads blocked out the overhead lighting so he couldn't see their faces. It was dark. Without warning, he felt an intense pain in his side. He cried out.

Someone kicked him again. "Shut up!"

The now-familiar pain inflicted on his other side.

Something wet and unpleasant hit him in the face and started trailing down his cheek. He hoped it wasn't spit.

"You're so lame."

"Dork."

"Fag."

Each utterance, followed by a kick, composed an off-beat rhythm to their attack. The boys continued to converse.

He was not invited to participate.

"Retard."

"You take up space."

"Wasted oxygen."

"Everybody hates you."

"Everyone wishes you were dead."

"Why don't you go choke on some pills like your cousin?"

Someone crouched beside him. "Your dad should mind his own business." Mark thought he recognized the voice. Losing consciousness, he couldn't process it.

He was punched in the face.

Whimpering, he tasted something like metal. Blood. His tongue touched the top of a tooth where it met his gums. It was loose.

He tried to raise his arms, but to no avail. The punching and kicking continued. He gave up. He lay still, praying it would end soon.

I wonder how many pages Mrs. Johnson will make me write?

And then, mercifully, darkness.

CHAPTER THIRTY-EIGHT

SEATTLE, WASHINGTON

JADE HAD NEVER watched a WNBA game from a courtside seat. During her playing days, she hadn't spent much time on the bench. Located in the Uptown—or as the locals called it, Lower Queen Anne—neighborhood just north of downtown, the antiquated Key Arena was packed for the first basketball game of the season. The Seattle Storm were hosting the Los Angeles Sparks.

The environment evoked a small rush of emotion within her: the squeak of the sneakers on the court, the thump as the basketballs bounced off the floor, the high fives, the half hugs. This was the game she'd loved and had spent a significant portion of her life playing. Just a small rush. That part of her life was over.

She didn't live in the past.

Many fans shook Kyle's hand as they walked by. Others called out to her from the seats behind them.

Storm players nodded and smiled at Kyle during warmups. Star player Sky Williams jogged over, a basketball under her arm. "Hey, Kyle." She stopped in front of Jade and held out her hand. Jade shook it.

"I'm a big fan of yours," the player said. "You're the reason why I went to Stanford." She pointed to her jersey. "And the reason why I've worn number twenty-two since middle school. Thanks for coming." Sky pivoted and dribbled away.

Middle school.

For the first time, Jade felt old. She looked at Kyle. "I give. Are you famous or something?"

Kyle smiled. "Or something."

"Hey, you."

The voice was out of place. Like way out of place. Like the wrong coast or the distance of a continent out of place. *Zoe?* Jade turned in her seat, puzzled. "What are you doing here?"

Zoe pointed at the back of Sky Williams. "Let's just say, I'm a fan."

"You're dating her?"

"'Dating' might be a little strong. We met at a party last year. In DC. After a Storm-Mystics game."

Jade shouldn't have been shocked. She had long since lost track of Zoe's copious number of exes. Jade just hadn't realized until now how geographically dispersed they were.

Zoe glanced at Kyle before asking Jade: "What are you doing here?"

Good question.

"She's with me," Kyle said, reaching across Jade to shake Zoe's hand. "Kyle Madison."

Zoe hesitated. "Zoe." They shook, their eyes held each other's gaze.

"How do you two know each other?" Zoe asked.

Jade was curious about the look they shared. Had they hooked up in the past, or were they attracted to each other now?

Neither Jade nor Kyle responded to Zoe's question.

Zoe fidgeted. After a while, she said, "I see. Well, we're going to a party after, if you want to join us."

"We have plans," Kyle said.

Jade glanced at Kyle, but said nothing.

Zoe looked at Jade. "When are you going home?"

"Tomorrow."

"Who's taking care of Card?"

"I got a neighbor to check on him. Since you weren't around."

Zoe shrugged and looked out on the court. "I had plans." She winked. "I need to get back to my seat."

More fans stopped by to say hello before the game started. Mostly for Kyle, but some acknowledged Jade as well. She was rarely recognized anymore for her basketball exploits. And she was okay with that.

Her phone vibrated. A text. From Zoe. Are you dating her?

Jade laughed.

"What is it?" Kyle asked.

"Nothing," she said. She texted back: Mind your business. You're my BFF. You are my business.

The first half, an exciting one with a lot of fast breaks and even a dunk by Seattle's six-foot-eight center, ended. At half-time, Kyle excused herself, and Jade trekked to the concession stand for popcorn. She resettled in her seat and scanned the crowd for danger. Professional habit. The arena didn't have much of a security presence. She worried about a major terrorist attack targeting a US sporting event, and was surprised there hadn't been one yet.

When she looked back toward the court, Kyle stood at the half-court line next to two other people and a cardboard check. Jade stopped chewing the stale, salty popcorn.

Into a microphone, Kyle said, "On behalf of the entire Seattle Storm organization, I present this check for ten thousand dollars to the Make-A-Wish Foundation."

Seizing the program on the seat next to her, Jade flipped through it until she came to a profile of Kyle with a quarter-page picture of her. Kyle was a minority owner of the Storm.

Kyle waved to the crowd and strolled back to her seat, a mischievous smile forming as she caught Jade watching her.

Kyle grabbed a handful of popcorn out of Jade's bag. "I've been a PAC-Ten, Twelve, whatever, fan all of my life."

"You knew who I was," Jade said.

"Of course I did."

*

"I would've been okay," Jade said. "I think I can take care of myself."

Kyle adjusted her hair under the hood of her North Face jacket. "I'm sure you can. But this is my town. I don't mind walking you."

"Where'd you park?"

"I didn't. This is a city for walking."

The night air had turned chilly since they'd entered the arena. A light drizzle fell as they strolled the twelve-block walk to Jade's hotel downtown.

"I enjoyed the game. Thanks for inviting me."

"My pleasure," Kyle said. "Do you ever miss it?"

"Some parts I miss. There are few things in life that compare to hitting a shot at the buzzer to win a big game or threading the needle with a perfect, no-look pass. But what I miss most is the time that I spent with my teammates off the court. The bus trips. Airplane rides. Team meals. Hanging out in the hotel."

"I wish we could have won for you tonight."

"LA is always tough. You know a lot about the game. Did you play?"

"No. I've always been more of an outdoor enthusiast: skier, hiker, cyclist."

"Not much of a team player, are you?"

This made Kyle smile. "I guess not."

In front of the hotel, Jade stopped. "Well, thanks again. I'll be in touch with you about the case." She yawned. "Time difference." She extended her hand. Instead of a firm handshake this time, Kyle simply held it. Her hand, soft.

Kyle gazed at her.

Those eyes.

"I travel to DC on occasion. I'll look you up next time I'm there. To check out the status of my case in person." A slight tilt of the head. "Perhaps we can have dinner."

Anything related to the case could be discussed over the phone. Before Jade could voice this, Kyle gave her hand a light squeeze and turned and walked away.

She didn't look back.

CHAPTER THIRTY-NINE

THE WHITE HOUSE, WASHINGTON, DC

"HOW MANY?"

"Maybe ten," responded her chief of staff.

"Still?" Ten out of a hundred senators. Whitney looked at Sasha, who sat across from her in the Oval Office. "We have a long way to go, don't we?"

"For so many things. But you're right. We need Hampton."

"That will make him happy."

"And maybe Sampson."

Whitney held up her hand like a crossing guard. "Let's try to do this without him."

"I do have some good news. Gas prices are at a three-year low."

"Why are presidents blamed when gas prices go up, but receive none of the credit when they go down?"

"Politics 101. Bad news is always the president's fault. Judy from ABC called me."

"Nice segue."

"She wants to interview you. About your childhood. Teenage years. Confirmation on some details. A fluff piece. I think it's a good idea."

"I think we should focus on the legislation, not me." Whitney's phone buzzed. She pressed the blinking line. "Yes?"

"The First Gentleman's assistant, Madam President," Sean, her secretary said.

Sasha rose, but hesitated. Whitney waved her to stay.

She leaned back in her chair, waiting for Grayson's assistant to connect them. "Yes, darling."

"What's this I hear about this new legislation?"

"Which one? There are many."

"This New Deal Coalition. Tell me about it."

"The New New Deal Coalition." She summarized the bill for him.

"I see," Grayson said. "What businesses will be regulated by it?"

There it is. The real reason for his call.

"Almost every business in the United States will be touched by it. And, yes, agribusiness is included."

Silence. Then softly, he said, "Touched."

"Businesses must pay their fair share. Even your business."

"This bill will hurt businesses. Our business. Have you thought about the unintended consequences?"

"Don't talk to me as if I'm an idiot. This legislation will right a wrong. It will bring a measure of fairness and equity into the economic system."

"I provide thousands of jobs. Treat my employees well. Pay them fairly. I don't need interference from the government. Let me do my job. Let me run my business."

Whitney felt her blood pressure start to rise. "This country is my business, and I must do what is right for the country, not Fairchild Industries."

"You should've talked to me about this first. Don't do this."

"Darling, I don't need to run my decisions by you. That's not how this works."

She hung up.

Sasha was nodding, a hint of a smile on her face.

Whitney forced thoughts of Grayson from her mind. "Where were we?"

"What do you want me to tell Judy?"

"Put her off."

CHAPTER FORTY

FAIRFAX, VIRGINIA

JADE DRUMMED HER fingers on the steering wheel. She drove faster than normal.

When she had returned to her hotel room last night after the game, she finally checked her smartphone. Christian had texted her. Multiple times.

His son Mark had been rushed to the hospital. The final tally: two black eyes, a few broken ribs, and bruising all over his face. Luckily, there was no internal bleeding or liver damage. Released, he was home, resting.

Instead of taking the morning flight as planned, she had taken the last flight out and was now driving straight to Christian's house from National Airport.

He answered the doorbell.

She entered without being asked. "How is he?"

She turned when he didn't respond. His eyes were hard, his jaw flexing. "The doctor said he's going to be okay." He lifted his chin. "He's in his room."

"Did he say anything?"

"I tried to talk to him about it, just like I tried to talk to him after what happened to Tyler. He didn't say much. He's afraid of something."

"Or someone."

Jade headed up the stairs, Christian's soft footsteps behind her. She knocked at the closed door on the second floor.

A weak "yeah" in response.

Opening the door, slow and cautious, she poked her head inside. Mark lay on his bed. The TV off. She didn't see a cell phone, electronic tablet, or game console.

What had he been doing? "Hey, guy."

"Hey, Mrs. Harrington."

Jade didn't correct the boy's inaccurate characterization of her marital status. "Can we come in?"

He shrugged. She sat on the bed, careful not to jar him. His face and arms sported bruises, some more purple than others. He looked bad. She noted the absence of faded cuts or scratches.

Mark didn't play on the baseball team.

She tried to quell the rage building inside her. He was a good kid. Polite. Respectful.

Christian didn't enter the room. Instead, he leaned against the door frame, his hands clasped in front of him. His head down.

"I'd hate to see the other guy," Jade said.

The boy gave her a weak smile. "It hurts to laugh."

"You're lucky then. Because I'm not that funny."

This time he did laugh, stopping as suddenly as he started. He winced and touched a rib. "My dad said you were in Seattle. Did you catch the bad guys?"

Instead of cyber perpetrators, his question conjured up

thoughts of Kyle. "Something like that. Do you want to tell me what happened?"

A brief shadow of fear crossed the boy's face.

"You can trust me," she said.

The boy looked from her to his dad and back to her. "I was getting ready to take the stairs to my sixth period, when someone grabbed me. Tripped me. They dragged me under the stairs and beat the crap out of me."

"Did you see who it was?"

"No."

"How many were there?"

"Three or four," he said.

"All boys?"

"I think so. It happened so fast, I didn't see their faces. It was dark under there."

"Did you recognize any of their voices?"

The boy's eyes shifted infinitesimally to the left. He swallowed. "No."

"Are you sure, Mark?"

"Yeah, I'm sure." He grimaced, and held his side.

"Why you? Why did they choose you?"

He glanced at his father and then back at Jade. He shrugged.

The kid was hiding something from his father. Or did it have something to do with Christian? Was that possible?

"What about Tyler? Do you know what happened to him?"

He slid farther down into the comfort of his bed. He closed his eyes. "I'm tired."

"Can you tell me anything else about the attack? We want to find the kids who did this to you."

He opened his eyes. "I thought I was going to die."

Mark's eyes closed again. Jade turned to glance at Christian, his face a dark mask. She'd never seen him this angry. She felt pity for what he and his family were going through.

She also pitied whoever had done this to his son, oblivious to what they had unleashed.

CHAPTER FORTY-ONE

THE WHITE HOUSE, WASHINGTON, DC

"MAYBE WE SHOULD change the name."

Whitney shook her head. "Nonnegotiable. The New New Deal Coalition represents our future, and serves as a reminder of a time in our history when we came together to change the course of this country."

Sasha nodded. "That's good."

As they walked down a hall in the West Wing, Whitney and Sasha continued to debate strategies for selling the legislation to Congress and the American people.

Sasha stopped.

"What is it?" Whitney asked.

Her chief of staff glanced up and down the hallway and lowered her voice. "I had lunch at the Four Seasons today."

"When did I start giving you time off to eat?"

"Sampson, Hampton, and Bell were having lunch with Xavi."

Xavier "Xavi" Fernandez, the former Independent governor of Florida, was now the vice president of the United States.

"Brutus isn't trying too hard to hide his plot against me, I see."

"The conversation seemed pretty intense. Hampton did most of the talking."

Sampson's presence didn't surprise Whitney. He had never forgiven her for breaking her implicit promise to name him as her vice president after he dropped out of the closely contested Democratic primary in exchange for her support for a bill that he'd sponsored. He still blamed her for his unnecessary sacrifice. This was one of the reasons he had switched parties. Maybe the only reason. "See if you can find out the purpose of the meeting."

"Yes, Madam President." They resumed walking. "What do you want to do about the situation in Colorado?"

A dozen armed ranchers, calling themselves The Last Patriots, were squatting on federal property in Colorado protesting the federal government's decision—her decision—to designate more land as national parks. They threatened to annex the land and secede from the union. The FBI had surrounded the ranchers, but had been instructed to wait it out. No shots had been fired, yet.

"Let them secede?" Whitney joked.

"I wonder what the Second Amendment crowd would say if it were a bunch of African Americans with assault rifles squatting on federal property?"

She didn't bother to answer Sasha's question. She knew white privilege existed. "Our Founding Fathers gave us the right to bear arms, not arsenals."

"Tell that to the militia."

"Let's not move in, yet," Whitney said. "But keep me posted."

"Did you see Sampson's press conference in support of the 'patriots'?"

"Contrary to what they profess, Republicans—even newly declared ones—do not have a monopoly on patriotism."

Descending the steps to the basement, they continued walking until they arrived at an unassuming door. Josh McPherson opened the door that led into the Sit Room. The Situation Room.

Although she had selected Xavi as her running mate to attract the Hispanic and independent vote, she had never trusted her ambitious vice president. On Election Night, after the results were in, she reminded him that Hispanics were not the only minority in this country. She envisioned providing opportunities for all minorities. He responded that Hispanics were the only minority that mattered.

And now that man stood to her left at the table dominating the diminutive room. With dark hair and eyes and a trim build, Xavi's smile never quite reached his eyes.

What are you up to, Xavi?

"Good afternoon," she said. "Ladies and gentlemen, shall we begin? Please be seated."

CHAPTER FORTY-TWO

FAIRFAX, VIRGINIA

"IT'S TEN O'CLOCK in the morning," Christian said.

"So?" Jade pushed open the door to The Stratford Arms, a bar a few miles from Christian's house. Near a strip mall, the English-style pub was a standalone building surrounded by its own parking lot.

The inside was dark. Pictures of current and former members of the royal family, prime ministers, English celebrities, pennants of all the English Premier League teams, and English quotes and slogans covered almost every inch of the dark brown, wood-paneled walls.

Christian cocked his head. "Please, don't tell me it's five o'clock somewhere."

"Then pretend we're in Prague."

He shrugged. "Never been. As good a place as any, though."

The place was understandably empty, since most normal people were at work. With no one behind the bar, she called out, "Hello?"

A female bartender slammed through the swinging saloon doors, wiping her hands with a white towel. "May I help you?"

Jade pointed to the tap, as she and Christian grabbed stools at the bar. "Two Guinnesses."

"And a shot," he added.

"You came around quickly." Jade signaled a peace sign to the bartender. "Two shots. Of whiskey."

The bartender set her palms on the bar, taking in the two of them. "Rough day already?"

"Something like that," Christian mumbled.

"Then, I'll make it a double." She pushed away from the bar. "If you're going to do it, do it right."

"My kind of woman," Jade said, turning to Christian. "I thought it was too early."

"Well . . . since we're here."

The bartender placed their drinks in front of them. Jade picked up her pint-size glass and motioned for Christian to do the same. "To Mark."

Christian's jaw tensed. He looked down for a moment and back at her. "To Mark."

They clinked glasses, and each took a gulp. They picked up their shot glasses and drained the whiskey.

She grimaced at the bitter, unfamiliar burn. "This was not a good idea."

"Actually," he said, "it's the best idea you've had this year."

"Thanks a lot," she said, punching his shoulder harder than intended.

"Ouch."

The bartender stood a few feet away, wiping pint glasses. Christian twirled his finger for another round.

They sipped their beers in silence, as the bartender placed another beer and shot in front of them.

In a quiet voice, he said, "I want to kill them."

She placed her hand on his arm, and stared into his anguished, angry eyes.

"We'll find out who did this."

"I'm an FBI agent," he said, "sworn to protect and defend the United States of America." He rubbed his eyes, hard, as if he no longer wanted to see. "And I can't even protect my own son." He stared at his glass. "Amanda told me that when Mark gets home from school, he runs to the bathroom. Do you know why?"

She shook her head.

"Because he holds in his pee all day long, too afraid to use the bathrooms at school." He took another sip of beer. "He flinches every time he receives a text message."

"He's lying about not knowing who did this to him." She gulped another swig of beer. "I think it has something to do with you."

"He's afraid I'll kick their asses if I find out their names. It's not like back in the day. If another student hit you, you'd hit him back. Today, you'd get in trouble for that. Suspended, because you're trying to defend yourself. Ridiculous." He drained the second beer and signaled for a third. "How was Seattle?"

Jade filled him in on the electronic theft at Kyle's company. She didn't mention the Storm game. Or the walk back to the hotel.

"Could it have been an inside job?"

"Not sure yet. We interviewed the accounting staff and those with access and authorization to make a transfer of that amount: the CFO, CTO, and Ky—the managing director.

Could another insider have done it? Maybe. Haven't had a chance to send my report to Cyber."

"Funny how you keep getting drawn back to Seattle. Ethan was in a funk while you were gone."

"I wonder why."

"Maybe it had something to do with your threatening to leave the Bureau. Or your slamming the door on him."

Or maybe it had something to do with receiving a call from POTUS requesting my services by name.

"Well," she hiccupped, "he had it coming. I'm hungry. We should order some fish and chips or something."

"Going all-in on this English thing, eh?"

She called their order down to the bartender, now at the end of the bar making calculations on a pad of paper.

The bartender stopped writing. "We're not serving lunch yet."

Jade leaned over the bar to look at her. The bartender hesitated and then put the pad down. She went into the kitchen, the doors swinging behind her.

"Case in point," Christian said. "Because you're Jade Harrington, you don't need to say a word for someone to do your bidding. You're already a legend at the Bureau. Ethan doesn't want to lose you. No matter what." He motioned for her to pick up her refilled shot glass. "To the good guys!"

"We usually save that toast for when we win a case."

"We're going to win both of these."

Jade belched. "Excuse me." She picked up her glass. "Both? Ethan says the bullying case isn't our case."

"It is now."

"In that case . . . " She twirled her finger for another round, as the bartender came back out to retrieve her writing pad.

"Make it shots two," she said to the bartender, holding up three fingers. "I mean two shots."

She snatched the first shot glass before the bartender placed it on the bar. Jade downed it, loving the burn as it went down. She grabbed the second shot glass and nodded at Christian's first.

"Catch up."

CHAPTER FORTY-THREE

THE WHITE HOUSE, WASHINGTON, DC

"MADAM PRESIDENT, YOU might want to turn on the news," Sasha said.

Whitney gave her a questioning look, before turning on the television on the credenza in her study right off the Oval Office. Although the internal TV system in the White House showed CNN Headline News day and night, the TV in the study was normally tuned to MSNBC.

"ABC," Sasha said.

On the screen, Judy Porter stood in front of an older house, one somehow familiar to Whitney. She moved closer to the TV.

"Yes, Glenn, ABC News has been working on a feature about the president's early years. We've been focusing on her aunt, Mary Churchill. President Fairchild has never spoken publicly about their relationship, or why she lived with her for a year during high school."

My God. That's my aunt's house.

The reporter continued. "Churchill died at the age of forty-one, a year before the president was elected to her first term in the US House of Representatives."

Whitney stared at the house behind the reporter. The memories of her nine months there—repressed since her stay—assailed her in a way that was almost physical. Her aunt had been good to her. And there for her when her parents were not.

"Interesting," said Glenn, the anchorman.

"It is, Glenn. We will continue to delve into this relationship and its impact on the president's life."

"Thanks, Judy. And now to Robert in Glendale, Missouri."

The TV screen switched to a man in shirtsleeves standing on a road in a wooded area holding a microphone with ABC in big letters. "And that's not the only mystery we're trying to solve tonight, Glenn. Through our intensive investigative efforts, ABC News now believes that the death of US Representative Steven Barrett wasn't an accident.

"To remind our viewers, Congressman Barrett died in a one-car collision late one night on this road"—he gestured behind him with his other arm—"in 2005. Soon thereafter, Missouri State Representative Whitney Fairchild ran in, and then won, the special election to replace him."

"Can you give us any details of what brought you to that conclusion?"

"Not at this time, Glenn. We've turned over our investigative documents to the local police. We believe they will reopen the investigation into his death, and change the cause of death from an accident to murder."

"Thanks, Robert," Glenn said. His expression turned serious. "It sounds as if anyone who stood in President Whitney Fairchild's way didn't have much time left in this world. Was it luck that propelled a state senator—and former housewife—to the highest office in the land? Or something else? We'll talk about it after the break. Don't go away."

Without turning around, Whitney waved her hand at Sasha. "Change it."

Whitney tried to still her heart. *What was going on?* She didn't trust herself to move for fear her legs would fail her.

Sasha tried to laugh it off. "There is no end to the media's conspiracy theories." When she didn't respond, Sasha's laugh subsided. "Madam President, is there something I should know?"

Whitney still did not turn around. "Find Agent Harrington. I need to talk to her. Now."

CHAPTER FORTY-FOUR

ARLINGTON, VIRGINIA

CHRISTIAN LUMBERED UP the walkway to his house. His wife, Amanda, would not be happy. Jade watched and waited for him to open his front door before indicating that they could go.

In the driver's seat, Zoe was leaning forward watching him, too. "I know I'm not supposed to ask any questions, but why were the two of you getting drunk on a Wednesday morning? And, most importantly, why didn't you call me to join you?"

Jade turned to her. The best decision she had made this morning—contrary to what Christian had said—was realizing that she was too drunk to drive. She had called Zoe to come pick them up at the pub.

Jade burped. "I'm. Not. Sure."

Zoe laughed and put the car in drive. The acceleration caught Jade by surprise. The back of her head bounced off the headrest. She cracked up laughing. Zoe glanced over at her before turning her attention back to the road.

Mesmerized by the numerous colorful bracelets on Zoe's

arm, Jade stole a glance at her friend. Zoe's hair stuck up all over the place. On purpose. Stopping at a traffic light, Zoe turned to her and smiled, brightening up the car's interior.

"You're beautiful," Jade said.

Her best friend in college—and since—shook her head and laughed again. She turned on the radio.

Jade started moving her head to the beat of the music. "Uh, uh." She sang the first line of the song.

Zoe stared at Jade, her mouth open. "You must be drunk."

"I. Think. You're. Right."

As the Nelly song, "Hot In Herre" played, Jade sang and danced and tried to take her shirt off. Zoe laughed until she cried, trying to keep Jade's shirt on with one hand while driving with the other. Eventually, after Jade promised not to undress, Zoe joined in.

Windows down, they sang classic R&B songs at the top of their lungs and chair-danced, just like they did in college. Their own version of car karaoke.

*

Parked in front of the townhouse, Zoe glanced at Jade's door. "I'm not carrying you in there."

Zoe, at five three, weighed no more than one-ten. At slightly over six feet, one hundred and sixty pounds, Jade towered over her.

She uncharacteristically put an arm around Zoe, and they zigzagged into the house. Jade zeroed in on the Japanese journal on the sofa, open to the latest haiku she'd written. She grabbed it before Zoe could notice it and stuffed it under a cushion, before stumbling onto the couch, willing herself not to throw up.

She hadn't told Zoe about her poetry hobby.

Zoe left and returned with a thin, worn blanket from the upstairs hall closet. When she bent over to lay the cover on her, Jade glimpsed a tattoo on Zoe's chest.

進 捗

"What's that?"

Zoe glanced to where Jade pointed. "Oh. I got a new tattoo."

Jade peered closer, but the design became less focused rather than more. "It doesn't look new."

"Because you're drunk. Be right back."

She left again and came back with three Advil tablets and a glass of water. "Swallow."

"Thank. You."

Zoe strolled over to Jade's bookcase. The books were arranged in alphabetical order and aligned at the edge, library style. "Next time you're out of town, I'm going to rearrange these."

"Where's my phone?" Jade had not checked her voicemail messages in Seattle. She wouldn't make the same mistake again.

Zoe dug through Jade's jacket, thrown in a heap in the foyer. She brought the phone to her.

"I'm going to go," Zoe said. "I need to get back to work. Eat something when you wake up. Call if you need me."

She headed for the front door.

"Okay." Jade navigated to her voicemail messages, an almost insurmountable task in her condition. She checked the screen. Ethan. Ethan. Ethan. She couldn't talk to him drunk. She'd call him later.

She frowned at a 206 number she didn't recognize.

It wasn't McClaine. She didn't think so, anyway. Pressing the voicemail icon and speakerphone, she placed the phone on the hardwood floor.

"Hi. This is Kyle." Jade's eyes popped open. Too late to grab the phone to click it off. "I'm calling to make sure you arrived safely back in Washington, and to tell you how much I enjoyed last night. I'll see you again soon."

She stared at the ceiling. Waiting. The front door had not opened. A creak from one of the wood panels on the floor in the foyer. The jangling of Zoe's bracelets slowly drew closer, and then her face filled Jade's line of vision.

"Why is Kyle calling you?"

CHAPTER FORTY-FIVE

FAIRFAX, VIRGINIA

"MAN, I GOTTA go," Joshua Stewart said.

"We just tapped a new keg," said the boy hosting the party who had been talking to Kaylee Taylor. "Come on, man. One more beer."

"Nah. I can't. I'm leaving with my parents to go visit my aunt and uncle in Bel Air tomorrow morning. Early."

"Okay. Hold up. I'll walk you out." To Kaylee, he said, "Be right back."

The living room looked nothing like it did when Joshua arrived. All the furniture was pushed against the walls, including a lamp without its lampshade. The plush white carpet was now spotted with yellow splotches of draft beer.

William Chaney-Frost surveyed the damage. "My parents are going to kill me."

"Yep."

Outside, they crossed the front porch and bounded down the stairs, stopping at the end of the walkway that bisected the yard.

"Great party, man," Joshua said, although he hadn't had a

good time at all. Same shit, same people. Staring down at the sidewalk, he kicked at a small rock wedged between the cracks. "Do you ever . . . think about T?"

William glanced around the deserted suburban street. "Yeah. All the time."

"He wasn't a bad guy."

"No."

"Sometimes, I can't sleep. I have nightmares."

"Easy. It wasn't your fault."

"Of course it was. I—"

"It was an accident."

"I think about what happened to Z and Nic . . . Aren't you scared?"

William put his hand on Joshua's shoulder and squeezed. Comforting at first. Until it hurt. "No. It's just a coincidence. Our boys were in the wrong place at the wrong time. No one's coming after us. Take it easy." He gave Joshua the killer smile that drove the girls at school crazy. William could have any girl he wanted. Must be nice. Another squeeze of his shoulder commanded Joshua's attention. "Got it?"

Joshua shrugged him away. "I got it. What about that kid?"

"He's young. He'll get over it."

"That lady FBI agent made me nervous."

"She made me hot." William patted Joshua's shoulder. "Everything's going to be okay. Trust me. Go have fun with your family. I'll catch ya on Monday."

"Okay. Later."

Joshua ambled down the sidewalk in the direction of his house.

"Hey!" William shouted. Joshua stopped and turned. "The cage is a go next weekend."

Joshua nodded without enthusiasm and resumed walking.

He popped an Altoids mint in his mouth to cover up the beer smell in case his parents were still up. They usually didn't wait up for him.

The conversation with William hadn't made him feel better. He'd been T's best friend on the team, though that wasn't saying much. They hadn't been that close. But still. Joshua's face grew warm remembering the shame he felt when he saw the pictures of T circulating on the Internet. Tyler didn't deserve to be treated like that. No one did.

A car started up behind him, but Joshua paid no attention to it. Probably one of his classmates who shouldn't be driving. They had all seen the don't-drink-and-drive videos.

He didn't agree with what his teammates had done to T. What he had done to T.

I should've spoken up. Should've stopped it.

Now, instead of the quasi-friendship with T, shame was his constant companion.

He passed the last house on William's street and kept walking. In the new subdivision, Joshua's parents had built a house one street over on Cedarbrook Way, the lone house on the street so far. He stepped off the curb to cross. Still lost in his thoughts, he didn't bother to look both ways.

He didn't hear the car coming.

And then he did.

It accelerated toward him, its headlights blinding.

Joshua froze in the intense light.

The driver saw him. Right? "Stop! You drunk ass!"

He realized—too late—the car was not stopping and not going to swerve around him. The automobile hit him. As he propelled upward on impact, his coat caught on the emblem of the car's hood. The coat ripped away. He continued to roll over the hood and up the windshield. And then he was airborne. His head smacked the asphalt. Every bone in his body felt broken. And he had a massive headache. A pool of liquid spread under his head, seeping into his shirt. He felt all these things, which meant—

—he was still alive.

Maybe after realizing he accidentally hit someone, the drunk driver would help him. Or maybe someone heard the impact, although it had happened down the street from the last house on the block. Maybe William was still outside.

Help me!

Losing consciousness, the cry for help heard only in his mind.

The car idled.

No sound of a car door opening.

He called out again, but still no sound came. He tried to lift his hand, but it wouldn't budge.

Don't leave me.

The engine revved.

Please, don't go.

The tires squealed.

Help me.

He exhaled, his hopes fading.

But wait. Something wasn't right.

The car sounded as if . . . as if . . . it was getting closer.

That can't be.

The car accelerated backward. Joshua felt the heat of the exhaust burning his face, right before the back tires ran over it.

I'm sorry, T.

And then he felt nothing at all.

CHAPTER FORTY-SIX

WASHINGTON, DC

THE BOOKSTORE ON Connecticut Avenue was empty. Whitney stopped to scan the biography section before choosing a book on Franklin D. Roosevelt she had not read. If she were going to resurrect him now, it behooved her to learn everything about him.

The Secret Service had cleared the store of patrons and staff before her arrival, except for one employee. An avid reader, Whitney visited one of the local independent bookstores at least once a month, schedule permitting.

She moved on to the glass case where they kept the first editions. Collecting them was her hobby. She pointed to and examined and returned several books to the employee before selecting a first edition of *Emma* by Jane Austen.

The book was in good condition. Touching the slightly worn cover, she thought about her son, who seemed to be getting his act together; her activist daughter whose name in script she stared at on the cover; and the media who had seemed out to get her ever since she declared her candidacy for the presidency.

Family came first. Perhaps, it was time they all got together. She made a mental note to tell Sean to schedule it.

Her thoughts turned to her vice president, Xavi Fernandez. What was he up to? Whatever it was, it wasn't good. Was it the New New Deal legislation? Or something more sinister? She could ask him directly; he would just lie about it. She shouldn't have to deal with this now.

Trust between a president and vice president was vital and the only way they could work together. He should have been her partner, as Al Gore was to Bill Clinton. Then again, if she wanted a partner, she should have selected someone else. But she had gotten greedy.

She wanted Florida.

Since the inauguration, she had continued to meet with Xavi every Tuesday for lunch. No minutes were kept. Not much was accomplished. But she liked to keep her friends close and her enemies closer.

Which was Xavi?

Conflict in the workplace didn't bother her. A difference of opinion was a good thing. Healthy. It improved decision-making. As long as the conflict stayed within the White House. Beyond, the two of them needed to present a united front.

Moving to the young adult section, she smiled as she passed the *Twilight* books. "Twilight" was the Secret Service agents' code name for her, because of her weakness for young-adult fiction. She spotted Josh near the front door and winked. The agent returned the wink with a smile. She stopped when she saw an interesting book cover: *The Running Dream* by Wendelin Van Draanen. She grabbed it.

She headed down an aisle toward the cash register, where the employee stood, waiting for her. Whitney handed her the book to add to the almost-filled white bag with the bookstore's green logo, and strolled around the store one final time.

As she passed the politics section, a title caught her eye.

Why not?

She selected a recent edition of *The Prince* by Niccolo Machiavelli and smiled. She had read the political treatise many times. If Xavi Fernandez were present to witness her smile, he would be concerned.

And nervous. Maybe even afraid.

"Madam President?" Josh called out to her, still near the door. She turned to see the tall woman nod at him, the look that passed between law enforcement officers that were good at their jobs. "Agent Harrington is here."

CHAPTER FORTY-SEVEN

WASHINGTON, DC

"THANK YOU FOR coming."

"Sorry, I couldn't make it yesterday. I was . . . uh . . . busy."

"I understand."

I don't think you do.

Jade glanced around the store, gingerly, her head still pounding from the whiskey. "It must be nice to have a bookstore to yourself."

The president smiled. "The presidency has its privileges." Her expression changed to concern. "Are you all right?"

They sat in two overused comfortable chairs in the center of the store, the bag of books next to Fairchild's feet.

"Never better." Jade raised her chin at the bag. "You had a successful day."

The president glanced at the books and back at her. "Agent Harrington, I need your help."

"Did you already talk to my boss?"

Fairchild shook her head, laughing. "I apologize for that. I guess that was cheating, but I don't like to be told no. I'm sure you can understand that."

Jade conceded the point. "We checked out Stevens. He's been arrested several times for disturbing the peace. Protests. Sit-ins."

The president seemed distracted. "Good." She paused. "Have you been watching the news? About me? My aunt? The congressman?"

"No, ma'am."

The president hesitated. "I may be opening Pandora's box here, but I need to know."

Jade waited.

"ABC News is reporting that my aunt and my predecessor in Congress died under mysterious circumstances."

"Did they?"

"Aunt Mary died a year before I was elected to Congress. She lived in a suburb outside of Chicago. My parents told me at the time she died from natural causes. Congressman Barrett died in a one-car accident in Missouri. I know that stretch of road. It's curvy and dangerous. Especially at night."

"And ABC is insinuating that you had something to do with their deaths. That you profited in some way?"

"My aunt was a widow, who took me in when I needed her. That's not common knowledge, by the way. I had nothing to gain from her passing. The rep's death gave me the opportunity to run in the special election to replace him. But I was not thinking of running for national office when he died. I was happy working for the state government."

"Why did she take you in? Your aunt."

"Let's just say I needed time away from my parents."

Jade believed there was more to the story. She let it go for now.

"Why are you telling me this?"

"I need you to find out what ABC has. They claim to have investigative materials on Congressman Barrett's death, which they turned over to the local police. I want to be informed of everything they have before it becomes public."

What am I? J. Edgar Hoover?

"You have people who can take care of this for you. Why me?"

"Because I trust you," said the most powerful person in the world. "And in this job, I can't say that about too many people."

*

After leaving the bookstore, she returned to the Bureau. The conversation with the president had unsettled her. She stopped by Pat Turner's cubicle. "I need to talk to you."

She headed to her office.

Jade sat behind her desk. "Shut the door and have a seat."

Pat cocked her head, but did as she was told. Jade told her about the meeting with President Fairchild and the president's request for her help.

Pat processed the information in silence and then said, "Do you think this has something to do with the TSK case?"

Jade had wondered the same thing.

"I don't know."

CHAPTER FORTY-EIGHT

WASHINGTON, DC

"JADE, COME TO my office. Bring Merritt."

She had just booted up her computer. Frowning, she locked the system and left her office. She pointed at Christian sitting in his cubicle and pointed toward Ethan's office, as if she were still a point guard directing a play on the basketball court. She knocked once on Ethan's door and strolled in, Christian right behind her.

She sat in one of the guest chairs.

In a wry tone, Ethan said, "Come in."

She gave him an unapologetic smile. They waited for Christian to settle in the chair next to her.

"What's wrong with you two?" Ethan asked.

"Nothing," Christian said.

"I need more coffee," she said.

"I don't think that's it." He scrutinized them. "Are you hungover?"

"No," said Christian.

"Not really," Jade added.

"I need you to sober up," Ethan said, a sad look crossing his face. "A teenage boy was murdered late last night. Hit-and-run."

She sat up. "Where?"

"Virginia. Fairfax."

Christian leaned in. "Did he go to Randolph?"

"Yes."

Christian pounded his fist on the armrest.

Jade felt sadness for the murdered boy's parents. And then, just as quickly, anger at whoever took these young persons' lives.

She stared at Ethan, as her pulse quickened, knowing what was coming. "And?"

"Fairfax County police have requested our assistance." He handed her a thin folder. "It's your case now."

CHAPTER FORTY-NINE

FAIRFAX, VIRGINIA

JADE DROVE THROUGH the new subdivision, Dante in the passenger seat beside her, Micah in back. Christian had taken personal leave for the afternoon to attend a conference with a school guidance counselor about his son, Mark.

Joshua Stewart's parents lived in an upper-middle-class neighborhood with ample yards, but the houses in this neighborhood were not as big as the ones in the Rawlins's neighborhood. Sod had not been laid yet in some of the lots. Empty lots separated homes at various stages of construction. They wouldn't be empty for long. The real-estate market in the DC area, especially at the upper end of the market, was hot.

She drove down Meadowbrook Drive, but slowed when she saw a familiar figure washing a car. Shirtless and barefooted, he wore baseball pants.

She lowered the window. "I didn't know you lived in this neighborhood."

William Chaney-Frost walked toward them, stopping at

the curb. "That surprises me, Agent Harrington. I thought you knew everything."

"Not everything." She looked up at the gathering clouds. "It's going to rain."

He followed her gaze. "My dad doesn't care." He waved the sponge at the car behind him. "His new wheels. He's trying to keep me busy. I'm grounded indefinitely. 'Cause of the party." He inched up his chin. "Going to the Stewarts?"

"Mind if I look?"

"At what? The car?"

She nodded.

He squinted at her. "Never seen a Porsche up close before?"

"Something like that."

She didn't have a warrant, but she interpreted his question as an invitation. She hopped out of the car and started walking to the front of the Porsche. Another car door opened and closed behind her.

She squatted and examined the bumper, Micah next to her. He looked at her and at the bumper but said nothing.

No dents. No chipped paint. This wasn't the car that hit Joshua Stewart.

"Nice, huh?" William said.

"What about you? Where's your car?"

"Don't have one. Not sixteen yet."

Jade headed back to her car.

"Agent Harrington?"

She turned.

William glanced down the street and back at her. "I hope you catch who did it. J-man was my friend."

*

"Anything we need to know?" Micah asked from the back seat.

"Not sure yet."

She turned right onto Cedarbrook Way.

"These street names are peaceful," she said.

"Makes you want to puke," Dante replied.

She glanced at him. "Lovely."

Dante's left hand was resting on the dashboard. His fingers were long, his hands graceful. She hadn't noticed this about him before.

"I think the names are quite lovely," Micah said from behind them.

She could listen to his accent all day.

Dante turned in his seat. "What are you, queer?"

"Shut up, Dante," she said.

"You don't have to be gay to like nice things," Micah said, in a quiet voice, his eyes meeting Jade's in the rearview mirror.

She cut her eyes back to the road.

She parked at the curb in front of the lone house, midway down the street.

The door opened to a slender man with glasses.

"Mr. Stewart? I spoke to your wife earlier. May we come in and talk to you about your son?"

The man exhaled. "Sure."

Stepping aside, he led them into a generous living room. A leather sectional sofa took up most of the room, facing a flat-screen TV that hung on the wall over the fireplace.

"My wife will be down soon."

Situated, she said, "Mr. Stewart, can you tell us what happened?"

"Please, call me Joe."

He repeated what she had already learned from Det.

Chutimant on the phone that morning. That Joshua went to a party and never came home. A parent's worst nightmare. He didn't mention that his son was struck by a hit-and-run driver, or rather, a hit-and-hit-and-run driver. Per Chutimant, the driver had been going over forty miles an hour. She also mentioned that Joshua still possessed his private parts.

"The time of death was close to midnight," Jade said. "Weren't you concerned that he was out late?"

"Not really. He was just down the street. Wasn't driving. Joshua never gave us any trouble."

"Did your son have any enemies?"

Before he could answer, a woman descended the staircase and entered the living room. She didn't bother to shake their hands. She sat near her husband.

Jade repeated her question.

"Well—" Joe Stewart said.

"Of course not," his wife said. "He was a good kid, a baseball player. Smart. He planned to go to UVA or William and Mary."

"Mr. Stewart?"

He glanced at his wife, then back at Jade. "Sometimes I noticed bruises and scratches. On his arm and—"

"That's from playing sports. Everyone who plays a contact sport gets bruises."

"Baseball isn't really a contact sport," Joe Stewart replied. "He had this cut on his forehead. We had to take him to the doctor. I asked Joshua how he got it. He said he ran into a door."

"See!" his wife said.

"He didn't run into a door, Cindy," Stewart said. He looked at Jade. "Lately, he had become withdrawn, thoughtful, more"—he paused, searching for the right word—"*introspective* over the last year."

"He was finally growing up," his wife said.

Joe Stewart continued to stare at Jade. "No, I don't think that's it. I think he was being bullied."

"By whom?"

"If I had to guess, I would say Zach Rawlins."

A pinch came to Cindy Stewart's lips. "Zach . . . He never lived up to his mother's high standards . . . until he died. And then he became the perfect son." She confided to Jade. "His parents pressured him to succeed at sports."

Joe Stewart scoffed. "His mother wasn't the problem. It was his father. Always yelling at his son. The refs. Coaches. Players. Even other parents. He acted as if they were playing in the World Series instead of a JV game."

"He was just passionate," his wife said. "She, on the other hand, bullied her son with silence."

The agents' heads swiveled like at a tennis match. Jade was okay with that. She let them speak. You learned more by listening than speaking.

"I never liked the way he spoke to Joshua," Joe Stewart said.

"Zach?" Jade asked.

"The father."

From Dante: "Was your son a bully?"

"This is ridiculous," Cindy Stewart said. "It's just a bunch of boys being boys. You're too sensitive, Joe, really."

"I may be sensitive, but I'll tell you one thing. I'll bet Zach Rawlins had something to do with Tyler Thompson's death. And my son's."

"Why is that?" asked Micah.

"That boy was trouble."

CHAPTER FIFTY

THE WHITE HOUSE, WASHINGTON, DC

WHITNEY DROPPED THE *Los Angeles Times* on the table, among the other newspapers she perused every morning with her breakfast in the residence kitchen: the *New York Times,* the *Wall Street Journal,* the *Washington Post,* the *Chicago Tribune,* and the *Guardian.*

She refilled her coffee, inhaling the rich aroma before taking a sip.

The lead story in every paper was the same: income-inequality protests in its own city and other major cities. The number of people participating increased with each successive protest. And the tenor was changing. She felt it.

Violence was coming.

She muted the television.

ABC News's stories about the deaths of her aunt and the congressman had not been reported widely by the rest of the media. The story wasn't dead. Judy would never let it go.

Whitney wanted to chastise the veteran reporter. In public. Hold a press conference. There were more important things going on in this country than digging into her past: homelessness, economic insecurity, inequity, racial injustice.

Judy knew that. A competent reporter, she was well-respected in the journalistic and political community.

Judy could become a problem.

Meanwhile, the numerous protests across the country were still not enough to convince Congress to consider, much less pass, Whitney's legislation.

Frustrated, Whitney needed a Plan B.

She called Sean, already at the office. "Schedule a meeting with Evan Stevens. Today."

*

"Thanks for coming."

"Did I have the option to refuse?"

"Of course. This isn't Communist Russia or Nazi Germany."

"Sometimes, I'm not so sure."

Evan Stevens glanced down at the badge sporting a red-letter A clipped to his black turtleneck shirt. "*The Scarlet Letter?*"

"That depends. Have you sinned?"

"The day's still early."

Sarah placed a tea service on the coffee table.

"Thank you, Sarah," Whitney said.

Sarah poured tea for them and left.

Evan picked up his cup. "You called this meeting."

"These protests," she said. "What are your thoughts about them?"

Evan sipped his tea and then placed the cup and saucer on the thigh of his jeans, his legs crossed. "People are frustrated, Madam

President. Wealth is concentrated at the top. The rest of us are working harder for the same or less money. The cost of living is far outpacing wages. Since the founding of this country, the American Dream was never as attainable as the American people were led to believe, and now, even less so."

"What's the solution?"

"I've read your New New Deal plan. I like it. I think it will help. Do I think it will be enough? No."

"What would you do differently?"

"Are you familiar with the works of Thomas Paine?"

She smiled and nodded at the rhetorical question.

"Paine advocated that citizens should receive a basic income whether they work or not. Some of our manufacturing jobs are never coming back. They've been automated. A universal basic income would remove the stigma of welfare for the long-term unemployed and combat poverty and social inequality."

"That's fair."

"For Paine, it wasn't about fairness. It was about equality. Natural rights."

"I stand corrected. Please continue."

"I would also peg CEO compensation to a multiple of the lowest-earning employees' wages, remove the cap on the Social Security tax, and provide universal childcare and pre-K so that parents can work, and tuition-free college so that our children can enter adulthood debt-free."

"I see you haven't thought about this." Whitney sipped her tea. "A lot of those reforms won't be popular. CEOs aren't going to go along quietly."

"Corporate profits are at an all-time high. The ratio of wages to profits is at its lowest level in over fifty years. It's not sustainable. The workers will revolt."

"And you're going to help them?"

Evan set his cup and saucer on the table. "I'm just a blogger."

Whitney smiled. "And I'm just a bureaucrat. The cost for universal college education alone would be upwards of sixty billion dollars. How would I ever get that through Congress?"

"We spend sixty-nine billion on subsidies. Universal college may be a bargain." He leaned forward in earnest. "Only thirty percent of students enrolled in college today will graduate. How many more would graduate in four years—instead of the current average of six—if they didn't need to work?

"Unemployment would be reduced, state funding could be used for other pressing needs, and there would be fewer people on public assistance." Evan's eyes shone with an intensity that bordered on the maniacal. "Students who graduate from college, on average, make more than a million dollars over their lifetimes than those who don't. Highly educated people are happier and healthier. It's harder for our students to compete with those countries who offer free education, like Germany, Finland, and Norway. Some US states spend more money funding their prison system than education."

She and Sasha had discussed and dismissed universal college education, but his unwavering passion stirred something within her. She recognized it. The same passion that had driven her to enter politics in the first place. Back then, she was going to change the world. Start a revolution. Like Emma.

"The other party will say that students should have some skin in the game. I am inclined to agree with them. Those students would benefit the most from a free education."

Evan waved away this detail. "I'm not just talking about a more educated workforce, but an educated citizenry. So, that when we discuss issues like climate change there will no longer be a debate about whether it exists, but the more important question: what are we going to do about it?"

"Spending all that money on education, during a time of pervasive homelessness and a crumbling infrastructure . . . That's a tough sell."

Evan's eyes blazed. "I don't think you're listening, Madam President. Outstanding student loans total over one-point-four *trillion* dollars. A higher education is almost out of reach for the poor and now some of the middle class. We *must* do this." Abruptly, Evan relaxed and offered her a sheepish smile. "I'm sorry. I get worked up about this stuff. Look. Almost half of the members of Congress are millionaires. They're out of touch with the rest of us. They don't know what it's like to struggle. To live paycheck to paycheck. There's other alternatives. We could tax pollution. Carbon emissions. Raise taxes on the wealthy."

"That too should go over well," Whitney said.

Evan's eyes flared again. "There's a benefit from being born in this country. Taxation is a responsibility and a privilege of citizenship."

"I don't think a lot of people see it that way."

"Well, they should."

They discussed his ideas for another ten minutes. She placed her cup on the table. "If we don't pass my legislation or implement your ideas, what do you think will happen?"

"Capitalism leads to greater and greater levels of income inequality. The United States has reached a level at which soon it will be unable to function. Historically, when inequality increases unabated, something horrible happens. The Great Depression. The Great Recession." Evan stared at her, unblinking. "This time, I predict there will be a Civil War. But it will not be a war between the states. Between the North and the South.

"No. It will be a war between the wealthy and everyone else."

CHAPTER FIFTY-ONE

ARLINGTON, VIRGINIA

AFTER DROPPING DANTE and Micah off at the Bureau, Jade drove home. Her phone rang. Christian.

"How's Mark?"

"He's okay. The ribs are healing. He goes back to school tomorrow. They're beefing up student patrols in the hallways. Not sure how much good it'll do. How did the interview go?"

"The dad believes the son was bullied. The mother doesn't believe it or doesn't want to believe it."

"Well, if their son was a bully, then he got what he deserved."

"Christian," Jade said. A warning.

"I'm serious. This has got to stop."

"We don't know if it was the same killer. Different MO."

"What I said still stands."

"Justice isn't served by some vigilante knocking off teenage bullies. There's the rule of law. Our job is to uphold it, by the way."

"At this point, I don't care how it's upheld."

Jade understood why someone would want to take the law into his own hands. It's how she would feel if someone hurt someone she loved. But the legal system of this country was built on the rule of law principle. That we are a nation governed by laws, not the arbitrary decisions of individuals. Vigilantes assumed the role of police officer, judge, jury, and in this case, executioner. She believed vigilantism had no place in a civilized society.

"You don't mean that."

"An eye for an eye. It's in the Bible."

She closed her eyes at his words. "Then we'd all be blind."

Parked in front of her townhouse for the last few minutes of their conversation, Jade watched her neighbors arrive home from work and enter their houses, oblivious to the turmoil roiling inside the car. Inside her.

He had lost all objectivity.

"Christian?"

"Yeah?"

With reluctance, she said, "You're off the case."

*

Jade returned to the living room of her townhouse with a bag. Eating the delivered pad thai straight from the carton, she chased it with a Tsingtao, the cold beer refreshing after the day she'd had. The week. The month. She was frustrated with her lack of progress on the bullying case, even though officially, she'd only been on it for a day. No progress on the cybertheft case, either, for that matter.

Oh-for-two.

She spent some time connecting the PlayStation to the television. At her request, Christian had brought in the system earlier that day. She hoped Mark could live without it for one night. Slipping in the disc, she settled back into the sofa.

She couldn't think about Christian now.

The game's logo, *Bully*, filled her screen. Never much of a video-game player, like some of her teammates back in college, it took her some time to figure out the instructions and how to navigate the controls to do what she wanted.

The name of the game brought back memories. Childhood memories she would rather forget.

Her phone rang.

Pat spoke without preamble. "The death of Rep. Steven Barrett wasn't an accident. Someone tampered with his brakes. He didn't stand a chance going around that curve."

"Why didn't the detectives discover this at the time?"

"They should've."

"Anything else? Anything on the aunt?"

"Not yet."

"Thanks." Jade hung up.

Who would gain from Barrett's death? Fairchild wasn't assured of winning the election for the seat to replace him. Maybe it didn't have anything to do with Fairchild. It could've been Barrett's wife, a disgruntled husband, or an unhappy constituent. She made a mental note to call the local detective on the case tomorrow.

Glancing around her living room, the word "minimalist" sprang to mind. She had remarked that Kyle's office was bereft of tombstones, but Jade's home, too, displayed no evidence of her past glories.

Back to the game. The objective was for a teenager, involuntarily enrolled in a boarding school filled with bullies, to bring peace to the school and the town. Who would want to play this game for fun?

Based on her research of the game's sales, a lot of people.

An hour in, she was hooked.

The still half-full carton of Thai food rested on the wooden coffee table, ignored, as she negotiated teenage cliques, completed missions, attended classes, and used a wide variety of weapons to vanquish her opponents. She wondered, briefly, whether William Chaney-Frost was like the protagonist or one of the bullies.

She played until well past midnight. Being as competitive as she was, by the end of the night, she had become quite good at *Bully*. She didn't know if that was good or bad.

She did, though, have trouble falling asleep that night.

CHAPTER FIFTY-TWO

FAIRFAX, VIRGINIA

THERE IS NOTHING sadder than the funeral of a child.

Jade stood with Dante and Micah, away from the grieving family and friends, as Joshua Stewart was laid to rest at Fairfax Memorial Park. Earlier, the clouds, dark and ominous, threatened the gathered mourners with a thunderstorm, but a light rain had fallen instead during the service. Now, as if cognizant of the occasion, the sky cleared and the sun appeared, as the procession made its way to the cemetery. The park, with its rolling hills and impeccable landscaping, was peaceful. It turned out to be a beautiful day.

Most of the mourners had journeyed here from the church. A dozen teenage boys stood together, wearing their best black suits. Suits that were getting a lot of wear lately. A few of them were pallbearers, including William Chaney-Frost. Jade recognized some of them from interviews at the school.

From behind dark oversized sunglasses, she catalogued each of the attendees in her mind. After offering her condolences to Joshua's parents, she inclined her head to the car, signaling to Dante and Micah that it was time to go.

"Agent Harrington!"

She turned, expecting William, but it was one of the other boys she had interviewed. She allowed her mental Rolodex to come up with his name. "Andrew."

"Yeah."

The boy was larger than his teammates. He glimpsed over his shoulder at the still-gathered mourners. "There's something we—I—didn't tell you."

She waited.

"Something's going on with our team." He looked over his shoulder again. "It's gotten out of hand."

"What is it?"

"One of our best players, Sam, is going to quit because of it."

"Tell me what's going on."

William called out to him.

Andrew's eyes widened. "I gotta go."

"Andrew, how did you get those scratches on your face?"

Although Joshua's casket was closed, Jade read in his autopsy report that he'd had stitches removed over one eyebrow. The injury his mother said he received from colliding with a door.

Andrew mumbled something, eyes imploring her of—something—before he took off running up the hill.

William seemed to chew him out before smiling and waving at her.

She didn't wave back.

"What did Andrew say?" Dante asked.

"Not sure. It sounded like 'age,'" she said.

"That kid was scared to death," said Micah.

"I think we need to take a closer look at Mr. William Chaney-Frost," she said. She turned to Micah. "You game?"

CHAPTER FIFTY-THREE

THE WHITE HOUSE, WASHINGTON, DC

SHE GLANCED AT the stack of bios of congressmen and congresswomen she needed to convince to support the New New Deal Coalition legislation. Picking up the phone, she started to dial the first name on the list.

"Do you have a minute?" Sasha asked.

Whitney hung up and beckoned her in. "Good. You saved me from making these dreaded calls."

Sasha sat in the chair across from her. "I found out what Xavi is up to. He's shopping his own proposal. A competing income-equality plan."

"I'm surrounded by Judases. What's in it?"

Sasha shook her head. "Don't know yet. I'm meeting someone later this afternoon to find out."

Whitney didn't bother to ask from whom. If Sasha wanted her to know, she would tell her.

"He's receiving some support from the Republicans," Sasha said. "Hampton, Bell." She hesitated. "Sampson."

"What do they want in return?"

Always quid pro quo in this political game they played.

"My source tells me that Xavi promised to work with them on comprehensive illegal-immigration reform,"—Sasha hesitated—"when he becomes president. He's willing to compromise on some points Hispanics have demanded in the past."

Whitney smiled without mirth. "That makes a lot of sense. I don't think that will be popular with his Hispanic brothers and sisters."

Sasha pursed her lips. "I don't think he worries too much about the welfare of his brothers and sisters. The only person Xavi worries about is Xavi. Are you going to confront him?"

Whitney knew Xavi's goal wasn't to be president eight years from now. Or four years from now. He wanted her job now.

"Judas Iscariot purportedly committed suicide. Xavi may do the same."

Sasha gave her a questioning look.

Whitney picked up the phone again to call the first congressman on the list. Before dialing, she said, "Political suicide, of course. What were you thinking?"

CHAPTER FIFTY-FOUR

FAIRFAX, VIRGINIA

BASEBALL PLAYERS STREAMED out of the gate that separated the outdoor athletic complex from the school parking lot.

In ones, twos, and threes, they slowed and gawked at each other at the sight of Jade perched on the front end of her car, one foot on the ground. Micah leaned against the car next to her, looking like a model in his fitted suit and Ray-Ban sunglasses.

At the end of the pack was William, who broke into a cocky smile. He sauntered over to her. "You two look like a GQ ad for FBI agents. Where's Howie Long?"

She couldn't help smiling. Christian *did* look like the Hall of Fame defensive end for the Oakland Raiders and NFL commentator.

"He wishes he could be here."

"I bet. He seems to be MIA lately."

She didn't explain it was probably for the best that Christian wasn't here. She glanced over at the players who were huddled halfway between them and the school. "Nothing to see here!"

She waited until she saw their backs before turning to

William. His uniform was filthy. His face streaked with dirt. His blue and gold baseball cap looked brand new compared to the rest of his uniform. "FC" was written in black magic marker just over the bill.

"Shouldn't that be 'CF' for Chaney-Frost?"

"I really need to catch up with my team," he said.

"How do you do it?"

"Do what?"

"Keep your face so smooth, while your teammates' faces are scratched and bruised?"

He stroked his chin and perched his cleat on her bumper, resting his arms on his thigh. "They're clumsy?"

She glanced down at the dusty cleat.

He hesitated and then removed it.

"What position do you play?" Micah asked.

"Why? Are you planning on coming to a game?"

"Answer the question, William," Jade said.

"Shortstop."

"Tell me about your teammates who died," Jade said.

"Haven't we gone over this?"

She had debated whether to bring him down to FBI HQ to shake him up a bit, but decided it was premature. "I want to go over it again."

"Zach was a bully, you know that. Nic, too, but . . . "

She waited him out.

" . . . he was bullied as well. By Z." He kicked at an imaginary rock on the asphalt. "Joshman was weak, but a bully, too. He would do whatever Z said."

"Sounds like a team full of bullies."

"Are you one?" Micah asked.

"Do I look like a bully?"

Jade thought back to their original interview and Andrew Huffman's reaction after the funeral.

"Yes."

*

"It's late."

"Thanks for seeing us."

Jade sat in an institutional-gray chair across from Coach Lane Daniel in his cramped office on a lower floor near the gymnasium. Micah stood next to her, the room not large enough for another chair.

Daniel was barrel-chested, a former athlete who still ate—but didn't exercise—like one. He was dressed in the same uniform as his players. Jade always wondered why baseball was the only sport in which that happened.

He observed her taking in his office. "Yeah. It'd be bigger if I coached football."

"We won't take up a lot of your time. We'd like to ask you a few questions."

"Saw you talking to Chaney-Frost. Did he say anything that could help you?"

"What do you think is going on with your baseball team?"

The big man leaned back in his chair. "Hell, if I know. I told the police it must be a rival team. No one likes to see a successful man."

"You think this is about you?"

"I didn't say that. Someone's just out to get us. Since this is my team, it means they're out to get me."

"Do your players get along?"

"As well as any team. It's not peaches and cream all the time. These guys want to win. They won't hesitate to get in each other's faces, if necessary. But off the field every-thing's forgotten."

"Is that why so many of your players have bruises and scratches on their faces? Black eyes?"

"Baseball is a tough sport. We play hard every day. Doesn't matter if it's practice or game day."

"Seems like it's more than that." She paused to see if he would respond. He didn't. "Do you think there's bullying going on? Hazing? Anything like that?"

"Missy," he said, "I'm trying to raise men here, not pu— pansies."

"It's Agent Harrington."

"What?"

"My name is not 'Missy.' It's Agent Harrington."

She asked him his whereabouts the nights of the four murders. The coach leaned forward and paged through an opened school calendar on his desk. "The first night I was at a coaches' meeting." Licking his finger, he paged to the next date. She tried not to grimace. His hands were still dirty from practice. "Here." He showed her the date. "My daughter's soccer game. These other two nights aren't marked, so I was probably at home. In my home office. I'm pretty much all-in during the season. Watching tape. Working on practice plans."

"Do you think someone on your team could be killing his teammates?"

Daniel looked at her, incredulous. "The teams at this school are expected to win. Every player knows that when he signs up. To be a part of that tradition. That would be self-defeating, wouldn't it?"

"What do you think of Chaney-Frost?"

"Solid player. He's gotten some PT—playing time—as a

sophomore on varsity, too. Better with the bat than in the field. Better talker than doer."

"What about as a person?" Micah asked.

"He's bought into the program. That's all I care about."

CHAPTER FIFTY-FIVE

WASHINGTON, DC

COLE BRENNAN SAUNTERED past the crowded bar to a table around the corner, where Republican Senator Paul Sampson sat nursing a drink. Judging from the redness of his face, it wasn't his first of the evening.

Cole's drink waited for him at the table. Most nights, he rushed home from the studio to be with his family, but on occasion he held business meetings at the Capital Grille on Pennsylvania Avenue near the Newseum.

Sampson looked up. "What do you want to talk about?"

"Can't a man sit down first?"

Cole made a show of scanning the menu, even though he had ordered ahead. He didn't like to wait. "Try the porter-house. Amazing."

The waiter materialized and took Sampson's order.

"Can we talk now?"

Cole glanced around to see if anybody else was here. Anybody who was somebody. Politicians frequented this place.

A congressman or one of his staffers could be sitting next to you. Yeah, yeah, congresswomen, too.

"Look here," Cole said, "if you're going to be 'my guy,' you've got to become a populist."

"Okay . . . "

Cole paused as the waiter set down his food.

The aroma of his steak compelled him to take a bite.

"Don't wait for me," Sampson said, his tone sarcastic.

Cole ignored him. "If you want to be president you need to become folksier. More likable by the people."

"How do I do that?"

"You say what they want to hear. Anything against Muslims or minorities or illegal immigrants is usually a winner."

"Got it. What else?"

"Intellectuals, the media, and women are all good targets."

"Women?"

"September twenty-first, nineteen eighty-one. The beginning of the end."

"What're you talking about? What happened on that date?"

"Sandra Day O'Connor was nominated to the Supreme Court."

Sampson appeared baffled.

"And if you really want to endear yourself to the good folks on the right," Cole continued, "just mention abortion. They'll love you. Even better, all the Feminazis will come out of the woodwork. That's always fun."

The waiter set down Sampson's plate and withdrew.

"What about the gays?"

Cole thought about his son. "Them, too."

"What about Hampton? Why aren't you backing him?"

Cole waved his fork, dismissing the suggestion. "He's too

uptight. Too full of himself. He's also an intellectual. No one likes an intellectual."

Stabbing another piece of steak, he pointed at Sampson's plate. "Good, huh?" He stuffed the morsel in his mouth.

Sampson scanned the restaurant. "I've been here before, Cole."

"Yeah, but not with me."

The waiter asked how their steaks were. "Great," Cole said, pointing to his drink. "Bring us another round."

He had heard the rumors that Sampson was a lush. He didn't mind. In fact, it would make it easier to control him.

"Now, where were we?" Cole said. "Disagree with everything the president says. Everything. Even, if you agree with her. Especially anything about raising the minimum wage or government intervention. Your constituency will be with you, even though she wants to give them a raise. It doesn't make sense, but that's okay. It helps us. Also, it doesn't matter if what you say is the truth or not. You can say one thing one day and the complete opposite the next day, and your followers won't care. They don't care about the truth. They want to be with you. They want—no, they need—to believe in someone. To believe in something. Again. Like Reagan."

Sampson was nodding at everything he said. Cole had him.

"You should declare your candidacy about a year from now," Cole said. "The people must be on your side by then."

Sampson looked doubtful. "I don't know if I can make people love me like that."

Cole bestowed a broad smile. "You're probably right. But I can. Now, how about a cognac?"

CHAPTER FIFTY-SIX

WASHINGTON, DC

JADE BLEW HER whistle from the sideline. All ten players on the court stopped running and turned to her.

She addressed her point guard. "LaKeisha, I want ten passes before a shot is taken."

LaKeisha flashed her a questioning look. "Ten passes, Coach? That's a lifetime."

"Just do it, LaKeisha. I know we can score. I want to see you run the offense."

LaKeisha grinned at her and bounced the ball in place. "You got it, Coach." Facing her teammates, she held up her fist. "Stanford!"

The team ran their flex offense, named after Jade's alma mater. Last year, LaKeisha played on Jade's team of middle-school girls. She'd had a good freshman year, averaging ten points a game, leading her team to the city championship, and earning the *Washington Post*'s third-team All-Met honors. Jade now coached the high school's spring-league team.

After practice, Jade stuffed basketballs into a bag, LaKeisha lingering nearby.

"How's school?"

LaKeisha untied her low-tops. The mini-twist hairstyle of last year had grown out to dreadlocks. Her hair now hid her face. "It's okay."

Jade set the bag aside and sat on the bench next to her. "Let me ask you something."

LaKeisha tensed, still fiddling with her laces.

"Is bullying prevalent in your school?" LaKeisha relaxed. "I mean, is there a lot of it?"

LaKeisha sat up and shrugged, flipping the hair off her face. "I guess so."

"Have you ever been bullied?"

"Nah. No one messes with me. I'd fuck them up." She glanced at Jade. "Sorry, Coach."

"Ever witness someone else being victimized?"

LaKeisha hesitated, knowing what Jade did for a living. "I won't testify to anything, but yeah. It's everywhere. In the halls. In the locker rooms. In class. Online."

"And I suppose the school's anti-bullying policies don't help."

LaKeisha gaped at her. "There's policies against it?"

CHAPTER FIFTY-SEVEN

THE WHITE HOUSE, WASHINGTON, DC

THE NEXT AFTERNOON, Whitney disembarked from Marine One onto the helipad on the South Lawn. Sasha and Sarah came down the stairs behind her. As she walked toward the White House, Sean hurried toward her.

Unusual.

"Madam President, something is happening in Seattle."

Whitney glanced at Sasha before hurrying after him.

The television was on in her study off the Oval Office, the screen filled with police officers in riot gear shooting pepper spray at protesters on a city street. The protesters threw rocks and cans and other objects at the officers. A bottle shattered against an officer's helmet. At the bottom of the screen, the caption read Seattle Protest Turns Deadly.

Whitney motioned for Sean to turn up the volume.

"If you're just tuning in," said the voiceover, "we are looking at Pine Street in downtown Seattle, witnessing what at one time had been a peaceful march against income inequality. In the last hour, however, the march has spiraled into a deadly protest. At least three people are confirmed dead after being trampled in the crowd." A gasp from Sarah behind her. "Seven more have been injured."

"Damn!" Sasha said.

The announcer continued. "Those numbers may escalate. The mayor has called for a peaceful resolution and cautioned the police to respect the rights of protesters—"

"What about the rights of police officers?" Whitney murmured.

Although Whitney's attention didn't waver from the screen, she could feel the intensity of Sasha's glare. "Police officers' rights are protected well enough. Don't you think?"

"Not now, Sasha."

Sasha put her hands on her hips. "When then? When is a good time to talk about police brutality? I think now is as good a time as any."

"The coverage is everywhere," Sean said, oblivious to the growing tension between the two women. "Twitter's blowing up and—"

"Thank you, Sean," Whitney said, interrupting and dismissing him at the same time. "That will be all, Sarah."

After they left, Whitney shook her head, sickened by what she was witnessing on the screen. She held Sasha's gaze. "I want you to stay on top of this and keep me updated."

"Black lives matter."

"I know."

"It's happening every week now."

The week before, three black women, college students, were critically injured on a Mississippi university campus at a police brutality protest. A protest that went horribly wrong.

"We'll address it," Whitney said.

Sasha pursed her lips and crossed her arms. "Hmph. When?"

"In this term. I promise." She pointed at the screen. "But first we must address this. Perhaps, this will finally get Congress's attention."

"It hasn't yet," Sasha said, still staring at the television.

Whitney's intercom buzzed.

"Madam President," Sean said. "Senator Hampton is on the line for you."

CHAPTER FIFTY-EIGHT

WASHINGTON, DC

"WELL, ISN'T THIS a nice surprise!"

Jade turned to find Cole Brennan standing near her, his arms wide ready to envelop her in a hug. She braced herself and held her glass high in the air, as he hugged her.

They had not seen each other since the night TSK had paid him a visit, with almost tragic consequences for his family. The animosity he had shown toward her during that case had vanished. If she wasn't mistaken, he was now looking at her with respect. Possibly affection.

"Mr. Brennan. Mrs. Brennan."

His wife reached out and touched Jade's arm. "It's good to see you."

"How's Kaitlin?" Jade asked.

The woman gave her a vacant smile. "You remember her name . . . She's back to normal. As if it never happened. We'll never forget what you did."

"Hmph!" Cole said. "You're a hero to my kids. But things

aren't back to normal. My oldest son, CJ, and Kaitlin are liberals. That ain't normal."

He guffawed. Despite herself, Jade joined in his laughter.

"Well, I'm glad she's okay. It was good seeing you both."

She moved off to a space near a large window to watch people arrive at the Washington Hilton on Connecticut Avenue. The White House Correspondents' Dinner had transformed into a red-carpet event, with more celebrities—actors, athletes, performing artists—in attendance than reporters.

Wearing a gray suit, crisp white shirt, and black shoes, Jade enjoyed watching other people garner the attention for a change.

She sipped her beer. She'd never been invited to this dinner before. But this year, her invitation had come from the top.

"First time?"

Turning from the window, she scrutinized the gentleman next to her. Attractive, with short, sandy, gelled hair, he wore designer glasses and a well-cut suit.

He held out his hand. "Jade Harrington, it's an honor."

"Thank you, Mr. Haynes." They shook. "I watch you sometimes on MSNBC."

He smiled. "Sometimes?"

"I don't watch much TV."

"Do you follow politics?"

"Some," she said. "My best friend is into it."

"Who's that?"

"Zoe."

He sipped his drink. "I know her. We worked together occasionally when I lived in DC."

"I should ask 'Who hasn't worked with Zoe?'"

"May save you some time. Me, too, by the way."

"Me, too, what?"

"This is my first time." He waved his glass at the photographers and the famous attendees posing on the red carpet. "Quite a spectacle."

"Not really my thing."

"Mine either."

They stood comfortably next to each other, observing others.

"What do you think about the protests?" he asked.

"They're intensifying."

He nodded. "The deaths were inevitable. The rhetoric is getting out of hand. I'd be surprised if we didn't see more violence."

"If anyone can bring this country together, Fairchild can."

"You sound like an 'FOW.'"

"FOW?"

"Friend of Whitney. I am by the way."

Since my invitation came from her, I guess, I am, too. That and her personal FBI agent.

She kept these thoughts to herself.

"We better go in." He tilted his head toward the ballroom where the other attendees had started to migrate. "What are you doing later? There's an after-party at a bar down the street."

"I can't. Early day tomorrow."

"That's too bad."

Before they parted to go to their assigned tables, he said, "It's been a pleasure. I hope to—"

She held out her hand. "Me, too."

She turned to head toward her table, and then back to him. "What's the name of the bar?"

He told her.

After President Whitney Fairchild roasted herself, the current male host of a late-night TV show began the traditional roast of the president. She sat next to the podium with a tense smile on her face, as if bracing for the onslaught.

"Now," the comedian said, "thanks to President Fairchild, and passage of the ERA amendment, women are entitled to the same rights as men. Thank God. Now, my wife can have an erection lasting four hours . . . "

CHAPTER FIFTY-NINE

WASHINGTON, DC

" . . . twenty-eight, twenty-nine, thirty."

She released the chin-up bar and dropped to the mat.

The Bureau gym, after lunch, was nearly empty. Jade liked it that way. She didn't like to wait on machines. She didn't like to wait for anything. Period.

She grabbed a towel to blot the sweat on her face and neck and under her ponytail. She was working hard, punishing herself for staying out late. She ended up joining Blake Haynes at the bar for a drink. One drink. Charming, intelligent, well-read, she enjoyed his company. And did she say he was attractive?

"Not bad," came a voice from behind her.

She turned. "And you can do better?"

Micah grinned. Pulling off his gray FBI t-shirt, he jumped and grasped the bar, his hands facing him. As he pulled himself up and started to count, the muscles in his arms, chest, and back rippled. His body, a work of art. He passed fifty with ease.

"Showoff," she said, throwing her towel at him.

She headed toward the leg-press machine.

After their workout, she sat on a bench up against the wall. Micah sat next to her on the matted floor, his back leaning against the bench.

She capped her Gatorade. "You don't say much during interviews. You know you have the green light, right?"

"I'll ask a question when I want to know something."

She nodded, pleased. "Anything on Chaney-Frost?"

"We've been trailing the kid every night for the last two weeks. His parents must have him on lockdown."

She had assigned a veteran agent to accompany him. Still, she couldn't resist needling him. "And you're sure he hasn't given you the slip?"

Micah gave her a look.

She believed William was involved somehow. "Okay. Let's give it another week."

*

"I need to ask you something," Jade said, leaning against Pat's cubicle.

Special Agent Pat Turner turned away from her computer. "Sure, boss, what's up?"

Although Pat appeared older than her fifty-one years, and most of the staff treated her like a favorite grandmother, she had a sharp mind and an unwavering tenacity to complete any project she was assigned. Possessing a vast knowledge of the Bureau's history, she knew its policies and procedures and the way the place worked better than anyone. She could run the Bureau, in Jade's opinion.

Her only weakness was that Pat didn't want to supervise people, a career-limiting predilection at the FBI. She would rather spend her day hunched over her computer, as she had been doing before Jade had interrupted her.

Jade pulled up a chair just outside the cubicle, her arms on her thighs. She felt refreshed after her workout and recovered from her late night with Blake. She scanned pictures of characters from the *Star Trek*, *Twilight Zone*, and *The Big Bang Theory* TV series, pinned to the cubicle's three walls.

"You've read what we have on the cybertheft case. How do you think they're doing it?"

Pat thought for a moment. "About a decade ago, a Trojan horse malware package called Zeus was used to steal banking information through keystroke logging and form grabbing."

"What's form grabbing?"

"Appropriating the authorization and log-in credentials before they reach a secure server to avoid HTTPS encryption. It can be more effective than keystroke logging, because it can capture copy-and-paste or auto-fill entries."

"How was it installed?"

Pat shrugged. "A download. Or phishing email. After the software installed itself on the victim's computer, it captured passwords, account numbers, and any other information needed to access online banking sites."

"And then the perp could transfer the money to his or her own account?"

"Pretty much. Before his arrest, the person who created Zeus sold his code to a Russian national who created its successor, SpyEye. It targeted financial institutions, and used a form-grabbing technique while the victims conducted banking business online. The victim was on the bank's website, but some of the fields were fake. The malware was difficult to detect."

"What about antivirus and other security software?"

Pat shook her head. "Nothing could detect it. Caught the

perpetrator a couple of years ago when he tried to sell one of his kits to an undercover agent."

"I believe our perp is using something similar. Whoever it is has a high level of technical skills."

"Could be one of the employees of the victim organizations, a hacker acting alone, or a foreign agent: Russian mafia, European criminal outfit, China."

"Is that your short list?" Jade said, wryly, rising.

"Wait. I have something for you, too." Pat handed her a file. "Haven't had a chance to review it in detail."

"What is it?"

"The autopsy report on Mary Churchill. The president's aunt."

CHAPTER SIXTY

WASHINGTON, DC

IN THE BACK seats of the presidential limousine—"The Beast," as the Secret Service called it—Whitney and Sasha conversed in low tones. Sarah reviewed their daily schedule on the adjacent sofa seat. En route to the Holocaust Museum, Whitney planned to give a major speech on the future of Palestinian and Jewish relations.

Her phone buzzed. Her daughter.

After their usual chitchat about school and friends, she asked Emma if she had talked to her brother.

Silence greeted her on the other end.

"Emma, what is it?"

"Nothing, Mom."

"Obviously, it's something."

"You're busy. It can wait."

"Tell me."

"Chandler's . . . changing."

"In what way?"

"He's not . . . nice! He's dismissive when I talk to him

about my participation in the protests. Actually, 'condescending' might be a better word."

"That doesn't sound like him."

"That's why I said he's changing."

"When was the last time you spoke to him?"

"It's been a while," Emma said. "When's the last time *you* spoke to him?"

"Two weeks ago."

"And you didn't notice anything?"

Her son *was* different. He wasn't his usual jovial self. More serious. She had hoped that he was maturing. "Perhaps."

"To be honest, Mom, I'm not speaking to him."

"You're always honest, Emma. You don't need to use that phrase."

"Mom! I'm having a serious conversation with you. I don't need a lecture on word choice."

She smoothed the leather on the seat's armrest. "You're right. Why aren't you speaking to each other?"

"He called minorities, 'those people.'"

She sat up. "What!"

"He's going to these crazy meetings. The Young Conservatives or something like that. The words that come out of his mouth are outrageous. Every time we talk, we fight. I don't enjoy talking to him anymore. I'm supposed to go home next week, and I'm not looking forward to it. I don't want to go."

Prior to his political awakening, Chandler never cared about anything except girls, skateboarding, and video games.

"I'll talk to him."

"I don't think it'll help."

"We need to get together as a family soon." Whitney sighed. "I meant to have Sean schedule something."

"What did we do before we had Sean to schedule our lives? I need to go study, Mom. Love you!"

"Love you, too."

Whitney stared at the phone a moment, pressing End before handing it to Sarah. She turned to gaze out the window at the Smithsonian National Museum of Natural History, Emma's question hurting her more than her daughter probably had intended.

How will I bring this country together if I can't do the same for my own family?

CHAPTER SIXTY-ONE

WASHINGTON, DC

SHE IGNORED THE knock at her office door.

Sheepish, Christian said, "You got a minute?"

She continued to ignore him. When he didn't leave, she gestured to the lone guest chair in the office. "What's up?"

He sat. "What's the latest with the bullying case?"

Jade said nothing.

"Look," he said. "I lost it after what happened to Mark. He's my son. My job is to protect him and the rest of my family. I felt . . . helpless."

She slipped a red peanut M&M in her mouth from the large bag she kept in the center drawer of her desk. She was not going to make this easy for him. "Our core values include respect for the dignity of all those we protect and uncompromising personal integrity. That's nonnegotiable with me."

The anguish was evident on his face. "I'm sorry. Okay? Rule of law and all that. I get it. It won't happen again."

She looked at him for several moments. "Apology accepted."

Christian seemed to be waiting. "Aren't you going to ask me something?"

"Like what?"

Exasperated, he said, "The case. Aren't you going to welcome me back to the team?"

"Oh." She wasn't going to make it *that* easy.

"Lawson has me working on a lot of BS stuff. Filing. Follow-ups. I want to catch the person who is killing these kids. Even if they deserved it." He waved his hands. "Not deserved to be killed, but deserved to be taught a lesson."

"I don't know . . . Dante is turning out to be a pleasure to work with. And Micah's learning quickly."

"Sometimes, I wonder how Dante got in. Must've been a tough recruiting year."

"He has his useful qualities." *Isn't that what Ethan said last year?*

"Like what?"

She frowned. "Still haven't figured that out yet."

They laughed and gave each other an exploding fist bump.

Jade picked up some files from her desk and handed them to him. "Welcome back."

CHAPTER SIXTY-TWO

THE WHITE HOUSE, WASHINGTON, DC

"WELCOME BACK. MADAM President, during the presidential election, different solutions were proposed for dealing with illegal immigration. What are your thoughts on building a one-thousand, nine-hundred-and-fifty-four-mile wall or fence?"

"Well, Blake, it's impractical, and doesn't address the root cause of immigration. A wall won't stop someone who is desperate to feed his or her family. Increasing the number of Border Patrol agents and erecting more barriers will only result in more people dying trying to cross over into this country with the hope of attaining a better life."

"And setting up an operation to deport eleven million people?"

Whitney crossed her legs. "That will turn us into a society we probably don't want to live in."

The interview was being aired live on MSNBC. They sat

in two chairs facing each other in front of the unlit fireplace in the White House Library. Portraits of Franklin D. Roosevelt and Woodrow Wilson adorned the walls. During the transition, she had retrieved Eleanor Roosevelt's portrait from storage in the basement of her Senate office building. It now hung in the place of prominence over the mantle. And rightfully so.

"How do you feel your first year in office is going?"

"We're not accomplishing as much as I'd hoped, but I'm excited as people become familiar with and understand the New New Deal, and what it will mean for jobs, improving the economy, rebuilding our infrastructure, and expanding access to education. We'll be able to help millions of people."

"I don't doubt you. You're a fighter. You never give up."

"This is true."

"Any surprises so far? About the job?"

"No one can know what the job is like, until you sit in that chair in the Oval Office."

She didn't mention how scary the view of the world was from that chair.

Blake steepled his fingers against his lips while she spoke. He removed them. "By sitting in that chair, you have shattered the glass ceiling. How does that make you feel?"

"Wonderful, of course. But it was never about me, Blake. It's about all the girls out there who can now grow up believing that, if they work hard, they can be whatever they want to be."

"Switching topics. What are your thoughts on Senator Sampson switching parties?"

"I'm sure children are watching this broadcast. Next question."

He laughed. "Okay . . . "

He asked her several questions about the specifics of the

New New Deal Coalition legislation. Whitney presented her plan, but not its tepid reception so far, by Congress or the American people.

Five minutes before the top of the hour, Blake wrapped up the interview. "Madam President, it was a delight having you on the show today. I hope we can do it again soon."

"I believe that can be arranged, Blake."

He turned and faced the camera. "This is Blake Haynes with *The Haynes Report*. Good night, everyone."

The interview had gone well. They had an easy rapport with each other that she believed would come across well on camera.

He did not push back on the lukewarm response to her legislation. Or bring up that another two protesters in Seattle had died from their injuries. He also didn't mention the speculation around why she had lived with her aunt for a year or her aunt's subsequent death. Or the mysterious death of the congressman from her district on a dark and winding road near her home in Missouri.

Blake had promised a softball interview.

He had kept his word.

And could be useful to her in the future.

CHAPTER SIXTY-THREE

THE WHITE HOUSE, WASHINGTON, DC

"WHAT ARE YOU doing here?"

"I could ask you the same thing."

He hooked his thumb over his shoulder. "Interviewing the president."

"How did it go?"

"Wonderfully," said Whitney Fairchild from behind him. She glanced at both of them. "I did not know the two of you knew each other."

"We don't," Jade said.

"We do," Blake Haynes said.

The president smiled. "Which is it?"

Jade willed herself to stop blushing. "We met at the Correspondents' dinner, but we don't *know* each other."

"I see. That's what that dinner is all about. Bringing people together. Well, I'll leave you two to continue your conversation."

She handed the president a file, detailing Cyber's analysis

on the cyberthefts. Their report was conjecture at this point. "This is for you. The documents you requested."

Fairchild held her gaze. "Thank you. Stop by my office when you're finished here."

"Yes, Madam President."

Blake nodded toward the receding back of Fairchild. "I guess that's what you're doing here. How close are the two of you anyway?"

She reminded herself that he was a reporter. "She's the boss."

"What are you doing after you meet with the president? My flight back to New York doesn't take off for several hours."

"I have plans." She didn't, but she didn't want to give him the wrong idea. They'd had a drink together. A quiet conversation in a noisy bar. She wanted to leave it at that.

His eyes twinkled behind his glasses. "I don't give up easily."

Jade started to walk away. "Neither do I."

CHAPTER SIXTY-FOUR

THE WHITE HOUSE, WASHINGTON, DC

AFTER THE INTERVIEW, Whitney returned to her study next to the Oval Office. The television was on, the volume low. She grabbed the top one off the ever-present stack of briefing books, and began to read it in more detail.

Something on the TV captured her attention. The banner on the lower part of the screen said State Legislator Pushes for Investigation.

Her breath caught.

With a shaking hand, she turned up the volume with the remote.

The mid-day news anchor spoke into the camera. In the box next to him, a handsome, middle-aged man addressed a crowd of reporters.

"Cameron Kelly," said the anchor, "a Missouri representative from the Eighty-Seventh District, is advocating for an investigation by the FBI into the mysterious death of United States Representative Steven Barrett. Let's listen in."

The legislator was the picture of a hard-working politician fighting for the people he represented. He wore a white shirt with the sleeves rolled up, red tie, and dark slacks.

"Congressman Barrett was a Missouri son," Kelly said. "He was born here. Raised here. And represented our district and our state admirably for most of his adult life. He deserves better than this. He deserves justice. And I won't rest until he gets it."

Whitney stared at the screen, her hand over her mouth. She resisted the urge to scream.

She knew Cameron Kelly well. He had been a classmate of hers in high school.

He had been her boyfriend.

He was also a monster.

She didn't hear the knock.

"You wanted to see me, Madam President?" Agent Harrington looked at her expression and then at the television. "What happened?"

CHAPTER SIXTY-FIVE

SEATTLE, WASHINGTON

HE OPENED THE front door of his home in Madison Park to Blayze Tishman, recently retired CEO of the number-three software company in the Fortune 500, now searching for a professional football team to buy.

Noah waved him in.

Tishman had been there before. He headed down the hall to the rear of the house before Noah had closed the door and followed him.

Pausing at the entrance to the great room, Noah admired the panoramic view of Lake Washington through the floor-to-ceiling windows. That view never got old.

The temporary bartender served Tishman a whiskey sour from the permanent bar in the corner. Noah clapped his hands once. "Let's get started."

"What are we, at camp?" Tishman chortled, gazing around at the others.

No one else laughed.

Noah scanned the faces of the men and one woman sitting

on the sofas and chairs. In addition to Tishman, in attendance was a real estate developer who had built more than one million square feet of office space in the city; the CEO of the online conglomerate which handled transactions for almost every individual and business in the world and was—as of this morning—the second most valued company on the New York Stock Exchange; the mayor of Seattle; and Kyle Madison. The combined net worth of the people sitting in Noah's living room was somewhere north of a hundred billion dollars.

"Welcome," Noah said. "You all know why you're here today. Our president needs us. Our country needs us—"

"Aren't you being a little melodramatic, Blakeley?" Tishman interrupted.

"No, I'm not. We're facing an issue that can tear this country apart. How can we help her fight income inequality?"

"Seattle has led the way on income inequality," the mayor said. "We were the first city to raise the minimum wage to fifteen dollars an hour. And now all the other major cities are following suit."

"We don't need a stump speech, man," Tishman said, as he struggled up from the couch to fetch another drink. "All you politicians do is talk. It's time to *do*."

"I've *done* a lot," the mayor retorted. "You're just not paying attention." He paused. "I'm getting ready to launch an extensive initiative around equity. I'd like for all of you to be a part of it."

"We must figure out how to stop these protests, before they impact businesses and tourism," the real-estate developer said, "in *your* city."

"*Our* city," the mayor said. "My point is that we need to show America the way again. We can enact progressive measures here in Seattle that will demonstrate to other areas of the country that they work."

The developer shook his head. "But that will take time. Anything like that won't be felt for years."

"Are the protests such a bad thing?" the CEO of the online conglomerate asked. "They're keeping the issue in the public eye."

The wealthy progressives debated for over an hour. Noah listened to the powerful people around him. He noticed Kyle Madison didn't say much either, her eyes on him for most of the evening. She didn't bother disguising her distaste. Or was he imagining it? She wore a smart black business suit and matching Gucci shoes. His wife had a pair just like them.

After a time, they quieted, the conversation exhausted. A rare time when this group had nothing to say.

Finally, Kyle spoke into the void. "Have any of you heard of the Equality One Foundation?"

CHAPTER SIXTY-SIX

WASHINGTON, DC

"THIS IS NOT a good idea," Sasha said.

"Getting out and walking or going to see Hampton?"

"Both. The former makes us look stupid. The latter makes you look weak."

Her driver let them out at the corner of Louisiana and Constitution Avenues in Northwest Washington. Whitney had insisted it would be fine if they walked the rest of the way. Imploring her to reconsider, Josh McPherson argued that she was making a mistake and taking an unnecessary security risk. The look of consternation on his face made her almost laugh out loud. Josh and the Secret Service agents scrambled at the change of plans.

Whitney and Sasha passed through the ninety-foot atrium, which afforded an abundance of natural light into the building. The Hart Senate Office Building was the most contemporary of the three Senate buildings. Whitney, however, preferred the neoclassical architectural style of her former workplace, the Russell Senate Office Building.

The two of them were ushered into Senator Hampton's office on the seventh floor. His staff formed a line and stood respectfully to shake her hand. It was not often that a sitting president visited the Hill except for the annual State of the Union address.

The senator rose as she entered, arm extended. "Madam President."

"Senator."

Representative Howard Bell and Senator Paul Sampson sat in chairs opposite the desk. Bell rose, slow and reticent, to shake her hand, as did Sampson. Hampton returned to the chair behind his desk. A power move.

Bell and Sampson glanced at each other.

"I'm the senator," Sampson said.

Bell stared at him for a beat, and then scanned the room for another chair. A quick-thinking staffer brought him one.

Sasha continued to stand, staring at Hampton. He hesitated and then plastered a smile on his face. "Madam President. Please." A chivalrous gesture toward his desk chair. He settled in the chair next to Sampson. Sasha moved to a sofa behind them.

Whitney wasted no time. "Something needs to be done."

Hampton tilted his head back, the ever-present smirk on his face. "To what are you referring?"

"The unrest in this country," she said. "Nine people lost their lives in Seattle. The widening gap of income and wealth among our citizens. Take your pick."

"What are you suggesting?"

"Pass the legislation I put before your chamber."

"Isn't it our job to create legislation?"

"It used to be. How many bills have you passed this year?"

"Now, see here—" Bell said.

Hampton waved him to keep quiet. "Instead of always penalizing the people who reach the top, why don't we find ways to empower those at the bottom. Provide opportunity. And help people rise up out of poverty."

"Save it for your constituents. You don't really believe that anyway."

"My anti-poverty initiative is starting to gain some traction."

"But how long will it take before we'll see the impact? What about the middle class?" Whitney looked at Hampton. Although the Speaker of the House had the most power over legislation—arguably more than the president—Eric Hampton was the leader of the Republican Party, since former President Richard Ellison left office. "It's a good bill, Eric."

He held her eyes for a beat. She rarely used his first name. He leaned back in the chair, smoothing his tie. "I concede that there is an inequality of *opportunity*. Let's work on the portions of your bill that address that. But, let's get down to it, shall we? What's in it for us?"

Meaning, what's in it for *him*. He wanted her to betray one of the values she had built her career on. Campaigning against pork. "What do you want?"

Hampton stared off into some middle distance, and then turned around in his chair. To his staff: "Leave the room."

They quickly shuffled out of the office. He turned to Sasha.

"She stays," Whitney said.

He hesitated and then nodded. He gestured toward Bell and Sampson. "Our districts and states need infrastructural improvements. With interest rates at historic lows, now is the time to invest. I get that. If you could see your way to allocate a significant portion of federal funds to us, we can make this happen."

She glanced at Sampson, wondering what had happened to him. Their political stances used to be more alike than different. He shrugged, his hands in their customary position on top of his stomach. "You owe me."

"Paul, I owe you nothing."

Whitney looked back at Hampton. She would need to amend the proposal just enough so that he would receive some of the credit. Still, she hesitated. He had reneged on deals with her before. Unfortunately, she didn't have a choice. He was her only option.

"A senator once said, 'There are two things that are important in politics. The first is money, and I can't remember what the second one is.'" She came around Hampton's desk to shake his hand, aware that she was making a pact with the devil. "You have a deal."

She pivoted to leave, staring straight ahead. Ignoring Sasha, still seated, whose head shook vigorously in dissent.

CHAPTER SIXTY-SEVEN

ARLINGTON, VIRGINIA

CHRISTIAN SHIFTED IN the passenger seat and glimpsed back at his son. "Excited?"

Jade glanced up at the rearview mirror. Mark shrugged, but didn't respond. He continued to stare out the window. She looked over at Christian and mouthed, "Chill."

Parking at a strip mall near her home, she strode toward a nondescript storefront with a faded Won Ho Tae Kwon Do Academy stenciled in the glass. Christian and Mark ambled behind her.

They were greeted in the lobby by a diminutive, athletic man with short-cropped gray hair in his mid-sixties wearing the blue *dobak* (uniform) of the school. His black belt sported six thin gold stripes at the end of the right side of the belt, his full name in cursive stitched on the left.

Jade bowed, barely bending. She straightened. "Master Ho, I would like to introduce you to Mark."

Mark Merritt extended his hand dutifully for a handshake. Master Ho ignored the hand and gave Mark a slight bow. "I bow to show my respect to you and to our art. You should do the same."

Mark imitated him. His arms flat against his sides, his hands pointing down.

"Very good." Master Ho looked at Jade. "Excellent timing. I have time before my next class. He'll be done in a half hour."

Jade's instructor pointed at a small room, the interior of which could be seen through a square window from the lobby. Mark glanced up at his dad, reluctant.

Christian touched his shoulder. "Go on."

The boy followed the older man through the door, glancing back at his dad before entering the room. Christian started for the window.

Jade reached out and grabbed his wrist, tugging him in the opposite direction. Toward the front door.

"I want to stay," he said.

"That's why we need to leave," she said, smiling. "He'll be okay, Dad."

He appeared unconvinced.

She let go of his wrist. "Come on. I'll buy you a cup of coffee next door."

CHAPTER SIXTY-EIGHT

WASHINGTON, DC

AFTER DROPPING MARK off at home, Jade and Christian returned to the Bureau. In her office, she went over the police reports from the three murdered bullies. She had lost count of how many times she'd reviewed the case files, hoping to find something she had missed. The cases were linked, but she needed evidence. The last few weeks had offered none. Her office phone rang.

"Agent Harrington."

"Good afternoon, Agent Harrington," came the smooth, confident female voice.

A stirring in her stomach.

The voice continued. "This is Kyle Madison."

Jade aligned the five pens on her desk in perfect formation. "Ms. Madison, how can I help you?"

"We enjoyed a wonderful evening together. I think you can call me Kyle."

"Okay, Kyle. What can I do for you?"

"So formal. Okay. I'm in town on business. Did you receive my message?"

That would be the message Zoe overheard the day Christian and Jade got drunk. She hadn't returned the call.

"I did."

"I'm staying at the Hay-Adams hotel. I was hoping you could meet me for dinner tonight."

"Tonight . . . "

"We could discuss the case."

"Do you have additional information pertinent to your case?"

"I may."

"Ms. Madison—Kyle—if you have information material to your case, tell me now."

"Ms. Harrington—Jade—I'll meet you at the restaurant in the lobby of the hotel at seven. Don't be late."

"Kyle—"

Jade looked at her phone. Call Ended.

CHAPTER SIXTY-NINE

THE WHITE HOUSE, WASHINGTON, DC

SASHA GLANCED OVER at her, as if to say something, but remained silent.

"What's on your mind?" said Whitney.

"What's wrong with you? Is everything all right?"

"Why do you ask?"

After enjoying a working dinner in the residence, the two women sat on matching sofas in the sitting area. The window allowed an unobstructed view of the Washington Monument and the National Mall. A bottle of wine rested on the glass table between them.

"You're more pensive than usual," Sasha said. "Notwithstanding the weight of the world on your shoulders, I think it's something else. Xavi?"

Whitney flicked her hand as if shooing a gnat. "I wouldn't waste my time."

She couldn't tell Sasha the truth. That Cameron Kelly, the state representative fighting for justice for a murdered congressman, was a rapist. And the father of the baby she gave up for adoption.

Instead, she said, "My kids. They're not speaking to each other."

"Is that all? I don't always speak to my siblings, either. They get on my nerves."

"No. It's more than that. They have always been close. I think politics, of all things, is getting between them. Emma is becoming more liberal every day, and Chandler is heading in the opposite direction. Any day now, I expect to hear him call into Cole's radio show. If he does, I'll disown him."

Whitney smiled to indicate she was kidding.

"It may be just part of growing up. Trying to find their own way. Striving to find their own identities, separate from yours. And the First Gentleman's."

Whitney stared out at the Monument. Constructed in two phases, pre- and post-Civil War, the structure was built with marble from three different quarries. The spotlights now made the bottom third of the structure appear pure white against the purple sky. "Perhaps. Sometimes, it feels as if I am losing my son. As if I have to choose between him and the presidency."

"If you were a man, you wouldn't need to make a choice. We wouldn't even be having this conversation."

"Maybe. But I feel this way just the same. My family means everything to me. I don't want my legacy to be that 'she was a great president, but a lousy mother.'"

"When was the last time you saw them?"

Whitney opened her mouth and then closed it. "I don't know. Easter? I've been meaning to . . . " She shook her head. "They're busy now. Chandler's in summer school, and Emma's in New York interning for a nonprofit that focuses on income equality."

"Madam President, you're an amazing mother, and a role model that both of your children are trying to emulate. They want to leave their mark on the world. Not sit around and rest on *your* laurels. You should be proud of them."

Surprised by the tears pressing against her eyelids, Whitney had never cried in front of Sasha or any of her staff. She was not about to start now. She did not speak, afraid her voice would betray her.

Sasha reached out and took her hand and stared deep into her eyes. "Remember why you entered politics in the first place. To help people. And you've done that. You continue to do that. You have many things you want to accomplish. I believe in you. Many Americans believe in you. You need to finish what you started." Sasha released her hand. "Be more gangsta."

"Gangsta? What? Are you going all 'Sasha Fierce' on me now?"

"What do you know about 'Sasha Fierce'?" Sasha stopped smiling. "This New New Deal legislation is your legacy. You can't beg for it. You must *take* it."

Whitney understood, with a deep certainty, that Sasha was right.

"Eisenhower said that 'every president needs an SOB.'" She smiled at Sasha. "I guess you're mine."

"I would be honored. You can start calling me 'Fierce,' if you'd like." She winked.

Whitney smiled. After a moment, she said, "As the first woman president, I can't fail. I would be crippling every woman who tried to run after me."

"Then, we just can't let that happen, can we?"

Whitney held up her glass. "No, we can't. Now, how about some more wine . . . Fierce?"

CHAPTER SEVENTY

WASHINGTON, DC

"TO WHAT DO I owe this visit, now that you're famous?"

"I was in the neighborhood?"

"Yeah, right," Zoe said, opening the front door wider to let Jade by. The explosion of colors in Zoe's Adams Morgan apartment never ceased to overwhelm Jade's senses at first, and then the colorful ambiance embraced and drew her in. The walls displayed framed posters from various local and national political campaigns she had worked on: marriage equality, taxation without representation of DC citizens, and the Equal Rights Amendment that passed six months ago.

The bookshelves reflected her fascination with all things African: Nigerian statues, Ghanaian mementos from Zoe's time with the Peace Corps, and Ivory Coast knickknacks, including swaths of Kente cloth.

Jade moved to the sofa. A big round orange throw pillow rested in its corner. She held it under one arm like a basketball.

"One day, I'm going to get rid of that thing," Zoe said. "Beer?"

Jade nodded, throwing her suit jacket on a chair. After Zoe

left the room, she lay down and started shooting the pillow straight up in the air to herself.

Zoe returned. "I knew it. Here." Jade sat up and took a sip of the India pale ale.

Zoe flopped onto a cushioned circular wicker chair. "By the way, I 'liked' your fan page on Facebook."

Jade thought about the high school girls' comments about Facebook. "It's all so ridiculous. I'm not even on Facebook."

"You're famous, your Highn-ass."

"Nice . . . "

"You have a following. Get over it. You're a verb. A guy at work the other day said he 'Jaded' a presentation."

Jade set down the beer, lay back, and resumed shooting. She changed the subject. "What've you been up to?"

"Enough."

Jade cocked an eyebrow.

"Enough gun violence. Our goal is to reduce the number of mass shootings. Create a national database, implement universal background checks, and resurrect the assault weapons ban."

Zoe worked for a nonprofit organization that advocated for pro-choice, Democratic female federal and state candidates.

Still shooting the pillow, Jade looked at Zoe. "Why will it be different this time?"

Zoe stared at her for a moment. "How do you do that? Anyway, after that lone, white gunman gunned down over one hundred elementary-school kids playing at recess, even some Republicans have had enough. We'll get it this time. You'll see."

Jade stopped shooting, raising her hands in surrender. "I hope you're right."

The best friends lapsed into a shared silence. Comfortable. Unhurried.

"What about you? What's happenin'?"

"I'm working on two major cases. Both stalled."

"Can I help you this time?"

Jade sat up again for another sip of beer. "Maybe. You were clutch on the TSK case."

Zoe beamed. Jade gave her a brief description of both cases without revealing any confidential information.

"And you have no idea who could be behind the cyberthefts?"

Jade shook her head.

"Have you spoken to Kyle?" Zoe drew Kyle's name out. A smile, mischievous and deadly, spread across her face.

"Only about the case."

"Huh."

"Why 'huh'?" Jade paused, then, "She did ask me out to dinner tonight."

Zoe's smile disappeared. "Oh?" She frowned. "She's here?"

"On business."

"She must have had a lot of information about the case to take up an entire dinner."

"I didn't show."

"Why not?"

"Let's just say I don't like being told what to do."

"I Googled her, by the way. Your Kyle gets around."

"She's not mine." Jade placed her beer carefully on the table. "What do you mean?"

"Not like that. She attends fundraisers and other events in Seattle. Sometimes with an attractive man—or woman—on her arm. Most often alone." Zoe swigged her beer, eyeing Jade. "Is she gay?"

A question lobbed casually with the explosive weight of a grenade.

"I wouldn't know."

"Are you?"

Jade flashed her a warning look.

"I'm your best friend. You can tell me."

Instead, Jade swiped her bottle off the table and held out her hand. "Finish."

Zoe drained the last of her beer. Jade went to the kitchen to retrieve a fresh round. She selected a couple of German hefeweizens this time. She handed one to Zoe and returned to the sofa. After a moment, "Why did you research Kyle?"

"I was bored."

"Yeah, right. You didn't need to do that. We checked her out when we first took on the case." She picked lint off the pillow, not looking at Zoe. "What else did you find out?"

"I knew it!"

Zoe regaled Jade with Kyle's family history and her successful business exploits.

When she finished, Jade said, "How did you find out some of that information?"

"You know I have skillz," Zoe grinned.

"You're still doing that?"

"Not really. I couldn't find where she's been romantically linked with anyone. I don't think she's ever been married."

"Huh," Jade said, not sure why this pleased her.

"But there's a problem."

"What's that?"

"You know how many people in DC act as if they're in the one percent and they're not?"

"Sure."

"And that most one-percenters are men."

"If you say so."

"And that you and I are proud card-carrying members of the ninety-nine percent?"

"Get to the point, Zoe."

"Your Kyle Madison is not like us. She is definitely in the one percent."

CHAPTER SEVENTY-ONE

WASHINGTON, DC

JADE SPENT THE following day in her office, reviewing both the murdered bullies and the cybertheft cases. As she told Zoe, the bully case had stalled. There hadn't been another death for weeks, but there hadn't been any new clues either as to who was killing suburban teenage boys.

Two of the murders were linked. That the wounds in two of them were consistent with damage caused by a blunt instrument had been released to the media. The severing of the baseball players' penises had not. What was the significance of that?

On the other hand, there had been movement in the cyberthefts case. In the wrong direction. Not only had three more significant thefts occurred in the Emerald City—an online retail company, a real estate developer, and a Fortune 500 software company—but also, the crimes were no longer isolated to Seattle. They had spread to other cities. Incidents of significant unauthorized bank transfers had been reported in Oklahoma City, Anaheim, Omaha, and San Antonio.

What was the motive here? Was it one of the crime

syndicates from the Ukraine? Russia? A political statement from the Chinese? Simple greed? Or something else?

Although she had initially explored whether one of the employees of a Seattle organization could be responsible, she had eliminated them as suspects. They had investigated the CFO, CIO, accounting, and IT personnel of every firm where a theft had occurred. All of them clean.

These were not inside jobs.

Mid-morning, McClaine called, asking her to return to Seattle to interview additional victims.

Leaning back in her chair, she rubbed her eyes. When she opened them, her gaze fell on the Churchill file, kept separate from the other files on her desk. She hadn't had a chance to review it. What the hell? She wasn't making any progress on her cases. She might as well be useful to the president.

Jade took her time studying the case file, starting with the autopsy report. Cause of death was a heart attack, not natural causes as Fairchild was led to believe. Pretty straight forward.

A co-worker had found Mary Churchill—concerned when she didn't show up for her job three days in a row as head librarian at the public library—dead in her bed. She was forty-one years old.

Jade reviewed the toxicology report. Halfway down the page, she stopped.

Oleander.

She read the word again, thinking she misread it. Four grams of oleander were found among the contents of Churchill's stomach. She needed to be sure. She fired up her computer. All parts of the shrub—the flowers, leaves, stem, roots—were poisonous, and could be found in an ordinary garden. Ingesting honey created by bees that consume the nectar from oleander plants could also be toxic. When a chemical in the plant, oleandrin, was absorbed into the blood stream, it could cause irregular heartbeats or stop the heart from beating altogether. Jade scanned the autopsy report for Churchill's weight. 105 pounds. It wouldn't take a large dose of oleander to be fatal for a woman of her size.

Did Mary Churchill, the president's aunt, commit suicide? Was it an accidental poisoning? Or was she murdered?

She picked up the handset to call the local police department in the Chicago suburb, and then replaced the receiver in the cradle without dialing.

She left her office and paced up and down the hallway. Other agents—used to Jade's habits—ignored her. She thought about what she'd discovered, and what she was going to do about it.

Back in her office, she picked up the handset again. What she was about to do went against her grain as a sworn agent of the Federal Bureau of Investigation of the United States of America.

She dialed.

"This is Agent Harrington. I need to speak to the president."

*

After she hung up with the president, she called the local police department in the Chicago suburb. She relayed her discovery to the officer in charge of the case.

She had a feeling that Churchill had not committed suicide. The president didn't believe it when she told her. She said her aunt always had a positive outlook. Jade put Pat to work, scouring the manifests of flights and train schedules into and out of Chicago and hotel registrations in the surrounding sub-urbs around the time of the president's aunt's death in 2001.

While she waited for an update from Pat, Jade checked her email inbox. Earlier in the day, Pat had sent a list of the latest victims in the cyber case:

Capstone Energy Partners, Oklahoma City, OK, $1,500,000

BMR Aviation, San Antonio, TX, $1,250,000

TVX Corporation, Anaheim, CA, $10,000,000

Third Data Corp., Omaha, NE, $1,125,000

What was the significance of the amounts, if any? She opened a spreadsheet on her computer and entered the four companies' names, locations, and amounts. She then entered Kyle's—Ms. Madison's—organization, Madison Ventures, Seattle, WA, $1,000,000 and the other Seattle organizations that had been victimized. She stared at the numbers, then opened her web browser to further research each company.

Her cell phone vibrated on her desk. A text message.

This is Kyle. I missed you the other night.

Jade typed back: Too busy. Then. And now.

I'll let you go then. Until next time.

She stared at Kyle's last text for a minute. And then two.

Don't do it. Don't do it.

She didn't like anyone telling her what to do. Even herself.

Jade texted: I'll be in Seattle the day after tomorrow.

I'll see you then.

Her face flushed. She looked up at the knock on her door. Christian leaned against the door frame, staring at her.

"What's up with you?" He peered at her strangely. "Are you . . . blushing?"

CHAPTER SEVENTY-TWO

THE WHITE HOUSE, WASHINGTON, DC

"I UNDERSTAND, GOVERNOR."

My aunt died from poisoning?

Into the phone, she said, "Yes. You will have the full support of the federal government behind you." Whitney spotted Sasha standing at a door to the Oval Office, an anxious expression on her face. The Republican governor of Alabama thanked her for her help in dealing with its latest hurricane and the flooding aftermath. "You're welcome. Good day."

She waved Sasha in.

"Are you okay, Madam President?"

"I'm fine. What's wrong?"

Sasha remained standing in front of her desk. "I have some bad news."

"What is it now?"

"It's Emma."

Whitney froze. She had witnessed and read about many

atrocities in this office, but when it came to the well-being of her own children, the world stopped.

"Is she all right?"

"I'm not sure."

"What do you mean? Spit it out, Sasha."

"She's been arrested."

"Arrested!"

"She was picked up at an income-equality rally in New York City. She and about fifteen thousand other people. The largest mass arrest in US history, by the way. The media will find out about Emma shortly. We need to prepare a response for Lena."

Lena was the White House Press Secretary.

"I don't give a shit about the media right now." She pressed the button to call Sean. "Get Mayor Nasir on the phone. Now!"

"Do you think that's a good idea?"

"What?" Whitney snapped.

"Emma wouldn't want to be treated differently than any of the other protesters."

"I don't care—"

Whitney stopped and thought about it. Sasha was right. Into the phone, she said, "Sean, hold off on that call for now." She said to Sasha. "I need to call Gray—The First Gentleman."

CHAPTER SEVENTY-THREE

WASHINGTON, DC

"IT TOOK YOU long enough to say 'yes.'"

"I've been busy," she said. "I can't tell you the last time I was in a museum."

"I wanted to do something different."

Blake Haynes didn't know that Jade didn't date much. So, this was different.

Strolling through the National Gallery of Art at Sixth and Constitution, they stopped to gaze at a huge painting of Phillip II of Spain—his face replaced by the face of pop star Michael Jackson—clothed in 16th-century battle gear, sword and all, astride a gigantic horse. Two cherubs hovered over his head.

"This is dope," she said.

"The colors are vibrant," he agreed.

He waited for her to finish reading the museum label. They moved to the next painting in Kehinde Wiley's collection, a black woman in a black dress with an exaggerated bouffant hairstyle, shrouded in flowers.

"He should paint you," he said.

"He'd have to lose the flowers."

"I envision a royal officer headed into battle."

Me, too. "How often do you come to DC?"

"Not often," he said, still staring at the painting. "But that could change."

Jade's face grew warm. Without waiting for him, she moved on to *Bound*, a sculpture of three black women bound together by their interlocking braids.

He joined her. "Okay . . . let's not be different. How about dinner?"

Jade hesitated. "Sure. Give me a call next time you're in town."

"I was thinking we could go now."

CHAPTER SEVENTY-FOUR

ARLINGTON, VIRGINIA

STILL THINKING ABOUT her dinner with Blake, she stopped short. "You shouldn't be here."

That smile. "I missed you."

She continued walking toward her townhouse, car keys in her left hand, stopping several yards away. Her right hand was at her side, loose, not too far from the gun in her holster. "What are you doing here, William?"

"I have some information."

"You could have called me."

"Aren't you happy to see me?"

"I guess I don't have to ask how you know where I live."

"Same way you have pretty boy following me around." Sitting on the top step to her front porch, he scooted over. "Want to sit?"

I guess Micah isn't that good, Max. But then again maybe I'm not either.

"I'm fine right here."

He glanced around. "It must suck for you to live in this

area. Most of your victims and—what do you call them?—perpetrators make more money than you do."

"Including you?"

He shook his head. "I was lucky to be the offspring of a couple of high-priced lawyers, who married later in life. The DC way."

Jade had checked into William's background. His father was a corporate attorney at a prestigious law firm in DC. His mother was the top defense attorney in the Northern Virginia area.

"It's late. What do you need to tell me?"

He stared at a long blade of grass in his hand, an unwitting reminder that she needed to mow. "It's about Tyler."

The Thompson case was still with Fairfax PD. With Chutimant. And, as far as Jade knew, growing colder by the day. "What about him?"

"There's a reason why Zach bullied him. Why others bullied him." William placed the grass between his thumbs and blew until it made a musical note. "He was queer."

"How do you know that?"

He flicked the grass away and stood. "Because he was sleeping with my best friend." He started to walk past her. "He and Joshua had a"—he whispered in her ear—"thing." He kept walking. "Goodnight, Agent Harrington."

CHAPTER SEVENTY-FIVE

BELLEVUE, WASHINGTON

THE NEXT MORNING, Jade breezed by the airline ticket counters at National Airport. She didn't check a bag. She wouldn't be in Seattle that long. She was glad she didn't have to wait. The queue for the main-cabin service was long. There was no line for first-class customers.

At the gate, first class was called to board, followed by Platinum and MVP passengers.

If you ever want to feel like a second-class citizen, travel by air.

Six hours later, the plane descended into a blanket of clouds. McClaine picked her up from Sea-Tac airport and headed north on I-5. The sleepy, cloudy, overcast day seemed conducive to curling up in a chair with a cup of hot chocolate and a good book.

She turned from the window. "What do we have?"

"A CFO named David Smith called us," he said. "He was fired from his job for embezzlement. Swears he's innocent."

"How much?"

"One million. Even."

"Where are we headed?"

"To his house."

Forty minutes later, they arrived at the Seattle suburb of Bellevue. Smith's neighborhood was a study in contrasting styles. Time periods. Big houses, like Smith's, towered next to small houses that appeared over a century old.

"This used to be a small ranch house like the others. Throughout the Seattle area, but especially here on the Eastside, they're tearing down all the little old houses and building tall boxy new ones."

"Sounds as if you don't approve."

McClaine shrugged. "Seattle is destroying its history. One house at a time."

A thin man in his mid-fifties, wearing blue track-suit bottoms and a Seahawks t-shirt, greeted them at the door. He showed them to the living room, his movements slow and measured.

After initial pleasantries and their denial of refreshments, McClaine said, "Mr. Smith, tell us about the money."

Smith scratched the stubble on his cheek. "I was in my office. Downtown. And in a hurry. A plane to catch. I opened the browser on my computer and clicked on the website for our bank—"

"Was the website saved in your browser?" asked Jade.

"Yes."

From McClaine: "Which bank?"

"Pacific Coast Bank. The company maintains both of their checking accounts there: operating and payroll."

"Go on," McClaine said.

"I transferred a million dollars from the operating to the payroll account. I used to transfer payroll every two weeks."

"Anyone else authorized to make transfers?" Jade asked.

"Only my controller, but she needed a dual authorization from me."

"What was the company's revenue last year?"

"About seventy million."

"And payroll?"

"About seven hundred thousand a pay period. I transferred additional funds because I was going out of town, and I wanted to make sure taxes were covered. Planned to transfer the excess back when I returned from my trip."

"Where did you go?" McClaine asked.

"Chicago. Where the parent company is."

Jade pressed. "Did you need to enter an additional password or use a security token? Anything like that?"

"The bank provided a security token. It displayed a six-digit authentication code prior to transfer."

"Where did you keep it?"

"In the center drawer of my desk at work."

McClaine and Jade shared a glance.

From McClaine: "Who had access to your office?"

Smith shrugged. "A lot of people. I had an open-door policy. Kept it locked at night, though. And when I was away on travel."

"Anyone have a master key?" McClaine asked.

"The office manager. My controller. The rest of the exec team. The cleaning staff."

"Who knew that you kept the token in the drawer of your desk?"

"My controller, for sure. No one else, unless they went through my things."

"Anything else, Mr. Smith?" she asked.

"I logged out of the bank's website and closed the browser. I always do. I take security very seriously."

"Was it a laptop?" This from Jade.

"Yes."

"Did you take it with you?"

"Yes. I took it home every night. The day after, I had meetings all day in Chicago."

"Who did you meet with?"

"CFOs of all the subsidiaries. I couldn't check our accounts until that evening. We weren't allowed to bring cell phones into the meeting." He turned his dead eyes to Jade. "One million dollars had been deducted from the checking account. The payroll account had a zero balance. When I got out of the meeting, I had received over a hundred text messages from my office."

"I don't understand," Jade said. "If you were at corporate, why didn't your office try to reach you there?"

"They did. They were told I couldn't be disturbed." He hacked out a laugh. "Well, I'm disturbed now."

"If you didn't embezzle the money, who did?" McClaine asked.

David Smith glanced around the room, his eyes tearing. "I have no idea. Wish I knew. I've lost everything. My job. No one will hire me. I'm not sure how long I can keep this house. What's going to happen to me and my family? Whoever did this ruined me."

*

"Harrington."

"What time will you be finished?"

"Why?"

Jade gazed out the passenger window at the pedestrians striding down Fifth Avenue. She and McClaine had just wrapped up interviewing David Smith's former co-workers at the technology company and were headed back to the police station.

"I'm picking you up from your hotel in an hour," Kyle said.

"For what? And how do you know where I'm staying?"

"I'm taking you to a fundraiser. For our mayor's equity initiative."

"But I didn't bring anything to wear."

"This is Seattle. It doesn't matter what you wear." Kyle hung up.

Jade waited a beat before looking over at McClaine.

He was grinning. "I think we're done for today."

"What are you talking about? We have interview reports to finish and—"

"It can wait until tomorrow. I'll drop you off at your hotel."

CHAPTER SEVENTY-SIX

AIR FORCE ONE

"HOW'S EMMA?" SASHA asked.

Her chief of staff sat across from Whitney's desk in her spacious office in the presidential suite. The 747-200B airplane was en route to the West Coast for a three-day trip where Whitney would speak about income equality in Seattle, Portland, San Francisco, Sacramento, San Jose, Los Angeles, and San Diego. They had just wrapped up her daily briefing.

"None the worse for wear."

"And the experience of getting arrested?"

"She said the police treated them decently throughout the entire process."

"The protesters must've all been white."

"Sasha . . . "

"I'm just saying . . . " Quietly, she said, "Regardless, getting arrested is never easy."

Whitney masked her feelings. It sounded as if Sasha were speaking from experience.

"Yes, me, too," Sasha said. "I was the cool kid with the

Walkman at the University of Texas, participating in a sit-in in front of The Tower."

"Against what?"

"The lack of faculty diversity. We overstayed our welcome and spent a night in jail." Sasha shrugged. "Glad it wasn't another part of Texas. Could've ended up like Sandra Bland."

During the last few years, reports of healthy black women dying under mysterious circumstances in Texas jails had reached the national news. Bland, arrested for a minor traffic violation, allegedly committed suicide in her jail cell.

Sasha still didn't rise to leave.

"What is it now?"

"Xavi."

Whitney threw her hands into the air. "It's like *Peyton Place* around here."

"He's making quiet innuendos, suggestions," Sasha said, "that given your daughter's arrest . . . it's your duty, as a mother, to step down and take care of her and your family."

Whitney's face got hot. "His concern for my family is touching, and I'm sure, genuine."

If Xavi believed this would make her second-guess herself about her purpose—her destiny—he was wrong. His actions were having the opposite effect. Her pity party was over. She could take care of her family. And her country.

"And one more thing."

Whitney pinched the bridge of her nose. "What is it?"

Sasha gestured with her thumb toward the back of the plane. Toward the press. "FOX is running another story about the year you spent with your aunt. There's a lot of speculation out there. Not only on FOX. But on Twitter. Facebook." When Whitney didn't say anything, Sasha continued. "They've also interviewed some of your classmates who recalled that you were shy and kept to yourself. That you didn't make any friends during your year there."

"Really. Don't they have anything more important to report on? They're on Air Force One, for God's sake." Whitney leaned back in her chair and closed her eyes. After a moment, she opened one eye. "Anything else?"

Sasha shook her head.

Whitney closed the eye again. "Then I'm hitting the gym."

The gym on Air Force One was quickly becoming her go-to refuge.

Sasha hesitated. "Is there something you need to tell me about your aunt?"

CHAPTER SEVENTY-SEVEN

SEATTLE, WASHINGTON

NOAH STOOD AT a window overlooking Eighth Avenue in a ballroom at the sleek and modern Hyatt Olive 8 hotel downtown. As he sipped white wine, he surveyed the crowd over the lip of his glass.

He swallowed hard as he saw Kyle Madison snake her way through the room. People parted for her like the Red Sea did for Moses. In her wake was a tall woman, beautiful in her own right, mocha-skinned, medium-length light brown hair, wearing a black business suit. She strode with confidence. Her eyes took in her surroundings, missing nothing.

Noah wasn't the only one staring at them.

After Kyle introduced the woman to the mayor, they waited in line at the bar for several minutes talking to each other, as if no one else were in the room. After receiving their drinks, Kyle began to work the room, introducing her companion along the way.

She looked familiar, but Noah couldn't quite place her.

Finally, Kyle stood before him. "Noah."

"Kyle."

"This is Jade."

"How do you do?" he asked, shaking her hand. "What do you do on weekends?"

She appeared puzzled by the question.

"It's different here than on the East Coast," Kyle explained. "Where your first question upon meeting strangers is 'What do you do?' Here, our hobbies are more important than our occupations."

Someone struck a spoon against a glass several times.

At the front of the room, the mayor spoke into a microphone. "You may have wondered about the extra security tonight. It's not for me." He paused as the crowd laughed. "But for a special guest who's here to help me introduce the Seattle Progressive Equity Initiative. Someone who is rectifying inequities across this country. Ladies and Gentleman, the president of the United States of America."

The three of them were as surprised as everyone else. After a moment of silence, the attendees applauded.

As President Whitney Fairchild navigated through the ballroom surrounded by a large coterie of Secret Service agents, conversation ceased.

"Agent Harrington," the president said when she arrived at the threesome. "What a pleasant surprise."

"The surprise is mine, Madam President."

"I'm sorry I was rude the last time we saw each other. I had just received some bad news."

"No apology necessary."

The president took both of Kyle's hands in hers. "Kyle Madison. Good to see you again. Thank you for your considerable support during the campaign."

"My pleasure."

President Fairchild turned to him. "And you are?"

Noah's face burned. "Noah Blakeley."

The president didn't react.

"I had a fundraiser for you at my house," he said. "During the campaign."

"Of course. My apologies. Thanks for your support."

The president moved on quickly to shake other hands.

"You all right there, Noah?" Kyle asked.

His face felt warm. "I'm fine." He gawked at the FBI agent. "*You're* Jade Harrington?"

She nodded, her smile modest.

"Noah's the president of AMB International," Kyle said.

He continued to stare at Jade. "Why are you here?"

"Don't be rude, Noah," Kyle said.

Puzzled, the agent said, "For a good cause?"

"No. I mean why are you here in Seattle?"

"She's looking into some thefts," Kyle said. "Cyberthefts. Come to think of it . . . weren't you asking—"

He barely registered the angry look the agent gave Kyle. "How much money?"

"Millions," Kyle said.

Jade looked at her sharply. "That's enough."

The ballroom seemed warm. He wiped his brow and murmured, "I wasn't the only one."

"What are you talking about, Mr. Blakeley?" the agent asked.

"We had a problem, too. My firm. Money stolen, I mean."

"Did you report it?"

"No."

She stepped closer, invading his space. "When did this happen?"

"I don't know. A couple months ago."

"Why didn't you report it?"

His eyes darted around the room, as if someone would throw him a lifeline. "I . . . uh . . . "

"How much was stolen—"

"Excuse me, I need to go to the restroom."

Noah walked away. He placed his half-full glass on a tray table near the wall and headed toward the stairs down to the main lobby. He didn't bother to retrieve his black North Face jacket from the coat check. He had an old one just like it at home.

He struggled through the revolving door and motioned for one of the valets to flag down a taxi. He didn't want to wait for a Lyft.

His father was going to kill him. He didn't like negative publicity concerning the family firm. Much less attention from law enforcement.

Why hadn't he kept his big mouth shut?

CHAPTER SEVENTY-EIGHT

SEATTLE, WASHINGTON

"HOW BORING WAS it?"

"It was okay."

"Liar."

Jade smiled. "I did like the basketball game better."

"How do you know the president?"

"She's my boss."

"Right," Kyle said.

"What about you?"

"What about me?"

"How do you know the president?"

Kyle waved her hand. "Connected her with some donors here in Seattle."

"I have a feeling you weren't one of the millions of small-dollar contributors."

Kyle smiled, but said nothing.

They strolled down Olive Way in silence. The June evening air was cool, the street empty of traffic. Few pedestrians walked the sidewalks. This part of downtown was not a happening place. The night was quiet, save the click, click, click of Kyle's heels.

"The guy we met at the beginning," Jade said. "What's his story? The one who admitted to the theft at his company."

"Noah? He comes from one of the first families, too. Our families probably knew each other, but there haven't been any intermarriages. Thank God! Any that I'm aware of anyway. Noah's not much of a businessman, but supports a lot of causes. An odd bird."

"How so?"

Kyle laced the fingers of both hands behind her back. "Noah dresses as if he's homeless instead of a multimillionaire. Maybe billionaire. He keeps one hand in his pocket. I've always wondered what the hell he's doing down there."

Jade made a face. "Nice . . . "

"He's just odd. He's one of those guys that if you found out he was a serial killer, you wouldn't be surprised."

Jade stopped walking and glanced at her.

Kyle looped her arm through Jade's. "Oops, forgot who I was talking to."

They continued walking.

"What's AMB International?"

"Transportation. Shipping. His father is Augustus Mathias Blakeley, the CEO. Noah has an older brother Augustus Jr.— they call him August—who is the opposite of Noah. Handsome, self-assured, a good business mind. August oversees the family foundation, and Noah runs the family business." Kyle shook her head. "It should be the other way around."

"Maybe Noah is easier to control."

"Good point. Augustus Sr. is private. Very private. Almost Howard Hughes-like."

They passed a local credit union with an odd juxtaposition of large vases filled with colorful artificial carnations protected by security bars.

There was a loud cry.

Jade flinched and swiveled her head.

A black woman of indeterminate age—she could have been forty or seventy—shuffled toward them, her dark clothes tattered. Tears flowed down her face. Jade could not understand what she was saying.

The woman's hand was out, palm up, begging for money.

"Please help me. Please help me. Please help me."

The woman reached out and touched Jade's arm. Jade backed up, arms raised, per her Tae Kwon Do training. The gesture meant that she didn't mean any harm, but she could quickly get into sparring position, if necessary.

Jade dropped her arms. She was being ridiculous. This woman wasn't going to hurt her. Or anyone else. She was the one who had been hurt. She stared at the woman, almost paralyzed by her pain.

She felt a tug on her sleeve.

Kyle whispered, "Let's go."

She put her arm around Jade's waist and led her away.

After a few steps, Jade said, "Wait."

She jogged back to the woman. She pulled a twenty-dollar bill out of her pocket. "Here. Get yourself something to eat." Jade searched her eyes. "Take care."

The woman stopped crying and gave her a grateful nod. "Bless you."

In those eyes was the belief in something, or someone, Jade didn't understand.

Disquieted, she rejoined Kyle.

A block away, Jade glanced over her shoulder. "So much homelessness. How can you stand it?"

Kyle hesitated. "It's difficult. I'm sad for that woman. Heartbroken for her, really. I help where I can. But I can't help them all."

"What's the solution?"

Kyle sighed. "Jade Harrington, you like to solve things. The more unsolvable, the better. Probably why you're good at your job. I'm not sure what the answer is. There are organizations that help fund education and job opportunities. Provide mental-health services. Drug treatment. New construction in Seattle requires inclusion of affordable housing. But, at times, the problem seems insurmountable." Kyle stopped. "I see some beggars in the same place every morning at the same time without fail. They're more punctual than some of the people who work for me."

They stood in front of a white building, the word Escala displayed in large, black cursive letters near the entrance.

Jade noted the name and looked back at Kyle. "Isn't this where that movie took place? *Fifty Shades of Gray*?"

"Where it was set. Yes."

"And you live here?"

"I lived here long before that foolishness came out. And don't worry. I don't have a red room of pain."

"I'll take your word for it." Jade gazed up at the building, and then back down the street from which they came. "Such vastly different ways of life, only a block away from each other."

Kyle stared at her, her green eyes piercing. "Jade, I won't apologize for who I am, what I do, or how much money I make. I had a lot of advantages because of who my parents are, but I've worked hard my entire life and earned everything that I own."

"The one percent. The protests. That woman." Jade raised her hands. "People like you living like this. Worth millions. Sometimes it's hard for me to see where it will all end."

She was still unsettled by the homeless woman, alone, crying on a sidewalk in prosperous, downtown Seattle. This was why people were protesting across the country. Against a system that favored the one percent.

That favored people like Kyle.

"How would you know how much I'm worth?"

Jade glanced away briefly and back at her. "What?"

Kyle stepped back. "Have you been looking into my background?"

Jade remained silent.

"Why?" Kyle asked. "Am I a suspect?"

Jade hesitated. She'd ruled Kyle out, but something prevented her from revealing that to her now.

Kyle's eyes narrowed. "Do you think I stole the money from *myself*? To what end?" She backed away, and then hurried to the front door of her building.

Jade made no attempt to stop her. She watched Kyle enter, and then turned and headed south down Fourth Avenue toward her hotel, her heart heavy and troubled.

She wasn't thinking about Kyle. She couldn't stop thinking about that homeless woman and her river of tears.

She had cried like that once. In middle school, after she was bullied for the last time. Even when she received the phone call in her Stanford dorm room from Max, when he told her that her parents had been killed by a drunk driver, she hadn't shed a tear.

It wasn't until she had lost an agent during the TSK case that she had learned how to cry again.

CHAPTER SEVENTY-NINE

AIR FORCE ONE

"WHAT IS IT now?"

She peered at Sasha over her recently prescribed "progressive" glasses. The term "progressive" had replaced trifocals. All Whitney knew was that her eyesight was getting progressively worse.

"It's Xavi again. There's a situation."

"There always seems to be a situation with Xavi." Whitney glanced at how far she had cycled: 1.2 miles. "Not much of a workout."

She climbed off the stationary bike and followed Sasha back to her office.

They were headed home. The trip had surpassed expectations. Not wildly enthusiastic crowds, but they had listened.

Still in her workout tights, she sat behind her desk. "What is it?"

Sasha remained standing. "A satellite picked up troop movements into Iran. Speculation is that they're Russian. Xavi and the JCs are in the Situation Room waiting for your call."

"Xavi and the JCs. Sounds like a singing group."

"Not one I'd want to hear."

"Me, neither. I guess I don't need to ask what this is about."

"What else? Oil."

"Put me through."

While Sasha placed the call, Whitney thought about her vice president. Three days. She had only been gone three days and now faced a global crisis.

Over the last several years, Russia had been quietly building a significant military presence in Europe and the Middle East. A Russian strategic document surfaced last year purporting the United States' role in NATO threatened Russian national security. US-Russia relations had been deteriorating ever since. The Pentagon hadn't worried much about Russia since the Cold War ended in 1991, but had begun to develop a contingency plan if Russia decided to turn back the clock.

Her vice president came on the line. "Madam President, I understand you've been apprised of the situation."

"I have."

"I recommend that we prepare a military response," Xavi said.

"Frances," Whitney said, into the phone, "what do you recommend?"

General Frances Wilkerson, chairwoman of the Joint Chiefs of Staff, and the first woman to hold the title, possessed a high standard of integrity and guided the US military with restraint. Wilkerson despised partisan politics and believed it had no place in governance. Whitney trusted her implicitly.

The general hesitated. "Madam President, I would wait until we receive better intel to assess the situation. Confirm that those are, in fact, troop movements."

Xavi's frustration was evident through the phone. "What

else could they be? Cows? No, we need to be prepared in case the situation on the ground escalates."

Whitney considered. "I'm with Frances on this one. Let's stand down and see what happens."

"Madam President, I respectfully disagree with your decision."

"Mr. Vice President, my decision respectfully stands."

She disconnected.

"Boom!" Sasha said and laughed. Whitney broke out into a smile as well. Sasha extended her fist. They fist bumped.

Whitney spoke into the speakerphone. "Sarah, get Andrei on the phone." Sean had stayed behind in DC.

She stared at Sasha as the call went through to the president of the Russian Federation.

Sarah's voice came over the line. "Madam President, I have President Andrei Tamirov."

She picked up the handset. "Andrei, what the hell are you doing in Iran?"

CHAPTER EIGHTY

SEATTLE, WASHINGTON

IN THE CONFERENCE room she had been using as an office at the local FBI field office, Jade logged onto her laptop and opened the spreadsheet she had created in DC. She tapped into the Securities and Exchange Commission (SEC) database and brought up the 10-K for Capstone Energy Partners, the Oklahoma City victim of cybertheft.

She navigated through the company's annual report until she came to the financial statements. The company had earned $150 million in revenue last year on assets of $356 million. She typed those numbers into her spreadsheet. The San Antonio firm, BMR Aviation, had earned $125 million on $274 million. TVX Corporation, the Anaheim firm, $1 billion in revenue. Third Data Corp., $112.5 million in revenue.

It didn't take long for her to see a pattern. Under the column Amount Stolen, Jade had entered $1.5 million for Capstone Energy Partners, $1.25 million for BMR Aviation, $10 million for TVX, and $1.125 million for Third Data.

She added a column to the far right, titling it % of Revenue.

She divided the data in the Amount Stolen column by the Total Revenue figure. The number in the % of Revenue column was the same for every company.

One percent.

One percent of last year's revenues had been stolen from the bank account of each firm.

She and McClaine still believed the rash of cybercrimes had started in Seattle. Those firms were all private, their financial information not available in the SEC database. How would the perpetrators find out the organizations' revenues? It wasn't impossible. A lot of private and confidential information could be found on the Internet.

Maybe I should ask Zoe. Or there's always the old-fashioned way.

She went online to find the phone number of AMB International.

"Noah Blakeley, please," she said, when the receptionist answered.

"May I ask who's calling?"

Jade told her and waited. And waited.

After a long silence, the receptionist returned. "Mr. Blakeley is not available. May I take a message?"

"Please tell him I called." She gave the receptionist her cell phone number and the number of the Seattle FBI field office.

She held the phone in her lap. She navigated to the Recent Calls screen and hesitated, her thumb poised. She pressed on the name.

The number rang and rang. Jade started to think she wouldn't answer. Then, "I don't want to talk to you."

"This is business."

Kyle's voice was cool. "What can I do for you, Agent Harrington?"

"How much in revenue did your firm earn last year?"

"That's none of your business."

"Actually, it is. I can subpoena the information."

Kyle exhaled, irritated. "About a hundred million."

The perpetrator had stolen one million dollars.

One percent.

"That's all I needed. Thank you."

Before she pressed End—

"Wait a minute," Kyle said.

She brought the phone back to her ear, but Kyle didn't say anything.

"Kyle, I was just doing my job."

"I know. I just felt . . . invaded. You don't need to check me out. Or run a background check on me. Just ask me what you want to know."

"Okay."

The silence lingered. Jade said, "Well, I should go."

"What are you doing later?"

"I have a meeting."

"After your meeting."

"Getting ready for my flight back."

"I want to take you somewhere."

"Where?"

"Volunteer Park. There's a Tai Chi class there this evening."

Jade did not bother to hide her disappointment. "Tai Chi."

"It'll be good for you. Relaxing. You'll stretch your mind and your body."

Zoe had tried and failed numerous times to get her hooked on meditation. "Don't you have a dojang around here?"

"A what?"

"A dojang. A Tae Kwon Do school. I'd rather spar with someone. Work out. Hit people. Work on protecting myself."

"You don't need to protect yourself from me."

Au contraire.

Even so, she was tempted. "I can't. I have a lot of work to do. Rain check?"

"As you wish, Agent Harrington."

CHAPTER EIGHTY-ONE

CASPER, WYOMING

AIR FORCE ONE landed.

She scanned the near-empty tarmac. There was no crowd. No local officials to welcome her. No band. No cheerleaders. No banners. Good. It's what she wanted. No one knew about this last-minute, unscheduled visit.

The seven-car motorcade left Casper-Natrona County International Airport and drove east on US 26 before exiting south on a one-lane road. The landscape was dotted for miles with occasional cottonwood trees, ranches, and farms. The press and her staff, including Sasha, had been shuttled onto buses and taken into Casper, the nearest town, for lunch and an afternoon off.

Whitney didn't want an audience for this visit.

Twenty minutes after leaving the airport, the limousine pulled into a gravel driveway, which stretched a hundred yards to the ranch house in the distance.

A slender man dressed in jeans, a t-shirt, and cowboy boots stood on the front porch.

"Madam President," the former president of the United States, Richard Ellison, called out to her. "Welcome to Wyoming." He opened the screen door. "Come on in."

*

The Presidents Club started with the 34th president, Dwight D. Eisenhower, and solidified under his successor, John F. Kennedy. Ever since, the former living presidents of the United States had formed the most exclusive club in the world. It currently had three members. This was the first time she had called on one of them.

The club had an unspoken rule of not badmouthing the sitting president. During Whitney's first six months in office—despite the beating she had endured from the press, by the other party, and on social media—Ellison had remained mute.

Maybe he'd felt he didn't need to speak out. He had plenty of others to do it for him.

Ellison handed her a glass of iced tea, and sat next to her in the matching rocking chair on the back porch. He pointed. "That's Casper Mountain over there."

"Are you sure your wife doesn't mind?"

He laughed. "She's grateful for your visit. Now that my term's over, we spend a lot more time together. Too much, if you ask her. She's fine."

"It's peaceful here," she said. "No wonder you love this place. How's private life treating you?"

"I can sleep at night. And sleep through the whole night."

She took a sip of her drink. "Do you ever think about the decisions that you made? The ones you were unsure of?"

"Sure. But not much. Presidents need to take the long view."

She surveyed his property. There was land as far as she could see. "How so?"

"The pundits and the American people all have an opinion about you and your decisions. None of them are in the arena with you. The future will be the best judge."

She stared down at her glass, thinking about what he said.

Ellison leaned back to start the motion of his rocking chair. "Whitney, what's bothering you?"

She looked up at him. "The New New Deal. My legacy legislation. It would help so many people and move this country forward. I can't let it fail."

"Then, don't." He inclined his head. "Do you know what our state's nickname is?"

She smiled. "I'm going to go out on a limb here . . . the Cowboy State?"

"That's one of them. But the one I'm thinking of is The Equality State."

She gave him a questioning look.

"Our motto is 'Equal Rights.' Wyoming was the first state in the nation to give women the right to vote, to serve on juries, and to hold public office. In 1924, Mrs. Nellie Tayloe Ross was the first woman to be elected governor of a US state."

"I didn't know that."

"She was a Democrat, by the way."

"Even better."

"We haven't voted for a Democratic president since 1964. Our state was somewhat supportive of your work on women's rights, but this New New Deal." He shook his head. "Our unemployment rate is four percent. We don't need it."

"It's about more than creating jobs. It's about rebuilding America. Aspiring for something greater than ourselves.

Making us respected around the world again." She glanced at him. "No offense."

"None taken."

The global reputation of the United States had plummeted during the Ellison Administration. His neoconservative foreign policies, resurrected from the George W. Bush era, had become passé for the times.

"Sometimes . . . I feel all alone. Did you ever feel that way?"

"The loneliness of being president can kill you, if you let it. The buck really does stop with you." He stood. "I'll be right back."

The screen door slammed shut, as he went inside.

Just talking to Richard helped. He understood. There was strength in the club, and she wouldn't be afraid to rely on it in the future. The members were the only people in the world who had walked in her shoes.

He returned and handed her a glass. "I thought we could use something stronger."

The first sip of whiskey burned Whitney's throat.

"How did you feel when the first revelations about your past came out?"

He shook his head. "It was a dumb, youthful mistake. Whoever said, 'Youth is wasted on the young' had it right. I should've come forward, but I'd forgotten all about it."

Numerous scandals—about them both—had surfaced during the campaign. Although Whitney trusted Richard to a certain extent, she knew it would be political suicide to tell him her teenage secret. It had not come up last year, and she would do everything in her power to prevent it from coming out now. FOX be damned. She did not plan to tell him about her problems with Xavi either. She could handle Xavier Fernandez.

Richard left again and brought out a pitcher of beer, a shot of whiskey for each of them, and two bowls of chili.

"This should warm you up. Sorry, no wine. Not any that I could give you in good conscience anyway. Be right back."

He returned with a Native American blanket for her, and a light jacket for him, to ward off the encroaching evening chill.

After they ate, she and Richard spent another two hours on the back porch. The former president and his successor rocked in their chairs, as the sun set on the land of the free, drinking beer and talking about everything and nothing.

Finally, Whitney said, "Enough about me. What have you been up to?"

"Fly fishing. Walking around my property. Writing my memoirs. Planning my library." He leaned over putting his forearm on his leg propped up on a wooden box. "I have an idea. Will you come to the library opening next year? Perhaps, make the opening remarks?"

Whitney smiled at him. "I wouldn't miss it."

CHAPTER EIGHTY-TWO

FAIRFAX, VIRGINIA

THE FOLLOWING DAY, Jade pulled into the Kamp Washington Shopping Center parking lot on Fairfax Boulevard. "I'm hungry."

Christian smiled as he exited the car. "Multitasking. I love it."

The heavenly aroma of freshly baked bread enveloped them as they entered the Jimmy John's.

They ordered, but instead of moving away from the counter, she moved to stand in front of one of the employees making sandwiches.

It took a moment for the boy to raise his head from his work.

"What are you doing here?"

"We want to have a chat with you."

He glanced over his shoulder and back at her. "I'm working."

She pointed at a table. "You have until the time we finish eating to take a break. Ten minutes." She looked at Christian and back to the young man. "Maybe five. He eats fast."

Andrew Huffman nodded and turned his attention back to making her late lunch.

She'd been spending the last couple of weeks on the cybertheft case, not so much on the bullying case. She had decided to follow up with the players individually. Starting with Andrew.

She had just finished her sandwich when Andrew stood at the empty chair at their table. He hesitated, then sat.

She balled up the paper the sandwich had been wrapped in. "How do you like working here?"

"It's a job. I get a discount on food."

"It must be tough going to school, playing sports, and working."

He shrugged. "I wouldn't be a sandwich maker, if I didn't have to be. I don't have a choice. We're not rich like some of my classmates."

"Like William?"

He lowered his eyes and stared at the table.

"What were you going to tell me? At Joshua's funeral?"

He shrugged his big shoulders. "That was a month ago. I don't remember."

"What happened to Tyler, Andrew? Did William have something to do with his death? Did you?"

He lifted his head. "Do you ever feel a part of something and not a part of it at the same time?"

She thought about it. "Sure."

"I'm a part of something that I can't get out of. I'm sorry I can't help you."

"Andrew, we can help you."

He glanced out the window and stood suddenly,

knocking the chair to the floor. He looked back at Jade, and said, "Warriors don't run. I need to get back to work."

He righted the chair and hustled back behind the counter. She looked out the window.

William stared back at her. He raised his hand and waved.

CHAPTER EIGHTY-THREE

ARLINGTON, VIRGINIA

SHE COULDN'T BREATHE.

Jade's eyes popped open. Her cell phone was vibrating on the table. Card, her cat, had lately taken to sleeping on her neck. He had no concept of personal space. She gently pushed him off.

She grabbed the phone. Two missed calls. Ethan.

"Your vigilante struck again."

"Where?" she croaked.

"Not too far from you. A 7-Eleven in Arlington. I'll text you the address. The rest of your team is on their way."

She dropped the phone on the table among the files she'd been studying prior to nodding off on her living room couch last night.

It was ironic that it was just this afternoon she had turned her focus back to the bullying case. There hadn't been any reason to. There hadn't been any new leads. Or nothing new happening.

Until now.

*

Jade parked the Audi down the street from the 7-Eleven store, which was a mile from her house. She could have walked.

The night was lit up like day. She had no trouble spotting Christian among the police officers and detectives.

"You got here fast," she said.

Before he could answer, Dante and Micah came up to them. She rolled the sleeves of her shirt up her forearm. "What do we have?"

"I'll show you," Christian mumbled.

They followed him around the store to the small parking lot in back. Christian flashed the badge on a lanyard around his neck to a police officer, and slipped it back into his shirt pocket.

Two crime-scene technicians in protective gear bent over the body. Several others searched for evidence nearby. The crime scene photographer shot pictures of everything.

The condition of the corpse was like the other victims. Bruises and welts down the left side. The head, a bloody mess. The crotch area appeared worse.

Her eyes closed. A brief bow of her head. "Damn."

"Who is he?" Micah asked.

"Andrew Huffman," Christian said, quietly. "We just interviewed him today." He inclined his head toward the Arlington County police officers. "They notified his parents. They're on their way."

"Fairfax is pretty far from here," Jade said.

"There's a popular spot nearby where the Randolph kids hang out sometimes. Frankie's. Games. Pool. Heard of it?"

She nodded. "Did it happen here?"

Christian flicked his thumb at the techs. "They think so. It doesn't look like he was dumped."

She raised an eyebrow. "You think William's good for it?"

"What's his motive?"

"Not sure." She looked down at the body again. "But this warrior won't be running anymore."

CHAPTER EIGHTY-FOUR

WASHINGTON, DC

JADE POKED HER head into her boss's door. "You wanted to see me?"

Ethan Lawson looked up from the newspaper spread out on his desk. He showed her the front page. She walked in and sat across from him. The headline blared The Bully Killer Strikes Again; underneath, smaller type: Randolph High School Parents Frantic.

"Haven't had a chance to read it today," she said, taking it from him. She skimmed the article.

"Press office says its phones have been ringing off the hook," Ethan said. "Local media. National media. The local police. Parents of the students."

She gestured at the paper. "These headlines don't help."

"They've beefed up security around the school. Some of the parents of the baseball team are homeschooling their kids until this is over. The season has been suspended." He waited for her to finish reading. "What's the latest on your end?"

She updated him on the investigation into the murder of

Andrew Huffman. "We're headed over to the school now. To interview the students again."

"We need to solve this."

Jade returned his stare. "You sure have changed your tune."

"All right. You were right." He leaned back in his chair, twirling his ring. "How many bullies can there be in one school?"

"Looks like a lot. Are you asking me if there will be more deaths?"

He stared at her, waiting for an answer.

She put her hands on her thighs and pushed herself up from the chair. "If we don't catch him . . . yes."

CHAPTER EIGHTY-FIVE

FAIRFAX, VIRGINIA

CHRISTIAN SQUATTED IN a chair much too small for him and glanced around the room. "Déjà vu."

They then spent most of the afternoon in a conference room off Randolph Secondary School's main office, individually interviewing the same students they had talked to in groups two months ago. The students who were still alive anyway. The nonchalance that Jade and Christian had endured at those prior interviews had transformed into something else.

Fear.

Dante and Micah were in the other room also conducting interviews. Despite their intense questioning, they were no closer to discovering whether any other students were involved in bullying Tyler Thompson or who could be killing the boys who bullied him.

The final interview of the day was with William Chaney-Frost.

He strode into the room. "Howie's back!"

Most of the kids she'd interviewed earlier were visibly shaken. Not this one.

Jade ignored Christian's puzzled look. After William situated himself, she said, "Talk to me about Tyler."

He sighed and pulled a folded piece of paper out of his pocket. "I'm a year older." He created a paper football as he talked. "We didn't run in the same crowd."

She pointed. "I haven't seen one of those in a while."

The boy glanced at it. "My Dad showed me. He used to make them when he was in school. Now, I have everybody doing it. We have tournaments and stuff during class."

"Where were you last night?"

"Home. My parents are keeping me on a short leash these days."

"What were you doing at Jimmy John's?"

"Meeting up with Drew."

"I thought you were on a short leash."

"My parents were at work. I got home before they did."

"Who bullied Tyler Thompson?"

"I don't know."

"I think you do."

"It could've been a lot of people."

"Was it you?"

"I bet it was Zach and Andrew, but I don't know that for sure. Like I told you, they had a problem with Tyler being gay."

Christian looked up from his notebook, but didn't react. Jade had already told him about William's claim.

"Did you?" she said.

"No."

"That just doesn't sound like Andrew to me," she said. "And I can't ask either of them, because they're dead. I can only take your word for it." William gave her an exaggerated shrug. "Any idea who might be killing your teammates?"

"We won states last year and the year before that. We were projected to go again this year. Maybe a rival team? There are a lot of haters out there. You know what that's like."

"What do you mean?"

He gave her a shy, charming smile. "You're a badass, and you're beautiful. If you don't have haters, you ain't poppin'."

Badass enough to be inured to your charms.

Jade did know about haters. As an All-American basketball player at Stanford and a former WNBA player, a lot of people wanted to be her friend on the way up. The same people who couldn't wait to watch her fall. Some of those people tried to get back in touch with her after the notoriety of the TSK case. She hadn't returned any of their calls or texts.

"Your teammates are dying. How does that make you feel?"

The lingering smile evaporated. The bravado gone. "Scared."

"You don't look scared."

He put the football in his pocket. "I am. On the inside."

Jade stood, hands braced on the table, leaning toward him. "You don't seem too anxious to find out who's killing your teammates. Aren't you afraid this person will come after you?"

The kid slouched in his chair. "I shouldn't be. I didn't bully T. I haven't bullied anyone. I tried to get close to him. Become his friend."

"Why is that?"

He glanced over at Christian. "Because of his mom, man. She's fine."

Jade had heard this from some of the other male students, particularly the athletes. "Why would that make you want to be his friend?"

"So, he'd invite me to his house." He glanced over at

Christian again, giving him a man-to-man look. "Because she's a MILF."

Mom I'd Like to Fuck.

"You know what that means, right Howie?"

Jade reached over and caught Christian's forearm in a firm grip before he began to rise. If he could murder with his eyes, William Chaney-Frost would be dead.

Perhaps, the kid didn't realize he had just insulted the sister-in-law of a federal agent.

She looked at him. "I just saved your life." She rose. "I'm going to get some water. You want some?"

The teenager sat up. His eyes round, unblinking. "You're not leaving me alone with him. Are you?"

She walked toward the door. "I'll be right back."

Christian stood. The closer he came to William's chair, the more the boy leaned back in his seat, until he was almost horizontal. Christian stopped at the chair, raised his fists, and then flinched. "Boo!"

William recoiled.

Christian smiled before preceding Jade out the door.

She took one last look behind her.

William finally looked scared.

CHAPTER EIGHTY-SIX

WASHINGTON, DC

LATER THAT AFTERNOON, she and Pat Turner sat alone in a conference room at the Bureau. As Pat fiddled with a VCR playback recorder, Jade thought about William and the bullying case, trying to tease out how he was involved. After the interviews, Dante and Micah had interviewed William's parents. They vouched that he was home with them all night.

Pat finished setting up and put the first tape in. "I can't believe businesses still use this technology."

Jade slipped a small plastic yellow bag out of her pants pocket, and selected a red M&M. She returned the bag. "Start it at eight p.m."

A call mid-morning from the coroner had pegged Andrew Huffman's time of death between nine p.m. and midnight.

Pat fast-forwarded until the time stamp in the lower-right corner of the screen showed 20:00, and then pushed play. The view, from the ceiling, covered the 7-Eleven's entrance and the ATM just inside the store.

"Forward until you see movement."

At 20:11, a man walked in, his image grainy, his movements jerky because of the tape's low-quality. The picture was the opposite of hi-def.

"Stop," Jade said. She scrutinized the face, but didn't recognize him. "Mark the time. Go on."

They continued to watch the tape in this way, stopping and examining everyone who came in, fast-forwarding when the store was presumably empty.

At 22:50 on the time stamp, Jade sat up. Huffman entered wearing a t-shirt and ripped designer jeans. The same clothes he had worn when she viewed his body in the parking lot. He was out of the picture for a few minutes, but returned drinking a large Slurpee through a straw. Before he reached the door, two men came in. One wore khakis and a polo shirt with a baseball cap pulled down low on his forehead. The other, dark slacks and a white dress shirt and tie, as if he had just gotten off work. Baseball Cap's face was averted from the camera.

Did he realize the camera was there?

Huffman and White Shirt had a conversation, before the boy smiled at him and left.

"Stop," Jade said. "Rewind. Pause."

She drew closer to the projection screen. Huffman had known him. Without looking at Pat, Jade said, "Can you zoom in on the guy's face?" She studied the image. Although it was blurry, she recognized him.

"That's Matt," she said, her pulse racing. "Zoom in on the other guy."

Only his chin, lips, and the bottom of his nose were visible. The hat bore an old Redskins logo.

Huffman left. The men followed him soon thereafter, Matt carrying a paper bag.

No one else of note came into the store from then until the time of death.

Jade returned to her seat. "We need to find out who that other guy was, and whether he's a part of this. Can you try to get a hit on the lower portion of his face?"

Pat nodded. Later, she would attempt to match it with the five hundred million photographs in the FBI's facial-recognition database. It had taken them an hour to watch the tape.

"What about after the attack?" Jade said.

"I already checked. Nothing. No surveillance camera covered the parking lot out back, either," Pat said, "but this came from a competing convenience store across the street." She grabbed another tape, but hesitated before sliding it into the VCR machine. "Do you need a break?"

Jade gave her a look.

They went through the same process as the previous tape, but now the view was of customers entering and leaving the store from the outside.

At 22:45, a woman walked out of the store, as Huffman walked in.

"I don't remember seeing her on the 7-Eleven tape," Jade murmured.

A knock on the door.

She didn't bother to answer it.

Dante opened the door, glanced at the two of them, and then at the screen. He took a seat at the table without being asked.

On the screen, Huffman held the door for the woman, admiring the view from behind as she strutted away. He entered the store. The two men walked toward the store, passing the woman, but not acknowledging her.

After they entered the store, there was no activity on camera, except an occasional passing car. Jade couldn't see into the store from this angle.

Huffman came out. The men walked out a few minutes later.

Pat stopped the tape without being asked. Jade moved closer to the screen. "Enlarge it."

She peered again at the nose, the chin, the jaw. If she didn't know better, he looked like—

Dante moved next to her. "What's he doing there?"

"Who?"

He pointed to the screen. "Christian."

CHAPTER EIGHTY-SEVEN

WASHINGTON, DC

"SHUT THE DOOR."

Christian complied and sat down.

"Why didn't you tell me?"

He shrugged. "I don't know."

"Trust is everything," she said. "To me."

A painful expression crossed his face, but he said nothing.

"What were you doing there?" Jade asked.

"We met for a drink after work. He needed someone to talk to. Jenny's driving him crazy."

"You're not answering the question."

"Jenny called him. Asked him to pick up a few things before coming home. We said goodnight, got in our separate cars, and left."

"It looks bad. You arrived at the scene before I did."

"Hadn't gone far when I got the call." He looked at her. "Jade, you know I didn't have anything to do with murdering that kid. Any of those kids."

She didn't think so. But she'd made up her mind.

"Dante's going in with me."

*

In an interrogation room at FBI HQ, she stared across the table at Matt Thompson and his lawyer. Dante sat next to her taking notes. Behind her, Christian, along with Pat, Max, and Micah, observed them through the one-way glass.

After dispensing with the preliminaries, Jade said, "Why were you in the 7-Eleven that night?"

"Like I told the police and you many times already, I was on my way home from the Mercedes dealership in Arlington."

"Why were you there?"

"I had a meeting with the GM. General Manager. We meet occasionally to discuss sales, promotional tactics. Inventory issues. I didn't feel like going straight home so I asked Christian to meet me for a drink."

"Can you state Christian's last name for the record?"

"Merritt."

Jade felt Christian's eyes boring into the back of her head. "And what is his relationship to you?"

"He's my brother-in-law. Anyway, my wife called and asked me to pick up a few things at the store."

"Like what?"

"Some chips, popcorn, a liter of soda." *Easy to check.* "We were going to watch a movie after we put the kids to bed. A date night. We haven't had many since . . . "

His voice trailed off. Jade let the silence hang for a moment.

"Did you know Andrew Huffman would be there?"

"I didn't know who he was until he started talking. I thought he could've been one of Tyler's teammates, but wasn't sure. A lot of those guys look alike."

"What did you talk about?"

"He asked me how I was," Thompson said. "That he was sorry again about Tyler. He hoped I would make it out to a game next year."

Jade switched topics. "Don't you find it strange that every murdered boy allegedly bullied your son?"

He glanced at his attorney. The attorney nodded. "Sure. I won't lie and say I didn't want to beat the crap out of them, but I didn't kill them. Hell, I didn't even know who all the bullies were."

"Do you think your wife did?"

Thompson shrugged. "Maybe. She went to all his games. Sometimes, I had to miss games because of work, especially the away games. My wife," he hesitated, "is not well."

"What do you mean?" Jade asked.

Thompson's eyes watered. "She"—he gulped—"won't leave the house. She rarely showers. Wears that ratty old bathrobe and slippers most of the time. Watches TV all day. Or sleeps. I want her to see someone. A psychiatrist. She won't go. The only place she *will* go is the cemetery. I take her sometimes. She lays on Tyler's grave. She can lay there for hours."

CHAPTER EIGHTY-EIGHT

FAIRFAX, VIRGINIA

JADE EXITED THE car and strode up the sidewalk that bisected the yard. She knocked on the front door, turning to scope out the surrounding houses while she waited. They had been waiting in her car for over an hour. The neighborhood of Colonial homes—the keeper of lives and their secrets for longer than four decades—mostly quiet.

Now, at six a.m., the residents had started to stir. A few of the Thompsons' neighbors departed, commuters trying to beat Washington's insufferable early-morning traffic.

She knocked again. This time, Jenny Thompson answered the door. She stared at them vacantly, cinching the top of her bathrobe at the neck.

"Are you here to tell me who killed my son?"

Jade handed her the warrant. "Jennifer Thompson, we have a warrant to search your house and garage for the contents listed on that document."

Jade didn't wait for an invitation inside. She pushed past

the dazed woman, followed by Dante and Micah and forensic techs. The techs dispersed throughout the house.

Jenny caught up to her and grabbed Jade's arm. "What is this? Where's Christian?"

Jade stared at Jenny's hand until she removed it. "Where's your husband?"

"He's at work. Why?"

Jade had seen him leave. Other agents were simultaneously serving him a warrant at his office at the dealership. "I suggest you gather your children and stay in one room. One of our agents will keep you company."

Jade left her and followed the techs into the living room. They knew what to search for: any evidence linking Matt Thompson to the four murdered William Randolph Secondary School students.

She turned to Micah and Dante. "I'm going upstairs."

"I'll go with you," Micah said.

Dante shook his head, smirking.

To Micah, she said, "Suit yourself."

They watched the techs process the master bedroom and the bedrooms of the two youngest children.

The technicians hesitated at the last bedroom. Everyone knew that the Fairfax County police had processed the room after Tyler's case was ruled a homicide.

"Do it anyway," Jade said.

She glanced at the twin-size bed, neatly made, the nightstand, the dresser. Everything seemed in its place.

But something was off. She couldn't put her finger on what.

She moved to the dresser against one wall. On top of it were a few trophies—one of the plaques said Most Improved, another Best Attitude—several text books, and his baseball cap.

A forensic analyst turned off the overhead light and began spraying Luminol on the walls, the carpet, and the bed.

Expecting to find nothing, Jade turned to leave.

A blue glow glimmered on the wall behind the bed, followed shortly by the bedspread and the carpet nearby. As the photographer clicked away, Jade stopped, her mouth slightly open as she took in the scene. She stared at the light for the entire thirty seconds it took to fade away, her mind churning.

A chemical in Luminol reacted to iron, which was found in hemoglobin.

Jade looked at the tech for confirmation. He nodded.

She said to Micah, "That means—"

"—there's trace amounts of blood present," he finished. "What's the big deal, though? The victim was beaten up before he died."

"Yeah. But he didn't lay on the wall."

CHAPTER EIGHTY-NINE

SEATTLE, WASHINGTON

NOAH ENJOYED A turkey sandwich at an organic deli near his office in Pioneer Square. He sat at the counter at the front of the restaurant, staring out the window at the activity taking place among the trees, tables, and black streetlamps in Occidental Park.

Pioneer Square had begun as the city's center. Noah's ancestors had settled there in 1852. Most of the original wooden buildings erected at that time had been destroyed in the Great Seattle Fire of 1889. The neighborhood's current brick and stone buildings replicated that original architecture.

The vibrant area consisted of art galleries, nightclubs, sports bars, restaurants, and bookstores. But the neighborhood had its dark side: vandalism, prostitution, drug dealing, and, sometimes, homicides. A large population of homeless people also called Pioneer Square home. The area was beautiful and primed for revival. The transition had been a struggle. Noah wasn't sure the neighborhood would make it. He didn't spend much time here after dark.

His phone vibrated.

He looked down to see a text from Jack, one of his running buddies. A text from him was rare, unless it was to schedule a run or a bike ride for the upcoming weekend.

I heard about what happened. Let me know if I can do anything.

Noah stared at the message, wondering what Jack meant. He shrugged and took another bite of his sandwich. Jack had probably intended to send it to someone else. As Noah sipped his bottled water through a straw, he received another text, this one from a fellow member of a nonprofit board on which he served.

Horrible news. I'm here for you.

Had something happened to his father? After a few more texts from well-wishers, he returned Jack's text.

What are you talking about?

He bussed his table and left the restaurant. Office workers walked to and fro or ate lunch at the outside tables, sharing the busy park with the homeless, beggars, a couple of street performers, joggers, and CrossFit members swinging kettlebells. He thought the latter activity should be illegal. Someone could get hurt. His phone vibrated in his pocket. He dug it out and stared at the message.

The money stolen from your firm.

He frowned and then texted Jack back.

How do you know about that?

He kept walking, staring at his phone, oblivious to everything going on around him. The wait seemed interminable, but may have been only seconds.

The Times just posted a link to an article on Twitter, man.

Noah stopped and navigated to the *Seattle Times* app.

His father's face—his face!—was on the front page. The front page. Not the business section. For all the world to see. The article stated that one million dollars had been stolen. AMB International was listed with Kyle Madison's venture-capital firm, and other firms in Seattle and across the country, in a chart in the middle of the article.

Some people grumbled as they walked around him. He barely noticed. He fished his wallet out of his back pocket, and found the card the federal agent had given him at the fundraiser and dialed.

"Special Agent—"

"Did you tell the media?"

"Who is this?"

"Noah Blakeley."

"Took you long enough to return my call."

"I . . . uh . . . didn't get the message."

She paused. "Interesting . . . "

"You leaked it to the media. It's on the front page of the *Times*. Everyone's going to know now. Why did you do that? Because I didn't return your call?"

Noah could hear the hysteria in his own voice.

"Calm down, Mr. Blakeley. Why would I call you, if I already knew? Besides, I can assure you that no one from my office told anyone in the media about what happened at your firm."

Her politeness was increasing his blood pressure. "Who did?"

There was a moment of silence. "I don't know. This is the first I've heard of it. But I can try to find out."

"I don't believe you."

He pressed End. His hands shook. His father was going to

kill him. He had to figure out a way to avoid him for the rest of the day.

His phone buzzed again. Another well-wisher? No. This text was from his father.

Come back to the office. Now!

He glanced around him. He must look wild. Crazy. He jammed the phone and the wallet into his back pockets, spun, and took off in the other direction, barely missing a hard body swinging a kettlebell. Perhaps he should have let the Amazonian woman hit him. It would have felt better than what his father was going to do to him.

Instead, he swerved around the woman and speed-walked. Away from the office.

And his father.

CHAPTER NINETY

WASHINGTON, DC

AFTER THE ABRUPT, strange phone call from Noah Blakeley, she returned to the spreadsheet she had worked on in Seattle. She was trying to keep busy, while she waited for the lab results on the Thompson case.

Pat had long since provided the rest of the financial information Jade needed on the victimized Seattle firms.

She stared at the completely filled-out spreadsheet: the list of firms, locations, total assets, total liabilities, cash balances, last year's revenue and net income amounts, and the amount stolen.

She sat back. Exactly one percent in each case.

Was this some kind of Robin Hood thing? Steal from the rich and give to the poor? She shook her head. Was she allowing Zoe's lectures on the evils of the one-percenters to influence her? But, most important, who would have the capability to pull off heists of this magnitude?

She continued to stare at the computer screen, as questions

tumbled around in her brain and she tried to come up with logical answers.

Her cell phone vibrated. Kyle.

"I'm in the middle of something," Jade said. "Can I call you back?"

"I don't like this kind of publicity."

"I had nothing to do with the leak. I'm working on finding out who did."

"It's a little late now. My investors have been calling. They're spooked. And threatening to withdraw their money from our latest fund. I'm not happy."

"I'm sorry." Jade hung up.

She returned to examining her spreadsheet, but almost immediately her mind wandered back to Kyle.

Jade liked her. Enjoyed talking to her and spending time with her. Her feelings for Kyle were complicated, beyond professional. And wrong. Jade should have learned her lesson with Landon. She chastised herself. *Caleb Hewitt.*

She looked at the spreadsheet again.

She needed to stop seeing her, except for case-related business.

Or, at least, not until the perpetrator was caught.

Pat entered her office and sat down uninvited. "Michael Brown."

"What about him?"

Michael Brown had overseen the federal government's response to Hurricane Katrina. Hewitt had used the name as an alias during his killing spree.

"You asked me to look into transportation manifests in and out of Chicago around the time the president's aunt died. On a lark, I did a search on all of Hewitt's aliases: Michael Brown, Eddie Cullen, Caleb Hewitt, Landon Phillips, and any combinations thereof."

"And?"

"Nothing. There was an Eddie Brown, who flew from New Orleans to Chicago for a conference, but his whereabouts during that time are accounted for."

Jade's forearm tingled. "But you found something."

"Who did Caleb Hewitt hate more than anyone else?"

She thought back to the interview with Hewitt's parents. "George W. Bush. Caleb believed he stole the 2000 election."

Pat handed her a file. "Here is the manifest for a Southwest flight from Newark to Chicago Midway in 2001."

She stared at Pat an extra beat. She opened the file, her eyes scrolling down the list until she reached the name that Pat had highlighted. Her eyes widened, as a small fist formed in her gut, and started creeping its way upward.

She glanced at Pat, and back down at the list.

The highlighted name was Walker G. Bush.

She stared at the Pennsylvania driver's license photograph of Walker G. Bush. His hair was dirty blond and longish. The eyes brown. There was not a doubt in Jade's mind that she was looking at Caleb Hewitt before he had transformed into Landon Phillips.

"There's more." Pat handed her another file. "Given how Hewitt felt about Bush, I deduced he hated someone else just as much."

"The godfather of 'enhanced interrogation techniques'?"

Pat nodded. "Good guess."

"Or Sherlockian deduction."

"At any rate, you're right. Dick Cheney."

The folder contained an airline manifest from 2005 establishing that a Rick Cheney flew from Philadelphia to St. Louis. The photo on this driver's license was taken five years after the

Bush photo. The hair was shorter and light brown. The eyes were green. And the nose job was in place.

The face Jade knew as Landon Phillips.

The fact that Caleb Hewitt was in Clayton, Missouri at the same time Representative Barrett was killed couldn't have been a coincidence.

"What about hotels?" Jade asked.

"Once he arrived in St. Louis, the trail runs cold. No one by that name stayed at a hotel within a hundred and fifty miles of the city."

"And the Congressman's car is long gone, so we can't verify fingerprints."

"Since it was an accident, it wasn't retained as evidence. The family sold what was left of it to a mechanic. We followed up with him. He sold it for parts."

"Thanks, Pat," she said, wanting to be alone with the file.

This time, she didn't pace. As soon as Pat left, she picked up the handset. "This is Jade Harrington. I need to see the president."

CHAPTER NINETY-ONE

THE WHITE HOUSE, WASHINGTON, DC

"I HOPE YOU don't have any food restrictions."

"No, when it comes to food—just like anything else—I don't discriminate. My best friend, though, is always telling me that just because you look healthy doesn't mean you are."

"Good advice. And who is your best friend?"

"Her name is Zoe."

"Doesn't she have a last name?"

"She doesn't want anyone to know it." The agent shrugged. "Like Madonna, Cher, Beyoncé. You understand."

"I do."

"She does a lot of work for you, actually. Worked on many of your campaigns."

Jade told her the name of the organization Zoe worked for.

Whitney lifted her glass. "Then, here's to Zoe."

"To Zoe. She would love this by the way. The president of the United States toasting her."

They clinked glasses and drank. Hers was filled with wine. Agent Harrington's with sparkling water.

"I don't have dinner guests here often."

"I'm honored," Jade said.

Jade's eyes surveyed the beautiful place setting on the table in the President's Dining Room in the residence, the Sheraton chairs, the chandelier, the grandfather clock, the fireplace, and the painting over the mantle of a woman with a child sitting in her lap.

The young woman seemed to be waiting for her. Whitney picked up her knife and fork and began to eat.

"I wanted to give you an update on the case," Jade said.

Whitney held up her hand. "After dinner. I assume the news will not be pleasant, and I would like to enjoy this wonderful meal my cook prepared. Especially, if you're going to tell me this is my last."

"It's bad, Madam President, but not that bad. This pasta is delicious."

Whitney eyed her plate. "There's more, if you're hungry."

The agent reddened. "It's not often I eat a home-cooked meal. I'm not much of a cook."

"Last year, when we were together, you told me about your hobbies. If I remember correctly, you play basketball and practice Tae Kwon Do."

"Good memory. I'm afraid I haven't had much time for either."

"That's a shame. Hobbies are important."

"What's your hobby? Let me guess. Reading."

Whitney nodded. "First editions."

"Expensive hobby. I read through your New New Deal Coalition proposal."

"Then you must have a lot of free time. And?"

"I like the part about funding infrastructure projects. Can you add the Bureau to the mix?"

Whitney laughed. "I'll see what I can do."

It was no secret that FBI headquarters was falling apart. Literally. Netting had been installed along Ninth Street to prevent passersby from being hit by falling concrete. The interior was worse. The agency needed a new building to reflect and support its critical mission in the modern world. And to better protect the building and its employees from terrorism.

Despite the elephant in the room, Whitney tried to relax during dinner. They would talk about it soon enough.

Afterward, they retired to the living room. Jade sat in one of the two chairs facing the sofa. Whitney lifted the bottle of whiskey. "Drink?"

Jade held up a hand. "No, thank you."

"Come on. Let your guard down for a night."

"All right." Jade hesitated. "Do you have any beer?"

Whitney smiled. "I'm sure we can come up with something."

She called Jade's request down to the kitchen, and selected a tulip-shaped glass from a cart and returned to the sofa. She poured the whiskey and waited.

There was a discreet knock on the door.

"Come in," she said.

One of the butlers entered with a cart. On top of it sat an ice bucket with twelve different brands of beer nestled within. Jade selected one. The butler offered her a glass, but she waved it away.

After he left, Whitney raised her glass. "Now, we can have a proper toast."

"That's a lot of beer for one person."

"If you drink too much, I have plenty of bedrooms in which you can stay. Twenty, plus or minus."

"I don't think that will be necessary."

Whitney curled her legs under her on the sofa. "I guess we should get this over with. What did you discover?"

"We don't know for certain what happened to your aunt. We do know that Landon—Caleb Hewitt—was in the Chicago area at the time of her death."

Whitney set her glass down, horrified.

"He was also in Clayton, Missouri at the time of the Congressman's accident."

"That can't be a coincidence."

"We don't think so either," Jade said, quietly.

The agent filled in the details. As she spoke, Whitney thought about her Aunt Mary. She didn't deserve what had happened to her. She was sweet, and one of the most genuine people Whitney had ever met.

She moved to a table by the window and opened the humidor. She cut the cap of a cigar and grabbed a wooden match from a section of the humidor. She glanced over her shoulder at Jade. "Would you like one?"

The agent shook her head.

Whitney returned to her seat on the sofa. "Don't tell anyone."

"Your secrets are safe with me."

Whitney caught the full weight of her words.

Secrets. Plural.

"Landon worked for me for years," Whitney said. "He volunteered for my first congressional campaign, and eventually became indispensable. I thought of him as more than a staffer."

"He worked for you before that."

"What do you mean?"

"He paged for you when he was in high school."

Whitney's mind swirled with the implications of this information. She tried to fit it in with what she knew, some of which the agent did not. She picked up her glass and swallowed a large portion of her whiskey. She grimaced at the burning sensation in her throat. After a while, she said, "I didn't know."

"Are you sure?" the agent pressed. "He was fixated on you for a long time. Was he in love with you, Madam President?"

Whitney puffed on her cigar.

Your secrets are safe with me.

Could she trust her? She was going to find out. She exhaled. "In the second quarter of my junior year, my parents sent me to live with my aunt. She was a widow and worked as a librarian at the public library. She was always reading. The love of reading was something that we shared. Once a week, she volunteered as a librarian in a convent's library near her house. It was a cold winter. Have you ever been to Chicago in the winter?"

Jade nodded.

"I kept a coat on pretty much all the time. Even indoors."

"You were pregnant."

It wasn't a question.

Whitney nodded. "My aunt brought me to live in the convent under an assumed name. I stayed there for three months until the baby was born. I gave it up for adoption." She moved to a table against the wall and retrieved the letter from her purse. She walked over to the agent and handed it to her.

Jade's mouth parted as she read. She looked at Whitney. "Landon Phillips—I mean, Caleb Hewitt—was your biological son?"

"So he claimed. I prefer to call him Landon. Otherwise, I wouldn't be able to deal with this."

The agent drained the rest of her beer. She stared out the window at the Washington Monument in the distance. Almost to herself, she said, "Oedipus."

"What was that?"

"His alias—or handle—he used in a chat room we discovered. We thought he chose Oedipus to honor his adoptive mother, Maddy Hewitt." Jade's long arms reached for another beer in the bucket. She twisted off the cap and took a long swallow, wiping her lips with the back of her hand before turning to Whitney. "But we were wrong. He chose it because of you."

CHAPTER NINETY-TWO

WASHINGTON, DC

"LOOK WHO'S BACK," Dante said.

Christian entered the conference room at the Bureau and settled in the chair next to hers. At Jade's strong suggestion, he had taken a few days off.

Jade scanned the faces of her team around the table. On the wall, she had posted a photo of each of the victims in life and in death.

"Let's get started."

She pointed to the photos. "Zach Rawlins, Nicholas Campbell, Joshua Stewart, and Andrew Huffman. Four boys who will never get married, raise children, embark on a career, coach youth sports, or make their mark on the world.

She waved her hand behind her. "All students and base-ball teammates at William Randolph Secondary School. All believed to have bullied Tyler Thompson, who died from blunt-force trauma."

From Micah, "Do you think there are other bullies?"

"Yes."

"How are we going to protect these kids anyway?" asked Christian. "There are still nineteen kids left on that team."

"Good thing they didn't play football," Dante cracked.

No one laughed.

"Get it? A football team has—"

"That's not funny, man," Micah said.

Dante allowed his chair to drop from its forty-five-degree angle without softening its impact. "Just trying to lighten it up in here . . . man."

Pat tore her eyes away from her computer to look at Jade, a historic event. "What positions did they play?"

"Good question," Jade said, rummaging through her files. She found the one she was looking for and glanced at a document inside. "Rawlins, third base; Campbell, second; Stewart, first; and Huffman was the catcher."

Her team digested this information for a moment.

Christian tapped his pen on his notebook. "What do we have left? Pitcher? Shortstop?"

"Outfield," Dante said.

"It seems as if the killer is starting with the infield and working his way out," Max murmured.

"The infield players will be our priority," Jade said. "Chaney-Frost is the shortstop. We need the names of the players for the other positions. Their backups, too." She dropped the file.

"On it," Pat said.

From Christian: "Any leads in Tyler's death?"

Jade shook her head. "I talked to Chutimant this morning. Nothing. Let's move on." She nodded at Pat. "We've mapped out the murders."

Pat tapped several keys on her keyboard. On the screen

behind Jade, a map of Northern Virginia materialized with four dots glowing where each murder had taken place.

Jade pointed at each dot. "Rawlins was found outside his home in Fairfax. Campbell in Gravelly Point near National Airport."

"Reagan National Airport," corrected Dante.

"Stewart was also found in Fairfax a block away from his home. Huffman in Arlington behind a 7-Eleven."

Dante eyed Jade. "Don't you live in Arlington?"

Before she could answer, Christian said, "Campbell was the only one killed elsewhere and moved. I wonder why."

"My grandmother was an awesome cook," Dante said.

"Who cares?" Christian said.

"She told me that in the kitchen you 'waste nothing.'"

"What does that have to do with the price of eggs in China?" asked Christian.

Dante looked at him as if he were dense. "Because cooking is like an investigation. Don't waste information. You don't know where it may lead. In this case, the murders took place in different counties, which means more than one jurisdiction. Increasing the likelihood that we would be called in. I'm trying to tell you. Maybe, it has something to do with Jade."

"Not bad," said Max, nodding.

"Any results from the lab, yet, on the Thompson house?" asked Christian.

"Still waiting," Jade said. Besides the blood, the search warrant hadn't yielded anything else. "Zach, Nicholas, and Andrew were all bludgeoned by a blunt instrument predominately to the face, their penises severed." She turned to Max. "All of them had prior scratches and bruises on their bodies. Thoughts?"

"A lot going on here. Rage, revenge, envy. The severing of

the penises is beyond extreme. Reminiscent of the Bobbitt case, but obviously the motive is different."

"Bobbitt case?" asked Micah.

When no one spoke up, Dante said, "Back in the Nineties, Lorena Bobbitt whacked off her husband's penis."

"After years of alleged domestic abuse," Pat added.

"The dude was asleep," Dante continued. "She took his member and threw it out her car window."

Micah looked uncomfortable. "What happened? Did the guy bleed out?"

"No, someone found it, and the doctors put Humpty Dumpty back together again."

Max tried to steer them back on track. "The penis removal could be a result of the bullying. Perhaps Tyler Thompson was sexually abused. This killer may be a vigilante administering his own form of justice. A vigilante with a God complex. Or it could have something to do with the baseball team itself. Was there a lot of dissension on the team?"

"Not that I'm aware of," Jade said. "The coach and the principal denied that there was." She recalled the first interview at the school, and the boy—Joshua Stewart—who had reacted when she asked about fights. "Although, I'm not sure."

Max pushed his glasses up farther on his nose. "It may have nothing to do with bullying or baseball."

"Then, there's Joshua—" Jade said.

"Roadkill," Dante said.

Micah scowled. "You're a wanker."

"A what?"

"The killer probably thought running him over was faster," Max said, ignoring the younger agents, "less risky than getting out of the car, killing him, disposing of the body—"

"And fleeing the scene without being seen," Jade finished for him.

He nodded. "That is, if it's the same killer."

"There's not a lot of evidence," Dante said. "Maybe it's someone who knows criminal procedure. Someone in law enforcement."

He looked at Christian.

Jade's cell phone buzzed. She swiped it off the table. "Harrington."

"Hi," a boy's voice said.

Jade held up her hand for silence. She placed the phone back on the table and pressed Speaker. "Who's this?"

"William. Chaney-Frost."

"What do you have for me, William?"

"Have you found anything yet? Any evidence?"

"Why do you ask?"

"There's something I haven't told you."

"What?"

"Someone else was bullying T. Tyler. No one's saying anything, 'cause no one likes him. They're probably hoping he gets whacked."

"What's his name?"

"Carter. Sam Carter. He's the pitcher on the team."

She wrote the name down. "Got it. Anything else?"

"Nah, that's it . . . and, uh, Agent Harrington?"

"Yes?"

"Sorry for being crude the other day. About T's mom. I'm not even like that. Not sure why I said it. Just upset, I guess. About what's going on. It's crazy that I'm never going to see my teammates again. My friends."

He sounded teary. Her job wasn't to comfort him. "Thanks

for bringing this information to my attention. If you think of something else, call me."

"I will, Agent Harrington."

She pressed End.

"What did he say about Jenny Thompson?" Dante said.

She glanced at Christian. "Not now."

"Can we trust him?" asked Micah.

"I don't," Jade said. "He's a person of interest. I'm just not sure for what, yet. He's playing with us. With me." She thought for a moment. "Maybe we should shadow him again. And Carter."

"A waste of time," Dante said.

"Matt has motive," Christian agreed, quietly. "A huge motive."

"He's not the only one," Dante said.

Christian rose. "I'm sick of your insinuations."

Dante stood as well and stepped toward him. "Who's insinuating?"

The two men were the same height, but Christian had at least seventy-five pounds on him.

Micah grabbed Dante's arm. Dante shrugged him off.

"I don't think you should be here," Dante said. "You should be on leave until we know your involvement with this case."

"I'm trying to solve this case. That's my involvement. Why don't you butt out?"

Dante turned on her. "He's too close to this."

"And you're too close to me," Christian said. "Back off. It's not your call."

"It's mine," Jade said. The room felt smaller with the four of them standing. Pat and Max remained seated. Observing.

Anger surged through her. "These children are dead. And I

have a team of grown men acting like children. It pisses me off. We don't have time for this."

She looked at the three men. "This is a team. I don't care if we like each other. But we're going to work together. Understood?"

"But he shouldn't be on this case," Dante said. "If he wasn't Robin to your Batman, you would've already reassigned him."

Christian's eyes narrowed. He shook his head at Jade. "This isn't right."

Her partner—her rock—opened the door and left the room.

The door clicked softly behind him.

After a moment, a quiet, British voice, said, "Some team."

CHAPTER NINETY-THREE

ARLINGTON, VIRGINIA

AFTER THE MEETING, Jade returned to her office, her adrenaline dissipated after the confrontation in the conference room. Her stomach growled. That was the fifth time in the last hour. She glanced at her watch. 8:30 p.m.

She needed to find something to eat.

She drove across the Memorial Bridge into Virginia. Instead of taking 395 South toward home, she headed south on GW Parkway. Shortly thereafter, she pulled in to the lot of a nearby park and got out. It was vacant.

The park was closed. Officially, she was trespassing. She sat on a stone bench, not too far away from where the second victim, Nicholas Campbell, had been found. She gazed up at the sky and waited. She didn't have to wait long.

A passenger jet roared overhead as it began its descent into National. As planes continued to land, she thought about how she would bring her team together.

She thought about Matt Thompson. Even if these boys bullied his son, was he capable of killing kids? What was he hoping to accomplish? These murders would not provide closure for him.

It seemed as if there had always been bullies—since the beginning of mankind—and there always would be. What could she, Jade Harrington, one FBI agent, do about it? Probably, not much.

She had not heard from Kyle since the story broke. Or Blake.

She thought about her conversation with the president. Did Caleb Hewitt clear her path to the presidency by methodically eliminating anyone who could say or do something damaging to her presidential aspirations? Or was he upset that Churchill allowed Fairchild to give her baby—him—up for adoption?

She had a lot of questions. But no answers.

Although watching the planes land was fascinating, she could no longer ignore the pains in her stomach. She headed back to her car.

Her phone buzzed in her pocket. A text from Pat.

I may have something. Talk to you tomorrow.

CHAPTER NINETY-FOUR

ARLINGTON, VIRGINIA

AT HOME THAT night, surrounded by folders, Jade reviewed rows upon rows of electronic funds transfers on her laptop. Prince's "Baby, I'm a Star" played at a low volume on her turntable.

A couple hours later, bleary-eyed, she set down her third cup of coffee. She checked the numbers again to be sure. All the cyberthefts, after flowing through many accounts in different countries, seemed to all end up in the same bank. In the same account. In the Cayman Islands. She wrote down her findings in an email and sent the records to Pat to find out who owned the account.

Jade's phone rang. A 206 number displayed on the caller ID. It wasn't Detective McClaine. And it wasn't Kyle.

"Agent Harrington, this is Iyanna Adey from KIRO 7. In Seattle."

"How did you get this number?"

"I'm calling for an update on the cybertheft case. I haven't heard anything lately."

"No comment at this time."

"That's a shame. Agent Lawson was so kind as to provide information on the Madison Ventures, AMB International, and other thefts. I thought you would be just as helpful. I promise not to attribute anything to you. Perhaps we can meet next time you're in Seattle."

She sat up. "Ethan Lawson?"

"He helped me out with the TSK case last year as well, and now he's always unavailable."

Jade tested pieces in different spaces of the mental puzzle. She tried to remember the chronology of the TSK case. She had suspected other people of leaking details of the investigation to the media. Ethan wasn't one of them.

The reporter was still talking. "I think he's avoiding me. Are you sure you don't have any information to share? Even off the record?"

CHAPTER NINETY-FIVE

WASHINGTON, DC

"DO YOU HAVE time now?"

Jade looked up from the computer in her office. She tore her eyes away from the same records she had worked on last night, the call from the Seattle reporter, Iyanna Adey, not far from her mind.

She followed Pat to her cubicle. Pat started typing on her keyboard before she sat down. Sometimes it was hard to tell where Pat's fingers ended and the keyboard began.

"I've been working with CART"—the FBI's Computer Analysis Response Team—"on the records you sent over last night." She pointed to the screen. "Most, but not all, of the victims share conservative political leanings."

Jade pondered this. "Most, but not all."

Pat clicked to different websites as she talked. "They donated to conservative Super PACs, candidates, foundations, organizations. We're still waiting on the registration papers for the bank account in the Cayman Islands."

Jade started to return to her office. "Okay, thanks."

Pat didn't bother to turn around. "That's not all." She brought up another screen. "The money didn't stay in the Cayman Islands. We traced it to its destination. The money ended up in one account. In Seattle."

Jade pulled up a chair. "Where?"

"The Puget Sound Bank. The account is registered to a nonprofit organization called The Equality One Foundation."

Pat brought up the foundation's home page, and then navigated to the About Us page. She clicked on the Board of Directors and pointed at the screen.

Jade leaned in and scanned the list of twelve names. Noah Blakeley was the chairman. David Smith, the CFO cybertheft victim, and Evan Stevens, the blogger, were on the board as well. The rest of the names she did not know, until she reached the bottom.

Her breath caught.

The last name on the list was Kyle Madison.

CHAPTER NINETY-SIX

THE WHITE HOUSE, WASHINGTON, DC

THE VICE PRESIDENT slowed when he saw Sasha sitting in a chair across from Whitney's desk in the Oval Office.

"I thought we were meeting alone."

"Xavi, have a seat," Whitney said, not bothering to rise. "Welcome back. How was China? Fruitful, I hope?"

He sat in the chair next to Sasha and crossed his legs. "Of course."

"And Lei Min?"

Min was the president of the People's Republic of China.

"He sends his regards. I laid the groundwork for a new trade deal and a bilateral agreement forbidding government-sanctioned cyberespionage. He understood our position."

Our. "Tell me about it."

"I'll draft up a memo for your review."

He didn't share any specifics. He never did. Whitney leaned

back in her chair. "I've been sitting here thinking about where I've come from."

Her handsome vice president's smile did not quite reach his eyes. "You have time for that?"

"Sometimes, I like to think about where I've been, to know where I'm going."

Xavi nodded, a skeptical look on his face. "I like to look forward, not backward."

"I'm sure you do," Whitney said. "Let me tell you what I've been thinking about. I had a talk with Eric Hampton."

"Oh?"

"He told me about your willingness to work across the aisle on comprehensive illegal-immigration reform."

Humbled, he said, "I believe we can find common ground. Hispanics want reform just like everyone else. It's a matter of compromising. Like you're always saying."

"When is the last time you spoke to Eric, by the way?"

He examined his cuticles. "I can't recall."

Whitney leaned forward, her eyes hardening. "Compromise. Such as not allowing a pathway to legalization for undocumented immigrants? Agreeing with Sampson on building the wall? Placing a moratorium on all non-Christian immigration? You told him that Americans need to defend their country from Hispanics taking over. All those babies, you know. That we don't need any more 'Mexican'ts.' Shall I go on?"

Xavi's face stilled. "Is that why you sent me to China?"

"Our relationship with China is important. I needed you there."

"Bullshit."

Whitney stood and went to the window. She glanced out at the Rose Garden: the grandiflora, tea roses, white shrub roses, and seasonal flowers. She could stare at the beautiful colors all day, but only stayed in that position for a moment. She did not want her back to Xavi for too long.

She turned. "Washington is such an interesting place to work. Politics makes strange bedfellows. Eric and I are bedfellows. For now."

He dropped the respectful pretense. "What do you want?"

"When I added you to the ticket, I did so because of your compelling story. Both of your parents had escaped from the Castro regime by boat, traveling across treacherous waters. The boat sunk a few hundred yards off the coast of Key West, Florida. Your parents swam the rest of the way, eventually migrating to Miami. Your father found a job in construction. Your mother became a housekeeper. They built a life for you and your four brothers and sisters. Born in America, and therefore an American citizen, you were the first person in your family to graduate from high school, college, and graduate school. You became a self-made man in your own right. The epitome of the American Dream. Your story was inspirational. To millions of Hispanic-Americans and Americans in general. To me."

His eyes blazed with an undisguised hatred he'd never revealed before. He remained silent.

Whitney returned to her seat, and rested both of her arms on the desk, her hands clasped. "Under your 'compromise,' you would have been deported." She stared at Xavi so that there was no misunderstanding her intent. "I won't tell anyone that you want to prevent other immigrant families from attaining the success yours has had. That you have had. Or your true feelings about Mexicans. In return, you will cease going behind my back to sabotage my legislative agenda. You will stop pushing your own. And, finally, you will support this legislation fully and unequivocally and with a smile on your face."

"And if I don't?"

"I will make your life so uncomfortable that you will resign the vice presidency and return to your insignificant life in disgrace."

"My children look up to me. I am a hero to my community and Hispanics everywhere. You captured the Hispanic vote because of me. You wouldn't do that."

She straightened. "Watch me."

Xavi stared at her.

Sasha stood, a smirk on her face. "I'll show you out, Mr. Vice President."

CHAPTER NINETY-SEVEN

ARLINGTON, VIRGINIA

IN HER BEDROOM a few days later, Jade packed for her evening flight to Seattle. She'd asked Christian to accompany her. He would be by soon to pick her up.

She stuffed the rest of her clothes into the open carry-on bag on her queen-size mission bed and allowed herself to think about Kyle Madison.

The two of them came from different worlds: Kyle went sailing and skiing, attended symphonies and the opera, was fluent in several languages, CEO of her own firm, owned a professional sports team and a second home in Palm Springs. Jade played pickup basketball, practiced Tae Kwon Do, listened to Seventies and Eighties music, and preferred a night out drinking beers with her fellow agents to going to a fancy gathering. The only property she owned was this small townhouse and her car. And even then, the bank still technically owned both of those.

She zipped up the bag and grabbed her phone. "Hey, you. I need a favor."

"And good evening to you, too," Zoe said. "I'm fine, by the way."

"I'm going to Seattle for a few days. Can you take care of Card?"

"Following up on a lead?"

"Something like that."

"Are you going to see your girlfriend?"

Jade snapped. "She's not my girlfriend."

Zoe paused. "The lady doth protest too much, methinks."

"Can you take care of Card or not?"

In her best *Downton Abbey* voice, Zoe said, "As you wish, my lady."

"Shut up."

Jade clicked off the phone, and allowed herself a small smile.

CHAPTER NINETY-EIGHT

SEATTLE, WASHINGTON

HE LOVED THIS time of the morning.

North of downtown, Green Lake was surrounded by a three-mile path. The air, crisp and cool at six a.m., caressed his face as he biked along the outer path for cyclists and runners. The inner lane was designated for walkers. The early hour allowed him to enjoy the relative quiet, and the space to maneuver.

He felt good.

He had told his father last night that he was retiring from the firm. He couldn't take another day working in a job for which he had no passion.

Besides, his nonprofit was keeping him busy.

His father had accepted his resignation, not even trying to hide his pleasure at the unexpected gift. He wasted no time appointing Noah's older brother, August, as president of the company, and hired an outsider to run the foundation. He never considered Noah for the foundation's executive director position. The position at one time Noah had coveted.

His father had never forgiven him for allowing the cybertheft to become public and bringing unwanted attention to the firm. He hadn't wanted the additional shame of firing his younger son. Now, he wouldn't need to.

It didn't matter now. Noah had been serving as the president of the Equality One Foundation, in addition to his role as chairman, and now would be able to do the job full time. He had been working out of his home, but recently found a suite of offices nearby. He planned to move the foundation's headquarters from New York to Seattle.

As he rounded a bend, he happened to notice the woman. *What is she doing here?*

The FBI agent, Jade Harrington, stepped out from behind a copse of trees ten yards off the path, her badge held high in one hand. A gun was lowered to the ground in the other.

He almost lost control of his bike.

"Noah Blakeley, you're under arrest."

It took him a moment to stop the bike and another to realize she was talking to him. *Arrest?*

He tried to unclip his cycling shoes from the pedals, but it just wasn't happening. He braced himself as he hit the asphalt hard, still clipped in, the bicycle between his legs.

Someone laughed.

The agent approached. The heat rose in his face, as he gazed up at her. Not from exertion, but from embarrassment. He still couldn't clip out of the pedals.

Sweat started to trickle down his face, into his eyes. Other agents in blue FBI jackets came out from behind nearby trees. One guy, jacketless, wore a t-shirt and jeans. He looked like Kurt Cobain with a badge. Strange.

"Don't move," Agent Harrington said to him.

A big blond male agent moved next to her.

"Is that a joke?" Noah tried to appear dignified, despite the decidedly undignified position he was in. "What is this about?"

"Equality One."

"I don't understand."

"You're in violation of sections ten twenty-eight, ten twenty-nine, ten thirty, and thirteen forty-one of the US Code title eighteen."

He shook his head, hitting his temple on the bike path. "Ouch! Goddamnit! I still don't understand. What are all those numbers?"

"Your organization is a fraud. You've obtained funding illegally. Agent Merritt?"

The nonprofit? Could his dream of making the world a better place, including being his own man, be over already?

Noah allowed his head to hit the pavement again, not caring.

His life was over.

The blond man walked over and crouched next to him, handcuffing his arms behind him. "Before I read you your rights, you want some help getting out of those clips, buddy?"

CHAPTER NINETY-NINE

SEATTLE, WASHINGTON

JADE GOT TO the point. "Why did you steal the money?"

"Don't answer that," the attorney said. Noah's father had not hired him. Noah had had to retain one on his own.

"I didn't do what you're accusing me of."

"Then explain how these thefts were initiated from your computer."

"For the last time," he yelled. "I don't know!"

He seemed genuinely perplexed. Jade stood in the interrogation room of the Seattle FBI field office. She started to pace.

She needed to calm him down. She returned to her seat. "Okay. Let's start from the beginning. Tell me about Equality One."

He exhaled. "It's a nonprofit. Its purpose is to provide jobs and homes for the homeless, low- and middle-income families, and the long-term unemployed. We do a lot of good. A lot of good. I'm the president and chairman of the board."

"That must have pleased your father."

He stared at her, as if she were insane. "I failed PE in

school. I could never please my father. No. He didn't know. He wouldn't have cared." He gazed through the observation glass. "My father had other plans for me."

"Like what?"

Noah gave Jade a rueful smile and shook his head, his eyes kept fluttering to the one-way mirror. "I still don't know. Surely, he didn't think I was the best person to take over the firm when he died." He noticed Jade's expression. "My great-great-grandfather started the business. My father would have never entrusted it to me."

"What about your mother?"

Noah looked down at the table. "After I was born, I'm not sure she knew I existed."

This guy is sad. She wanted to tell him to man up. "How is it funded? Equality One."

"May I have some water?"

Jade nodded.

Detective McClaine went to the door. After a moment, he returned with the glass, setting it down in front of Blakeley.

Noah took a sip. "Mostly through donations. We receive large gifts from progressives and liberals across the country, but primarily New York, DC, San Francisco, and here in Seattle."

Jade listened to the sound of Christian's pen scratching on his notepad, as she thought of her next question. "Why are you the only signatory on Equality One's bank account?"

Noah dropped one hand under the table. She remembered Kyle telling her he liked to keep it in his pocket.

"Because I oversaw the operations of the organization."

He told her that David Smith raised funds and attended board meetings, but wasn't heavily involved.

As evenly as she could, Jade said, "Tell me about Kyle Madison's involvement."

"She's an officer and contributes money," he said. He smiled ruefully. "In fact, she was the one who told me about Equality One in the first place."

"And Evan Stevens's?"

He shrugged. "The same."

She glanced at McClaine. "Anything?"

He shook his head.

"Okay. That's it for now."

Agents came into the room to take Noah away.

"Give me a minute," she said to Christian and McClaine.

After they left, she stared at the table. It was an enormous relief that Noah hadn't implicated Kyle.

She didn't ask herself what she would have done if he had.

SEATTLE, WASHINGTON

"I'M GETTING READY to head out."

She looked up from her paperwork and smiled.

Detective Kurt McClaine entered the conference room Jade had commandeered as an office. Still wearing the same jeans and Bumbershoot Festival 2014 t-shirt from that morning, he sat across from her at the table.

"You need to move to Seattle. You could solve all my cases."

"Then what would you do?"

"Good point." He glanced at her paperwork. "You guys taking the red-eye?"

"Christian is." Jade hesitated. "I'm leaving tomorrow."

McClaine rapped his knuckles on the table. He came around and stood in front of her. "Have fun your last night in Seattle. I enjoyed working with you again, Agent Harrington. Until next time."

"How do you know there'll be a next time?"

"I'm a detective." He waved off her outstretched hand, and gave her a brief hug.

When he got to the door, he turned, his hand on the knob. He gave her a slight smile. "Give my best to Ms. Madison."

*

"I've never seen so many coffee shops in my life," Jade said.

"We do love our coffee in Seattle," Kyle said.

From their table next to the window, Jade glanced around the empty, independent café on Sixth Avenue.

"Tell me about Equality One."

"My mistake. I thought we were just having coffee."

"I don't like loose ends."

"Very well. As I told you before, I try to do what I can. Homelessness is pervasive here. The mission of Equality One is one in which I strongly believe."

"But not Noah. You don't seem to care for him much."

A slight move of her shoulders. "There was something about him." She shook her head. "And now he has used our organization to commit crimes."

"It's Raining Men" began to blare from the coffee shop's speakers. The lone barista pirouetted in cabaret fashion, eyes closed, as he sang the chorus of The Weather Girls' song at full volume into a long spoon to an imaginary audience.

"He actually has a good voice," Jade said.

"His dance moves aren't bad either."

They watched him in silence for a few minutes, the young man oblivious to them. A line of customers could have been waiting in front of him, and he wouldn't have known. Or cared. After the song, he lowered the music to a conversational level.

Kyle sipped her coffee, and then placed her cup on the table. "I can't get away from Eighties music when you're around."

"One of the reasons why I like Seattle."

Chin in hand, Kyle smiled. "I hope that's not the only reason."

Jade's cheeks warmed. She stared into her wide cup, the latte-art heart mocking her. She didn't trust herself enough to answer.

Her phone vibrated.

Saved by the buzz.

A text. From Blake.

In town. Can I see you tonight?

She texted him back. Out of town.

"Is everything all right?" Kyle asked.

Jade pocketed her phone. "Never better."

THE WHITE HOUSE, WASHINGTON, DC

IN THE EAST Room, Whitney listened as the prime minister of Thailand leaned toward her and told a joke in flawless English. She was enjoying herself. The prime minister and his wife had been in DC the last two days for a state visit, staying at the Blair House across the street. He was charismatic and funny; she was graceful and kind.

Attending the event were athletes, entertainers, diplomats, businessmen, and fellow politicians. After a four-course meal that showcased cuisine from different geographical regions of the United States, an up-and-coming band from Fairfax County, Virginia—which has a large Thai community—played a variety of Thai and American music. From her vantage point at the center of the raised table, Whitney enjoyed a decaf coffee as the prime minister rose to go dance with his wife.

She wished Grayson were here.

In this room, presidents such as Abraham Lincoln, Franklin

D. Roosevelt, and John F. Kennedy had lain in repose, children of presidents had been married, and significant legislation such as the Civil Rights Act of 1964 had been signed. But when Whitney moved in, she thought this room would be perfect for dancing. She'd replaced the carpet installed by her predecessor with hardwood floors. The walls were repainted a stone color, the gold floor-to-ceiling draperies replaced with light blue ones. A gigantic mirror hung over the fireplace next to a portrait of Martha Washington.

Whitney spotted Senator Eric Hampton dancing stiffly with his wife. She had read once that how a man danced is how he made love. If that were so, she could only assume watching him make love would be a painful experience. During the planning for this event, she'd told Sasha to make sure that he and Xavi were seated at tables on opposite sides of the room.

Sasha walked over from her table on the outer edges, and bent down to whisper in Whitney's ear. "The poll's in."

"And?"

"Fifty-six percent in favor."

Whitney smiled and did a fist pump under the table, her actions obscured by the table cloth. A nationwide poll on her income-equality legislation taken today showed the public now favored it by a slight majority, a huge improvement over its polling in the high teens earlier this spring. The mood on the Hill had shifted dramatically as well. Xavi had lived up to his end of the bargain, crisscrossing the country touting the legislation as if he had drafted it himself.

More power to him.

If that's what it took to get it passed, then so be it. With passage more likely, the violent protests had subsided. And the media had moved on to other things.

The band segued into "Wobble" by V.I.C.

Whitney clapped. "I love this song. Let's dance."

Sasha looked out on the dance floor, and shook her head firmly. "I'm not dancing with you. Besides, there's something else I need to tell you."

"It can wait. Come on, it'll be fun." Whitney pulled her down the few stairs to join the front of the line dance.

Whitney hadn't danced since the Inaugural balls, but the rust wore off quickly. Next to her, Sasha dropped it down and wobbled lower than anyone else.

After the song, Sasha waited for Whitney to settle in her seat, and leaned down to whisper in her ear. "Now, I really need to tell you something."

Whitney reached for her glass of water. "What now?"

"FOX News is reporting that the reason you lived with your aunt for a year is because you were an unwed pregnant teenager and had a baby. No wonder you and the First Gentleman live apart. He's mad about your having a baby out of wedlock."

Whitney set the glass on the table with a slight tremor in her hand.

"Everyone wants to know, Madam President."

"Know what?"

"The number-one trending hashtag on Twitter. *#WheresTheBaby.*"

WASHINGTON, DC

ON THE WAY to work, Jade had stopped by the 7-Eleven where Andrew Huffman's body had been found to purchase a big bag of peanut M&Ms. The store had reopened the afternoon after the murder. Life goes on. She slipped an M&M into her mouth and stuffed the bag in her center drawer.

Mid-morning, she looked up from the file she was reviewing at Christian's knock.

"Hey," he said, as he leaned against the door frame. Since returning to the team, Christian had been working to the point of exhaustion.

"Get some sleep."

"I can't. I keep thinking about Andrew Huffman. That could've been Mark."

She knew he didn't need comfort. He wanted to solve this case. "What's up?"

"I got a hit on the blood."

"Whose is it?"

"Nicholas Campbell."

It took a few seconds for the information to click into place. "The second victim?" Jade straightened in her chair. "What the—?"

He sat across from her. "Not just blood. Other bodily fluids were found on the sheets."

"Semen?"

Christian handed her a file. "Yes." He picked up a basketball paperweight on her desk. "And on the bedspread. On the carpet. The wall."

"On the wall?" She shook her head in disbelief or disgust. She wasn't sure which. Or both. "And they're sure it wasn't Tyler's?"

He nodded, averting his eyes.

She sat back. "You think he was raped."

He tossed the paperweight back and forth between his hands. "Or, maybe he was . . . gay."

She banged her palm on the table. "How did Fairfax miss this?"

Christian set the paperweight back on the desk. "I don't know. Chutimant seemed really sharp."

She leaned forward and moved the paperweight to its original position. "Let's have another talk with Matt."

*

"Was Tyler close friends with anyone on the team? Did he have a best friend? Or a special friend?"

Matt Thompson scowled. "Special friend? What does that mean? I don't think he had a lot of friends. But Jenny would know better. He didn't talk about his teammates. At least, to me."

He sat across from Christian and her in the same interrogation room at the FBI. Same lawyer.

Thompson didn't seem to know what had occurred in his son's bedroom. She thought about how to broach the subject now.

"What about his room?"

"What about it?"

"You mentioned the last time we spoke that Jenny spent hours on his gravesite. Does she ever sit in there? In his room?"

A vigorous shake of the head. "Neither of us can go in there."

She began carefully. "Mr. Thompson, did Tyler ever have someone come over? Spend the night?"

"No. Like I said, I don't think he had a lot of friends. Why? Why do you keep asking about this?"

"We found semen in your son's bedroom."

He blinked. Thompson rose, making his chair tip to the floor. The impact was loud in the quiet room. "Wh— what did you say?"

"Please sit down, Mr. Thompson."

"I don't understand what you're saying."

Jade gestured to the space where his chair had been. "Please."

He retrieved the chair and sat.

"We believe your son had sexual intercourse in his room."

"And you're trying to find out—"

"The semen belonged to Nicholas Campbell."

He started to rise again, but his attorney placed a hand on Thompson's forearm, restraining him. "None of this is making sense. And what? Are you thinking he was gay?"

"Possibly," she said. More quietly, "Or raped."

Matt Thompson's eyes darted around the room with nowhere to land. She gave him a moment to process what he'd just heard. If he already knew this information about Tyler, he deserved an Academy award.

Christian looked up from his notebook, his eyes anguished. "Did you kill those kids, Matt?"

Thompson stared back at him, unflinching. "No, I did not." His eyes pleaded. "You know me, man."

"Mr. Thompson." Jade waited for him to look at her. "Would you be willing to take a polygraph test to prove it?"

WASHINGTON, DC

JADE, PAT, CHRISTIAN, Max, Dante, and Micah were back in the same conference room at the Bureau discussing a surveillance plan for William Chaney-Frost and Sam Carter.

They never had celebrated the resolution of the cybertheft case. There hadn't been time.

Max pushed up his glasses. "Are you more concerned that William will get killed or that he's the killer?"

Jade paused. "Either we're going to protect him or we're going to arrest him."

"Or both." Pat typed on her computer. "He doesn't seem too concerned about getting whacked himself."

"I still say this is a waste of time," Dante said.

"You're welcome to leave," Jade said.

Dante remained in his seat.

She rested her forearms on the table. "I believe this is what we need to do to catch this killer. Does anyone have a better idea?"

She looked at each of them in turn.

No one said anything.

"That's what I thought," she said. "Crickets."

"I think we should shadow Carter," Christian said.

"And William," said Micah.

The team spent the rest of the afternoon planning the Carter-Chaney operation.

At one point, Christian threw his pen onto his notebook. "Dante might be right for once. This could be a waste of time."

"I'll take that as a compliment," Dante said.

"I'd rather be safe than sorry," Jade said. "Especially with kids' lives at stake."

Christian shook his head. "You're right. But how long can we protect these kids, though?"

"As long as it takes."

"Or until Finance tells us to stop," Pat said, typing.

Max, always soft-spoken, said, "This vigilante will not stop until he has accomplished his mission." The other agents quieted and turned to him. "If there are any other bullies out there that victimized the Thompson boy, their lives are in danger."

"Then, we can't stop until we've accomplished *our* mission," Jade said. "Dante, you and Micah shadow William."

Dante stood and looked at Micah. "Let's go."

Micah remained seated. "I want to stay here with Jade."

Dante laughed. "What? You have a thing for the boss?"

"Shut up, Dante," Jade said.

"I just want to learn from the best," Micah said.

Dante stopped smiling, his expression almost hurt.

Micah was right. He was a junior agent assigned to her. She had an obligation to teach him all she could. She also thought it would be good for Christian and Dante to work together. She looked at Christian. "Go with Dante."

Christian's eyes questioned hers, as he pushed back from the table. "Sure."

Dante glanced at Micah as he followed Christian to the door, humming the chorus to "When a Man Loves a Woman."

FAIRFAX, VIRGINIA

JADE DRUMMED HER fingers on top of the door near the driver's side-view mirror. Her open window let in the mild night air, the temperature breaking after another scorching summer day. "How long does an AAU basketball practice take?"

Micah glanced over at her. "I would think you should know."

"The time seemed to go faster when I played."

"Do you miss it?"

Jade shrugged. "Sometimes."

"What do you do to fill that void?"

Those eyes. "I work."

He got the hint. He scrunched down in his seat. "Thompson passed. What now?"

The results from Thompson's polygraph had come through that morning. Unless he was a gifted actor or found a way to cheat the test, Matt Thompson was innocent of the murders of Zach Rawlins, Nicholas Campbell, Joshua Stewart, and Andrew Huffman.

"Back to square one."

They returned their gaze to the building just as a bunch of tall boys walked out of the gym.

"I guess practice is over," Micah said. "Why didn't you want to shadow William?"

Jade wasn't sure herself. "Wanted to check this kid out myself."

One of the kids headed toward a used Volvo. He waved goodbye to his teammates, glanced around the parking lot, and then opened his car door. The boy was handsome. With a skin tone the color of sand, he could pass for Caucasian at this time of night and at this distance.

They were parked several rows away from the Volvo.

"That was odd," Micah said. "What was he looking for?"

The Volvo entered the line of cars to exit the parking lot. She put her car in reverse, and joined the line as well, several cars behind the Volvo.

From the lot, they followed Sam Carter at a discreet distance. The kid drove perfectly, using his turn signal when appropriate, stopping at every stop sign without rolling, demonstrating all the Virginia DMV rules to perfection. His driver's ed teacher would be proud.

He parked on the street in front of his parents' house. Jade parked two blocks away. The tall, lanky kid sauntered up the driveway and disappeared into the house.

Two hours later, he hadn't reappeared.

THE WHITE HOUSE, WASHINGTON, DC

SEAN BUZZED HER. "Madam President, someone is here to see you."

"Someone, Sean? Really!"

He had already hung up.

Whitney was surprised. Sean's professionalism was normally impeccable. She replaced the handset a little harder than necessary.

Before the interruption, she had been gloating. Privately. Earlier that day, she had invited a reticent Senator Eric Hampton to the Briefing Room as a sponsor of the New New Deal Coalition legislation. He wouldn't be able to resist a photo op with her. Or, more accurately, a photo op televised to a nationwide audience.

He hadn't disappointed her. He accepted.

One of the doors to the Oval Office opened. She started to

rise, still not understanding—and disturbed—that Sean hadn't announced her guest according to protocol.

Wearing a gray business suit, white shirt with a spread collar, black silk tie, and carrying a matching gray fedora hat, her husband walked in with one arm behind his back.

"Grayson?" she asked, shocked.

She came around her desk and met him halfway. He whipped his arm in front of him. Flowers. Lilies. Her favorite.

She accepted the bouquet, breathing in the sweet, heavy aroma. "What is this? Why didn't you tell me you were coming? It's not on the schedule."

"Schedule, schmedule. We've been living according to schedules for too long, my darling. Surprise!"

He hugged her. She breathed in his familiar scent.

"I'm going to kill Sean." She pulled away slightly. "You're smiling, so the kids must be okay. Why are you here?"

"To see you. Can't I surprise my wife?"

"I have never known you to do anything without a reason. How long will you be visiting?"

"It's not a visit." He sat, crossed his legs, and draped both arms over the top of the sofa. "I'm here to stay."

"Stay?"

"I've heard about the rumors. About the baby. And your aunt."

Whitney's heart dropped. She was not ready to have this conversation. "I've been meaning—"

"I turned over the reins of Fairchild Industries to my younger brother for the duration of your presidency. Whether that's four years or eight. I realized that my family needs me. My immediate family. That you need me. You're more important to me than the business."

Whitney was still trying to comprehend this turn of events. "Are you sick?"

He laughed. "No. I'm in perfect health."

"But what are you going to *do*?"

"What the First Ladies did before me. Get involved in causes. Maybe take up golf."

"Golf?"

She was conflicted. The joy of him living with her was off-set by the fact that they hadn't lived together for years, not since Whitney left Missouri to join the United States Congress.

She was used to living alone.

Sean entered carrying a vase, two glasses, and a bottle. "Trade."

He handed her the Taittinger and the glasses and took the flowers from her. He arranged them in the vase on an end table.

When he finished, he said, "I've cleared your schedule for the next hour."

He gave her a sly smile and left.

Grayson reached for the bottle.

"Wait," she said.

She sat next to him, took his hand, and stared into his eyes. "I need to tell you something."

He searched her face. "Aren't you happy?"

"I am," she said. "I'm glad you'll be here. In fact, I'll love it. To share this"—she motioned with her hand to take in the room, the Oval Office, her presidency—"with you. It's not about that. It's about Landon."

"Landon?"

"Open the champagne. This may take a while."

*

Grayson spooned ice cream into her mouth. "You need to tell the kids at some point."

"I know."

Whitney tasted his strawberry ice cream, for once not caring about her weight or that she was eating after eight p.m. Food consumed after eight inevitably stuck to her hips forever.

It was now after nine.

She sat on a stool at a stainless-steel table in the kitchen on the lower level of the White House. She had dismissed the remaining kitchen staff. She didn't come down here often, the eeriness unsettling in such a large empty space late at night.

Grayson sat on a counter, his ankles crossed. He had changed into jeans and a t-shirt. His sandals lay stacked on the floor beneath him, where he had kicked them off earlier.

He finished the rest of the ice cream, jumped off the counter, and placed his bowl in the massive industrial sink.

Sitting on a stool beside her, he gently took the spoon from her hand. He scooped up the last of her mint chocolate chip ice cream and slipped it between her lips.

She swallowed. "I can't remember the last time you fed me. Are you sure you're not sick? Are you really Grayson Fairchild? What's your middle name?"

"Spencer."

An old joke between them.

He grabbed her chin and gazed into her eyes. His hands, soft. Gentle. Strong.

"Don't worry," he said. "Our children love you. They'll accept this. None of this is your fault."

"I still feel responsible."

"Because that's who you are. Does Kelly know that he's the father?"

She shook her head.

He came closer and licked just to the left of her lips. "Yum. That's good."

Whitney was shocked at Grayson's uncharacteristic displays of intimacy.

Grayson placed the spoon back in the bowl, giving her a mischievous smile. "And, no, I'm not having an affair. I just couldn't stand being away from you for another minute. I think you're finished with your ice cream. Let's go to bed. I want to show you how much I missed you."

As he leaned down to kiss her, she heard footsteps at the kitchen's entrance.

"Mom, I'm home!" yelled her daughter. She stopped short when she saw them. "Save room for Jesus, you two!"

Whitney and Grayson laughed. She shrugged at him with regret, and ran to kiss her baby.

FAIRFAX, VIRGINIA

"I THINK I like soccer better. Baseball is so boring."

"I sort of miss Zach."

"And soccer players have great legs. Did you see—? Oh, there's my mom! I'll see you tomorrow!"

Grace ran to the car and jumped into the passenger seat.

Her mom leaned forward. "You need a ride?"

Kaylee knew she was just being nice. Taking her home would have been out of their way.

"That's okay, Mrs. Angleton. My mom will be here soon."

"I hate leaving you here alone."

"It's still light out. I'll be okay."

As the car pulled away, Grace quick-waved at Kaylee through the open window, and then went back to snapchatting on her smartphone.

Kaylee plopped down on the curb in front of the school's main entrance and shrugged off her backpack. She had a driver's license, but she was in the doghouse because of her grades last semester. The only reason her mom had allowed her to attend summer cheer camp was so Kaylee could try out next month for fall sports. Her mom, not used to picking her up anymore, was always late.

She wasn't kidding about Zach. Even though she had played hard to get—and he never "got"—she had liked him. And enjoyed their game of cat-and-mouse. Who knew? They might have become a couple. High school sweethearts. Maybe even married.

A car she recognized stopped in front of her. The window slid down. "Do you need a ride home?"

"My mom will be here soon."

"Hop in. I'll take you."

"You sure?"

"It's on my way."

This would save her mom a trip. She could text her from the car. "Okay."

She hopped in the front seat, dropping her backpack on the floor between her legs.

Kaylee, hands poised on her phone ready to text, said, "Thanks—"

The driver slapped metal handcuffs onto her wrists. Their grinding clicks a finality. The steel cold. Kaylee's phone was ripped out of her hands and thrown out the window.

"You're not going to need that."

Before Kaylee understood what was happening, a soft cloth covered her mouth. A sweet unfamiliar smell tingled her nose.

The window closed.

And then nothing.

PART III

THE WHITE HOUSE, WASHINGTON, DC

SHE LOOKED AT the phone display. Chandler.

"Mom!"

In the gym, she signaled the private yoga instructor to take a break.

Whitney was relieved. She had told Emma about Landon this past weekend during her visit. Emma was shocked, understandably, but hugged her and told Whitney she loved her. Afterward, Whitney had called Chandler. His reaction was different. He was distant, as if he thought it was her fault she had been raped and impregnated.

She had also talked to him about the use of the phrase, "those people." He had said he had been caught up in the excitement of the club. He had quit soon thereafter. She was glad.

Now, he sounded happy again, like the son she knew. She sat cross-legged on the mat.

"Are you at school?" she said into the phone.

"I'm on the downslide, Mom. One more week of summer school, then finals, and then I'm out of here."

"Your dad can't wait for you to join the firm. Are you taking some time off first? Because once you start working, you won't stop for a long time."

Her son was silent for a moment. "That's why I'm calling, Mom. So you'll hear it from me."

"Hear what from you?"

"I changed my mind. About working for Fairchild after I graduate."

"Oh? What did your father say?"

"I wanted to tell you first."

"He'll be disappointed, but I'm sure he'll be okay with your decision. You should tell him."

"It's not that . . . "

"He had to realize that you wouldn't necessarily follow in his footsteps. Are you joining another firm?"

"I decided to do something else. Go in a different direction."

Whitney couldn't suppress the sense of foreboding. She worried about his decision-making abilities. He made judgments based on the moment, instead of what was best for the long term. If she voiced disapproval or disagreed with his early career choices, however, she may lose him forever. She would give him her full support, no matter what. She smiled so that he could hear it in her voice.

"What did you decide? Who will be the lucky employer? Or will you take a year off to travel? Volunteer?"

"I decided to enter politics. I'm coming to Washington."

"Politics?" Except for dabbling with the group Emma had told her about, Chandler's interest in politics had been nonexistent, even though his mother had been a politician for most of his life.

She wasn't sure she wanted a political life for her children.

"I got a job as a legislative assistant," he said, hesitating. "I'm joining the staff of Senator Paul Sampson."

At first, she thought she'd misheard. She was silent for a few moments. She couldn't forbid him from working for Sampson.

Distracted, she said, "That's wonderful, son. I'll see you at graduation." She hung up without thinking.

She resumed the downward-facing dog pose, waiting for the instructor to return.

Instead of relaxing her mind, her thoughts wandered. Why did she beam with pride when Emma stood for what she believed in, but couldn't conjure up the same feelings for her son? Because his political views were different from hers? Was he getting back at her for some perceived slight?

Or was she upset because the media was going to have a field day over the career choice of the president's son?

FAIRFAX, VIRGINIA

"THIS PERP IS sick," Christian said, his voice muffled by a handkerchief.

Jade, Dante, and Micah stood next to him, staring down at the body hidden under a fallen tree. Partially decomposed, the body had been discovered in the middle of Van Dyck Park. Kaylee Taylor had been missing for three days. She had been found by a dog with the Fairfax County canine unit. The temperature for those days had been over ninety degrees, the odor emanating from the corpse almost unbearable.

Jade's eyes watered from the smell. "What else do we know?"

Dante's eyes were watering, too. "That she smells."

Micah's eyes flashed above the protective mask he wore. "Your use of humor to compensate for your inadequacies is getting old."

"What? Are you vying for Max's job now?"

"Cut it out," Jade said.

"They found her phone in front of the school," Christian said. "Forensics is examining it now."

She pointed. "Check out the hands. Max'll have his work cut out for him with this one."

Dante laughed, but stopped when he realized she wasn't joking.

Like the other victims, all the damage had been inflicted on the left side of the girl's head. Her wounds appeared worse, if that were possible. Unlike the boys, however, Kaylee's genitals were intact. But her fingers were gone.

"Give me a minute," she said to them.

Jade crouched next to the body. The right side was free of bruises and scratches. She glanced briefly at the crime-scene techs ten yards away, waiting to finish their work.

"Speak to me, Kaylee," she said, her voice low. "Who did this to you?"

She stared at the young girl's once-pretty face. A face that would never wrinkle. Jade's eyes trailed down the decomposed body to the damaged hands. The missing fingers.

She stood. To Christian, she said, "I need to see her phone."

*

The data from Kaylee's phone was in her email inbox when she arrived at the office. She spent most of the day viewing what felt like millions of texts and photographs. A lot of pictures of Kaylee and Grace. Other cheerleaders. Friends. And, of course, boys. Lots of boys. But nothing helpful.

Jade started going through the saved Snapchats. Again, teenage stuff. Kaylee and Grace. Grace and Kaylee. She swiped through them quickly. Something caught her eye. She swiped in the other direction.

And stopped.

The school loomed in the background behind the two girls.

Someone else was in the picture. Behind them. They may have not known he was there.

His face was partially cut off.

Jade smiled. "Thanks, Kaylee."

THE WHITE HOUSE, WASHINGTON, DC

WHITNEY AND GRAYSON had fallen into a daily routine. Every morning, they ate breakfast and read the newspapers before she headed down to the Oval Office. Living together every day had been an adjustment for them both, but they were getting used to it. He had even found a cause to lead: overseeing a major initiative to provide job and business training to the long-term unemployed.

He slipped a forkful of eggs into his mouth. "How are you feeling?"

"Now that my son is a Republican?"

"Yes."

"I keep asking myself, 'Where did we go wrong?'"

They shared a laugh.

"He's still young," Grayson said. "He may grow out of it." He picked up the *Washington Post* from the table. "How's Emma?"

"She says her activist days are over. For now."

"She seems more mature."

"Being arrested can do that to you."

He peered at her over the paper. He hesitated. He seemed to be trying to get the words just right. "Do you ever think about what might have been?"

He was referring to Landon. After the initial surprise at learning the truth, Grayson had taken her revelation about Landon in stride.

She pushed her fruit plate away. "In the beginning. Yes. But we raised two beautiful children that I love with every fiber of my being. They are enough for me."

She kissed him on the cheek and moved to the living area. Picking up her purse from the table, she opened it to retrieve her lipstick.

Her hand stilled, and then a frantic search. The lipstick forgotten.

Landon's letter was gone.

FAIRFAX, VIRGINIA

NO ONE TALKS about the monotony of a stakeout. They don't show it on the cable TV shows or in the movies.

They had been shadowing Sam Carter for two weeks. Dante and Christian were surveilling William Chaney-Frost. She planned to confront William in the morning.

As they waited for practice to finish, Jade said, "What about you?"

"What about me?" Micah asked, surprised.

"What do you like to do? For fun."

"I'm a football fan. What you Yanks call soccer."

"Team?"

"Arsenal. Maybe we can catch a game together some time. There's an English pub by my house that shows all the EPL games."

Jade feared that she'd been to that pub before with Christian. "Maybe."

She put the car in drive and followed Carter, pulling over

two blocks down from his parents' house. As they had done every night. They settled in for a long night.

Tonight, however, he stopped in front of the house, but the car was still idling.

Jade and Micah glanced at each other.

A minute later, the boy resumed driving. They followed.

Carter left the subdivision via a different exit. After a few miles on Jackson Parkway, he exited and took the first right into Oak Creek Park, a Fairfax County public park. Officially closed at dusk, lights illuminated a couple of soccer games still in play.

"What's this kid up to?"

Micah shook his head. "Nothing good."

Carter drove past the soccer fields and turned into one of the many small parking lots that dotted the park. She parked on the side of the road about thirty yards from the lot entrance. She looked at Micah and brought a finger to her lips. They gently eased the car doors shut but did not close them all the way. Just enough for the interior lights to go off.

They approached the entrance on foot. It was dark here. If there were lights, they hadn't come on yet.

She spotted the Volvo parked at the other end of the lot next to another car. She couldn't see the make and model. She debated whether to draw her weapon. The kid could be just meeting a girl here. Or a friend.

Better to be safe.

She drew her Glock, the weapon pointed at the ground. From the side, she peered into the backseat of the Volvo and then the front.

Empty.

The other car was an older Mercedes. Ducking between the

cars, she peered into its back and front seats as well. Empty. She crouched as she walked to the front of the Mercedes and put her hand on the hood.

It was cold.

She scanned the area, but didn't see anyone. She glanced back at Micah and pointed to the woods with her index and middle fingers, indicating where she was headed. There was a break in the trees. Despite sticks and a few fallen leaves, they walked toward the opening as silently as they could.

In the center of a small clearing was a playground set with a slide, climbers, and swings. Carter was pressed against the beams supporting the slide, whoever was with him was barely visible, and at least a foot shorter than he was.

She felt stupid, but headed toward the couple anyway. They were kissing.

Jade shone her flashlight, stopping several yards away from them.

Carter swung around, his face pale with fear. He put his hand up to protect his eyes from the glare, while shielding the person behind him.

"Sam, my name is Special Agent Jade Harrington with the FBI. I need you to step away."

"FBI?"

"Sam, please step away."

"What do you want? I didn't do anything."

"Your teammates are being murdered. We're trying to protect you."

"I don't need protection."

"We think you do. Now, step away."

He glanced behind him at his companion and whispered something, before taking several steps away from the other person.

The girl glared at Jade. Rather, *woman.*

The last piece of the puzzle slid into place, as Jade stared not at the fearful, but the defiant expression on Jenny Thompson's face.

FAIRFAX, VIRGINIA

"'THE FIRST RULE of fight club—"

"—is you do not talk about fight club,'" Micah finished. He explained to Jade. "It was popular in the UK, too."

Sam gave him a small smile. "Yeah, William saw that movie a thousand times. Ours is called the WRSS FC—William Randolph Secondary School Fight Club. 'FC' for short. Every fight night, he starts with, 'Welcome to fight club.' He has all these rules. None of them are written down. We can't post videos or anything on social media. New players on the team fight the first night. I went only once." He shrugged. "I broke all the rules. I was out."

The night had turned unseasonably cool.

"You sure you don't want to sit in the car?" Jade asked.

Jenny had been whisked away to the local FBI office in Fairfax. She would be transferred downtown tomorrow.

He glanced at the Audi. "No, thanks."

It was dark in this part of the park. She suspected the darkness made it more conducive for Sam to talk to them.

"All right," she said. "What did you see when you went?"

"William likes to wear old-school knickers. The rest of us wore baseball pants. We were allowed to use MMA gloves. Nothing else. He beat the crap out of Joshua, who's supposed to be his best friend. J-man held the netting like he was holding on for his life. Then, William threw him on the ground, and kept hitting him and hitting him. Supposed to be when you go limp, you tap out, and the round is over." He shook his head, an expression of incredulousness. "William wouldn't stop." Carter looked at her. "But what was worse was the chanting. 'Loser! Loser! Loser!' Like a cult. Tyler threw up and ran when he saw what happened to his friend. Big mistake."

"Why didn't someone tell the coach? Call the police?"

"Tell them what?"

"About what was happening."

Sam wagged his finger at her. "Remember the first rule. Besides, the coach . . . Let's just say, snitches get stitches. The thing is FC, for those who belong, helps the team form a closer bond. The club represents something bigger than themselves."

"More than a normal team."

"Yeah. William has his own army. Disciples. What do you call them?"

"Acolytes?" Micah offered.

"Yeah."

"How so?" Jade said.

"The guys in the club would do whatever he said. Batshit crazy stuff. Like the SS during the Third Reich. Some of the players really got off on it. If you aren't in, though, you're terrified. They can come after you. Your sisters. Your girlfriend. Your mother. Kids rat each other out. After I left the club, I couldn't eat. Couldn't sleep. I almost quit the team. And baseball's my life. You know what's funny? The guy in the movie? Brad Pitt? His name was Tyler. William hated that Tyler Thompson had the same name. The name William wanted."

"What about Jenny? Mrs. Thompson?"

Sam's face reddened, visible even in the dark. "She came on to me. What was I supposed to do?"

"Say 'no'?" Jade said.

"Easy for you to say. You're older. You're smart enough not to be tempted by someone who isn't good for you."

Well . . .

Sam explained that Jenny had started texting him. She was upset about losing her son, and needed someone to talk to who knew him.

"Did you know him well?" Jade asked.

"No. But hey . . . " He smiled, sheepish. "Anyway, tonight was going to be our first night together."

"And, maybe, your last. On earth."

Sam stopped smiling.

FAIRFAX, VIRGINIA

CHRISTIAN SAT ON a big blue concrete ball, one of three in front of William Randolph Secondary School, which protected the building from someone trying to drive through the main entrance. Jade stood near him scanning the faces of the students as they hurried to their summer-school classes that morning. They had arrived early, but she had a feeling that the person they were waiting for was not an early bird. Her dress shirt stuck to her back, the humidity not taking a day off this summer.

Finally, William Chaney-Frost sauntered toward them. He had alighted from a new BMW M4. He slowed as he saw the agents. He glanced back at his car and back at her, his smile wide. "Agent Harrington! Howie! Nice, huh? Present for my sixteenth birthday."

She could never afford a car like that on her bureaucrat salary.

"It's Agent Merritt," Jade said. "We need to talk to you."

"Sure."

Instead of heading inside to the conference room with the little chairs, they led him to a backless steel bench away from the front entrance. She sat next to him. Christian stood beside her, arms crossed over his chest.

"What's up?" William asked.

"We need to ask you some more questions."

"I've told you everything I know."

"Not everything," she said. "Can you remove your sunglasses?"

"No, I'm good."

"That wasn't a request."

He hesitated, then did what he was told.

"Besides Grace and her mother, you were the last person to see Kaylee alive."

"How do you know that?"

"Did you kill her?"

"Of course not."

"What was she to you?"

"We were just friends."

"Just friends?"

"She was dating one of my teammates. I don't roll like that."

"But he's dead."

"Doesn't matter."

"Why didn't you come forward about being there?"

William's head drooped. "I was in shock. I thought you'd think I had something to do with it."

"Why were you at school?"

"Lifting."

"Anyone see you?"

"Yeah." He rattled off some names.

"I had a long talk with Sam Carter last night," she said.

A tightening of the eyes, but the boy's facial expression remained cool. "What did he say?"

"That he didn't bully Tyler. In fact, he said *you* were involved. Not only that, but you were the boss."

"He's lying."

"He told us something else."

William remained silent for as long as he could. "What?"

"About the fight club. The batting cages"—she pointed toward the baseball fields in the distance—"where you beat the crap out of each other. About how the teammates who didn't want to participate were bullied outside the club."

"We messed around. So what?"

"It looked like more than messing around to me. Sam showed us a video he took with his phone the night he was there."

"He recorded us?"

Jade nodded.

William swore, but regained his composure quickly. This was one cool kid. "Fighting's not illegal."

"Trespassing is."

"Our coach said . . . "

"What?"

"He said it was okay. If we used the cages at night to fight."

Christian stepped forward. "Sam also told us something else. You beat up my son. You and Andrew and Joshua."

Christian was acting and not well. He hadn't even been there last night to interview Carter. They had planned the bad cop/good cop routine earlier.

William's eyes widened. He glanced at her. "Isn't it a conflict of interest for him to be here?"

Christian inched closer. "Are you a lawyer now?"

"Do you know who my mother is?"

"I don't care who your mother is." He removed his badge and his gun and handed them to Jade. "You think you're tough. You've only been fighting boys in your little club. Why don't you fight a real man?"

William's eyes bulged. He turned to her, his eyes pleading. "Do something!"

She held up Christian's gun and badge. "He doesn't work for me anymore."

"Hey, man," William said. "I'm sorry."

The kid was shaking. Jade reached out and grasped Christian's wrist. "William, why don't you tell me everything from the beginning, and Agent Merritt will take a step back and let you."

Christian hesitated and then stepped back. She returned his badge and gun.

And William started talking.

WASHINGTON, DC

JADE HAD JUST settled into her seat in an interrogation room at FBI HQ. Jenny needed no prompting.

"Zach was slow. I've been watching him play sports for years. I knew I could take him."

"Why is that?"

"You weren't the only one who played ball. I played softball in high school. A small town in Iowa. Catcher. Got a partial scholarship to GMU. I know how to handle my son's bat."

Technicians found a baseball bat with Jenny's fingerprints at the top of the slide at the park. On the bat, they found hair and fibers from Zach Rawlins, Nicholas Campbell, Andrew Huffman, and Kaylee Taylor. Jade and Micah had arrived in time, before Carter had become a statistic. And not of the baseball kind.

"Was it your Vicodin your son took?"

Jenny nodded, a sad look crossing her face. "Bad knees."

"Is that where you met Matt? At George Mason University?"

"Yeah. We got married right after I graduated, and I never went home."

"Tell us about Nicholas."

"He was easy. Tyler told me the guys on the team said I was a MILF. He was embarrassed." Christian paused in his writing. He stared at Jenny. "I asked Nicholas to come over and help me pack up Tyler's things. He got off on doing it in Tyler's room. I didn't care. It was a means to an end. While he was on top of me, I hit him on the head with the lamp."

No wonder Fairfax County PD didn't discover the blood and semen. Jenny had had sex with Nicholas after they had processed the scene.

She was still talking.

" . . . and then dragged him to my car and dumped him in the park by Reagan."

"By yourself?" Jade asked, doubtful.

"I'm stronger than I look. When someone messes with your kids, you develop a strength you can't even imagine. I suppose you wouldn't know about that."

Jade ignored the barb. "And you had no help from your husband?"

"Matt's weak. He isn't strong enough to protect our family. I'm the strong one. No one is going to fuck with my kids."

So, you fuck someone else's kids?

Jade recalled the gnawing feeling that something was off when she was standing in Tyler's bedroom. Now she knew what it was: the circle, absent of dust, on the nightstand. There was something else off in that room, as well. She had thought about it a lot. But try as she might, whatever it was remained elusive.

"What did you do with the lamp?"

"I cleaned it, and dropped it off at Goodwill. I support the causes I believe in."

She was serious.

"Why did you cut off the victims' penises?" Christian asked.

"They were not the victims here," Jenny snapped. "I didn't want them spawning demon seeds."

The chill in her voice produced goose bumps on Jade's arms.

"Tell us about Andrew Huffman," Jade said.

She shrugged. "I flirted with him like the others. I saw how they used to look at me. When I sat in the stands. I could see it in their eyes. All of them. They wanted to fuck me. I could've had them all."

This was one sick woman. "I'm sure you could have."

"Are you mocking me?"

Jade let the question hang in the air for a moment. "Finish telling me about Andrew."

"I arranged to meet him behind the 7-Eleven."

"What was your husband doing there?"

"I knew you suspected him. He was my . . . what do you call it? Red herring."

"You blame Matt for Tyler's death?"

"He should've taught Tyler to be tougher. To fight back. Like I said, he's weak. I made him think I was going crazy. Wearing a bathrobe all the time. Not showering. I was sleeping during the day. At night, I would follow those boys around. Watch them. Watch their stupid fight club. Learn their habits. And then I picked them off one by one."

Jenny spat on the floor.

Christian stared at his sister-in-law, as if she were an extraterrestrial being who just landed from outer space.

William had corroborated Sam Carter's story about

the fight club and that he was its leader. He downplayed its viciousness.

"How did you find out which kids bullied Tyler?" Jade asked.

"The fight club. They did as much talking as fighting. I found out everything."

Not everything.

"How come Matt didn't recognize you at the 7-Eleven?"

"I was wearing a lot of makeup. And a wig."

"Why the 7-Eleven? There are lots of places closer to your house. To Huffman's house."

Jenny looked at her oddly. "Because it was closer to yours."

Dante was right.

Jade realized what Ethan had been trying to tell her about Dante. One of his useful qualities was his ability to take disparate information and make it fit together. Make something out of nothing. Like any good cook.

Christian stopped writing and stared at Jenny. "Explain."

"I wanted to make sure she noticed." She nodded at Jade. "The great Jade Harrington. Super FBI agent. I read everything about the TSK case. Where do you think I got the idea to use the bat? I wanted her to catch me. I wanted everyone to know. To read about it. Just like her TSK case. Now, Tyler will live forever."

"That doesn't make any sense, Jenny," Christian said, exasperated.

"Why did you kill Kaylee?" Jade asked.

"That bitch texted my son. Pretended to like him. I cut her fingers off so she would never be able to text anyone again. Even in the afterlife. I also found out she was the one who created that awful Twitter account. That whore got what she deserved."

She continued to talk, as if they weren't there. "I don't care what happens to me. I did the world a service. All those boys and that bitch who bullied my son will never hurt anyone again, and will not beget more bullies. I stopped the cycle."

Jade waited for Jenny's head to start spinning like the character in *The Exorcist*.

"Except one. We believe one other boy was involved in bullying your son."

Jenny snapped out of it. "Who?"

Jade stood, a sudden need to be out of Jenny's presence. "It wasn't Carter. You almost murdered an innocent kid."

Jenny digested this information. A manic expression returned to her face. She tried to stand, the manacles restraining her.

"Who? Who was it?"

Jade signaled to the window for Dante and Micah to remove Jenny.

"Answer me!" Jenny screamed.

They entered, each agent holding one of her arms. She fought them, as they pulled her toward the door.

"I won't be in jail forever," she said, her eyes never leaving Jade's. "I'll find out who it was! And when I do I'll—"

Mercifully, Micah closed the door behind them. Jade would never know what Jenny would do.

THE WHITE HOUSE, WASHINGTON, DC

"I DON'T THINK he's ready," Sasha said.

"Who could ever be ready for that job?"

"Lena is doing a good job. Why make a change? There are other unfilled positions that are a higher priority."

Whitney fiddled with the pen on her desk. "He thinks well on his feet. He's well-spoken, and he could sell ice cream to Eskimos. He has a prodigious memory, which will come in handy. He doesn't need to write anything down, so notes from our conversations would never be subpoenaed. He's perfect."

"Isn't it my responsibility to make hiring decisions?"

"My mind is made up."

"Do you really want a man speaking for you?"

"I am not going to dignify that question with a response." Her phone buzzed. "Yes, Sean."

"Madam President, Mr. Blake Haynes is here to see you."

Whitney looked at Sasha, as she spoke into the speakerphone. "Send him in."

A minute later, he crossed the room, taking in the Oval Office before he shook her hand.

"I wish I had seen your office when I was here for the interview." He glanced around again. "Amazing."

"Take a seat." She waited for him to sit in the chair next to Sasha. "Mr. Haynes, I have a proposition for you."

"Another interview?"

"Something like that."

He leaned forward. "I'm intrigued."

She glanced at Sasha, whose pursed lips were hard to ignore. Whitney turned back to Blake. "How would you like to be the White House Press Secretary?"

His mouth opened in surprise.

She would never forget the expression on his face as long as she lived. The young man with the gift of gab was speechless.

WASHINGTON, DC

"I NEED TO see you when you get in."

"I'm on my way."

Jade tapped the button near the car radio to end the call. What could Ethan want first thing in the morning?

When she arrived at the Bureau, she dropped her briefcase in her office.

She stood in his doorway for a moment watching him work. In a starched white shirt and maroon tie, he marked up a document, oblivious to her presence.

She had suspected Dante of leaking details about the TSK investigation to the media, but he'd been off the case at the time, and wouldn't have had access to the information. She never suspected her boss. A man she admired and respected for his work ethic, integrity, and loyalty to the agency.

She knocked.

He looked up from his writing. "Shut the door."

She sat across from him and began updating him on Jenny's interrogation.

He interrupted her. "That's not why I called you in here." He spun his wedding ring once. Twice. "I'm leaving the Bureau."

Jade opened her mouth and closed it. She had not expected this. At all. "What do you mean?"

"In all the years I've been here, I can count on one hand the number of times I've had dinner with my family."

"You're not answering my question."

"It's personal."

"Does it have anything to do with the leaks?"

"How did you find out?"

"So, it's not personal. A reporter called me. From Seattle."

Ethan, with an uncharacteristic display of anger, slammed his hand on the table, startling her.

"This is crazy," he said.

"She said that you provided her information about the TSK case."

"I didn't leak anything."

"You think someone set you up?" Jade asked, doubtful.

He let out a lungful of air. "Now, you think I'm crazy. Why would I leak it? I would be jeopardizing an operation. One of my agent's cases, which is a reflection on me. It doesn't make sense."

He had a point.

Realization dawned. "This isn't voluntary."

He didn't respond.

"Can we fight it?" she said.

He shook his head. "The decision's been made. I'm out of here."

She remained silent. She hadn't known an FBI without

Senior Supervisory Special Agent Ethan Lawson. "I don't know what to say. Is this permanent or a leave of absence?"

"I don't know."

"When are you leaving?"

"Not sure yet. Probably in a few weeks."

Jade started to rise. "This is a lot to process." At the door, she thought of something. "Who's going to take your place?"

"You are."

THE WHITE HOUSE, WASHINGTON, DC

"CONGRATULATIONS," THE PRESIDENT said, as she walked around her desk, hand extended.

"Thank you."

"You're batting a thousand."

Jade shrugged. "I win more than I lose."

"And modest. Please have a seat. I was just about to have tea. Care to join me?"

"That would be nice."

President Fairchild placed the order and returned to the chair next to the sofa. A woman brought in the tea service and placed it on the table between them. She poured for both of them.

"Thank you, Sarah." The woman left. "And to you for solving the 'Robin Hood' case." The president lifted her cup and toasted Jade. "Well done."

The cups, fragile and expensive, displayed an exquisite

design. Jade added a spoonful of sugar to hers before taking a sip.

"There is a reason why I asked for this private meeting with you," President Fairchild continued.

Jade wondered what it could be. With Ethan leaving, he couldn't have volunteered her services for another case.

Or could he?

"I haven't forgotten my promise to you," the president said.

"What promise?"

"The one I made to you over a year ago."

Puzzled, she said, "I apologize, Madam President. I don't remember."

"I told you that perhaps you would come work for me someday." The president replaced her cup in the saucer and placed it on the table. "That someday is today. I'd like for you to join my staff."

Jade glanced around the Oval Office. Not one to impress easily, she was impressed. The elegance. The power.

Work here?

"Why me?"

"As I said before, I trust you, and I need strong people around me. I have big plans for you, Jade Harrington."

QUANTICO, VIRGINIA

"THANKS FOR COMING."

"Not often a beautiful woman asks me out to lunch."

She looked askance at Max. "But it does happen?"

"What a beautiful day," he said, ignoring her question. "The dog days of August are finally over."

They sat next to each other on a bench. He glanced around the small park she had chosen near the FBI Academy. At this hour, they were the only two people in the park, except for a young woman pushing a toddler on a swing. "This is nice. I didn't know this park existed."

"You need to get out more," she said.

"The day all the serial killers take a day off, is when I'll take a day off."

"You might need to take a day off before then." She handed him a sandwich she'd picked up at a deli down the street. "I wanted to talk to you about something."

She told him about her career choices: joining the

president's staff as a special assistant or staying with the Bureau and filling in for Ethan while he was on leave.

Max chewed his egg-salad sandwich. "They both sound like great opportunities." He swallowed, thoughtful. "Aren't you forgetting one?"

She frowned. "No."

"What about moving to Seattle? We have a local office there."

Jade's cheeks grew warm. "Why would I do that?"

He shot her a look. "You forget I study human behavior for a living."

She bit into her Italian sandwich. Squeals of laughter emanated from the child on the swing. Jade never thought much about having children. A family. She hadn't thought about it at all.

"I don't know what you're talking about."

"Look at me," he said.

She stopped eating and complied.

"My wife left me after thirty years of marriage. Because I was committed to the job. My vows to the Bureau more important than my vows to her. Do I regret the choice I made? Sometimes." He gestured at the child. "But look at her. She doesn't have a care in the world. She's free. Safe. That's why I do what I do." He turned to her. "You've been chosen. To serve the president or the Bureau. You don't have a choice. You're made like me."

She balled up her sandwich wrapper and shot it at a nearby trash can. Good. "You're my godfather. You're supposed to guide me. Which position should I choose?"

"Duty is your only choice."

WASHINGTON, DC

TONIGHT, HE DINED alone at the Capital Grille. The crowd seemed light, even for a week night. He read the *Washington Times* as he ate. The only legitimate paper in DC. He stared at a photograph of the happy couple.

He glanced around. The restaurant was empty.

Odd.

"They say you shouldn't drink alone."

"They're probably right," Cole said, "but they never said anything about eating." He held up the newspaper. "Nice picture."

"Thank you," the president said. "May I sit down?"

"Knock yourself out." He circled his fork in the air. "I suppose you had something to do with this?"

"The Service takes my safety seriously."

He laid the paper on the table. "Well, I'm glad the Homo Erectus came home. Your daughter is an agitator with an arrest record. You had an illegitimate child who's gone missing. And your son has jumped ship to the good side. You need a man around the house."

"No one's here. You can drop the act."

"What act?"

"Do you really believe all the stuff that you say?"

He dropped his fork. "What did you say?"

"What's wrong? You look as if you've seen a ghost."

More like heard one.

Landon Phillips had said almost those exact words to him. Right before he shot Cole's daughter. He pushed his plate away. He was no longer hungry. He dabbed his mouth with a napkin and then wiped his forehead.

"Whitney, why are you here?"

"It's Madam President, Cole. Your wife came to visit me several months ago. Did she tell you?"

"Ashley? What for?"

"She told me about your son. CJ, isn't it?"

He nodded. "She didn't tell me."

"Your wife is a strong woman."

He had never thought of Ashley as strong. He remembered her bravery when their home was invaded by that monster. And how she was always there for him. And his family.

"What did she say?"

The president said, "She asked me whether I could put forth a federal anti-bullying law."

This was interesting. "Can you?"

"I can, but I'll need your help."

"I'm listening."

WASHINGTON, DC

"JADE, I THINK you're going to want to see this."

"I'll be right there."

Jade frowned as she replaced the handset. She locked her computer, left her office, and stopped at Pat's cubicle.

"What is it?"

Pat turned in her chair. "I know the Robin Hood case is closed, but something about it kept nagging at me. You might want to pull up a seat."

Jade looked around, but didn't see a vacant chair. She eyed the agent in the next cubicle.

He stood and grabbed his coffee mug. "I need a break anyway."

She scooted his chair next to Pat's. Pat's fingers flew across the keyboard at the speed of sound.

"The hack was sophisticated. The perpetrator created a malware program and sent it to potential donors in an email asking them for money."

"Wouldn't that be double-dipping?"

A slight smile from Pat. "Good one. He named it Astrea."

"Goddess of Justice."

"Correct. Astrea detected the passwords to the victims' banking sites stored on their computers." Pat stopped typing. "I watched a recording of your interview with Blakeley and, between that and what you told me, he just doesn't seem to possess the skills or background to pull off something like this."

"Noah didn't seem technically proficient to be the brainchild behind this," Jade conceded.

"I don't think he was. I've been working with CART on his computer. His password was 'equalityone.'"

"There's that."

"At first, we thought that since he was one of the victims, the likelihood of him being the perpetrator was small. Then, conveniently, all the evidence pointed to him. But now I think he was not only the victim of theft, but that he was set up to take the fall for a crime he didn't commit."

Jade sat back in her chair. "Why do you think that?"

"I believe someone hacked into Blakeley's computer a second time and installed a file that would make it appear as if all the transactions were conducted from his computer."

"Can you prove it?"

"Not yet."

"If it wasn't him, who was it?"

Pat's fingers stilled. "That, we don't know."

*

Back in her office, Jade packed up her briefcase and thought about Noah Blakeley.

He had been charged with ninety-nine counts of wire, bank, and computer fraud; computer intrusion; aggravated identity theft; computer hacking; and violation of numerous other federal laws. If convicted, he would spend the rest of his life in prison.

If Pat were right, she could never live with herself. She had told Pat to quietly continue the investigation while she untangled all the "good" Equality One had done.

"Outta here?"

Micah joined her in the hallway as she headed for the elevator.

"Kind of late for you," she said.

He grinned. "Trying to impress the boss."

She pressed the down button. "I think you've already done that."

He looked at her. "Not him. You."

Her heart may have skipped a beat, but she ignored it.

They both stared at the numbers above the door, as the elevator descended. He smelled faintly of cologne. Micah wasn't encroaching on her personal space, but she was cognizant of his lean, muscular body just the same.

At the second level of the parking garage, he hesitated, allowing her to exit first.

"You parked on this level, too?"

"No," he said.

"I don't need you to walk me to my car."

He shrugged. "I'm not doing it for you. I'm doing it for my mum."

"Huh?"

"She raised me right." He smiled. "Isn't that what you Yanks say?"

She couldn't help smiling. "I guess."

"I've been meaning to tell you. Great work on the Robin Hood case."

He didn't know she had authorized Pat to continue working on it. "Thanks."

They stopped behind her car.

"On to the next one," he said, his look intense.

"Yep."

He cocked his head. "You mean it?"

"Sure."

"Good."

"Where's this coming from, Micah?"

"I just think you need to focus on your next case. Let Robin Hood go. Move on."

"Thanks for the advice."

"That's what I'm here for. Good night, Agent Harrington."

He strode toward the elevator. As he got on, he turned and held up a hand. He stared at her until the doors closed.

She felt an inexplicable chill, as she opened her car door.

Why did his advice feel more like a warning?

ARLINGTON, VIRGINIA

PRESIDENT WHITNEY FAIRCHILD said something to Senator Eric Hampton, who gave her a false smile.

"I wonder what she said?"

Zoe swallowed a sip of her beer from a microbrewery in nearby Burke. "Not sure. But he's not happy. The legislation had originally been a few votes shy. He was pressured into making it happen."

"By the president?"

Zoe shook her head. "Cole Brennan."

"Interesting."

The two friends were sprawled on Jade's living-room couch watching the news. After her weird run-in with Micah, she wanted some company. On the TV screen, the president moved to a table where a blue hardcover folio held the New New Deal Coalition Act.

"Hampton will smile to her face today, and be back at her throat tomorrow."

Jade took a pull of her beer. "Is he worse than Sampson?"

"Not even close. When we lie, we get fired. Since he switched parties, Sampson lies every time he opens his mouth. That's not just my opinion either. *Politico* recently ranked him one of the least honest politicians."

"That's saying something."

"He'll get his, though."

"Why do you say that?"

"Word on the street is that his farming corporation in Nebraska employs illegal workers."

"Mexicans?"

Zoe nodded. "Guess he didn't build that wall fast enough."

The president selected a pen, and smiled, as she signed the New New Deal Coalition Act, the most extensive—and expensive—economic legislation in this country's history. Standing behind her was former President Richard Ellison, who had flown in for the occasion.

"Ellison being there is huge," Zoe said. "Bipartisan cooperation. If only the rest of his party could follow suit."

Jade sipped her beer. With Zoe, she didn't need to say much.

"I guess she's not going to mention Xavi," Zoe said.

"Not today."

A competing story to the signing of the historic legislation was the announcement that the vice president of the United States, Xavi Fernandez, had resigned for personal reasons. This was only the third time a vice president had resigned in US history.

"I'm glad she finally stood up for herself and got rid of that misogynistic ass."

Jade glanced over at her friend. "It was forced?"

"That's what I hear. He's such a potato." She gave Zoe a

questioning look. "Someone who has lost his heritage. Brown on the outside. White on the inside."

"Got it," Jade said. "Your 'word on the street' seems pretty informed. Anyway, I think Fairchild can take care of herself. Maybe she was waiting for the right time."

"I just wish she'd take a stand against special interests. Wall Street. Getting big money out of politics. Everyone needs to stand for something." She glanced at Jade. "Even you."

"What do you mean?"

"You can't be middle-of-the-road on everything. Are you a progressive? A liberal? Gay? Straight?"

Jade smiled. "Nice try. I don't do labels."

"But you must stand for something."

"I do. I stand for justice." She thought of her last conversation with Max. "Duty."

"Barf." Zoe made a gagging motion. "You're such a Bureau poster child." Zoe sat up, placing her beer on the table in front of them, and stared at Jade. "That's not good enough, though." She placed her hand over her own heart. "You have to stand for something that's personal. That matters. That hurts, if you don't say something."

"Why are you saying this?"

"Because we're family."

"We're not related, Zoe."

"Blood doesn't mean family. Blood is just blood. You're my chosen family, which means more to me."

Jade was touched. Besides Max, Zoe was the only family she had. She should respond in kind. Instead, she lifted Zoe's bottle and used a napkin to wipe the condensation off the table until it was spotless. She wiped the bottle's bottom before placing it on the napkin.

She was saved from responding by a knock on the door.

"You expecting someone?" asked Zoe.

Jade shook her head, as she moved to the door. She returned with a large box and set it on the hardwood living room floor.

The packing slip contained a note:

> Jade,
>
> Thank you for solving my case. I hope these remind you of Seattle.
>
> Always,
>
> Kyle

"Aren't you going to open it?" Zoe said, her tone, mischievous.

Jade had to be careful. Zoe knew her. If Zoe sensed that there was anything between Kyle and her, Zoe would tear her apart for information, like a starving Rottweiler left alone with a steak. She feigned nonchalance. "I'll open it later."

"Like hell you will."

Zoe started tearing off the packaging. Jade hesitated, and then knelt to help her.

"Wow," Zoe said.

Inside the box were dozens of original Motown albums from the Sixties through the Eighties. The sight brought an unusual pang to Jade's heart. She missed Seattle. Missed the attention.

Missed Kyle.

Jade didn't dare look at Zoe.

Zoe stared at the vinyls in disbelief or confusion. Jade couldn't tell which. She turned to Jade, her eyes huge. "Why is she sending you these?"

THE WHITE HOUSE, WASHINGTON, DC

WHITNEY GLANCED AROUND his office. "When are you going to settle in?"

Blake laughed. "I live here now."

In between the Press Briefing Room and the Oval Office were the White House Press Secretary's office and those of his large staff, which was appropriate since the press secretary served both the president and the press. Her official presidential portrait hung on one wall, as did the portraits of JFK and Bill Clinton. Another wall displayed a panoramic photograph of the pre-9/11 New York City skyline. Blake's desk was covered with briefing books, reports, transcripts, and a few bottles of water. Papers covered the entire surface of his desk, the round table he used for meetings, and his credenza. She also spotted a couple of gourmet-food magazines.

She inclined her head toward the skyline. "Do you miss it?"

"Sometimes. As a foodie, I miss the restaurants. But I like

the West End. Everything is within walking distance, and I can walk to work. A lot of great places to run. Maybe we should run sometime."

"I'm sure Josh would love that. No, I prefer my elliptical. Less stress for all of us."

Whitney sat on the edge of his desk and crossed her legs. She checked the flat-screen TV. The CNN caption blared Killer Momma Arraignment at the bottom of the screen.

"How are you settling in at home?" she asked.

"Not as well as here. I'm never there."

"No social life?"

"As I said, I'm always here."

"Pity. I thought you and Ms. Harrington made a striking pair. How did the gaggle go this morning?"

The press gaggle was the daily briefing he gave from the desk in his office. The press gathered around him, as he took them through her schedule, measured their temperature about what stories they were following, which in turn helped him plan his day. Although what he said was on the record, these briefings—unlike in the Briefing Room—were not recorded or televised.

"It was fine. A lot of questions about Chandler's first day of work. I handled it."

"Good. I need you to do the talk-show circuit soon. Educate people on what they can expect from the New New Deal and our other legislative initiatives."

Blake smiled. "Got it, boss."

At the door, she turned. "I'm glad you're here. We're going to make a great team."

ALEXANDRIA, VIRGINIA

WEARING AN EXPENSIVE black suit, her makeup flawless, Rachel Chaney sat at the table across from her. Her hair was brown, cut just above the shoulders.

Like Jenny's.

Jenny had known William's mother of course. Had seen her at the baseball games dressed in her suits, just so. She had always showed up late—the fourth or fifth inning—when she bothered to show up at all.

The small room off the courtroom barely had enough space for the rectangular table and two chairs.

She rubbed her wrists, grateful that Rachel had asked for the handcuffs to be removed.

Rachel pulled out a legal pad and a fancy pen from her briefcase. She opened her mouth to tell Jenny about the process for her arraignment at the United States District Court for the Eastern District of Virginia.

Jenny didn't have much time. But she did have the element of surprise.

On the count of three to herself, she exploded from her chair and wrapped her hands around her attorney's neck in a vise grip. And squeezed.

Rachel Chaney's eyes bulged.

The rage coursing within Jenny threatened to explode. Everything her family had suffered. She had suffered.

Her little boy, her angel, had suffered.

The woman's body finally relaxed.

Jenny had to move quickly.

When Jade Harrington had told Jenny that her son's killer was still alive, she realized she needed an attorney after all. She had remembered William's mother from the games. That she was a defense attorney. That they looked alike. And were nearly the same height.

She switched clothes with her. The suit was loose, but fit well enough. She set the attorney upright, now with her back facing the door.

She left the pad of paper where it was. And the woman's briefcase. She adjusted the suit skirt, and slapped the door as she had seen on TV. The bailiff opened it, looking in on the defendant.

She breezed past him. "I need to use the bathroom. I'll be right back."

He closed the door behind her.

Jenny walked down the commodious hallway, her newly acquired high heels clicking on the floor. She passed benches where defendants and their lawyers waited. Passed courtrooms. She cruised on past the ladies' room.

And walked out of the courthouse into a beautiful autumn day.

WASHINGTON, DC

SHE FELT A presence.

Christian filled the door frame.

"What's up?"

"Did you see the news this morning?" he said.

Jade nodded. Jenny Thompson, now forevermore dubbed "Killer Momma," perp-walked into the US District Courthouse for her first court appearance. The video had been plastered on cable and local news and social media throughout the morning.

Half the public demonized her. The other half considered her a hero.

He sat in the only other chair in her office.

"Matt wants to take the kids and move to Minnesota."

"Minnesota?"

He shrugged. "He thinks they can live a normal life there."

"Maybe. Any family there?"

"Nope. But they could never return to a normal life here."

The "Killer Momma" stigma would probably follow

Thompson and his kids around for some time. Maybe the rest of their lives.

"How's Amanda?"

"My wife is a strong woman. I think she's accepted what happened. That her sister could commit these murders. The statutory rapes."

"Matt say anything else?"

"Only that Jenny can rot in prison forever as far as he cares." Christian pushed off to leave. "He's already taken Mia and Matt Jr., and moved out of the house. They're living in a hotel now. Said he can't stand to be there."

"Because of Jenny?"

"Yeah. But Tyler, too. He can't even go into his room."

Dante entered her office without knocking, his face unusually pale. "You haven't heard."

Jade started to rise, a horrible premonition overcoming her. "What?"

"Jenny Thompson escaped."

FAIRFAX, VIRGINIA

HE WIPED A tear from his eye. He and his mother hadn't been close. She was never around. Always working. His dad had told him the story multiple times that when his mother was pregnant with him, she took only one day off work for maternity leave. The day he was born.

Still. The thought of never seeing her again . . .

He parked the BMW near the gate in the vast, empty lot. Grabbing his cap and gloves, he exited the car and jogged toward the field in the distance.

Earlier, he had called the team—what was left of it—together for a fight night. He needed to work off the emotions from his mother's death. But it was more than that. She never saw him fight. And, now, she never would. He was good. Really good. This was a way, for him, to honor her.

He was early.

He stripped off his baseball shirt and shoved the cap back on his head. He donned the MMA gloves and removed his shoes.

He entered the cage.

In the fading light, he spotted an object in the middle of the turf.

It was a cap. He wondered which of his idiot teammates had left it. He picked it up.

And his hand began to shake.

The faded "FC" was written in black magic marker over the bill where he had written it before last season. Seven months ago. He turned it over. Inside the bill, written in the same magic marker, were his initials "WCF."

It was the cap he had lost the night they had beaten up Tyler.

"My son was wearing that when he died."

William spun, dropping the cap.

Mrs. Thompson stood in the darkness at the end of the cage. She held a baseball bat relaxed against her shoulder, as if she were on deck.

Before he could react, she took several quick steps toward him and swung the bat. He didn't get his arms up in time, and the bat smashed into his left temple.

"Fuck!" he yelled as he clutched his head.

"That was for Tyler."

He hit the turf. Head throbbing, the blood seeped through his hands. Another blow to the kidney.

"Ow!"

"You killed my baby!" Whack.

"You took my family away from me!" Whack.

"You even hit on me. You pig!" Whack.

Where's the damn FBI when you need them?

Whack.

Whack.

Whack.

Before the next blow came, a massive body flew over him and tackled Mrs. Thompson.

"Howie?" William whispered. "What took you so long?"

ARLINGTON, VIRGINIA

SATURDAY MORNING, SHE sat with Christian, his wife, Amanda, and three of their kids in the stands of the same arena where Jade had received her fourth-degree black belt two years ago. A lifetime ago. She should be testing for senior fourth-degree by now, but had scarcely trained.

The attention of the three adults was focused on a ring where twelve-year-old boy and girl blue belts competed in a *poomsae* (forms) and sparring tournament. Christian's son, Mark, had not done well in the *poomsae* competition. In fact, none of the boys had finished in the top three. The girls performed the patterns unerringly and with precision, in a way the boys hadn't yet mastered.

Mark competed against a much taller boy for the sparring championship. The score was two to one, in favor of the other boy.

Christian turned to Jade. "Tyler must've lost his cap running away from the cages, or when they beat him up afterward. William accidentally dropped his when he and Andrew dumped Tyler in the front yard."

"That's why William had a brand-new cap with 'FC' on it when Micah and I interviewed him."

He turned back to the match. Three to one. "Jenny figured it out in jail."

Jenny had told them that Tyler had been proud of his baseball cap and had worn it everywhere. That as soon as he'd gotten it, he'd put his initials on it. Though a meticulous housekeeper, in her grief, she hadn't realized it wasn't Tyler's cap on his dresser. Jail had given her plenty of time to remember.

"He almost committed the perfect crime," Christian said. "His fists were his instrument. He didn't leave fingerprints. The witnesses are dead." Three to two. "Way to go, Mark!"

"I wonder why William told me that Tyler and Joshua were gay."

"He was just trying to throw us off. Did you hear about Daniel?"

William wasn't the only one who wouldn't be returning to the team. Coach Lane Daniel had been placed on administrative leave pending an investigation. Based on information supplied by William and Sam and corroborated by their teammates, Daniel had encouraged an environment of hazing. Players had hurled racist, homophobic, and religious insults at each other. The coach had humiliated them for poor play and getting injured. It had become a game to see who could say the meanest, most hurtful things. Although the head coach and assistant coaches hadn't been present during the fight club sessions in the batting cages, they were being held liable because they'd known about them.

At a press conference yesterday, Mr. Trussell, the principal of William Randolph Secondary School, had renamed the baseball complex Tyler's Diamond. The team would play again next year, and he would expect nothing less than another state championship. He'd also announced his retirement from the county school system, effective immediately.

"Mark was afraid of William," Christian said.

"He wanted to send you a message through your son."

"After he gets out of the hospital, I don't think he's going to like prison much."

Four to two.

"I think you're right."

"He's going to be engaging in a whole new level of fight club in a different kind of cage."

Jade grimaced. "Ouch."

"Oh, and the handcuffs Jenny used. An old pair of mine. She must've lifted them from my house." Four to three. "Yes!"

Amanda leaned over. "Can you two stop talking shop for once?" Her smile gave away the fruitlessness of her request.

The judge happened to be Master Won Ho, Jade's instructor. He said, "*Sijak!*"

Mark rushed in and punched the other boy in the abdomen before he had a chance to react. Four to four.

The next point won.

Christian stood. "You got this, Mark!"

Jade grabbed his forearm and guided him down, knowing his muscular frame blocked the view of at least three spectators behind him.

Before Mark could rush in to surprise the boy again, the taller kid used his long leg to fire a side kick to Mark's abdomen. His body lifted in the air, and flew a few feet. His "Oof!" was audible to them in the stands. He fell on his back, clutching his stomach.

Christian started to rise again, and again she forced him to sit. "Like you said, he's got this."

Mark's opponent reached down with both hands to help him up. Mark tapped the boy on the shoulder, thanking him.

During the medal ceremony afterward, the Merritt family and Jade cheered wildly, as Mark bowed for the judge to put the ribbon attached to the silver medal around his neck. The boy's face, unhidden now by headgear, looked as if it would burst with pride.

As she clapped, Jade said to Christian, "I don't think you need to worry about him being bullied in the future. He can take care of himself."

"I didn't tell you what happened a few weeks ago. Mark was drinking from the water fountain, and a couple of guys were giving him a hard time. Mark, still drinking, mind you, lifted his leg and shot a back kick right into the privates of one of them. No one has bothered him since."

Jade nodded, still clapping. "A kid after my own heart."

THE WHITE HOUSE, WASHINGTON, DC

SHE STARED OUT at the array of flowers and the gathered reporters in front of them. She fingered the index cards in her hand. She had occasionally spoken to the press in her role at the FBI, but never to this many. The cameras shuttered, unceasing, like the sound of an old movie projector. Never in her wildest dreams did she think she would ever stand here. In the Rose Garden.

As she stood next to President Whitney Fairchild and the radio talk-show host, Cole Brennan, a young woman spoke from the podium. She had spent her high-school years bullied repeatedly because of her sexual orientation. She recounted the broken noses, the cracked ribs, the bruises, the fear, the anguish, the loneliness. Wanting to die.

Most of those years, she had spent hiding behind a book, a safe place where she could go anywhere she wanted, unmolested. Anywhere but school.

Her story had a happy ending. The girl had persevered through her time in high school, gone on to college, majored in sociology, and was now a counselor working with bullied youth.

The president spoke next.

"October is National Bullying Prevention Month. How appropriate and right that I will be signing legislation that will do just that on this glorious day." She raised her hands, taking in the seventy-five-degree weather. "But first, I want to say a few words and then introduce another special guest.

"Bullying is a major public-health issue. What at one time may have seemed innocuous or just part of growing up, has been proven to have long-term health consequences, such as head-aches, stomachaches, sleep deficiencies, and academic failure.

"Thirteen million kids in America are bullied every year. One third of all children. Our children.

"Two hundred and eighty-two thousand kids are bullied each month. One hundred and sixty thousand kids skip school *every day* in this country for fear of being bullied. Ten percent of them drop out or change schools. The leading cause of death for kids under the age of fourteen is suicide.

"It doesn't have to be this way. And it's not a coincidence."

"Everything is connected. When the leaders and potential leaders of this country speak to each other and about each other with disrespect and vitriol, it trickles down through the popu-lace. Civility matters.

"Until our leaders embrace tolerance and inclusion—no matter if you are LGBTQ, overweight, Muslim, physically challenged—none of us will be accepted as individuals. And bystanders do not receive a free pass. Silence equals acquies-cence. When a bystander gets involved, bullying stops.

"Now, I would like to bring up a special guest. She is with

the Federal Bureau of Investigation. She apprehended the Talk Show Killer, the modern-day Robin Hood, and Killer Momma. May I introduce Special Agent Jade Harrington?"

Fairchild turned to her and smiled, and beckoned her forward.

Jade stood at the podium as the president moved behind her. She placed the index cards with her remarks on the flat surface and raised the microphone.

She did not like to talk about herself, and now she was about to tell the entire world something she had never admitted in public—or private—to anyone but Max.

"Good afternoon. My name is Jade Harrington, and as President Fairchild said, I am an FBI agent." She stood proud and strong. "And I was bullied as a kid."

She relayed to the journalists present and to the nation the story of when she had been beaten up by three of her classmates and left alone in the woods. How a stranger had come by to help. And how she had learned to protect herself by participating in Tae Kwon Do.

"They say what doesn't kill you makes you stronger. If you were bullied as a child, you never forget it. Some of the physical scars may heal, but the emotional ones never do.

"Kids need our protection. I'm proud to be standing here today to witness President Whitney Fairchild's signing of the Federal Anti-Bullying Act, the toughest anti-bullying legislation ever created.

"This bill includes cyberbullying. And it not only protects kids. It will also be a federal crime to bully teachers.

"And to all the kids out there watching, ask for help if you need it. Check out stopbullying.gov. Accept who you are. Find a passion. Be confident. It's okay to be different.

"And, remember, you're not alone."

Jade stepped back from the podium, surprised and pleased at the applause. She joined the group standing behind the president, who moved to sit at a nearby table. She glanced at Cole Brennan next to her and smiled at him.

He leaned toward her. "How's my favorite FBI agent?"

"How's my favorite conservative talk-show host?"

He displayed mock surprise. "You have one?"

Jade smiled. "How's your son?"

"I'm proud of him. He's the lead in his school's musical."

She turned to the president who reached for one of the pens that her body woman, Sarah, had placed on the table.

After signing the document with a flourish, Fairchild beckoned Brennan, Jade, and the young woman who had spoken to join her. The president held out her hand, palm down, and looked at Jade. As a former athlete, Jade needed no instruction about what to do next. She placed her hand on top of the president's. The young woman placed her hand, the scars faint but still noticeable, on top of Jade's. Cole Brennan laid his beefy hand on top. The four of them held this position and smiled, as cameras from the White House press corps clicked away and saved the moment for posterity.

Afterward, Jade leaned close to the president. "May we talk privately? It's about the offer. I have an answer for you."

WASHINGTON, DC

OVER THE RAISED beer mugs, she scanned their faces: Christian, Amanda, Pat, Max, Micah, Blake, Dante, and his girlfriend, Laurie. Ethan couldn't make it. His leave had started last week.

"Although it was sometimes painful," Jade said, "we came together as a team and got it done. To the good guys!"

"To the good guys!" the agents in the group yelled.

Glasses clinked all around. At a sports bar across the street from the Bureau, they had annexed two long tables and pushed them together. The place was packed, the Wizards game on all the TVs.

On the screen, the Wizards' big man soared for an offensive rebound and dunked the ball before returning to the floor.

"Told ya!" Christian shouted to her from the other table.

"That condo is still for sale," she yelled back.

"Won't need it."

"No dancing on the table tonight, okay?"

He grinned. "I'll try to control myself."

As they waited for their food, the group sipped their beers and talked.

Blake leaned in to her. "I have to go out of town for a week or so. Business." He looked around at her rowdy crew. "Maybe, we can have a quiet dinner when I get back."

She had invited him to join them after the Rose Garden ceremony that afternoon. Now, she felt Micah, motionless, on the other side of her. Waiting for her answer.

"Maybe," she said.

When Blake turned to talk to Max, Micah lifted his chin toward Blake. "Why is he here?"

"He's a friend," she said.

"I wish I had friends who looked at me like that."

She was saved from responding, by Zoe walking through the front door. Jade smiled and waved her over.

She wasn't alone.

What the—

Behind her sashayed Kyle Madison, whose eyes never left Jade's.

"Look who I found standing in front of the Bureau!" Zoe raised her arms in a vee. "Surprise!"

Jade's mouth parted. And, for some reason, her eyes landed on Dante.

"I see you're taking the edge off just fine," he drawled, putting his arm around Laurie and looking from Micah to Blake to Zoe and, finally, to Kyle. He laughed. "Let me count the ways."

WASHINGTON, DC

SHE WOKE UP at her customary time of five a.m. and was at her desk by seven. A high-ranking analyst from the Office of the Director of National Intelligence had just left.

A door to the Oval Office opened. Whitney looked up, surprised that there had been no knock or warning from Sean.

She stood, a premonition, overwhelming her. "Sasha, what's wrong? Is it one of the children?"

She had left Grayson eating breakfast in the residence kitchen, so he was fine. She was scheduled to have lunch with Chandler today. Emma was back at Princeton for her junior year and studying for mid-terms.

Sasha shook her head and inclined her head toward the study. She grabbed the remote and hit the power button. The two women moved in front of the TV, although they both could have seen it perfectly from where they stood.

The channel was set to MSNBC. Rubble and smoke and ash filled the screen. The front of a building had been blown away.

"We're looking at a picture of 30 Rockefeller Plaza in Midtown Manhattan," said the voice-over. "Ten minutes ago, we received reports of a loud explosion. As you can see, it's utter chaos."

The camera cut to people running away from the building, most of them blanketed in gray ash. Some were limping. Some, bleeding. A mother ran with her daughter in her arms, the toddler's pink dress, a sharp contrast with the gray.

Whitney would not be having lunch with her son today.

"Why didn't we foresee this?" she said.

"I don't know."

Whitney moved to the desk and pressed the Intercom button on the phone. "Sean, get the ODNI guy back in here. Now!"

She disconnected and returned to stand next to Sasha. They watched the report in silence for several minutes.

"Sasha," she said, still looking at the television, "you asked me once whether I had something to tell you about the time I lived with my aunt."

"Yes, Madam President."

"I need to tell you something. About Landon Phillips."

Sarah materialized next to Sasha. She, too, stared at the screen in shock before addressing Whitney. "Madam President."

"Sarah, what is it? Sasha and I are in the middle of something."

"It's Blake."

"Tell him to come here ASAP. We should start working on a statement."

"I can't."

"For God's sakes, Sarah, get him in here. Now!"

"I can't, Madam President. He's not here."

"Where is he?" Whitney snapped.

Sarah's finger shook as she pointed at the screen. "He's there."

*

"My fellow Americans, today was a dark day in our nation's history. In New York City, a suicide bomber walked into the Lower Plaza at the center of the Rockefeller complex and not only took his own life, but killed and injured dozens of innocent people.

"Twenty-seven people were killed and another forty-five injured, five of them in critical condition. This was a terrorist attack. And mark my words, I will use all the powers vested in me and the United States government to track down and bring to justice any other individuals responsible for this heinous attack.

"Members of the press, Blake Haynes, our White House press secretary, stands here every day informing you of events, answering your questions, and speaking for me." Whitney paused. "This morning, he was at MSNBC giving an interview on my behalf about the recent passage of historic legislation: The New New Deal Coalition Act and the Federal Anti-Bullying Act. Blake was critically injured in today's attack." She swallowed. "I ask you to pray for him, and for everyone else who was injured or who lost their lives today at Rockefeller Center Plaza. Pray for their families."

She blamed herself.

He was at the MSNBC studio because of her. His last smile haunted her. The one he gave her the last time she visited his office. She scanned the solemn faces of the reporters scribbling furiously, most of them—if not friends with Blake—at least, shared a common bond with him: love for this country, communicating what was happening within it, the need to perfect the story every day, and the jokes, pranks, and arguments along the way.

She stood at the famous podium in the James S. Brady Press Briefing Room, with the presidential seal and the mock columns behind her. She wrapped up her address to the White House press corps before her, and the nation and the rest of the world through the cameras present in the rear of the room. Another set of cameras to the right of her was aimed at the press, normally ready to capture an aggressive reporter who asked a tough question.

She had insisted that those cameras be turned off today.

She stepped down from the dais and headed toward the door.

Sasha joined her in the hallway.

"Madam President, I need a word."

"It's been a long day. I'm going back to the residence. Can it wait until tomorrow?"

"I don't think it can."

Whitney stopped. "What is it?"

Sasha touched her arm and guided her to an alcove.

"What were you going to tell me about Landon Phillips?"

"It can wait. What's so important?"

"It's Blake."

Whitney felt the blood drain from her face. "He's not—"

Sasha squeezed Whitney's hand, her grip strong and reassuring. "He's still alive, but he's in bad shape."

"I wish there were something I could do."

"Maybe, you can."

Whitney looked at her sharply. "What? Anything. My resources are at his disposal."

"Blake needs a blood transfusion."

"Okay."

"He has a rare blood type that is only shared by two percent of the Caucasian population." Sasha hesitated. "It doesn't match either of his parents' types or his siblings'."

"What can we do for him? Can we find a matching donor quickly?"

"We've located two people with a matching blood type."

"Sasha, what are you waiting for? We can fly one of them or his or her blood to New York. At my personal expense. Do whatever it takes." She exhaled, trying to calm herself. "Who are they?"

Her chief of staff stared into her eyes.

"One is a state legislator in Missouri. The other is you, Madam President."

PHILADELPHIA, PENNSYLVANIA - ONE MONTH LATER

"THESE ARE THE times that try men's souls."

Thus began the 240th meeting.

Those famous words kicked off every meeting. The Paine Society, or The Society, as most of its members called it, met in person once a year at an undisclosed location.

A US-based secret group of like-minded individuals, The Society was founded by Thomas Paine in 1776. A founding father and the author of *Common Sense* and *The Age of Reason*, Paine was also the intellectual forefather to liberals, feminists, and progressives. An offshoot of the Illuminati, it was rumored that the two groups had partnered together to start the French revolution.

The Society's mission was to create a progressive new order.

Its current objectives, based on Paine's writings and beliefs, were to:

1. Remedy the evils of poverty, illiteracy, and unemployment
2. Provide education, a living wage, relief for the poor, pensions for the elderly, and work for the unemployed
3. Promote liberty, tolerance, community, and social progress

Like most secret organizations, The Society had its rituals, symbols, and passwords. Though every member used an alias, their true identities were not a secret from one another. The current leader glanced out at the ninety-eight members—and one other—seated in chairs throughout the great hall. In the front row sat Franklin, Jefferson (who hated the name, complaining "Might as well call me 'The Farmer.'"), Washington, and Hamilton, who oversaw The Society's finances. The leader also spotted Dickinson, Marshall, and Adams.

"First," Paine continued, "I wish to thank Adams for her service over the last year. Your plan was brilliant. Your execution flawless."

Adams raised a hand to her heart and bowed her head slightly at the praise. She would be quick to point out that her alias was based on Samuel, not John.

Although Adams had received a degree in poli sci at Stanford and a master's degree in public policy from Duke, she had also always loved to take things apart and put them back together. She had done that with her first computer in high school. Always up to mischief, she broke into her friends' AOL accounts and IM'ed crazy stuff to their girlfriends. A gifted hacker, she ventured on the dark side for a time, but then decided to use her skills for good. For social change. She referred to herself as a "white hat, with shades of gray."

It had been Adams's idea to form the Equality One Foundation. The mission of the organization was real: to provide jobs and homes for those who needed them. The source of revenue, donations and gifts from wealthy progressives and liberals, was real as well. The foundation was also used, however, as the vehicle to appropriate one percent of the revenues of conservative companies and foundations and those who supported them and redistribute that money to people in need. The targets each had more wealth than could be spent in a lifetime. It was money they wouldn't miss.

It was also her idea to initially steal from progressive Seattle corporations to throw off the scent for conservative conspiracy theorists.

Hamilton had suggested recruiting Noah Blakeley to be its chairman and then, eventually, president.

The leader thought of Noah Blakeley. While, regrettably, he would be spending the rest of his life in jail, sometimes a life had to be sacrificed for the greater good.

He wasn't, and wouldn't be, the only sacrifice.

Congressman Steven Barrett's death hadn't been an accident.

And Landon Phillips didn't kill him.

The airplane manifest had been altered. The driver's license fabricated to point law enforcement to the desired conclusion. Franklin had seen to it that the FBI's investigation into the death of Representative Barrett had been buried.

"But this was a team effort," the leader continued.

Supervisory Special Agent Ethan Lawson was a good man. His career wasn't over, just on hiatus. The leader nodded to

Franklin, who had leaked the information on the TSK and cybertheft cases to Dickinson, the recipient of those leaks.

The leader stood and raised a chalice of wine to the group. "To duty!"

"To duty!" ninety-eight voices responded.

"To preserve and protect our democracy."

"To preserve and protect our democracy," they repeated.

The leader took a sip of wine, and then beckoned to someone in the front row.

"And now, I'd like to welcome the newest member of The Paine Society. May I introduce Madison?"

As the other members clapped, the inductee stepped forward until he stood before her. Madison had been successful so far in deterring the FBI from pursuing the Noah Blakeley case any further.

The case needed to be closed.

The handsome man smiled, his mesmerizing gray eyes never leaving the leader's, as he slowly unbuttoned his shirt. He held it open to reveal the new tattoo he had received that morning, on the left side of his chiseled chest.

進捗

The End

ACKNOWLEDGEMENTS

MANY THANKS TO:

MY MAGNIFICENT EDITORS: Jim Thomsen and Christina Tinling.

My sons, Travis and Brandon, for their support and my daughter, Jaz, for her support and Jazisms.

My cat and the king of our household, Fitzgerald.

My mother, Julia, who bestowed on me the love of reading and, when I was a child, took me on weekly trips to the library.

My amazing wife, manager, and editor, Audi, who was with me through every page.

And last, but not least, to the readers of *Don't Speak*. For an author, releasing your baby to the world, especially your first, is a scary thing. I have been overwhelmed and honored by the positive reaction to the story and to Jade. Thank you for sharing the word about *Don't Speak*.

WHERE IT ALL BEGAN . . .

"A promising debut." – *Kirkus Reviews*

DON'T
SPEAK

A JADE HARRINGTON NOVEL

J. L. BROWN

ISBN 978-0-9969772-1-0 (paperback)
ISBN 978-0-9969772-0-3 (ebook)

Made in the USA
San Bernardino, CA
24 July 2018